Bollywood Wives

Bollywood Wives

Alex Khan

hera

First published in Great Britain in 2019 by Hera

This edition published in Great Britain in 2019 by

Hera Books
28b Cricketfield Road
London, E5 8NS
United Kingdom

A CIP catalogue record for this book is available from the British Library.

Print ISBN 978 1 78863 608 7
Ebook ISBN 978 1 91297 300 2

Printed and bound in Great Britain by Clays Ltd, Elcograf S.p.A.

To the Bollywood Wives in my life, Alison and Keshini, this wouldn't have been possible without you both.

And to all the stars, film makers and designers that have made Bollywood so amazing, always.

Prologue: Bollywood

Zara Das was nineteen when she saw Mumbai for the first time. The bus that brought her was dusty, cheap, packed. Mumbai was the same. And within seconds, she knew this was home. This was where she belonged. Among the dirt, the desperation and the dreams. Oh yes, the dreams. And Zara Das had the biggest dreams of them all. Desires that took her from her small provincial town, and led her to where she was now, standing on her twenty-seventh-floor balcony, watching the waters of the Arabian sea as they washed up against the bright golden sand. Palm trees added to the exoticism as they swayed on the horizon.

She could easily pretend, as she let the heat of the sun warm her body, that it was her own bit of ocean. Her apartment building was prime location in Mumbai, with a view that guaranteed privacy from the millions of people that were thronging the streets just the other side of the residential complex.

It was a decade since that wide-eyed innocent girl had stepped foot into the heaving mass of the city of stars. And now, aged twenty-nine, she was the brightest star in Bollywood. When the Indian heat abated that night, and the glitterati came out to play, it was to the premiere of Zara's new movie that they would go. A beeline to the hottest ticket in town. Ironically, the threat to her life had only made her stock rise. They all wanted to be there tonight, just in case. Sycophants. They had watched her claw her way to the top, resenting every success she had had, this two-bit nobody who had come from the backwaters of India, to rule over them. They were probably licking their

I

MAC-coated lips in anticipation, waiting for her to fall and implode. But they hadn't counted on Zara. She had fought hard for this view. And as the breeze danced with the palm trees, hypnotically, and the ocean waters cast a haze where they met the sands, Zara knew she would do everything to hold onto this view. Or die trying.

–

Zara looked at her reflection in the mirror, making sure she had checked every last detail. She had dressed herself for the premiere, with only her maid, Shanti, a woman in her early fifties who had spent the last decade serving Zara faithfully, assisting her. The bitchy make-up and hair artists – mostly men – often hired to polish Zara always looked down on Shanti. The woman had never let her village modesty slip, always wearing plain sarees with her hair in a knot on her head, no make-up of her own. Just the morning vermillion dot on her forehead from her *puja* and the aroma of *agarbatti* incense sticks. Yet it was Shanti who Zara trusted most, more than any of the vacuous glamour pusses who were attracted by the sheer brightness of Zara's star. Shanti had been through hell in life: born a mute, she had lived permanently in silence. A silence that hid the evil truths of her past.

After giving herself a facial, she had sat down to paint her face using Zara X, her own make-up brand that made her more money than even her movies did. Zara had become famous as being the only actress that regularly did her own hair and make-up, and even designed her own clothes. They all lauded her creativity, but in reality, she was always thinking of her future, of her brand, ready to advertise the products and outfits she wore. Plus, the bitchy make-up artists liked to rub her face in the fact that she wasn't from a rich or filmi background and always cast aspersions on her sophistication. Well, Zara was having the last laugh now, raking in the money from her trademark looks.

She issued instructions to Shanti, telling her what she needed. Zara had gone against the subtle naked look she normally wore when out in public, ramping up the glamour quotient for the premiere. Her lips were clotted-blood red, her eyes rimmed with thick black kohl, touches of rose-gold along her cheekbones and shoulders. Her eyelids were magenta, with diamanté encrusted eyelashes and matching stones sparkling in her hair, which she had pulled back into a thick plait. Diamond earrings from Mouawad were the only jewellery she was wearing. It was her outfit that would get everyone talking though, and would fill the column inches tomorrow, her image splashed across the Internet within seconds of her arriving at the venue as every smartphone in the crowd took a shot of her. When Zara was finished, Shanti put a small dot of black *kajal* on her cheek, to ward off the evil eye. And she was definitely at risk of that.

Those rich bitches of Malabar Hill who had looked down on her for years, the snobbish fashionista journalists who always said they could tell her breeding from her bad dress sense, and every armchair Internet troll who tore her to pieces online, while burning with envy at the price tags on her clothes, would all be left speechless tonight. In a coup fitting her superstar status, and bypassing her favourite Indian designer, Sabyasachi, for the night, Zara had been convinced by Laura Kim and Fernando Garcia, the heirs to Oscar de la Renta, to wear their first custom made saree. It was layers of white chiffon and silk, embroidered with real gold thread and finished with the same diamantés that were in her hair and eyelashes. It was her defence, keeping the eyes of the world on the outer shell, blinded by her battledress, so they didn't see the real Zara Das, the chinks in her emotional armour. She had turned to her favourite Indian shoe designer, Anita Dongre, for her exclusive white and gold sandals, covered with more of the diamantés. Zara had known Dongre long before the Duchess of Cambridge made her internationally famous.

Shanti handed Zara her iPhone X, in its exclusive Buccellati gold and diamond starburst cover, the left corner light flashing an alert. Social media messages. She should have switched them off today; cut herself off from the hatred. She couldn't though; like some slow-motion accident, she was drawn into the drama and felt unable to stop herself. As she read the messages of hate, the threats to torture and kill her, she was rendered powerless, unable to move. She felt the very air sucked out of her lungs, her world suddenly small and brittle.

Zara realised she was holding her breath, her fists clenched against her stomach, the image of herself in the mirror as false as a broken idol. The beautiful woman reflected back at her – this wasn't her true self. The real Zara was lurking somewhere close, always lurking, waiting to drown and suffocate her. Ten years of dragging herself to the top, and now, they were trying to drag her down again.

Zara opened the sliding doors in her bedroom and rushed to her balcony. She looked out at the water, suddenly menacing, purple-grey in the dark and fake lighting from the metropolis around her, the shadowy palm trees swaying like spectres. She closed her eyes, gripping the sides of the balcony and counting backwards from a hundred, trying to control her breathing. *Focus on the number, the breathing, just being. Let the anxiety go, let the darkness evaporate.* Only the darkness wasn't inside her, it was outside, and it was threatening to destroy her.

–

VJ was slouched in the living room, his dirty feet on the sofa that had been especially imported from Paris, like the rest of her lounge furniture. Zara had spent so long having to make do, that when she made it, she only wanted the best. Even if she couldn't afford it. Luckily for her, Mumbai was full of men who would give a beautiful woman like her anything she wanted. Stupid pricks. And here was the dumbest prick of them all, she thought, looking at VJ cracking monkey nuts, bits of shell falling over her baroque-inspired couch and handmade rugs from Istanbul.

'Get me some liquor,' he shouted at Shanti. The maid bristled, she loathed VJ, but she tolerated him for Zara's sake. Shanti shook her head, indicating there was no liquor. 'What are you saying? I don't understand you, you dumb cunt.'

'Don't speak to her like that. Shanti, get VJ some juice. There is no alcohol in the flat, I'm on a detox.'

VJ looked Zara over, smirking. VJ was from a small village outside Hyderabad and had come to Mumbai to make his own fortune. Zara had met him in her early days, and they had together made their steady climb to the top. The only difference, he had replaced his burner phone and clipboard with an iPhone X and a tablet computer. He was still the slimy bastard he had been back then.

'White again. Isn't that fraud?' he said bitterly, his eyes trailing her designer saree. 'The virginal Queen of Bollywood. Fake. Like the diamonds in your hair.'

She ignored him, thinking again that she desperately needed to get rid of him. He was becoming impossible, had been for years now. The more famous and rich she had become, the less she needed him. VJ knew this and clung to her like a leech. In his head lingered the secrets of Zara's past and how she had gone from a girl who had run away from home with nothing to being the highest paid actress in Bollywood. And she knew he wasn't afraid to use them against her.

Zara had already put plans into place to deal with him. She had been in talks with Kavita Ruia, the hottest talent manager in India, to take over her management. Zara had received a contract, and she just needed to work out the legal details in such a way that VJ would be left unable to stop her in any way. What he did after that, Zara didn't know.

'You need to have a word with that bitch on security. She wouldn't let me in. Said *Zara Ma'am* had forbidden anybody from coming up today. Zara *Ma'am*. "Madame" is more appropriate isn't it? Stupid whore.'

He looked directly at her as he threw out the Hindi word *randi*. Zara held his stare, her green eyes boring into his black ones full of hatred. He had lost his control, which made him angry and dangerous.

'And yet here you are,' Zara said bitterly.

'I called her manager, had him tell the bitch to let me up. I still have my passkey to the flat anyway.'

VJ clapped his hands, the debris from them falling onto her rug. He walked over to her. Zara froze as he approached, her heart hammering inside her head. She could smell nuts and cheap beer on his breath as he spoke into her face.

'Pull a trick like that again, and you watch what tricks I can pull. You understand?'

Zara stared at him, but didn't respond. She didn't trust herself to speak; fear would be laced into every word that came out, and she didn't want to give him the satisfaction. Not just him, but every man out there who thought they owned her. They were all the same: they saw her films, downloaded her pictures, read the gossip rags, and staked a claim. In moments like these she realised she had no one to turn to, no one to help her.

They were interrupted by the clink of glass as Shanti came back with the juice. Her eyes bored into VJ, reading the situation, then turned to Zara, who nodded her head subtly to indicate she was ok. VJ laughed and kissed Zara on the cheek, his hands squeezing her waist as he did so. Zara wanted to scream, to pick up one of the heavy metal awards in her cabinet and crush his skull. Only she couldn't. Not yet.

'Your car is here, waiting to take you to the premiere.'

'Are you coming with me?' she managed, her voice a whisper.

He looked at her with his empty eyes, snake's eyes, unblinking, dead.

'Not tonight,' he said.

She felt relief, then fear. VJ never passed up an opportunity to be at the centre of her success. Tonight was the premiere of her new movie, a biopic of the young queen who had helped lead the mutiny against the British. It was meant to be her big crossover breakthrough, the role that would get her movie an Oscar nomination which would lead to the Hollywood roles that only big names like Aishwarya Rai and Priyanka Chopra had managed so far. Only things hadn't panned out that way, and instead it was the movie that was threatening to destroy her completely.

VJ put on shades and escorted her to her front door.

'Have a blast tonight,' he said, smirking at her again.

She felt herself go cold and wished there was more than just the see-through Oscar de la Renta saree covering her.

–

Zara trembled as she read the message, seated in the back of the white Mercedes taking her through the busy streets of Bandra. The premiere was happening at the Juhu PVR theatre, famous for its Bollywood openings. She felt her stomach tighten, and felt so small in this city of twenty-two million people.

Zara looked at her phone screen, tracing the words with her fingers. Gone were the days of dead letter drops, paint daubed on walls, a physical intimidation needing a physical presence. Now, someone could be invisible and send their hatred and threats through the cloud, direct to the device that she kept close to her all day.

She zoomed into the screen:

> *I wonder what I would do if I only had moments to live.*
> *You don't have to wonder, Zara.*

The threat was nothing new. Since the trailer of the song had been revealed, Zara had gone from being the nation's sweetheart to being the most demonised woman in the country. And then an insider leaked the entire song online. All it had taken to undo the hard work of ten painful years was five minutes and thirty-six seconds.

She pressed the intercom and told her chauffeur to take a longer route. She needed time to compose herself. Zara had slowly removed VJ's henchmen from her life over the years, one by one. VJ had created hell, threatened to expose her, but she had called his bluff. She knew he was saving his ammunition for some other day. She instead hired her own staff, all of them women, including her driver tonight, a single mother with five kids and an elderly mother to feed.

Zara didn't know why this new message stood out. She had been trolled on Twitter and Facebook, had been parodied mercilessly on YouTube; there were Instagram accounts dedicated to slating her. One particular website had videos showing images of Zara with cello tape across her mouth which ended with her being burned alive. This had been a misfire though. It had led to feminists across the country taking up for her, angered by the idea that she was being told to keep quiet.

Despite the feminist protests and backlash against the video of mutilation, the campaign of hatred had continued on social media. Only Zara wasn't going to give in to the threats and hide away. She had worked too hard and gone through too much hardship to lose it all now. And she would do anything to stop that happening. Anything.

–

The flashes were bright, the voices deafening as her Mercedes stopped at the red carpet. The cinema security had told her not to risk doing her usual long walk up into the theatre, but to park her car right at the entrance so she would only be exposed for a few seconds at most. She was told not to stop for photographs and autographs, not to be her normal self.

Zara looked out at the throng of faces and felt relief. Her fans hadn't deserted her; she wasn't over, not for them. The young girls screaming her name, wanting selfies with her, the ones who bought her make-up, perfume, and clothes. The ones who followed her Instagram and watched her YouTube tutorials on how to recreate her looks. They were all still there, what did they care about the misogynistic campaign against her?

Still, they weren't enough to sustain her career. She knew that too. Once she had enough fame and power, Zara made sure that the women she played were tough, independent, not like the mother she had grown up with, happy to stay under her husband's thumb. No, she was speaking for the women of India today. Educated, hard-working, successful. They could be housewives or CEOs, but the bottom line was that not a single one of them would be abused, physically or mentally. And that was always the message.

That's why Zara was the reigning queen. She made sure her films were for women and about women, but put in enough sex appeal to get the men horny and into the cinema, and then she punched them in the face with her social messages mid-jerk.

And it was for the men that she had done the item song. The irony wasn't lost on her, as they were the ones who had reacted most against it. Hypocritical bastards. An onslaught had followed in the press and across the Internet, protestors on the streets burning effigies of her. Men with placards, saying she had tarnished the reputation of the nation's heroine, demanding her death, while still probably jerking off to her pictures on a regular basis. She had seen the images on the web, her face digitally remastered onto porn actresses' bodies. Zara had been disgusted at first, and then let it go. The men came in more ways than one, and as long as that meant her films were cashing in at the box office, she chose to ignore the obviously faked snuff.

The girls screaming her name weren't enough though. Women, men, young, old. She needed them all. To make it you had to appeal to everyone, producers needed to bank on you to bring in the masses. Hundreds of movies were released every year, only a few made money, and less still made the big bucks.

Zara's films had done just that. Now though, producers were all terrified, scared of being tarnished with the same infamy that was following her around.

Cowards. It was fine while they were pimping her out and making money from her, but when it got tough, they were nowhere to be found. If it hadn't been for the torture website, and the feminists, she would already have been finished. When you were hated in Mumbai, people could literally wipe you off the face of the earth.

Zara's phone beeped. It was a message from the same anonymous number she was sure had sent her the earlier threat. Only it was worse: *BOOM!*

That's all it said. Time seemed to slow down for her, as she looked at the crowds, the message, and the flashing lights. As though in a blinding fog, she sat immobilised for seconds, then she came to and reacted quickly. Opening the door to her car, she threw herself out, screaming at her driver to do the same. Zara landed heavily and thought she had broken a rib and maybe her elbow. The press went crazy, as did her fans. Hysteria filled the air as the hired event security desperately tried to keep everyone away from her. She forced herself up and ran as fast as she could away from the car, trying to alert everyone. The driver had got out and was shouting after her. How far were the crowd? She couldn't tell. She was pleading with them to go back, screaming as loud as she could. Her driver, wide-eyed and panicked, was rushing towards her as Zara tripped and fell, toppling a life-size cut-out of herself dressed in the armour of the warrior queen. She tried to see where her driver was, saw her still too close to the vehicle. *Get away! Run!* The words were loud in her head, but nothing came out of Zara's mouth.

Zara watched as the car exploded, as her driver was engulfed in a whirlwind of fire, flying debris, and smoke. As the world was filled with terror, all Zara could hear were screams, renting the air and deafening her. And then she realised they were her own, before her world went black.

Chapter One

Zara was pissed. Did they not fucking well know who she was? Actually, it seemed they didn't. Mumbai airport had been fine, they knew who they were dealing with. Zara Das. The woman they fantasised about when they were screwing their wives. Despite the controversy, and despite the myth that every Indian was after her blood, those guys had been busy taking selfies with her and getting her to sign their hands and chests. Then to land on English soil and be ignored and treated as a nobody? What a joke. The border patrol at Heathrow were asking her questions she shouldn't have to answer.

'How long will you be staying? Did you travel alone? Where in London will you reside?'

Zara was tempted to scream at them, 'Do you know who I am?' Only her ego might not take the blank stares that met her outburst. It was her own fault, she should have flown with the rest of the cast on the private jet her director Raj Dillon had arranged, except she didn't really want to travel with them. Her co-stars and their wives usually treated her like vaccinations: unpleasant but necessary. Zara didn't fancy eight hours of snide looks and whispered comments, so had come alone.

As if the humiliation of airport security wasn't bad enough, and despite travelling first class on BA, she then had to wait for her transport to turn up.

'Raj, this is not fucking ok,' she shouted into her phone. 'I don't give a fuck you just landed yourself, or you had to check your crew in. They wouldn't have jobs if I wasn't part of this project, you should be here.'

Raj arrived thirty minutes later, and she bawled him out all the way to the hotel. He was sweating in the unexpected heatwave that had London in its grip, dressed in jeans and a cotton shirt, wearing a baseball cap. The casual get-up couldn't hide his intelligent good looks, and she wondered again why he had settled for his wife. Raj had access to every beautiful woman in Bollywood, all of them creaming themselves to be in his movies, and he had chosen that average-looking American woman, Jackie, instead. Maybe he was secretly after a Green Card.

'What if something had happened to me?' she continued, her anger levels pushed up so high she knew she was going to take a while to come down. 'You know my life's in danger, you can't just leave me unprotected like this. And the racist bastards at the embassy wouldn't give Shanti a visa, so I had no one with me. I mean, what risk does she pose? Ridiculous!'

'I'm sorry, we arranged private security for you but they got confused and went to the hotel instead. It won't happen again.'

'It had better not,' she threatened.

'It won't, I promise. And you know I tried to get Shanti here, they wouldn't budge. She hasn't got any papers, or a passport. You don't usually travel with her anyway, why is it so important this time?'

'This time is different. I feel different, I need her. Nothing is the same since that night, why don't you get that? Why does nobody get that?'

'Look, we're nearly at the hotel. We are shooting tomorrow morning, so order room service this evening, relax and watch the free Netflix. They have a great spa, and everything is paid for us by James Kapoor and Sheikh Walid.'

'Are you kidding me? Is that freak sheikh staying at the hotel with us?' Zara had met enough sheikhs in the Middle East over the years. They were usually polite, respectful, fun even. Walid though? He had something loose in his head.

'He's bankrolling our movie, Zara, we've had this conversation before.'

He was right; she had already lambasted him in Mumbai. They had met on the thirty-eighth floor of the St Regis tower, with breathtaking views across the city skyline all the way to the sea.

'He's a fucking letch,' she had said. 'Find another sheikh, they all love me in the Emirates. Or find someone else. Someone who isn't going to attempt to grope me as reward for financing this film.'

Raj had been drinking water, she had gone for a Zara D, the cocktail named after her. It tasted disgusting – too much sugar not enough champagne –but every time she drank it she did it as though she was making love to the glass, while taking a selfie which she uploaded to Instagram and her millions of followers. She got a nice cut of the profits Zara D made.

'There aren't many choices, Zee,' Raj had said, sipping his water, avoiding her eyes. 'They're our executive producers now. James Kapoor will give us the majority of the budget we need; the rest is coming from Walid.'

Zara had groaned, slamming down her cocktail glass.

'Yeah, and what price is Kapoor extracting? Making you cast his fucking asshole son in the movie!'

'Come on, Zee. Kapoor is letting us stay in his seven-star hotel in London and paying for the London production unit. He pulled some strings and got us funding from the UK government as well. Casting his son for a secondary role isn't such a high price. And you had no issue with him when you were the face of Kapoor Steel for their media blitz.'

'That's different, all actors do endorsements. What I don't like is him and Walid having control over this movie.'

Zara had curled up into her seat, aware that everyone was secretly watching her. They would all be tweeting about it later no doubt, so she lowered her voice.

'I don't know why you're doing all this, Raj,' she had said. 'You could make this movie with any other actress, make it in India, and get funding the normal way. Casting me is forcing you to do all this.'

Raj had looked at her intensely. She remembered the days when they had begun their careers in Bollywood. It was her debut movie, and he was assistant director.

'I wrote this movie with you in mind, and I will make it with you in it or I won't make it at all.'

Raj had adapted Jane Austen's *Pride and Prejudice*, and called it *Kismet India*.

'It's been done so many times, I still don't get it,' she had bitched, while drinking Zara D and fake smiling for the onlookers. Despite the hip urban Mumbai socialites around them, nothing attracted attention like a Bollywood star.

'It's time to turn the tables. How many films have been made about poor, ignorant Indians falling for wealthy Westerners? Or in reality how many people in the past have had arranged marriages to their cousins abroad, to better their family's situation? Well fuck that shit, Zee. It's time we showed the world that India is back. I want to show it's the non-resident Indians who are desperate to marry our new rich; to show the world I grew up in.'

'Do you really think the NRIs will be that interested in your take on life, Raj? They live in their little closed bubbles in the West, born and brought up with their warped images of India. What can a producer's son have to show them? The parties, drinking, loose sex, and cocaine? The spoilt upbringing of a Bollywood Prince?'

'Come on, Zee, it wasn't that bad. You just see the worst of it.' He had gone quiet, not able to meet her eyes. She knew what was said about her, the murky stories about her rise up the greasy pole. If only they knew.

'You should have cast a British actress, or Katrina Kaif. She has the accent at least.'

'I wanted you. You are my Maya. My version of Elizabeth. If you had said no, I wouldn't have made this film.'

Zara had seen something in Raj that night she didn't see any more in most people she met. Loyalty and vision. Things that meant something. Things that set you apart, were testament to your strong moral core. They were also the things that got you killed easily.

–

Zara felt her anger subside, replaced by mounting excitement, as London opened itself up to her with its familiar landmarks. She never failed to be in thrall to it, as she followed the thick river glistening with reflected sunlight, staring out at St Paul's, Westminster Abbey, the Houses of Parliament, the London Eye, and the line of bridges that seemed endless. After Mumbai, she thought London was the best city in the world. Zara had made multiple trips over the years: as her star had risen, so had the pockets of producers and media moguls who were willing to pay her fares. She had done outdoor song shoots, press junkets, specials for the different media companies around; Sony, Zee, Colors, B4U, Star, and Eros. There had even been an International Bollywood Film awards ceremony at the O2, and she was told that if she came, at their expense, she would be given the best actress trophy. Since her last visit to the English capital, she noticed that more and more skyscrapers had infiltrated the classic skyline. She didn't mind them in Mumbai, but in London they seemed to represent an unwelcome corporate takeover.

The BMW Raj was driving crawled up Northumberland Avenue, until they were right at Trafalgar Square; the archway leading to St James's Park on one side, and the grand stucco Georgian building of the hotel in front, covered in ivy and with the British and Indian flags hanging from the roof. She suppressed a smile, her stressful journey all but forgotten. Until she saw VJ as the car came to a stop outside the hotel entrance. Zara felt her stomach tighten.

'What's he doing here? Did you invite him?'

'He's your secretary, I thought you wanted him here.'

'You know how I feel about him, why would I?'

'He insisted when I signed your contract and agreed your fee. I thought it was odd, but it was your signature on there.' The bastard must have tampered with it after she signed it, she thought.

'Is he staying here?' she spat. Zara had signed a contract with Kavita Ruia just before leaving for London, and was hoping to break the news to VJ via phone or text, while he was thousands of miles away. She had felt brave and reckless after the explosion, thinking, what could VJ do that was worse than someone trying to blow her up? Seeing him here, she felt the fear of having to tell him while he was close enough to do some real damage to her.

'No, he's staying with the crew in the Hilton,' Raj reassured her.

'You got something right at least.' Zara took a breath to let her anxiety drop a couple of ranges. Kavita had arranged for her London office head honcho, Collette Dove, to deal with her PR and itinerary while she was in town. That was how she knew she was dealing with a seasoned professional. Kavita not only had Mumbai in her hands, she had an international presence in London, Paris, New York, and Los Angeles.

Raj opened her car door and helped her out, then said he had to go to a meeting with the production manager responsible for the UK staff.

'Will you be ok? Checking in?'

'I will fucking well have to be, won't I?'

'What did I tell you about swearing in public?' said VJ, speaking the street Hindi he preferred. 'And I told you, don't speak English here, they will all understand you.'

Zara gave him a look, put on her Gucci shades, and let the emerging hotel staff deal with her Louis Vuitton embossed luggage.

'This hotel is for the stars, not the help,' she said, attempting to storm past him.

VJ bristled physically, taking a step to block her from entering. Looking at his cheap face in a city where he had no

16

power and no control, she saw him for the lowlife he was. And that gave her a dangerous confidence. She deliberately pushed him aside as she walked past him, but he had no shame and followed her into the hotel.

The porters were staring at her, all of them brown, all of them knowing exactly who she was. *That's right, boys, Zara fucking Das is in your orbit.* She smiled at them warmly. There was a correlation between how nice she was to people which was directly proportionate to what they could do for her career. The porters got a smile. They would watch her movies at least. VJ got nothing. The arsehole didn't even do that.

The Mirage definitely lived up to its name. A converted mansion block opposite Trafalgar Square, with St James Park and the Mall at its rear, a view directly onto the front of Buckingham Palace, it had been bought and revamped by James Kapoor, the billionaire industrialist and one of the richest men in the world. In the middle of classical London, Kapoor had built interiors worthy of a palace in the heyday of any Rajput Maharajah.

The vast spherical entrance lobby was marble floors and pillars, sweeping up into a giant chandelier with nine circles of crystals, the ceiling hung with smaller chandeliers. When you looked up, it was like the window display of a diamond jeweller's. Exotic palms were potted around the space, with divans, rugs, and drapes of maroon velvets and gold completing the opulent look. Reception itself was a solid marble block, with old style finger dial phones on the counter and smooth jazz infused with Indian music playing in the background. Zara felt as though she had walked into the 1920s.

The hotel manager, Gareth Jones, in his late fifties she guessed, came out especially to greet her, totally ignoring VJ. He presented her with a bouquet of flowers, before introducing her to a sweet-looking young man.

'This is Kasim Shah, he is your personal butler while you stay here. He will be staying in the staff quarters so feel free to call on him anytime,' Gareth said, almost bowing to her. Obviously, James Kapoor had given him special instructions.

'Anything at all you need, ma'am, please just ask of me,' Kasim said in heavily accented English. 'You are already checked in and I will have your luggage brought to your room, so all you need to do is follow me and then enjoy your stay please.'

Yes, that's how she should be treated, not looked at like some illegal immigrant by border control asking her how long she was staying. Yes, she would enjoy her stay here she knew, and if everyone was as ass-kissing as the hotel manager, she would *really* enjoy her stay.

'You can go,' she told VJ.

'I insist on staying, making sure you don't have any issues.' His voice was cold and full of rage, she didn't want to be alone with him, but didn't want to cause a public scene.

As her butler, Kasim, escorted her and VJ through the opulent glass and marble corridors, images from the past flitted through Zara's mind, they always did when she was surrounded by luxury like this: eating leftovers from fast food boxes others couldn't finish; days when she subsisted on three day old *daal* and stale *roti*. Her private suite was more like an upscale apartment than a hotel room, with a lounge, dining area, balcony, bathroom, a shower room, a walk-in closet with wall to wall mirrors, a separate dressing room, and a bedroom with a stylish four poster draped with red and gold velvet curtains. Her personal wardrobe of the latest designer clothes and her array of cosmetics had arrived with the rest of the equipment that would be used on the movie. Her clothes had been carefully hung in the closets, her shoes laid out in the racks provided, and her personal brand make-up and cosmetics placed on the dressing table. The perks of stardom, you didn't have to carry your own stuff or unpack it either.

Zara felt a sudden urgent desire to show her parents this place, to see the look on her mother's face as she walked around the palatial corridors, her mouth open in wonder at the display. Her mother, who had raised Zara somehow on nothing and less. Who had lived the dull life she had been allotted by fate without complaint. Zara felt sadness envelop her, feeling the chill of the luxury around her, cold like a mausoleum. Her parents deserved to see this, deserved to experience what their sacrifices had achieved. In a land where caste and the poverty you were born into could still be a barrier that couldn't be broken, Zara had done just that, escaping her destiny of living with just enough to having it all.

Her father wouldn't come though. Traditional, proud, and having just enough not to have to beg was a lethal combination. His small town conservative values had caused him to threaten her to come home when she had first left, then to accuse his only child of being a whore as soon as his friends first saw her ad campaigns. He had accused her of shaming him and his ancestors, and her mother had quietly accepted his verdict, because that was what still happened in some places. Places that seemed so alien to Mumbaikers, to Londoners. Instead of her parents, it was VJ who was experiencing the Mirage, always VJ who got to taste the finest things in life. Zara Das, the woman millions wanted to possess, had been completely rejected by the people closest to her. It always hurt when she thought about it.

'Would you like anything else?' Kasim asked, once he had given her a tour of her suite.

'No, it's perfect,' she said, meaning it. She went to get money from her Loewe purse to tip him, but he waved her off.

'There is no need. Mr Kapoor has forbidden staff from taking any gratuity from our special guests, ma'am. He will recompense us all once your stay has been a success.'

I bet he will, she thought. Kapoor Junior was going to get his big Bollywood break without even cutting a sweat, so daddy dearest would be paying out blindly, she had no doubt. Still, she liked the butler's honesty.

'Will sir also be staying here?' Kasim asked, looking amiably at VJ.

'No, he won't.' Zara's voice was cold and matter of fact, no room for misinterpretation of her intent.

'I will leave you to relax, ma'am. Please install the hotel app on your phone and you can use it to summon me anytime, or you may also call reception.'

When they were alone, VJ sprawled himself on her bed, his legs open.

'I need to shower and change. You can go.'

'You want to watch that attitude of yours, *Zara Ma'am*. You wouldn't want anything else leaking online, would you? Look at the mess you're already in.'

Zara narrowed her eyes at him as he taunted her with the video that had leaked online and was threatening to destroy her completely. It was the item number – the song filmmakers liked to put in their movie to attract the masses, the catchy song they hoped would burn up the charts, usually with scantily clad heroines and backing dancers – she had done for her last movie. Based on the life of the Rani of Jhansi, the queen who led the rebellion against the tyranny of the East India Company in 1857, it was a serious historical epic, a meaty role where Zara was the pivot to the whole film. It was her attempt to position herself as not just as the face of blockbuster fluff, but a high calibre performer. Only Zara had panicked. She thought the film might be too dry, too intense, excluding vast swathes of the audience, especially the pathetic men who wanted to let off some steam while watching her. To placate them, Zara had decided to spice up the serious movie with a song in which the queen, the heroine of the Indian freedom struggle, had decided to enjoy the monsoon. As the rains fell, Zara had danced provocatively in a saree that got wetter and clingier. Underneath the saree, rather than a full petticoat and blouse, Zara had worn a bejewelled bustier, barely hiding her cleavage.

The backlash to the song had culminated in the car bomb, and the death of her driver, whose elderly mother and five young kids had been left destitute. Zara had visited them in private and made sure they wouldn't starve. She did it away from the cameras, and the press had gone to town with stories about her selfishness at not visiting the family of her driver, a woman who had died in her service to protect her.

Zara had been a wreck after the attack, withdrawing into her apartment and not venturing out. Mumbai police and counter-terrorism had created a ring of steel around her building complex, until they had eventually caught the perpetrator. He was a young man from the slums, who had been acting on the orders of the supposed descendants of the heroine on India's struggle for independence. It was all a front though, the authorities later uncovered it was actually a wannabe Mumbai Mafia lynchpin, who wanted Zara's scalp to enter the underworld with a bang. Even when the don and most of his men were behind bars, Zara still felt anxious. The police could easily have missed one of his henchmen.

The video and its aftermath had been deadly, yet here was VJ, mocking her with the tragedy. Zara turned all her hatred towards him, this man who had usurped the place in her life that belonged to someone else. Anyone else. She deserved someone who cared, surely?

'Listen, VJ, I don't give a damn any more what you do or what leaks online. I've faced death and now nothing you or anyone else can do will scare me.'

'Cheap words from a cheap tramp,' he said, laughing in her face. 'I know you, Zara, every dirty-little-secret inch of you, and I will destroy you if you cross me.'

'Try me, you low rent asshole.'

VJ leapt to his feet, grabbing her wrists and twisting them roughly behind her back. Zara looked him straight in the eyes, not flinching despite the pain. She wouldn't give him the satisfaction.

'Listen to me, you pathetic little whore, this might not be Mumbai, but don't think I don't know people here. I don't like your behaviour of late, I'm watching you. And if you push me too far...'

'I suggest you let go of the lady, before I make you.'

Zara looked at the man who had just appeared in her room. He was well over six foot and broad, his black suit unable to hide his well-built body. He had the most piercing blue eyes and thick dark hair. Something about him told her instantly that he was someone you didn't mess with.

VJ stared at him, tightening his grip on Zara.

'I will count to five,' said the man, starting the countdown. At one, she felt VJ let go of her, and she moved away quickly. The man came closer, his eyes on VJ.

'Dan Rourke,' he said, 'responsible for your security, Miss Das. Apologies for the confusion this morning, there was a miscommunication about how you were arriving.'

'Anything could have happened to me,' Zara spat. She couldn't help directing the anger she felt towards VJ in Dan's direction instead. Cornered, she had returned to type. Striking out at everyone. 'Hardly fills me with confidence. Who hired you?'

'James Kapoor,' Dan said, unmoved by her attack.

'I will make sure he hears about your incompetence,' she told him. VJ watched their exchange, unsure of himself. Zara had seen that look before, and what followed was never pleasant. Zara narrowed her eyes at VJ and ordered him to go. VJ left, throwing a look of utter hatred at her, and the same towards Dan. She let herself enjoy the momentary triumph as he slinked away, all the while wondering what revenge VJ would exact from her in return.

Chapter Two

Zara sat on the lounge sofa, scrolling through her phone, looking disinterested, while Dan went through the security protocols he had put in place. Zara thought he might be ex-military, he was so stoic, not reacting to her nonchalant mood at all.

'The Mirage take their security extremely seriously, as you can imagine. London's only seven-star hotel is a target for a number of threats, from terrorists to international mafia.'

Zara snorted, Dan continued as though she wasn't there. 'They also respect their clientele's privacy, so there is a distinct lack of CCTV in private areas of the hotel. There is only one lift that can access this floor from reception or the lower ground floor where the staff are. If you wish to access any other floor, you need to go back to the reception area and take different lifts.'

Zara pulled off the pink Balenciaga platform shoes she had worn on the airplane. Her travel outfit consisted of shorts, topped off with a Prada poncho. Zara removed that now, revealing the thin material Fendi white blouse she had on underneath. The cold of the air con was making her nipples hard and show through her sheer bra. Dan didn't seem to notice, droning on about the lifts. Zara checked the itinerary Collette had sent through on her phone, listing the launches and events she was invited to attend. Zara had been asked to confirm which ones she was ok to go to, given the tight filming schedule. That was different. Normally VJ told her which ones she had to attend, or she went to parties hosted by industry colleagues.

She couldn't really call anybody in the film industry a friend and had always been wary of forming those sorts of relationships. At first it wasn't out of choice; she was given about as much respect as a street walker by some of the film fraternity, especially the ones who had been born into the grand movie dynasties or had won beauty pageants or been models in former lives. They had waltzed into the best roles while Zara had done it the hard way. As time moved on, Zara had become closed to any advances of friendliness, cutting off anyone before they had a chance to reject her, acting like a bitch so nobody had the chance to treat her like crap because she got in there first. And she had been right to, she thought, thinking of the way they had all turned on her when she was in need. A small voice told her maybe she should have been nicer to people and made some friendships she could have relied on now.

'Above you are the penthouse suites,' Dan was saying. 'Mr Kapoor keeps those for himself and his family, it is where they stay when they are in town. And there are two other suites on that floor which are given over to royals and presidential guests.'

Zara ran her fingers through her hair, and rubbed her arms, deliberately pushing her breasts forward. She kept her green eyes on his face, thinking how attractive he was, and how solid he looked.

'I have a team of six responsible for your safety while you are in London. I will be on duty during the day, but members of the team will always be available.'

'Available for what exactly?'

'You will have twenty-four-hour cover provided, just in case. This is my card, and on there is also a mobile number which is cleared for your use only. I will send you an app you can download onto your phone, it will work as an emergency button even if the phone is locked.' Zara smelled leather and citrus as he came close. 'Whoever is covering will be available to help when you need, and if you are unhappy with any of these arrangements, you can call me. Mr Kapoor has insisted we provide you with the best.'

'And how exactly will you provide crowd control? I attract masses of people sometimes, how will you make sure they don't harm me?'

'This isn't your home turf, so I expect crowds will be minimal.'

'I think that as well as your fuck-up this morning, Dan, you also didn't get the memo that Bollywood is a global brand now, has been for years. I get recognised from the streets of Marrakesh to the ski resorts of Val d'Isere. My fans are everywhere, eager to get near me.'

That wasn't exactly true; she had only even been to the ski resort for an outdoor song sequence shoot. And nobody had recognised her.

'If such a situation arises,' Dan still looked sceptical as he spoke, which irritated the hell out of her, 'I have a back-up team taken from Mr Kapoor's own security.'

'Well, looks like you've got me all tight and safe, Mr Rourke. I'd like to see anyone try to damage me while you're on the payroll. Let's just hope you don't keep going to the wrong location.'

There was a buzz at the door and Dan went to open it. For a moment Zara felt anxious that VJ had returned, instead from the commotion she knew exactly who it was.

'Zara, you old tart, finally made it to my home turf, eh? London better watch itself, me and you are going to tear it up bigtime.'

Ruby Dee was a British journalist who had tried her hand at Bollywood a couple of years earlier. She had interviewed Zara initially before spending six months in Mumbai trying to make it. Ruby had the arrogance her British passport gave her, not giving a damn who she was talking to, or about playing by the Bollywood rules.

'I don't blow smoke up anyone's ass,' she was always saying when people advised her to curb her style to get on. Zara had loved her fresh approach, had envied that level of self-belief, even. It was the bit parts and favours that Zara called in that had got Ruby any traction at all. Her career never even fizzled, but Ruby became practically the only female Zara could consider a friend of sorts, and now she had managed to get her a part in *Kismet India*.

'Ruby, where have you been? I have had such a shit start to my stay. Immigration treated me like some illegal immigrant trying to get in, despite flying first class, there was no security at the airport, and Raj made me wait for ages before turning up.'

'Obviously they didn't get the memo that the queen had arrived! Welcome to London, darling. You're just another brown face here, get ready for Brexit Britain. Although, hello, to your hunky security guard.'

Dan was clearly listening to their conversation, but didn't flinch. He left quickly though.

'Talking of queens, have you seen what that little cow Minnie Chopra tweeted?'

Jasmine 'Minnie' Chopra was the hottest new actress in Mumbai. Zara had seen the headline and the interview that claimed Minnie was going to be the new queen. Two hits and the media were ready to crown her already? Zara would see about that. Minnie was one of Bollywood's star children, her mother was the legendary diva Laila Chopra, who had ruled the box office in the late seventies and early eighties. Minnie had been given the best launch movie by her mother, followed by a number of starring roles that had propelled her up the rankings. Since her debut she had been baiting Zara on social media.

'What's she said now?'

'*London's full of washed-up queens, but the new Queen Bee is in town.*'

'Bitch,' muttered Zara.

'Uber-bitch,' agreed Ruby. 'Why haven't you slapped her yet?'

'I've managed to ignore her so far. Any parties or events I attend where she's present I pretend she doesn't exist and avoid her.'

'You need to start twit-slapping her online, your fans expect it. Put her in her place.'

'It's ok. I agreed to let Raj cast her in the movie. There is only one way to show her who the real queen is, Ruby dearest. I will out-act that spoilt little brat in every scene.'

'A slap on Twitter would be so much more fun, but whatever works for you. Thanks for getting me the role by the way.' Ruby popped open the complementary bottle of Bollinger that the Mirage had left in Zara's room. It wasn't a big role; Ruby was playing the character of Charlotte from the novel, but it was a big movie. 'Charlotte the Harlot, think that sounds just like me. I've given up acting though, I'm the entertainment editor for *Asian Eye* now. It's the best gig, I get to go to every celeb party for free, guzzle as much bubbly as I can, and get up close and personal to some very hot guys. And I get paid. It's like being a star only without the fame bullshit. Cheers.' Zara shook her head at the glass Ruby was offering her. 'Allow it, Zara, you still on that crazy detox plan? Live a little. You've done it, you're at the top.'

'Yes, but when you're at the top, there's only way to go.'

'Trust me, Zara, Whingy Minnie ain't gonna replace you. Wow, this place is actually amazing, why don't I get a suite? I'm part of the cast too.'

'Speak to Raj, or come and stay with me?'

'I'd love to, but I'm living with a man now. I know, I'm not telling anyone yet. He's a writer and Muslim and his parents don't know yet. That's right, darling, even in London in this day and age that's an issue. Go figure.'

'Trust you to break the rules even when you finally find someone you want to settle down with.'

'Settle down? Steady on, I'm not done yet. He's a trial guy; if it works with him, I'll find someone I really want to be with.'

Zara didn't reply. Ruby was so easy about her private life, about the men she dated and slept with. Zara was the opposite. She didn't know how to have a normal relationship, had never even been close to having one. She envied Ruby in that moment, and thought how she would give everything to have someone love her for herself. She put the thought away. It wasn't going to happen, so why dream of it, even?

–

Zara slept fitfully in the afternoon, jet lag catching her unawares. When her eyes opened, it was six p.m., and her mind and body were still tired from the shadowy threat of her nightmares. Zara spent the next few hours eradicating the travel from her. She stood under a cold shower for a few minutes, rubbing her body with a home-made pomade containing lemon, coconut, and an assortment of herbs. She avoided the harshness of chemicals in cosmetic soaps and shampoos, instead preferring her own natural formulas. Soon she would be launching Zara X2, a range of shower gels and hair products made from mainly natural Ayurveda inspired ingredients.

After the shower, she dried her body, and checked it over in the full-length mirror wall that made up one side of the second bathroom. It was a daily ritual, not born from utter vanity, but necessity. She needed to be sure there were no blemishes or marks that might show up on-screen or in pictures as she socialised in Mumbai. Happy everything was as it should be, she rubbed in another home-made lotion made from olive oil, coconut, ginseng, and patchouli. The moisturiser would be part of Zara X2. It was thick and creamy but also smelt amazing.

Zara massaged it into her body, enjoying the sensation of the gentle strokes of her fingers under her breasts, and over her thighs. She felt herself stir and thought about Dan. She wondered if he was still on duty, and if it was too soon and too risky to invite him to play her games. Although he hadn't seemed to be moved by her earlier display, unlike most men she encountered.

Zara hadn't always been so upfront about her sexuality. When she came to Mumbai, she was a virgin like every other decent young woman from a decent family like hers. There were boys at college, and there had been offers. But she was saving herself; she knew there would be someone one day actually worth giving herself to.

Mumbai had quickly taught her there was no place for those who tried to hold on to such ideals. She had lost her virginity quickly, painfully, and for all the wrong reasons. Like every other girl without connections, Mumbai had taken her on a dark road, a road that she didn't like to dwell on, but one that pulsed through her memory. Under the surface, the pain was just waiting to tear through her skin.

They said it so easily in the media. Struggle. *The actress Zara Das struggled for years before getting her big break under producer Amol Dillon, Raj Dillon's father.* The misery behind that word, they would never know and they would never understand.

When her father closed his doors to her, Zara was alone in a way she had never been before. Her situation had caused her to suffer anxiety and panic attacks, as the darkness of the open mouth of Mumbai's underbelly snapped at her. Without any skills or experience, without a godfather or mentor, Zara was at risk of being crushed, just like the thousands of other girls who came to Mumbai. She saw them in cafes, in department stores, working the streets as hookers. Their faces made-up with cheap lipsticks and powder foundations as their desperation clung to them like a stench.

Zara saw herself sliding that way. She wanted to make it so badly, but she soon found out it took more than just wanting a dream to escape a nightmare. Sharing hostel rooms with three other women, women studying and working in call centres, she didn't find any solace. They thought she was deluded, telling her she was no Aishwarya Rai on a regular basis. The same message came from the empty castings she attended, as hungry-eyed casting agents took in her modest small town outfits, and didn't find what they were looking for. The taunts mounted up, reminding her of school, as so-called professionals told her she was too old-fashioned, she needed to wear more modern outfits that revealed who she was – code for just revealing more skin. She complained to VJ, but he would just tell her to listen to the advice she was being given. The times she was told she was too ugly to even be cast as the heroine's friend, or that she should consider skin bleaching, were the worst of all. And yet she saw the average-looking daughters of movie stars being launched in big budget extravaganzas.

How was she meant to look good when she spent her meagre funds on clothes and make-up, with nothing left for food? The hostel provided breakfast and dinner, but her castings took so long and were so far away she went days sometimes without eating either. Zara had been so starved on days that she had eaten from bins and taken to stealing from the café she worked in part time between auditions. Mumbai wasn't cheap, and when you had nothing it was a daily grind.

VJ had played a blinder, waiting until Zara was on the wrong side of desperate to start dangling before her the sleazy meetings she had to endure just to get the small jobs that would mean she could afford the hovel she lived in, and still pretend she was treading water to get to her goal. Zara had fallen for the Bollywood dream like every naïve starlet before her, and had resigned herself to a future of nothingness and pain.

Only, the camera did love her, there was no denying it. VJ often told her how she was nothing special in real life, but on-screen she was spectacular. And as Zara crawled in the dirt, forced to do acts that meant she could survive another day not being homeless or hungry, one job had led to another, like dominoes, until she came to the attention of Raj's father. That break, if it was hers, would mean she had a real chance to make something of her life. To really escape the hell she had fallen into. Zara was willing to do virtually anything to secure it. Only she hadn't realised at the time just what she would have to give up to get the role, how low she would be forced to fall. Once it was done though, Zara made everything of it she could. Fate was finally on her side, and she thought she had passed the darkest times. The jaded heroine of Zara's debut movie, already so washed up through coke and partying although she was only in her early twenties, was too much of a risk, so producers and directors had flocked to Zara's door as the movie made more and more cash at the box office. Zara Das had arrived.

Only Zara saw how easily women, no matter how successful, were still judged, how easily, like vultures, men turned on them. She was a soft target, she had no filmi family to back her up, she had no mentor to shield her from the threats she was facing. The problem with being a self-made superstar was that you could be un-made far too easily.

Zara lay on her bed, her body exfoliated and pampered. She always slept naked, enjoying the feel of clean cotton and silk sheets against her skin. She stared at the ceiling, but it only provided a blank canvas for her thoughts. She decided to distract herself, and messaged her butler, Kasim, for some hot chocolate. He arrived fifteen minutes later, to find Zara dressed in her La Perla slip and robe on the lounge sofa. He had brought the drink on a tray and laid it down with such precision and rehearsed formality she laughed. Kasim blushed.

'It's ok, Kasim, you can drop the stiffness around me,' she said, her eyebrow arched, enjoying his deepening embarrassment. 'Please sit,' she added, taking the large hot cup in her palms. Immediately she felt the familiar comfort of its soothing warmth as the aroma reminded her of happier moments from earlier on in her life. Kasim had perched himself uncomfortably on the seat opposite her, torn between his training and the request of a VIP guest. Zara looked into his eyes. She had noticed them before when she had first met him. They were amber, like honey, and a memory hit her hard. One she didn't like to think about.

'Where are you from?' she asked him, to take her mind away from the abyss.

'I was born in Pakistan, ma'am. I came here six years ago, for work.'

'Six years? And in that time you have made your way up to the only seven-star hotel in London?'

Kasim reddened at the compliment, smiling as he did so.

'My mother told me when I was young that if you do anything, make sure you be the best at it. And if you can't be the best at it, make sure you work so hard that you seem to be the best at it.'

Zara thought of her own mother. The only advice she had given her of late was not to call home and provoke her father, and when Zara offered to send money to make their old age easier, she had simply refused.

'Tell her we don't need her whore money,' her father had been screaming in the background, as her mother ended the call.

'Your mother sounds like a wise woman,' Zara said softly to Kasim.

'She was. She passed this last year.'

Kasim's eyes reflected the sadness he was feeling.

'I'm sorry to hear that,' she said softly. 'You must miss her?'

'It was very hard for me, ma'am. I couldn't attend her funeral even.'

'That's awful. Why?'

'Just some visa issues,' he said without explaining.

'Don't worry, I understand. My maid Shanti was supposed to be here, but they wouldn't let her in. I say she's my maid, but she is so much more than that to me. Isn't that sad? My closest confidante is my maid?' Zara laughed bitterly, feeling odd for having shared so much with this man she had only met a few hours ago. It was the eyes, they brought back memories of someone else, and she was opening up to Kasim because of that.

'I think you are lucky you have somebody you trust, no matter who it is. So many people spend their lives not having even a single person they can turn to. And sometimes the people you should be able to rely on, they are the ones who hurt you the most.'

Zara was touched that Kasim was relaxing in front of her.

'Thank you, Kasim.'

'For what, ma'am?' he asked in surprise.

'Just being here tonight. I was feeling homesick.'

'I am paid to be here twenty-four seven, ma'am, so call on me anytime.'

And there it was, she thought. Her ugly truth. Who would choose to be with her unless they were getting something from it? Whether it was money or her looks.

'I'm tired, I think I'll go to sleep. Have a good night.'

With Kasim gone, her mind was more awake than ever. She stared at her bedroom ceiling, her head filled with the thoughts she wished would go, but which she knew never would.

—

Zara Das was no stranger to being judged for her looks. It had had happened all of her life, and none of it was pleasant. She had been born Parineeta Grover, Pari for short, to a Hindu Punjabi family on the outskirts of Delhi. There was nothing about her parents or family that made them stand out. Her father worked for the railways; her mother was a homemaker. They had two children, twins. Pari and her brother, Dev. There was never very much money to go around, but they weren't poor. In India when you had nothing you really had nothing. Her parents thanked their many gods every day in family puja for all that they did have. It had seemed so unbreakable at the time, Pari confident that she was looked after and safe at home, as she grew up with her best friend and playmate Dev.

As Pari grew older, she became aware of how differently her mother treated her and her brother. Ever since she could remember, she had been told that unlike Dev, she would be a burden on them. They would have to pay out a huge dowry for her, especially because she was so dark-skinned and fat, while Dev was thin and fair, and would marry a wife that would bring a dowry with her. Pari had felt like a burden from before she even started school. As a girl she was expected to help her mother with the chores while Dev was allowed to parade around the neighbourhood with his friends. He didn't neglect his twin sister though, making sure he still found time to play the games they always had. His favourite thing was to watch movies, with Pari at his side. He would narrate every scene to her as they watched, and he would always predict what would happen next. When it didn't, he would say his version would be better, and she agreed – Dev's version usually did sound more interesting. When she found out they would be attending separate single-sex schools, Pari was terrified. She wanted Dev to be with her, but despite a week of crying she was told it wouldn't happen. Dev had comforted her, telling her how she would make so many friends at school, filling her head with anticipation and potential.

Pari remembered how excited she was that first day, imagining at last girls her own age who would fill the gaps in her life that having no sisters had entrenched. They would play with dolls, play make-believe, share gossip and dreams, and she would walk arm in arm with them as she had seen older girls do when she was out and about with her mother. With her dreams bigger than her satchel, she had practically skipped to school. At the gates, her mother had seemed sad, stroking Pari's cheek and walking away quickly to hide her tears. Pari didn't understand what the tears meant until years later. Her mother had let her daughter go, away from the protection she had kept her in at home, and she was now going to face the world. And it was a cruel world.

Pari was wearing her homemade uniform, her oiled hair in pigtails, her books in her small bag, and her tiffin with her lunch. She didn't realise her father's employers were paying her school fees, as they had for her brother. Instead her eyes were full of fantasies of best friends and sisterhoods. Only this school was for girls who came from the next social level up and Pari, with her trademarks of a family that had to skimp and save, was an easy target. She had dreamed for years about the joy she would get from her time at school. But things didn't turn out the way she wanted.

She was short and dumpy, with dark skin and greasy hair. Almost immediately the other children made her the target of their jokes and venom. By the end of the first day someone had pulled her pigtails, pushed her over, emptied her tiffin box into the drains, and she had been called every hurtful name children aged six could know. She had cried at first, but as her tears fell, the girls that tormented her grew in their confidence. Alone, scared, and crushed, Pari had walked home with her head bowed and every ounce of excitement gone from her. Dev asked her if she was ok, and Pari had just stared out of eyes that knew that things would only get worse.

As the daily torment continued, Pari grew more and more insular, trying to be invisible in a school that had nowhere to hide. She became immune to the hatred eventually, expecting it, praying every day that she would survive and that it would end. Faking illnesses not to go to school, failing at her classwork, nothing seemed to ring the alarm bells at home. Except, maybe her parents didn't care, their focus was always on Dev and what he would achieve.

Dev had tried to comfort her, but what could a six-year-old boy really do? So, he soothed his sister the only way he knew how, by watching the latest Bollywood movies with her, never losing his passion and enthusiasm.

And then at nine, Pari had changed. She shot up during the holidays, and came back to school tall and skinny. She looked at herself in the mirror and convinced herself that things would be different. That now she would be accepted, she wouldn't be taunted any more. Dev told her she was beautiful, like a film star. Coming from her brother with his amber eyes, and his creamy skin, who really did look like a film star, Pari dared to hope that maybe now she would be left alone at least. She turned up to the new school year wearing a new uniform, her hair no longer oily but glossy and held back with a hairband. Only, when she walked into school, she soon realised nothing had changed apart from her physical form. The other girls compared her to a drainpipe, mocking her cheap hairbands and shoes. The name-calling was still there, but the girls were now too scared to harass her physically, as she was taller than most of them. They all still said how her green eyes were a joke in such an ugly, black girl like her, and Pari realised that she was still trapped in her torment even now.

Pari retreated even more into her secret world, her world of books that school had introduced her to, and Bollywood films. They were the only things that gave her joy, and she relished them both.

And then things went quickly from bleak to even worse for Pari, and her life entered a place she was still trying to surface from. A place in which she had lost the most precious thing to her. Dev.

–

Zara lay in the four-poster bed watching an old Bollywood movie on her phone. Watching Amitabh Bachchan and Rekha fill the screen, she was reminded of her brother still. Zara felt a tear crawl down her cheek and wished more than anything that he was there with her.

–

Dan Rourke stretched himself in the upholstered red chair that had been placed opposite Zara's door for her security, to keep an eye on anyone entering or leaving. He couldn't believe his life had come to this. His promising career in MI6 cut short through injury, Dan had started to freelance in security, quickly attracting big name clients thanks to some secret work he had done for his previous paymasters. You never really left MI6. And they certainly didn't leave you.

He had met James Kapoor a couple of years ago when the billionaire tycoon had needed some last-minute security for an impromptu trip with his long-term mistress. A week aboard a fancy yacht, sailing around the Mediterranean. Only he hadn't counted on being hijacked by pirates. Luckily for James, he had Dan on board, who had quickly managed to put into place a rescue mission. Which was lucky, given the negative publicity that would have resulted in the exposure of James's little tryst. His wife would have walked off with billions on top of the ordeal of being kidnapped and ransomed that James would have faced.

The details of the hijack stayed between them; there had only been a crew of four on board, all of whom were faithful employees of James Kapoor. And Dan became a staple of the Kapoor empire, being called on when the stakes were high. And with Zara Das, the stakes were higher than even she knew.

Still, she had played to type: arrogant, vain, narcissistic, condescending. Sure, she was a looker, and some hot shot star in Bollywood, but it didn't give her the right to look down on the world.

It was thirty days, he kept telling himself. Thirty days of excellent pay. Money that he desperately needed. Only nobody knew the reason why, not even James Kapoor himself. And Dan was willing to put up with any shit Zara Das threw at him in that time.

Dan's phone buzzed loudly in his hand, Zara's name flashing on the screen. He answered it immediately. Her voice was apprehensive but not worried or hysterical. She confirmed his identity and then asked him to come into her suite.

Zara was seated on the sofa where he had left her earlier, only now she was dressed in an outfit of feminine materials that left little to the imagination. Dan tried not to look, but despite himself he had to admit she was a beautiful woman. He wasn't fazed by this though, he had protected enough famous and powerful people, trophy wives and mistresses always came with the territory. But Zara was different. She wasn't anyone's wife or mistress, she was her own boss.

Zara held her phone out to Dan, and he read what was on her screen. It was a message from an unknown number, and he saw in her eyes the fear that had been caused by it.

YOU CAN RUN BUT YOU CAN'T HIDE. TIME'S UP BITCH. THIS TIME IT'S GOING TO BE YOU.

Chapter Three

They were in a cake shop in Marylebone, Feya, all pink walls and white flowers covering the ceiling. It felt like sitting in a giant cupcake. The staff were all extras, and the crew was minimal for the day, as the space was limited. Raj had discovered it on his recce trip earlier in the year when he had scoped out locations for the shoot. The scene was a confrontation between Darcy and Elizabeth – in Raj's version, rechristened Maya and Rahul – where they each misunderstand each other totally and their fledgling attraction falters.

There was a stone-cold coffee in front of her, and a triple chocolate bombe, which looked molten and glistening. Zara thought it was ironic that she would indulge in this on-screen, when in real life she wouldn't allow herself to go near anything that looked or tasted so good; the trauma of childhood taunts about her weight still haunting her.

'So, you finally decided to act with me?' she said archly, looking at her co-star, Imran Khan. He laughed at her, not taking offence at her implication. She had met him at a number of events and parties over the years, but they had never been cast opposite each other before. She liked Imran, he was unusual like her. His story really was rags to riches. He had been born in the slums and raised by his widowed mother until he had broken through and become Bollywood's most successful actor. The only real contender to the original Khans: Aamir, Salman, and Shah Rukh who had ruled Bollywood for thirty years, Imran had taken over the box office for the last five years.

'It's not like that, Zara, it's an honour for me,' he said in his usual charming lilt. 'You became too successful too quickly for any of us.'

She knew what he meant. She was the only actress who had really made it to the top without relying on famous co-stars. Raj's father had cast her in a secondary role in her debut film, it was just a song and a few scenes really, but it was enough to get her noticed and signed up for a series of what the industry termed 'B-grade' movies. Low on budget, high on entertainment, they had nonetheless cashed in bigtime and her videos had taken social media by storm. That led to more serious roles, but the big heroes shied away from playing second fiddle in a Zara Das movie. When the superstar heroes had finally agreed to act opposite her, Zara's career had imploded, and the actors had been scared off by the threats to her life. Only Imran had come through and accepted Raj's offer to star opposite her.

'I guess this is my unofficial acceptance, is it? *You've finally earned your place, Zara, you are now classy enough for even an A-lister like Imran Khan to star opposite you?*'

'Come on, Zee, you know I have no such hang-ups. I'm the *Slumdog Superstar* remember? They looked down on me for years.'

'I'm just teasing you,' she said. 'And that nickname hasn't done you any harm, in fact it's been a shot in the foot for your dickhead rivals who invented it. I think people find it endearing; you are the underdog and they support you where it matters.'

'Yes, I guess you're right. Still the press and those assholes who grew up in Juhu and Bandra love rubbing it in my face.'

'We've spoken about this so many times, Immy. They will never accept us – we made it when we shouldn't have. They can't cope with modern India. They're the ones who grew up with the Chanel bags at sixteen, the birthday parties at the hottest nightclubs. No one is as entitled as the elite in our country. They can't compute it when the strays bring down the marquee.'

'Nice, so we're the strays, are we?'

'In their eyes you know we are.'

'True. How are you now?'

Zara looked past Imran's shoulder where she saw Dan hovering outside Feya. He caught her eye, and for a moment the anxiety surfaced. The message, his worry. He had agreed with her not to tell the police yet, but he had increased her security team. She didn't know why, but she felt some sort of safety knowing he was there, and his concern seemed genuine. After all, if anything happened to her no doubt his pay cheque from James Kapoor would take a hit. Dan gave her a slight nod, his eyes bright in the London sunshine. They were a beautiful colour, she thought.

'I'm fine,' Zara said to Imran. 'I think things are getting better. There haven't been any more incidents since the…' She didn't need to talk about the explosion. It had been national news and film world gossip for months. 'Thank you for doing this movie.'

'Are you crazy? Zara's comeback movie? It's going to blow up the box office. Sorry.'

'It's ok,' she said laughing, as he grinned at her. 'You have to laugh about it, don't you? It's too terrifying otherwise.'

'Accept it all, though, Zara. Starring in a Raj Dillon movie is going to take you into a whole new bracket; it's what will keep you at the top. He will give you the sort of class you get when someone like Aditya Chopra, Karan Johar, or Sanjay Leela Bhansali casts you. If Raj didn't keep casting me, I would have fizzled out already. You're in the club.'

'Yes, although I see I'm still not trusted.'

'What do you mean?'

Zara looked over to the small table in the opposite corner to them. Imran and Raj's wives were sitting there, watching proceedings.

'Your wife feels she has to watch us,' she said to Imran. Sasha Khan was older than Imran, but they had met and married a long time before Imran had become an actor. He often said she was the one who encouraged him, but Zara knew never to believe anything stars said in their interviews. They were acting on and off screen, their realities hidden away in their marble mansions.

'Not at all, it's just a ritual we have. First day, first shoot. If she can, she is there. I owe her, Zara, you don't know what she did for me. No one does.'

Zara caught Sasha's eye and nodded towards her. Sasha responded in kind, but there was nothing behind it. No animosity or friendliness.

'You should stop by and say hello sometime, you'll see. Sasha's not a typical Bollywood wife, she hasn't grown up in that world.'

'Maybe not, but once you enter that world, you become a part of it. And to the Bollywood Wives I'm just a cheap tart who makes love to their husbands on-screen. They loathe me.'

Raj called them to attention, and the camera started to roll. Zara put away the threatening message, and the watchful eyes, and went into Zara Das mode.

-

On her way to her mobile vanity van, Zara stopped by the table occupied by Sasha Khan and Raj's wife, Jackie. Jackie Dillon was an American who had fallen in love with Raj and married him two years previously. She had auburn curls, olive skin, and bright blue eyes. She wasn't stunning, mainly because she played down her looks, dressing casually when she was usually surrounded by Mumbai's elite in designer labels. Still she stood out, as some sort of exotic creature built by the American dream, who had crashed into the middle of an Indian summer.

As she approached them, Zara noticed Jackie move her purse from the table to the other empty chair next to her. Zara felt the slight inside, but she was too used to such things to let them show on her face.

'How are you both? I hope you're enjoying the shoot,' she said without faltering, her smile plastered to her face and her acting prowess forcing it into her eyes.

'You look stunning,' said Sasha warmly. 'You and Imran did really well in that scene.' She had a quiet voice, and always seemed so calm. Jackie didn't say anything at all.

'Thank you. Yes, I think your husband and me make a really good couple. On screen.' Zara laughed, but her joke had been a misfire. She saw the pain flash across Sasha's eyes, and Jackie physically bristled.

'He's a professional, he can fake emotions for anyone,' said Jackie. 'I'm sure you get that. Fake emotions, I mean.'

'How are you enjoying London?' Zara asked her, ignoring the jibe.

'I'm jet lagged and my husband's stressed,' said Jackie. 'I don't know why he bothered filming in London, I told him he was taking too much on. Still he insisted, said he wanted Zara Das in his movie. I personally can't see why, but maybe you'll surprise me?' It was a pointed comment: Zara knew Raj was filming in London just for her. Despite the arrest of the people behind the car bomb, there was still so much antagonism against Zara from other quarters that nobody else was willing to risk filming with her in Mumbai. Even Raj wouldn't take the risk.

'I hope so. Raj is a good man, and a good friend,' said Zara. 'He's always been so kind, and the only one in our industry who is standing by me.'

Jackie looked away, rolling her eyes at Sasha, who looked embarrassed.

'It's a beautiful hotel, isn't it?' said Sasha.

'Yes, beyond my wildest dreams. I didn't expect it to be so lavish.'

'It's seven star, it was hardly going to be a roadside motel, was it?' quipped Jackie. 'Anyway, we are going to have a brilliant time, exploring the city, lunching, shopping, catching the shows. Right, Sasha?' Plans that didn't include Zara obviously.

She excused herself, but heard them both as she was leaving, Jackie's voice carrying across the small cake shop.

'Give her a chance, Jackie, we are going to be with her for a whole month,' said Sasha.

'You must be joking. She can flash her snatch at Raj and get him to roll over, but her fake tits and teeth aren't going to work on me.'

Zara didn't let the hurt show, retreating to her mobile vanity van to touch up her make-up before the next scene, Dan following her closely. One of his team was stationed outside the vehicle, but Zara ignored them both as she went inside. She stared at herself in the mirror, in her pastel coloured Marc Jacobs coat, her deep earth Lacroix dress underneath with autumn leaf prints. None of it could protect her, not if someone really wanted to hurt her. Zara checked over the make-up on the dressing table counter and called Dan. He knocked and then entered the van.

'Everything ok?' he said, looking her over. He really was attractive, she thought, so solid and yet his eyes were so alive.

'I'm not sure,' she said. 'I think… maybe the text message has just upset me more than I thought.'

'What's wrong?'

'I think, the make-up… it looks like it might have been moved?'

'What do you mean, moved?'

'It feels like it's not where I left it. You probably think I'm being paranoid, but I think it's just off slightly.'

'Are you sure?'

'No, that's just it. I'm not. It's just a feeling.'

Dan went out of the van and came back a few seconds later.

'No one has been inside, not since you left. I've had someone standing watch all day.'

'It must just be me,' she said apologetically.

'I think it's understandable, and I would rather you voiced your concerns to me than not,' he reassured her.

43

'Thank you,' she said. 'Are you sure no one could have gotten in, though?'

Dan looked around the small space which was a horse box that had been converted into a mobile dressing room for film stars on location.

'It's a closed box with one entrance,' he said at last.

Zara smiled, embarrassed, and went to work using the Zara X make-up products in front of her, and didn't think about it again until much later.

–

The evening scene was going to be the climax of the movie when Zara and Imran finally declared their love for each other. It seemed odd to film the last scene on the first day, but Zara didn't question Raj's plans.

He had chosen to film on Chelsea Embankment, with the bridge lit up behind them. Imran and Zara were dressed in winter outfits, which were causing them to swelter in the cloying July heat, which hadn't abated even into the evening.

'I thought I'd be wearing jumpers and jackets throughout the trip,' Imran said. 'I wasn't expecting it to be so hot.'

'I know, I'm actually sweating under here,' Zara said.

Sasha and Jackie were both on set too, looking tired but watching from afar. It was going to be an awkward scene, as Zara was meant to kiss Imran. Bollywood had evolved from hiding the intimacy behind flowers or hands, and it was now normal to see a brief smooch in the classier films, and full-on French kissing in the borderline soft porn trendy movies that had emerged of late, which featured simulated sex and tantalising exposure of flesh, without actual full-frontal nudity.

'I hope Sasha doesn't lynch me,' Zara said nervously to Imran.

'She's used to it, I've kissed half of Bollywood.' He was right; Imran was infamous for his on-screen kissing. 'She's fine with it, she knows she's the only one for me.'

Zara didn't correct him, letting him hold on to his fantasy that his wife didn't care about his on-screen shenanigans.

'Are you ok?' he asked.

'No, I feel off. It's been happening all day really, as though I've caught something. And my skin keeps itching in this heat, I don't think the make-up can cope.'

'I thought you used your own brand? I'm sure it's able to withstand the Mumbai sun, so this is nothing, right?'

'Yes, I must be getting climate flu or something,' she said.

Zara swayed slightly and Imran grabbed her arm to steady her.

'Hey, you don't look well at all. Shall I get Raj to cancel?'

'No, no, it's fine. Let's just wrap this up in one take if we can. I probably just need to get back to the hotel and rest.'

They cut a beautiful scene, the handsome couple against the brightly lit Chelsea Bridge behind them. Imran was definitely the best looking of the Khans, she thought, with his long lashes and naturally pink lips. Still she winced in between takes as she burned up.

'Seriously, Zee, shall we leave it?'

'What's wrong?' said Raj, coming up to them.

'Zara's feeling unwell,' said Imran.

'It's fine honestly, can we just finish? I need to have a bath and sleep, that's all.'

Raj didn't look convinced. 'Come on, Zee, let's call wrap up and finish this tomorrow. There isn't that much left to do.'

'No, I know you have a tight schedule, Raj. Let's just carry on.'

'No, I insist.'

'Raj, please. I'm absolutely fine. Let's do this.'

They argued for a while, but she convinced them both to finish the shot before calling an end to the day. All that was left was the kiss. Zara was apprehensive and despite not wanting to, her eyes flitted towards where Sasha was standing with Jackie. She felt guilty about what she was doing, it would be natural for Sasha to feel uncomfortable, then she remembered she was here to do a job, and so was Imran. As Raj called for action, Zara went in, kissing Imran with as much passion as decency on a film set would allow, knowing it would get her male viewers excited. Her triumph was momentary though. The look of embarrassment and unhappiness on Sasha's face cut her, as did the pure hatred on Jackie's face.

–

Sasha was edgy when they got back at the hotel, unable to get the image out of her head. She had seen Imran kiss dozens of heroines over the years, seen it on-screen and first hand. Yet Sasha still felt the pain each time, couldn't help the jealousy coursing through her.

Imran emerged from the bathroom, after brushing his teeth pointedly, and pushed her back on the bed, kissing her deeply, his hands reaching for her breasts, then moving down her stomach and between her legs. It was a rehearsed move, they had done it so many times during their marriage. Sasha tried to keep it interesting, testing out various tantric massage techniques, and experimental evenings when she introduced the Kama Sutra into their lives. Imran would go through the motions, oblige her, but he always seemed bored. She felt so unattractive in those moments that she stopped trying so hard. What Imran Khan, Bollywood's reigning superstar, seemed to enjoy was the same frantic routines they had perfected over time.

Imran's mouth moved from her own down her throat to her breasts. He took each enlarged nipple into his mouth, sucking on them hard. Sasha gasped, throwing her head back, and pulled at his hair. She knew he loved it. His mouth went further, kissing her body, as he pulled open her legs, his tongue tasting her inner thighs before plunging into her. She moaned as she rocked back and forth on his tongue, getting louder as his fingers started to enter her at the same time. When he was convinced she was wet enough, Imran pushed her back and entered her roughly. Sasha saw his toned body move over her, thrusting with frenzy. She cried out at every push, grabbing his lower back and moving her hands down to play with his arsehole. He loved it, closing his eyes as he pushed harder and faster into her. This was his way every time, having sex with her to reassure her, that no matter what happened, there was only ever one woman for him. Sasha didn't know how to explain to him that kissing another woman and then fucking your wife was not a good idea. The lingering thought was always there – is he thinking about her right now? Did the kiss turn him on that much?

Sasha knew Imran's rhythm well, and knew the moment when he collapsed on her, that it was time. Imran fell forward on her, biting her breasts, making guttural noises, and moments later she felt him come inside her. Sasha moaned loudly, holding his head to her, suffocating him, until he was done and rolled off her.

'Did you come?' he said.

'Always,' she lied.

–

Imran had gone to make use of the four-headed shower with more settings than Sasha knew what to do with, leaving her lying in the sheets. They felt sticky and warm after their love-making, and she could smell her husband on them. Inside, the anxiety was creeping to the surface.

It hadn't always been like this. Imran and Sasha had been incapable of being away from each other until they had had kids. Imran liked to boast how in twelve years of marriage they hadn't slept apart for a single night. She knew that wasn't true, but it was nearly true. And it had been great. Until the kids and until he became so successful it was hard to stay afloat in the tsunami of his career.

Imran came out of the shower, wrapped in a towel, the water still on his skin and in his hair. His body was ripped from a daily gym routine and complex diet plan that cost him a fortune; he had not a single ounce of fat on his six-pack, broad shoulders, and strong chest. He had a light down of hair across his creamy skin. Imran Khan was the man millions of women around the world wanted and dreamed of having inside them. She had him nearly every day, and couldn't get herself past zero.

He sat on the edge of the bed and kissed her hard. She smelt the cool scent of the shower gel on his skin and tasted the mint in his mouth from just brushing his teeth.

'Fuck, I'm horny again,' he said, pulling back the sheets, and sliding his hands down her body to between her legs.

Sasha shuddered under his touch, mainly from the cold of the air con. She had held her breath as his fingers went past her stomach, aware that while once it had been flat and toned, it was now anything but. It had been four years since the twins had been born, and she hadn't been able to shift her body back to how it had been. She hated looking at herself in the mirror, and hated Imran looking at her, seeing the stretch marks. He spent his life romancing and dancing with the most beautiful women in the world, kissing them passionately, women like Zara Das, and what did he come home to?

She abruptly removed his hand and pulled the sheets back up again.

'I love you, Sasha,' he whispered. 'You are the best thing that ever happened to me. If it wasn't for you...'

She touched his lips with her fingers, he had said it so many times over the years, and each time it rocked her sense of herself. Each time Sasha wondered if it really was love he felt for her, or just gratitude.

–

Dan had arranged a car to take her back to the hotel after the shoot, with just him and one of his team driving. Zara rubbed at her face, fanning herself and asking for the car's AC to be turned up full.

'Everything ok?' Dan asked.

'Can you get me back quickly? My face is burning and I feel ill. Really ill.'

Zara hunkered low in the Mercedes, as Dan sped her back to the Mirage, checking she was ok in the rear-view mirror throughout. By the time they got back to the hotel, Zara was shivering, wiping her make-up off against her coat sleeve.

Back in her suite, Zara rushed into her bathroom and washed her face in cold water. Her make-up was meant to last, and the water had no effect. Zara could feel her skin stinging and struggled to find her Zara X make-up remover among her bottles of products. She applied it like water, the make-up eventually rubbing off and her skin feeling the cool air of the bathroom against it. Still the burning continued, and when she was done, Zara saw her skin was raw and reddened. She called Dan, who was shocked by the colour of her face.

'I think we should take you to hospital,' he said, buzzing for Kasim to bring him some cold milk and butter.

'No, please. So many actors and actresses have been stung by revelations from hospital staff. I can't risk it, please.'

'Have you had a reaction before?' Dan asked.

'No, never. It's my own brand, I used all natural ingredients. I think… I know you said no one went into my van, but honestly I feel like someone's tampered with my make-up.'

Dan flinched, but didn't have time to respond as Kasim came in with the milk and butter.

'Look this is going to sound crazy, but trust me please,' Dan said. 'Do you mind if I apply this to your skin?' Zara shook her head, and Dan proceeded to wash her face gently in the milk. It felt cold but also reduced the heat she was feeling. Dan then took the butter and rubbed it into her skin, which further alleviated the pain. She tried not to notice the sensations his touch was causing in her. Kasim had meanwhile disappeared but returned with some hot chocolate for her.

49

'I thought this might help relax you,' he said, not asking what the problem was. 'Are you in pain, Zara ma'am?'

'A little,' she said. 'Thank you,' she said, addressing Dan.

'Can you give me the make-up you used?' he said. 'I want to get it tested.'

Zara nodded, acknowledging silently that Dan was beginning to believe someone had mixed something into her make-up which had caused her skin to burn. She may not be in Mumbai anymore, but the threat had followed her to London.

Chapter Four

As the morning dawned, the anxiety of the night seemed to inhabit a pocket in Zara's mind that she could shut off. She decided she wouldn't be beaten, no matter how scared she really was. Escapism was what Bollywood did better than anyone, and today she would do just that. Zara was going to hit London and burn up her credit cards. In Mumbai everything was on tap, she couldn't remember the last time she had paid for anything in a shopping mall. If she was shooting for a movie, any clothes or accessory shopping was billed to the producer. In between shoots, it would be whichever magazine was interviewing her or she would do some promotion for a product that meant again Zara got it for free. Her YouTube channel had been a stroke of genius, as was her Instagram. Zara saw how YouTubers were making money and getting millions of views putting up video tutorials showing women how to get the 'Zara look'. Zara decided to beat them at their own game and show everyone direct from her own bedroom how a movie star look was created. She was a sensation.

Zara got out of bed and used her app to summon Kasim. Raj had agreed to re-arrange the shoot, so she wasn't needed that day. Kasim turned up fifteen minutes later, giving her time to change into silk pyjamas provided by the hotel, and freshen up. Kasim brought her a trolley for breakfast, the contents of which he laid out on the dining table in the lounge of her suite.

'This is too much, please join me.'

'I cannot, ma'am, it is against hotel policy.'

'Have you eaten?'

'Yes, ma'am. Please, what can I get for you? I have fresh tea and coffee, there is eggs Benedict, eggs Florentine, smoked salmon, cereal, toast. All of it on heated trays so it stays warm.'

'I'll just have tea please, with almond or soya milk if you have any. And those strawberries with the low-fat yoghurt.' Kasim served her quickly and silently, smiling at her. Again, the amber eyes reminded her of Dev, and the memories of him jolted her.

'Are you married, Kasim?' she asked.

'Me, ma'am? No, not yet. I came here to work and build my career. Marriage is for when I am settled.'

'Will you marry a nice Pakistani girl an aunt chooses for you?' He blushed at her words. 'Or have you got a secret girlfriend tucked away, some hot English girl?' Kasim started to laugh, he was so embarrassed.

'No, ma'am, I am so busy working, there is no time.'

She felt a stab of envy. Men were allowed to venture out like this, even back in Mumbai. They struggled, worked hard, often got used and abused, but still they had a chance. Women were still at so much risk when they decided to try to make it.

'Do you hate Indians?' she asked suddenly. For a moment she looked at him, wondering if he was capable of harming her, this man with access to her room twenty-four seven. The hotel had given that role to a Pakistani? Then again, James Kapoor probably told the hotel manager to send the best butler for Zara, or he'd better have done, and Gareth Jones didn't really understand the India–Pakistan thing. The decades of animosity the two nations had engaged in since the 1947 Partition, when the British gave India its independence and created Pakistan at the same time. She knew that when she had suggested visiting Pakistan, there was a furore by the right-wing press who had labelled her a traitor, right-wing politicians saying she would be banned from returning if she did. And the Pakistani right-wing press said a death warrant was waiting for her if she did come.

'No, ma'am, why would I? We have more in common than we have that is different. Religion and politics I leave to the men who make their livelihood from creating hatred. The rest of us are only worried about feeding our families and giving them a future. I mean look at you, ma'am, Pakistanis love your movies. They call their daughters Zara after you, it is so popular a name now.'

Zara nodded politely and smiled at him. How naïve he was; the world was so much messier than he wanted it to be. Zara had learned that the hard way. She wondered then how someone who had managed to get from Pakistan to London could be that naïve. Maybe it was an act? She didn't want it to be. She wanted to hold on to a view of Kasim as decent and honourable because she felt in her emptiness that that was what Dev would have been.

–

Life was predictably bad for little Pari, the torment of school and the isolation worn like a second skin. It was strange how children could accept the worst conditions, so powerless to change them. That was exactly what Pari had done. Her solace was that at home with Dev she was safe at least; he at least cared about her and looked out for her. She knew in her parents' eyes what her worth was, she was a child not an idiot. Still she thought maybe if she started to try harder at school, they might see hope in her too.

So, she strived to achieve in class, but getting the best grades only made her a target again. So Pari stopped doing that too, learning that it was better to remain invisible. More and more the staple of Dev and his movies became her salve, and she would accept that lot in life, she thought.

It was August fifteenth, and India was alive with Independence Day celebrations. School was closed and Pari felt the happiness she usually did on such days, knowing she would be free from the hatred and torments for a few hours at least.

She had dressed in her white shalwar kameez, *with her* dupatta *coloured like the Indian flag – orange, green, and white; her hair held back with a hairband in the same tricolour. Dev had worn a white shirt* and black pants, with a flag painted on each of his cheeks. Her mother had told Pari that her skin was too dark for the flag to show properly. The day progressed as it always did, the family attending puja in the morning, followed by a military parade in Delhi. The evening would be a three-course meal, only done on festivals like Dussehra and Diwali, with lots of mithai. Pari loved it, and there was nothing but happiness in her memories of years past and she expected that year to be the same.

Only it wasn't. Dev had wanted to buy a kite; it was what the boys in their town did on Independence Day. Fly kites and play with firecrackers. He had rushed off before anyone could stop him when he saw the kite seller, but so had every other boy around them. Only, the other boys came back, Dev didn't.

Pari remembered how her parents had searched for him, her mother dragging her by the hand, Pari's heart trembling with fear and worry. Where was he? Every boy in the same white shirt as Dev had worn made them hope for a moment, was it him? None of them were. The day turned into evening, and evening into night. Her parents called Dev's name on the streets of Delhi, and lodged a complaint to the police. But they didn't seem to care about the missing nine-year-old son of a poor family, Dev was just another such case in a pile of them. And as the night turned again into morning, Dev was still gone. And Pari had never seen him again. Her best friend, her twin, her everything.

–

Zara's phone rang, making her jump. She had just convinced Kasim to eat some of the eggs, or they would go to waste. She watched him eat, tentatively, but saw the look of pleasure on his face. For a moment she wondered if Dev would have looked like Kasim, and if he would have pulled the same face when he tasted the fancy eggs. She pushed the thought aside. Kasim was not Dev, and she was being crazy for even thinking it. The call was from Collette Dove, from the Kavita Ruia London branch.

'Miss Das, pleasure to speak to you at last. Did you check the schedule I sent over? Anything on there you don't want to do, please just say. If there is anything else you *do* want to do let me know. Did you settle in ok to the hotel?'

'Please, call me Zara. Yes, the hotel is beautiful, I have my own butler.' She winked at Kasim. 'The itinerary is very detailed, and I have to say I am impressed already. I like the interview days being back to back, and the events seemed ok. I will be tired from shooting so if we can keep to the A-list ones, please. I'll leave it to you to judge which will work best for me.'

'Yes, of course, I'll refine the list for maximum impact events and cut them down. It's just so exciting to have you here for so many weeks, everybody wants to meet you.'

'Of course, I am Bollywood's top heroine,' she said, matter-of-factly.

'Yes, I know. I love your movies.'

'Oh, you watch them?'

'I am a huge Bollywood fan, have been for years. I dated an Indian boy in university and he introduced me to them. He didn't last, but my passion for Bollywood did. It's why Ms Ruia assigned me to you.'

'That's very thoughtful of her. Who else have you worked with?'

'The last client I managed was Angeline Jolie during her recent visit to London.'

Zara liked this piece of information. Yes, if anyone in the world could compete with her, maybe Jolie could. In her younger days.

'What have you planned for today? I believe you aren't filming?'

'I want to go shopping.'

'Give me an hour and I will send over a list of stores that are safe for you to visit, without being disturbed. I'll inform the staff you will be coming so they have their best on offer. Mr Kapoor has said he will cover the cost of all your personal shopping while you are in London.'

Zara had managed it then, even in London. She was going to get the Mumbai treatment. That would be fun. She was feeling reckless though, maybe because of the drama of the night before, she felt as though she wanted to push the boundaries today, too.

'Thank you. First though, I want to go to Tristan's.'

'On Oxford Street?' Zara heard the hesitation in Collette's voice, and then the immediate click into action. 'I'll make sure I have maximum press coverage for you, that can be one of your public appearances, and I'll inform management there—'

'No, Collette. I want to just go shopping there today.'

'It's one of the biggest stores in London, they claim they are bigger than Harrods and Selfridges. You will get recognised.'

'Maybe, but today I need some of that.'

'Of course. I'll arrange the private shopping for after your visit to Tristan's. Do you want any beauty treatments or spa sessions for later?'

'Thank you, but they have a spa here in the hotel. I will make use of that. I do need an appointment at a clinic on Harley Street though. A laser service, I'll send you the details. In a few days.'

'No problem. Do you have a security lead I can brief on where you are going today?'

Zara groaned inwardly, thinking of Dan. She didn't fancy spending the day with him shadowing her, but she knew she probably didn't have a choice. She gave Collette his details and ended the call, feeling light-headed but happy. This was how it was done. This was how it *should* be done. VJ was nothing more than a fixer, a thug. And yet he had helped her start her career. Would she have made it without his help? Was there another way for someone like her? Zara filled her mouth absent-mindedly with a strawberry, sucking on it.

Kasim had pressed the outfit she was going to wear shopping, and she again did her own hair and make-up. Ruby called at just the right moment.

'Fuckety-fuck, Zara I was so drunk last night I ended up shagging my Uber driver, he was so hot.'

'What about your boyfriend?'

'Allow that, Zara, it's open season until we get hitched. Anyway, tell me, love, are you ok?'

'Yes, but listen. I'm going shopping, so cancel all your plans, you're coming with me. We have James Kapoor's soirée tonight, and I want to look hot. And expensive.'

-

The Mercedes was cruising down Regent's Street, Londoners out with so much flesh on show, it brought home to Zara the difference between Mumbai and here. Men and women were dressed in barely there clothes as they tried to cope in the heatwave. Zara had to laugh, thinking how Indians dealt with extreme temperatures and still didn't think getting so naked was the way to do it. Only certain sections of the metropolis or stars like her on-screen would wear the sorts of clothes every other person was wearing on the streets here.

Dan was seated in the front with the driver supplied by the Mirage. He wasn't amused by Zara's insistence on going to Tristan's, and she became irritated with him. He had been so gentle the previous night, when he had washed her skin and massaged butter into it. She had to admit she had liked the touch of his skin, but today his controlling attitude was pissing her off. Another prick thinking he could order her around, just when she had managed to get rid of VJ.

'I just want to go in and be normal, I do not want a body-guard there with me,' she insisted, hearing the petulance in her voice. 'You will draw attention to me, and you will be the cause of any crowd trouble.'

'And if you are recognised? Or if whoever tampered with your make-up has followed you here? I can't take the risk. I'm going in with you.'

'No, you are not. You work for me. I give the orders.'

'I technically work for Mr Kapoor and he has given me a very clear remit.'

'You just got told, Zara,' Ruby muttered. She had made it to the Mirage in quick time from her Warwick Avenue flat.

'I'm not a prisoner,' Zara argued.

'Freedom is the price you have to pay for safety sometimes.'

'You sound like a Nazi,' Ruby said.

They parked up behind Tristan's, and Zara raced out of the Mercedes and into the busy store, with Ruby following. Dan was behind her, wearing his black suit, luckily no shades, but there was no mistaking what he was. Zara tried to keep as much distance between them as possible so people might just assume he wasn't with her. Dan assumed a respectable position away from her and Ruby, surveying the store, and giving them some space at least.

Zara stopped by the La Prairie counter, picking up a foundation which claimed to look invisible and didn't stain.

'Yeah right,' Ruby said, smearing it on her hand. It clashed badly with her fair skin. The woman behind the counter didn't even smile at Zara or Ruby, dismissing them no doubt as part of the unwashed masses that walked through stores using products for free.

'Hey, shop-girl, have you got the next shade up in this?' Ruby said to her.

'And can you get me some unopened one so I can try it?' Zara said. The shop assistant looked irritated with Zara and answered her as though it had taken all the effort in the world to do so.

'The foundation is nearly two hundred pounds,' she said. 'I can't just open one for you to try.'

'Why? Don't you like the look of me?'

'We don't do that for anyone,' the shop assistant insisted. And if she was Sarah Jessica Parker or some other recognisable fashion icon, Zara thought?

'I see,' Zara began, 'so do you have the shade I've asked for or not?'

The woman looked annoyed and sighed as she went to get it. Zara meanwhile tested a lipstick colour on some card. She didn't want to test it on her skin, who knew how many people had already used it? The woman came back with a packaged foundation bottle, but protested when Zara tried to open it.

'There's no tester for this shade,' Zara said.

'How else will she try it? Are you slow? Is that why you work in a shop?' Ruby said.

'I beg your pardon…'

'Yeah, yeah, granted. Now back up, we are testing this before we buy it.'

Zara opened the box and took out the foundation. The woman was about to explode she was so angry, and grabbed it from Zara's hands.

'Please don't violate the merchandise.'

'Violate the merchandise? Are you for real? Where's the manager?' Ruby demanded.

The woman was nonplussed, sure that the manager would take her side, no doubt.

'Call the flaming manager, now.' Ruby was authoritative, and the woman picked up a landline to do that.

Meanwhile a crowd had gathered, a brown crowd. They were loudly whispering among themselves, asking each other if that was Zara Das. One young girl came up to her and asked, 'Please can I get a selfie?'

Zara obliged, observing the confused look on the woman behind the counter. This was followed by more people asking the same until a lone middle-aged man came up to ask for a picture. Dan stepped in and asked everyone to please give Zara room as she was out doing personal errands.

'I can handle this,' Zara spat at him. Dan ignored her, but stood close by.

The manager came along, initially with the same attitude as his employee, but then saw Dan and took a closer look at Zara.

'Miss Das? I am so sorry for the mix-up. Collette called and informed the senior management you would be coming and to keep a look out for you. Please accept my apologies for the hassle, it was caused by miscommunication.'

'Miscommunication? I want to put in a formal complaint against your employee here, and get her fired,' said Ruby.

The woman behind the counter was now showing emotion at last – embarrassment and terror mainly. Zara said there was no need for that, and proceeded to be given as many products free of charge as she wanted.

—

Back in the Mercedes, driving the two women the short distance to Mayfair, Dan was seething. As the car pulled up outside Stella McCartney, he opened the door for them to climb out, not looking at either of them, slamming the door behind them.

'What's your problem?' Ruby said. 'Crack a smile, it won't kill you.'

'I get paid to protect you, not provide entertainment.'

'Allow it, you couldn't entertain a joker's funeral,' Ruby said, walking unsteadily towards the boutique entrance. She had just downed a mini bottle of whisky.

'If you have other things to do, feel free to leave us,' Zara said.

'I'll be here,' Dan replied, tersely. 'It was unfair what you did to that woman back there, though.'

'What did I do? Correct her attitude, that's all. If I was a Hollywood actress or royalty, I'm sure she would have let me test the foundation. The fact is she saw a brown face and made assumptions and didn't think I might be anything special.'

'How is she meant to know who you are? She would have behaved like that whatever colour you were. She was a snob, not a racist.'

'What would you know? I have seen women like her all my life, telling me I can't afford this, or I can't try that on. They work in shops, they don't own them.'

So, she had humiliated her, and taken a petty revenge for all the store assistants who had ever dismissed her in the past. Dan didn't

60

trust himself to speak, shutting the car door with more aggression that he should have. Zara looked at him with a flash of annoyance, but walked away from him quickly. He watched her enter the boutique and saw through the closing door how the staff welcomed her. This was what her visits were like, star treatment for the celebrity client. The display in Tristan's was a show, that's what irritated Dan the most.

Zara knew exactly what she was doing, it was a power play. Shame the attitude-laden retail staff. There was nothing surprising about the staff at these posh stores having an attitude, customers expected it. If Zara had properly arranged to meet the store management, she would have had no issues. She had done it this way though, the cheap, nasty way, to get a reaction. So she could act like a diva. And if Zara wasn't bad enough, Dan now had to deal with her co-diva, Ruby, as well.

He breathed in; he had to curtail his feelings. He had to do this job, he needed the money for something more important than the couple of spoilt bitches he was looking after. And only he knew just how much he needed it.

Chapter Five

There was a muted atmosphere in the room despite the music playing softly in the background, the waiting staff with their trays of drinks and food, Zara's fellow cast members, and James Kapoor's assorted guests.

'This is like the *Asian Eye* list of the richest Asians in the country, most of them are in the top hundred,' Ruby said, draining half a glass of her champagne. 'The stories I could tell you about this lot, but I think I'll keep them for when I'm destitute and need to write my tell-all book. Just look at them though. The combined wealth of these people is billions, but the women's faces are pulled back so tight they're going to snap like elastic bands any minute now and look at the men, so sleazy, their tongues are practically down the waitresses' throats. Probably desperate to kiss lips that don't feel like dead fish, they're so plumped up with filler. They're all so snooty as well, totally look down on film stars, but I bet they all still ask you for a picture. Oh, look I downgraded myself by taking a picture with a *Bollywood* star, *uff*, so tacky *na*!'

The suite they were in was exquisite, with panoramic views across London on three sides with viewing balconies. Zara sipped at the Dom Perignon, as she let her eyes drink in the opulence around her.

'I thought this was going to be a private soirée for the cast only. I'm so tired, really didn't want to stay too long, anyway. Now it will feel like work,' Zara complained. 'I know he's financing the movie, but he hasn't bought us all.'

'I think you'll find in his head he has.'

'Plus, I'm shooting again in the morning.'

'Oh shit, am I needed then?'

'Yes, it's an ensemble dance number. Didn't you get the schedule?'

'Yeah, but who has time to read detailed crap like that? Text me the address and time, I'll try to get an early night. Or just spend an extra two hours in make-up.'

'I got you this part so you could keep me sane, so please don't let me down.'

'Sorry, it's just a bit of a laugh for me, but I'll try. Oh, watch out, incoming. Can't tell if this one is even human she's had so much work done.'

'You are so beautiful in real life. Please may I take a selfie?' the woman guest was asking Zara, already taking her phone out to take the picture. She had the telltale look of plastic surgery, with a shiny veneer to her skin and fake boobs straining her dress. Zara used every natural product she could so she avoided looking like these women and dreaded the day she would succumb to the knife. She really didn't know if she was strong enough to resist and grow old gracefully, moving from leading lady to playing the wicked mother-in-law.

Zara smiled quickly as the woman's finger pressed her screen to take the shot. No matter how she hated it, there was never an excuse for a bad picture.

–

Sasha watched the consummate actress Zara take selfies with one of the wives gathered in James Kapoor's suite, fake smile showing her allegedly capped teeth. Her smile didn't reach her eyes, Sasha noted, there was no warmth in them. Sasha didn't hate Zara, but as she watched her interact with the guests, she did feel a familiar stab of envy. The kiss floated into her head.

Sasha thought how understated Zara's outfit was, making her own – which was a turquoise Ritu Kumar dress with costume jewellery – look as though she had tried too hard. Actually,

Zara made every woman in the room look like they had tried too hard, waltzing in and stealing their thunder with her casual glamour.

They had met at industry events and parties, but Sasha's path hadn't crossed with Zara's to this extent before.

'You want to watch that one. She has the soul of a crocodile.'

Sasha turned to see Jackie Dillon standing next to her, drinking a glass of what looked like water, but Sasha knew was neat gin. Jackie was notorious for her hard drinking, which was the only real thorn in her friendship with the teetotal Sasha. The two women otherwise gelled well, forming an alliance in Bollywood. Jackie was an outsider just like Sasha, but more than that, Jackie's liberal American values didn't care what social or economic background Imran and Sasha came from. The women who had grown up in tinsel town barely hid their disdain, Sasha could tell they were just waiting to make digs about her husband the *Slumdog Superstar*. Jackie's own Jewish–Hindu marriage to Raj also meant she didn't care that Sasha and Imran were from different faiths.

'Jackie, where have you been? I tried calling, but your phone was switched off. I figured you got a UK SIM card.'

Sasha air-kissed her, admiring how Jackie looked effort-lessly perfect, wearing a summer blue kurta with jeans, which brought out her eyes and auburn hair. She wore minimal make-up and looked fresh.

'I had something to do,' Jackie said, evasively. 'How are you settling in?'

'The hotel is amazing, it's like Scheherazade's *One Thousand and One Nights*, isn't it?'

'More like someone puked up after one thousand and one drinks. The word *kitsch* was made for this place. Someone said we're gonna spend millions and make it look like we did. They should have pasted dollar bills on the walls, it would have been less tacky.'

'You make me laugh, Jackie, don't let James Kapoor hear you say that.'

'I'm sorry, I wouldn't want to upset our paymaster for the next month.'

'He is funding your husband's movie.'

'More's the pity. I have no idea why Raj is doing this, especially for that two-bit little tramp. What hold she has on the Dillon family I will never know. Talking of tramps, will you look at that?'

Sasha turned to see Sheikh Walid enter. He had a woman who couldn't be older than twenty-five on his arm. He was wearing a Savile Row tailored suit, his dark hair brushed with grey, his pale grey eyes surveying the room.

'Not seen this one before,' drawled Jackie. 'Is there a factory, do you think, that churns out these brainless bimbos? And the men just order them online or something? All the money in the world and they can't spot a gold-digger when she's on her knees with their dick in her mouth.'

Sasha spat out her still water.

'I guess you haven't learnt how to swallow yet, dear,' Jackie quipped.

—

Zara listened to the woman beside her droning on about her love of Bollywood, and how she had wanted to be an actress when she was younger, but then had to do her economics degree and MBA and then she got married and being a millionaire's wife was so tough. *Someone shut her up*, Zara thought.

'Life is such a bitch sometimes,' Ruby drawled. 'How do you cope?'

The woman looked was unsure how to respond, so laughed nervously and left them. Imran was standing with Raj, surrounded by a circle of guests.

'I bet they're having an intelligent conversation about politics or sport or business,' Zara said.

'Check out the women though,' Ruby said. 'I bet they're creaming themselves standing so close to Imran.'

'He is very good-looking,' Zara admitted, checking out his smooth skin, dark hair, and light eyes.

'He doesn't quite have Aamir's acting prowess, Salman's body, or Shah Rukh's charisma, but yes he is beautiful. Although that stubble and gym body is all alpha. Shit, I'm getting horny, let's look at something else.'

'Great, it's Sheikh Walid's latest hooker,' Zara whispered, as the woman who had been on Walid's arm only moments before was walking towards her. She was stunning in an obvious way; high cheekbones, grey eyes, gold flecked hair. She was wearing a long-sleeved dress, which was clingy, but not transparent. 'I recognise that, it's Dior.'

'Maybe this one isn't as slutty or classless as Walid's usual women,' Ruby added.

'Ms Das? A pleasure to meet you at last. I've heard a lot about you,' the woman said.

'Pillow talk from the sheikh,' muttered Ruby. Zara held in her laughter, wondering if it was true though, and if this woman was here to invite Zara into their bedroom for a threesome?

'From my father,' the woman said with emphasis. 'He is very excited about this movie.'

Zara looked confused, then embarrassed. The woman laughed.

'Apologies, I didn't introduce myself properly. My name is Emel, I am Sheikh Walid's daughter.'

Zara couldn't hide the surprise from her face.

'I knew he had three wives, but didn't know about his children.'

'Yes, my mother and her co-wives are all kept back in the Emirates. They wear the full face veil in public, and when in London are only allowed out during the Harrods' sale. It's why they go so crazy, it's like their Olympics. My father on the other hand takes his mistresses to the most exclusive boutiques around the world. Believe me when I say most of the ateliers in Paris are only in business because of his whores.'

Zara kept her face neutral, but warmed to the no-nonsense Emel immediately. Ruby giggled openly.

'I refused to be like my mother or his other daughters. I was lucky, my brother is his favourite and heir, and he was on my side. I was allowed to study and when my father saw how capable I was, he let me into his business. I then made him send my sisters for an education. Two of them are now doctors. The girls are more capable than any of our brothers. Forgive me, I am getting carried away, boring you with my family dramas. I would like to speak to you about something when you have the time. Your filming schedule here is a month, I believe? I won't be in London for all of it, but I will fly in and out of the city for business. I hope I can catch you. I want to propose something that might benefit us both.' With that, Emel went back to her father.

'Maybe she's Walid's pimp really,' Ruby said. 'Make sure you ask for a million if he wants to fuck you. I'll take ten per cent, just because.' Zara laughed, but was left intrigued to discover what Emel might have to offer her.

–

'What happens when that much cheapness gets together? It's like whore squared.'

'Jackie, you are bad,' said Sasha.

'Zara and the sheikh's little slut. Maybe they're trading tips.'

'Zara's not so bad,' said Sasha.

'She slept her way to the top. That's not on. Women don't need to do that anymore. They shouldn't have to. If I find out she's fucking Raj…'

'Jackie, come on you don't really think that, do you?'

'Why else was he so adamant? Bringing his whole fucking unit to London so he could cast that tramp.'

'You've been married two years, and I've known Raj for a lot longer. I've never seen him as happy as he is with you. Trust me on this?'

'Has Imran ever said anything to you?'

'No.'

'I suppose he wouldn't. Him and Raj are the dream team aren't they, best friends. Why would he tell you if he did know anything?'

'Jackie, what's brought this on?'

Jackie was quiet, then emptied her glass, asking a passing waiter for another one, while picking up a designer mini chocolate cake from his raised tray.

'This is gorj, you should try some.'

'You're changing the subject, and I'm on a diet.'

'What for?'

Sasha shrugged, then caught sight of Imran. He was with two women, both rather stunning, obviously the trophy wives of James Kapoor's friends. They were fawning over him, their hands touching his arm and chest, inching closer as they spoke to him. Why did Imran not understand what it did to her when women touched him so casually, as though they owned him? It was one thing accepting his heroines doing it on-screen, but totally another when any random woman could do it. Imran always said he had to cater to his fans, it was part of the territory of being a star, but she didn't know if he secretly enjoyed it.

'Darling, you're his wife. Those women can get as close to him as they want, but in the end it's your bed he will sleep in. Take confidence from that. And these women? Come on, Sasha, you'll find more real body parts in Madame Tussaud's than this lot.'

Sasha smiled weakly, turning to look at Jackie.

'Is that all I am though, Jackie? The woman whose bed the great Imran Khan sleeps in at night?'

'Sure, you're the lucky gal who gets to hear him snore every night. Mazel. Is that why you're dieting? To try to compete with these pathetic creatures? Sasha, my dearest, you are so much more than just your body. It isn't about your vagina any more. Women aren't just about taking cock and pushing out kids any more. Stop this nonsense right now and have some cake.'

'Aren't you doing the same being paranoid about Zara?'

'Not really. The director–actress adultery story is a cliché for a reason, because it happens. You're randomly getting jealous of nobodies.'

Jackie would never understand, Sasha thought. Sasha had grown up being taught what a woman's role was, her mother had lived it for her. Yet she was so lost in playing that role, she sometimes couldn't even remember the dreams she had once had. Winning the Filmfare award for best screenplay, an invitation from the Academy Awards recognising her work. Instead she was worried about her body image. It was like a fog of chloroform that left her too lethargic to move beyond what she was used to.

'What do you want to do with your life?' Jackie asked.

'You already know what I want to do.'

'Then make it happen.'

'Imran won't even read my script. Without him, who is going to finance my movie?'

'Look at me. I get financing for my documentaries. Raj doesn't so much as piss funding in my direction.'

'That's different, you started before you met him. And I'm not being a bitch but the budgets you need are small in comparison.'

Jackie had met Raj in New York three years before when they were both teaching the directors of the future at a special film summer school.

'Ouch. But true. It's about economy of scale though, Sasha. You can do this if you really want it. The fact you haven't yet makes me question just how much you do. Have you really tried everything?'

Sasha hoped Jackie wasn't right. Because if she didn't have her dream, her ambition, then what exactly was left of her?

'India is changing, darling. You all don't see it sometimes because you grew up there. Even in the two years I've been married to Raj I've seen it transform.'

'It hasn't changed that much, that's why we're here in the first place. Zara offends millions with a five-minute dance sequence. Tradition isn't so easy to ignore.'

'Please, Zara is a self-serving little tramp, don't use her as an example for your state of the nation speech.'

'It's true though.'

'Maybe. Listen to me. Half a billion people in India are under the age of twenty-five. They've grown up on a diet of TV and films and music that my country churns out for them, they don't care about old school big budget movies or traditions. Target that audience, Sasha, they are desperate for someone to speak to them. Look at all these trendy films making money. Netflix and Prime are cornering the market globally now. Reese Witherspoon, Nicole Kidman, Sandra Bullock, even Julia Roberts. They do TV shows now as well as movies. It's hot to have a TV sensation. Look at Saif Ali Khan and *Sacred Games*.'

'I don't want to make a cable movie though or a TV series. I want to make a big budget blockbuster. An event. You know what I mean, the big releases at Diwali, Eid, Christmas.'

'Then congratulations, you're gonna be writing your script until you die. You found a job for life. Oh, watch out, incoming at nine o'clock.'

'Yours or mine?'

'We're facing the same way, darling.'

Sasha watched as Zara was walking towards them.

–

Zara didn't know what propelled her to talk to Sasha Khan, especially as Jackie Dillon was standing right next to her, not hiding the vehement hatred she felt for her. Still, the look on Sasha's face the day before was haunting her, and she wanted to try to defuse the situation. Sasha had been pleasant enough over the years, unlike the openly hostile women Zara regularly came across. Her co-star and so-called rival Minnie Chopra had been tweeting crap all day again, talking about how she was the star of *Kismet India*, and how London had gone crazy for her. Deluded brat, thought Zara.

'Can I have a word?' Zara said tentatively.

'I can give you a few,' muttered Jackie, swallowing her drink and staring at Zara hard.

'In private, if you don't mind?' said Zara.

Jackie rolled her eyes but left them alone.

'I know it might be presumptuous, but I just wanted to clear the air between us.'

'I don't understand?' said Sasha, looking genuinely confused.

'The other night, when Imran and I... the kissing scene. I didn't know you would be on set, and I felt awkward doing that. I know that it's our job, we are acting, and honestly no matter how attractive your husband is, I don't feel like that about him at all. Imran and I, we come from the wrong side of Mumbai. That is the only connection we have. I know what everyone says about me, but I'm not the man-eater the gossip mags and that online gossip bitch Miss X always portray me to be.'

Miss X had a website that printed the most salacious stories and supposed insider gossip on Bollywood stars. She was often called the Perez Hilton of India, but in reality she was a scurrilous bully who Zara would gladly throttle. If she ever found out who she was. Unlike Perez, Miss X didn't have the balls to show the world her identity.

'It's ok, I'm not so naïve. I trust my husband and my marriage, and you're not the first woman to kiss him on-screen.'

'Maybe, but it's my first time kissing him and in front of you. I just wanted to make sure everything was ok.'

Sasha looked at her oddly, and then smiled.

'You know, Zara, the sort of dances you've done with so many married actors over the years, did it really bother you?'

'Yes. Not because of the kiss. That was work. But it felt wrong because you were there. Anyway, I just wanted to apologise if it put you in an awkward situation.'

'It didn't, but I appreciate you saying this.'

71

'Imran's been really helpful since I started making movies. He understands what it's like to have nothing. Not many others do, and he is always giving me advice. He's one of the good guys, and trust me, I've seen the bad guys. Too many of them. So, I would never want to do anything that might harm him or those he loves.'

Sasha nodded, squeezing Zara's arm in a genuine gesture of affection.

'Look at that,' Zara said, her eyes following the guests who had just entered. 'There goes Bollywood history.'

Zara watched as three legends of Bollywood crossed paths. Playing her father in the film was Ajay Kumar, superstar of Bollywood cinema who had ruled the box office back in the eighties, at a time when Anil Kapoor, Sunny Deol, and Sanjay Dutt were taking the marquee by storm. Ajay didn't come from a film family and had still given the star sons a run for their money. The double standard of Bollywood meant that Ajay, who was nearly sixty, was still able to romance heroines who were in their early twenties and no one cared. Ajay was no Amitabh Bachchan, he didn't have that stature or legendary status, but he did have a statue in the Baker Street Madame Tussaud's and his name still got producers excited. Although the reality was that Ajay's last few films had barely made a return and only became profitable because of satellite and on demand deals being done by the producers.

With him was his wife, Rani Kumar. She had been a bigger star than him back in the early eighties, as Rekha, Hema Malini, Laila, and Zeenat Aman reached their peak. They said Rani was going to topple them all and was the only competition that Sridevi had to the throne of Bollywood. Only she had given it up when she became pregnant with her first child. She did the odd film now and then, mainly arthouse pictures, with meaty roles and social messages. Still, it wasn't a career. She instead indulged in charity work and lunching with the ladies.

'You think the kiss was awkward, I would hate to be Rani*ji* right now,' said Sasha.

Zara agreed, as walking across the room towards Ajay and Rani, and the actress chosen to play Zara's mother in the movie, was Laila Chopra. Bitch Minnie's mother, and more importantly, Ajay Kumar's first wife. They had had a torrid marriage that lasted barely six months, before an acrimonious divorce, and then he had married Rani very quickly. Ajay and Laila hadn't spoken since or worked together until now.

'I don't know how Raj convinced them to star opposite each other. Laila had said she would never share screen space with her ex-husband again,' said Zara.

Laila's back was straight, her head tilted back, exuding a self-assurance that Zara wished she had. Rani and Ajay were still, as every eye in the room turned to them, waiting to see their reactions. Zara too held her breath, curious to see what would happen. As she watched, she saw Rani make the first move, meeting Laila as she approached, and kissing her on the cheek. The audience seemed to deflate at the lack of fireworks between them, and then collective jaws dropped as Ajay too kissed his ex-wife on the cheek, as Rani looked on smiling. Zara silently applauded in her head, as the three legends had just given the performance of their lives.

—

VJ was pissed, quite literally. How had this happened? He had given that bitch everything. For ten years he had dragged her up from being some cheap slut to being the highest paid actress in the country. And she was daring to question him? She had the gall to ban him from visiting her. Who did she think she was?

VJ rubbed his greasy fingers across his smartphone screen, opening up his secure folder. There he opened the pictures and videos he had of Zara. Back when she was Pari, and she was sucking every man he put in her way. And that slut had the nerve to shout at him? To embarrass him in public?

VJ had tried visiting her earlier, but security had said nobody was allowed without permission. And she hadn't given him permission. So she had found her little castle, her little hide-away. What did she think, that she was safe? It might not be Mumbai, he might not have all his contacts here, but he had himself. And Zara Das wasn't safe from him anywhere. Not Mumbai and not London. And she would realise that soon enough.

Zara walked quickly down the corridor to her room, aware that she was being followed closely, his footsteps keeping pace with hers. She wanted to get away from him, hated his intrusion into her space and her life. There was enough security already in the hotel, he should just stick to protecting her when she needed it. Even at the party she had seen Dan watching her all night, discreetly mouthing words into his comms unit. The security detail for the other stars weren't present, so why did he have to be? She was still seething over his arrogance when she had gone shopping, judging her and presuming to know what was going on in her head.

'For God's sake, please can you just go,' she complained, stopping and turning on him so suddenly that he failed to notice and bumped into her. 'Great, looks like it's probably you I need protecting from.'

'Mr Kapoor's orders. As long as you are in London, I am to make sure nothing happens to you.'

'Why is he so bothered? He's got his son into the movie already.'

'It's his hotel, and his movie. Anything happens to the leading lady, it's not exactly going to go down well.'

'I don't know,' Zara arched an eyebrow, 'the publicity would mean he makes a killing.'

Zara walked quickly to her room. She was stuck with Dan it seemed, but rather than feeling safe she felt oppressed. What freedom would she have with him shadowing her every move, no doubt reporting back to James Kapoor? She used the electronic key on her iPhone X to open her room door, then stood in the doorway staring at him.

'Am I ok to go in alone, or do you want to do a sweep of the rooms? Make sure no one is lurking behind a curtain to slit my throat.'

'If it would make you feel safer,' Dan deadpanned, to which Zara responded by swearing and storming into her suite, pushing the door as far as it would go behind her.

–

Dan Rourke watched the door close slowly, the automatic springs preventing it being slammed. It was to keep the noise down for other guests, just one more perk of being aboard a seven-star hotel. Dan thought it was like the *Titanic*, everything so over the top, right down to having mini chandeliers in the pisser for crying out loud. Who needed to see crystal hanging over them while they took a dump? Obviously stuck-up arseholes like he had to protect.

–

Zara felt a chill as she wandered into her bedroom. The door to the terrace was open, allowing a breeze to come in, adding to the already cranked up air con. Zara had forgotten to close it when she was getting ready for the party. She walked out onto the balcony, breathing in the warm cloying air, and looked out across St James's Park, the Mall and Buckingham Palace. She had seen these places so often as a child in books and on TV, she still remembered the first time she had come to London on an outdoor shoot. She had been a newcomer then. They were only filming a dance number and their accommodation at the time had been a budget hotel in Earl's Court. Still, she had gone out every day after pack-up, exploring the city like a tourist, soaking in every inch of it.

As her star rose over the years, the accommodation for outdoor shoots became better, but so did her difficulty in disappearing into the city. It was full of immigrants and generations of settled children of immigrants from the Indian subcontinent. She found herself being recognised and stopped for autographs on Oxford Street, in Selfridges and Harrods and while she wandered around the British Museum. Eventually she could only ever visit the exclusive boutiques on New Bond Street and in Knightsbridge, or the really exclusive shops that were hidden away from the general public in London. There she still managed to remain anonymous.

Looking out now into the star-filled sky, Zara felt the ground from beneath her disappear. This really was the marker that she had made it. From sleazy rodent-ridden budget rooms, to a suite with a balcony looking over the queen's palace. Could anyone blame her then if she was willing to do everything to prevent it all slipping from her grasp? She went back to her room, remembering the early shoot she had.

Zara washed her face and applied some of her night make-up range. It was the naked subtle tones she liked, but they were all enriched with natural oils and moisturisers, so worked like the best night creams out there. She changed into a lace negligee and applied perfume to her wrists and between her breasts. She wondered if Dan was still outside, or if he had been replaced by one of his lackeys for the night. The very thought of him infuriated her.

Minutes later, Zara called his number frantically. When Dan ran into her room, using his emergency key, Zara was sitting on the bedroom floor, crying and rocking, her hands covered in blood.

Chapter Six

Zara sat still on the midnight blue sofa, staring into the fifty-two inch wall-mounted flat screen TV. Nothing was playing, except her own reflection. The two men were talking at her, around her. She wasn't paying attention, her body on mute. She rubbed her hands, the blood still smeared on them.

'Zara, come on, I need to take you to the hospital. Or at least get a doctor, you're in shock,' Raj was pleading with her. 'And we need to contact the police.'

'Please, Mr Dillon, I am sure we can deal with this, we do not need the police,' Gareth Jones, the hotel manager was begging him. 'It will create too much negative attention.'

'Someone just left a rose filled with blood in her bedroom. I'm sorry, Mr Jones, but I don't think your hotel security is up to much.'

'I have asked them to examine the CCTV. All key cards used on the lift to this floor are also monitored.'

'Can you see who entered her room?' There was just silence, interrupted by the background hum of the air con system.

'The cameras do not cover guest's suite doors, sir. It is for their own privacy…'

'So, no, then. I want the police…'

'Please, Mr Dillon, sir, let me speak to Mr Kapoor first…'

'I will explain to James Kapoor. You understand how serious this is? Someone entered her room and left that shit on her bed. Have you any inkling of how vulnerable she must be feeling?'

Zara thought Raj was being too harsh, and looked at the hotel manager, his shoulders slumped and his eyes downcast. Kasim, her Mirage butler, was standing with him.

Raj in contrast was very much displaying his brat prince South Mumbai attitude. The occasions were rare, but Raj couldn't shake off his upbringing, cloistered among Bollywood's inner circle and rubbing shoulders with the elite. She hated seeing him so agitated on her behalf.

Zara got off the sofa, suddenly galvanised by this thought. She had been shaking so badly earlier, she had wrapped herself in the thick white cotton bathrobe the hotel had provided.

'No police,' she commanded Raj. 'I don't want any more attention or publicity. I came here to get away from these people, and if they've found me, well, they don't know what they've taken on. I won't let them get me quietly.'

'Zara, please, this is serious.'

'Gareth, tell me, how easy is it to break down this door?'

'Ma'am. It is reinforced steel, ten inches thick. The wood panelling is just for effect. The door can only be opened with an electronic key card, and once you are in possession of that key card there are no other copies made. You will have a copy on the app on your phone, but that is all.'

'What about housekeeping?'

'No, ma'am, they don't have copies for any of the rooms on this floor. They will only service the rooms under Kasim's supervision...'

'So, you have a key card then?' snapped Raj at Kasim.

'Yes, sir, but that is only for... yes,' Kasim admitted.

'I thought you said no copies are made, Mr Jones? How do we know we can trust him?' Raj said.

'Raj, please. I'm sure James Kapoor wouldn't have hired anyone without the most stringent checks. For now, let's just keep this between ourselves, and carry on. Please.'

Raj shrugged his shoulders. 'As you wish, Zara. But if anything else happens, we are calling the police. Where the hell is that oaf security guard? Why wasn't he here to protect you?'

'He's in the bedroom, sir, checking how the… thing could have been left,' said Kasim.

'He should have done a sweep of the rooms before he let you in,' Raj fumed.

'He did offer, I'm the one that stopped him,' Zara whispered. 'He's done a good job protecting me.' Dan had walked back into the room, and it was his eyes she was staring into as she spoke.

'The hotel keeps an electronic log every time a key card is used, I've managed to check that. No one entered this room after you left,' he said.

'How is that possible for you to know? My staff are still checking their systems,' Gareth said.

Dan ignored him. 'There are only two options. The first is that someone used a manual key card, creating it without your knowledge.'

'That is not possible, we keep a very tight control…'

'It's not impossible though, is it?' said Raj. He was busy scrolling through his phone, looking anxious.

'And the other option?' Zara asked Dan.

'The second option is that somebody entered through the door to the terrace.'

'I think I left it open, I can't remember,' she admitted.

'Why would you think to close it?' Dan reassured her. 'You are on the tenth floor. Unless someone scaled the walls or used the rooms on either side of yours as an entry point, it shouldn't be an issue.'

'Are you saying someone had access via a neighbouring room?' Raj asked.

'Possibly. I had a look at the layout before Ms Das checked in. The top floor consists of the family suites, and then there is a gap. A whole floor that was filled with concrete, so there is no noise pollution. The same exists under this floor of suites too. The only real access point would be from the two rooms on either side.'

'Who occupies them?' Raj asked.

'Jasmine Chopra is on one side,' Gareth said reluctantly. 'And on the other, Ajay and Rani Kumar.'

'They were all at the party,' Raj sighed.

'I didn't see Minnie,' Zara countered. 'Maybe someone should ask her what she was doing and who she let into her bedroom.'

–

Jasmine 'Minnie' Chopra didn't think she should be in this position. She was lying on her back while Rocky Kapoor, son of the billionaire James Kapoor, was pounding away at her, as though he were entitled. Minnie wasn't into men like Rocky, but he was all that was available. She dug her nails into his back, and when he winced, she used her Pilates-strengthened hips to flip him over so she was straddling him.

'This is how I fuck, Rocky, on top and in control.'

Rocky seemed to be getting turned on by her attitude, pushing himself in deeper. He sat up, kissing Minnie's neck, as he moved inside her, taking her nipples into his mouth.

'Yes, that's better,' she gasped, as he sucked on her breasts, rubbing her clit with his fingers. Rocky was well versed on how to make a woman come, and Minnie was glad she had taken the risk with him. She pulled his head back and kissed him hard on the mouth, tasting herself on his tongue, from when it had been inside her earlier. Minnie had no time for romantic foreplay or passion, she wanted to feel raw and Rocky was responding to her in all the right ways.

Rocky fell back onto the bed, grabbing her hips, and began to slide her up and down his hardness, using his brute strength to lift her up and bring her back down again. Minnie loved the feeling, as Rocky entered her repeatedly, feeling her own body hit another level, as the waves of passion broke inside her. She heard his breathing grow shallow, and he started to cry out, getting close.

'Not fucking yet,' she screamed at him, as she moved his hands until his fingers were playing with her again, getting her closer. She moved one of his hands to her throat and clasped his fingers around her neck. Rocky got the hint and stroked her throat, tightening his fingers slightly. Minnie moaned, as the pain and pleasure mixed with the dangerous thought that Rocky might choke her, her body responding to his thrusting and his experienced fingers, until she felt herself unable to hold back, her body shaking and releasing as she came, feeling him climax at the same time, their bodies in perfect union.

–

Minnie yawned and switched on the wall-mounted TV, the screen coming to life with specially installed Indian channels. She surfed through the myriad Star channels, and Zee channels.

'Oh, look, Mummy, there's you and Ajay.'

Laila stopped mid-rant to look at an image of herself from over thirty years ago. She looked the same, as far as she was concerned. Sure, her skin was fresher then but even now she had no real lines or signs of age, or so she kept telling her daughter.

'Turn that nonsense off. I was mortified by your absence tonight, where were you? Do you have any idea how embarrassing it was having to give your excuses? And to the men who are making this movie?'

'I'm sure they don't give a fuck, Mummy.'

'Don't swear at me, you little ingrate. Where were you?'

Minnie flicked channels and ignored her mother. Superstar Laila, harlot of the eighties, the woman who had driven her father out of the house and out of her life.

'You have no right to ask me my whereabouts, I'm not a child.'

Minnie was tempted to tell the cow exactly what she had been doing just to see the look on her face. Her fake face with the layers of make-up, her hair that she washed only in rose-scented water every day, and the stupid massive flower she stuck over her ear. This woman was her mother?

Minnie was shocked by the slap. She was so lost in hate for her mother, she didn't see her approach and smack her across the face.

'You think this world revolves around you? Don't fool yourself. You've been lucky so far. I got you the breaks you've had. If it wasn't for me, do you think anyone would be interested in you? You're hardly Miss India material, and you can just about string a sentence together on camera because of the expensive acting coaches I sent you to. This film took a lot of negotiation on my part. They only cast you because of me, because I agreed to star opposite that man after all these years.'

'Whatever, you're probably glad you get to grope each other on-screen again, you disgusting people.' Minnie felt the tears sting her eyes, and pouted, trying to look petulant instead.

'And your behaviour,' continued Laila, ignoring her completely. 'Coming late to shootings, giving your directors attitude, telling them when to pack up. Who do you think you are?'

Minnie threw the remote control across the room and jumped off the bed, squaring up to Laila.

'Read the writing on the wall, Laila. Your time is over. You know what they're saying about me? They're saying I'm the first actress to come along that can challenge that bitch Zara Das for her crown. So keep your favours and your breaks, I don't need them.'

Laila started to clap. Slow and patronising.

'And, Minnie dearest… who do you think paid the journalist to write that headline?'

Minnie couldn't hide her shock, her confidence draining from her in an instant. Minnie was Laila's daughter, and that's all she would be known for. She stormed out of her mother's room, realising she had left her key card in her purse. She didn't want to go back and face round two, so instead she took the lift to the floor below. She knocked on the door. No answer. She knocked harder, hearing muffled voices and banging. A woman opened the door, dressed only in her bra and panties.

'Yes?' She was giggling as she spoke.

'Where's Rocky?' Minnie demanded.

'Who the fuck is it? Come back, Bailey, my dick needs sucking.'

Minnie strode into the room where she found Rocky with his jeans pulled down. He was tied to the bed with silk ties, his eyes also bound. Minnie turned to Bailey, pointed at her discarded clothes on the floor, and then pointed at the door. Bailey rubbed her fingers. She wanted cash. Rocky was into hookers? Minnie felt a bit sick, remembering she hadn't used a condom with him earlier. Minnie had no cash on her, so searched Rocky's pockets where she pulled out a handful of fifty-pound notes. She gave Bailey four of them, keeping the rest for herself.

When Bailey left, Minnie walked over to Rocky who was struggling against his binds, shouting for help. Minnie saw the line of coke on the bedside table too. She pulled at his erection gently, making him groan Bailey's name. There was a ring of lipstick on the head of his penis. She was damned if she was going to go there now. Instead she took off her Louboutin stiletto and gently tapped Rocky's legs with it. She then turned him onto his front, stroking his balls as she did so. Rocky was moaning with pleasure, begging her to suck him off. Minnie rolled the stiletto heel down his lower back, to his buttocks. Then in one quick rapid movement she inserted it into his anus. Rocky screamed in pain.

'Youfuckingbitchwhatthefuckdoyouthinkyou'redoingyou fuckinglowdownlittlecunt!'

'That, you slimy little shit, is for thinking it's ok to screw a prostitute hours after you've had sex with me. And if you do something like that to me or anyone else ever again, I'll send daddy dearest your dick in a Tiffany's box.'

Rocky went quiet, stifling his sobs in his pillow. When Minnie was angry, it made her crazy, and capable of anything.

–

Imran sat down to begin his complicated beauty routine, involving a dozen different products. They had showered together, making love in the heated water jets. Sasha pulled on her Carine Gilson silk kimono and came up behind him. She knew not to get too close while he put himself together, so she just massaged his shoulders gently.

'I've been thinking,' she began cautiously. 'I met Tanuja before we left for London.'

Imran's eyes immediately darkened, and a firmness set in his jaw. He knew what she was going to say, and she could sense his response already. Still, she pursued her conversation.

'She's made some really good edits. From what you said last time, *jaan*. I think it works now, it's more commercial. It's more your sort of film. If you would just take a look?'

'Tanuja is a fucking dyke and hasn't got a clue what anybody wants,' he shouted, slamming the foundation bottle onto his dressing table. 'I don't get it, Sasha. Isn't what I've given you enough? What about the children?'

'The children? You brought me to London for a month without them.'

'I needed you. And my mum will look after them.'

'I'm their mother…'

'I needed you,' he insisted.

'Your mother can help out while I'm making the movie. I'm only going to produce, I won't be needed every day. Please just read it.'

Imran picked up his eye gel, starting to dab the thick substance under his eyes. 'I don't have the time right now, Sasha. When we get back, maybe?'

'This is the best time. We are away from the craziness of Mumbai. There your time is taken virtually every day. This is a place where I can have you to myself for a while.'

'So, let's enjoy that. Just us. We haven't had that since the kids have been born. I wanted this for us. Please don't spoil it.'

Don't spoil it? Sasha didn't trust herself to speak. She tried Jackie's phone, feeling so alone and lost. Jackie wasn't answering, in fact Sasha hadn't seen her since the party.

-

Jackie was on a corner sofa by the fire, the flames throwing orange and red shadows across the bar that had resorted to mood lighting a while back. There were mini chandeliers throughout, chaise longes of blue velvet and gold trim, smoked glass tables, and a bar that belonged in a Vegas nightclub. A sheer crystal wall showcased shelves full of the most expensive drinks in the world. The waitresses looked like out of work actresses, and the bar tender was hot.

Jackie stuck to her gin, pacing herself as she hit her own limits. She had worn an embroidered Sabyasachi kurta to the soirée, summer blue with a heavy gold neck, matched with a skirt from a street trader. The kurta had been a gift although Jackie was too normal for the designer world. Despite the wealth she had grown up with in Franklin Lakes, her parents managed to keep her from being another spoilt New Jersey princess. She didn't want for anything, but she wasn't smothered in indulgence either.

Still, the absolute poverty she had faced in Mumbai made her appreciate just how fortunate she had been. Most of all for the choices she had been allowed to make. Choices of where to study, what to do for work, and who to love. And that was the issue, wasn't it?

Jackie was by no imagination a loose woman, she had only had three major loves in her life. Three boyfriends, and the occasional casual fuck when circumstance, alcohol, and opportunity all came together. But those three men were enough to destroy what she and Raj had managed to build.

Jackie didn't know when it had all started. Raj knew about her past when they met, she hadn't hidden anything from him, she was in her mid-thirties after all, he didn't seriously expect her to be a virgin. He was no wilting wallflower either, having grown up in Mumbai's party circuit. Back in their halcyon days in New York when they had met, it all seemed so civilised and so romantic. They had been through the rubbish, done the dating, fucking, heart-breaking. They had both crossed thirty, and were looking at settling down. That's what had worked, that sense of wanting to settle. Not for second best or comfort, but for really finding the one you could spend the rest of your life with.

And she believed that when they had met. She was the daughter of a Jewish New Jersey businessman, he was the son of a faded Bollywood producer who had turned around his father's production house by making commercial extravaganzas. They were both at New York University's Tisch School of the Arts, only he was there as break from his routine as he worked on his next script, while Jackie was there to teach students how to make the sort of documentaries she did, the sort that were her voice to change the world.

It was at an academic mixer, a place for new and temporary staff to meet the old hats, where she had first laid eyes on Raj. He was good-looking, with a slightly tubby frame, nursing a drink and looking around the room. He was smiling even though he was on his own, and then he laughed. Jackie thought he was either crazy or fascinating. She decided to take the risk and speak to him.

'What's the joke?' she said.

'That I'm in a city of millions and I was feeling lonely. How does that happen?'

'Easily.'

'Yes. I felt the same in Mumbai too. As though I was standing still, and the world was moving on and around me without involving me or caring.'

Jackie looked into his dark eyes and saw beyond the black and felt something inside her move.

'Jackie Newman.'

'Raj Dillon.'

'What brings you to New York?'

'I wanted a break from Mumbai. So, I chose a city that was just as busy and chaotic.'

Jackie had laughed. And she had carried on laughing all night. Raj was sweet and charming and innocent, so different to the men she was used to. As the party ended, and the stragglers all decided to go home or sleep at someone else's home, Raj and Jackie had gone for bagels and a walk along the Hudson.

'What's India like?' she had asked him.

'You can't describe India. You have to experience it.'

And she had. She took off for three months and spent the time with Raj, as India invaded her every cell. And by the end of the three months she was in love with Raj and she was completely devoted to the country. Marriage and a move followed.

They had done it quickly, quietly, and with no fuss, sorting the legal formalities without bothering about involving their respective faiths. They planned the same in America, and when she called to tell her parents, they had been happy she'd finally found someone who shared her passions.

Passions that extended to each other as they found their souls and their bodies intertwining. It had seemed so easy back then when she agreed to give up New York for Mumbai. Despite his parents having major reservations about him marrying such an unsuitable girl – forget caste, he had gone to a totally different faith – they had eased into life among Bollywood's jet set. Raj had delivered another blockbuster soon after their marriage, while Jackie had been nominated for an Academy Award for her latest documentary on the female entrepreneurs in the slums, and they were soon touted as Bollywood's most loved up and approachable couple.

Then just as suddenly things weren't so easy any more, and what happened away from the world's eyes was anything but normal. As time went by, something ugly began to fester inside Raj. It was as though he became obsessed, possessed even, and anything could trigger him off.

Jackie had tried to understand at first, trying to talk to him about his mood swings, trying to help him. None of it mattered though. He was impenetrable in his rage and darkness. Jackie had never felt so alone in her life. She had no close family, friends that were as fake as the sets in her husband's movies, and an emotional turmoil that came from her inability to have children. She felt like such a cliché as she found herself turning into a drunken lush who would have put Sue Ellen from *Dallas* to shame. And she couldn't see how anything would change.

This whole thing with Zara Das was making her have irrational thoughts. Was that why he was behaving like this? Driving her insane with his jealousy which was actually masking his guilt? No, he wouldn't. She thought then about what was happening between them in the bedroom. Was Zara the real reason? How much had she drunk, she wondered, having thoughts like this? Sasha was right, Raj just wouldn't.

'A beautiful woman like you shouldn't be drinking alone.' The man was six foot something, with broad shoulders, and a narrow waist. He was wearing a suit, his tie undone, his blazer over his shoulder. His blonde hair was tousled slightly, his eyes piercing and blue as he stared into hers. He must have been in his late twenties at best.

'Purrlease, has that bullshit line ever worked on anyone?' she quipped.

'You'd be surprised. Although usually I don't need a line. I only save them for the women I know will be hard to get.'

'Yeah, because I'm just sitting waiting here for a man to *get* me.'

'I knew irritating you would be the only way to get more than one sentence out of you. I'm Ryan Matthews.' He held out his hand, which was tanned and smooth, the veins visible under his perfect skin. Jackie was too drunk to even deny the attraction, and with her gin specs the gorgeous Ryan was looking like a supermodel. Still, she really shouldn't. If Raj saw her even speaking to him... no fuck him, he could have his little clas Zara. Jackie would not be cowed.

'I'll have another gin, and don't talk to me if you're going to bore me,' she ordered.

Ryan gestured to the barman to repeat Jackie's order, and sat down on the same sofa as her, one knee drawn up so it was inches from Jackie's own.

'I wish they'd turn that goddamn fire off, it's already roasting in here. London in a heatwave, who knew?'

'Yes, it's extremely uncomfortable, but has its advantages,' said Ryan. He had a clipped accent, the sort you'd imagine Prince William to have. 'I usually fly out to my parents' villa in Dubai to get a top up of my tan. These days I've been lazing around in Hyde Park when I can.'

'Dubai is too sanitised for me.'

'My parents have a holiday home there, but I grew up in Chelsea. Now I travel across the world for my father's business.'

'What does he do? What do you do, even?'

A waitress brought their drinks over, giving Ryan the biggest 'fuck me please' look Jackie had seen in a while. Ryan either didn't notice or pretended not to.

'You'll judge me if I say.'

'Go on, try me. I don't bite. Unless I want to.'

'Hedge fund management.'

Jackie laughed, spilling her drink over her chin as she did. *Classy*, she thought. 'Sorry, but you're right. I am judging you. If there is a soulless profession...'

'A man's got to eat.'

'A man can survive on burgers, he doesn't need caviar for breakfast.'

Ryan swigged from his glass, looking embarrassed.

'So, if you live in Chelsea, why are you staying at this monstrosity?'

'You don't like it?'

'Are you kidding me? I expect this came straight out of a Kardashian rear end, it's so full of itself.'

'I find it quite exotic, a little Arabian oasis in the madness of London.'

'You can't buy taste, obviously.'

'No, but you can buy everything else. Everything except for you.'

Jackie didn't know if he was flirting with her or actually propositioning her.

'Look, Brian…'

'It's Ryan…'

'Whatever, sweets, I'm not on the market. I'm a happily married woman, and this ain't going anywhere. Go play your prince charming on some dumb little girl who will appreciate it.'

'That's just it, those sorts of girls don't interest me. You do.'

Jackie put her glass down hard.

'I'm married.'

'Happily. You said.'

'Take the hint.'

'And yet here you are, at 2 a.m., drinking alone in the city's most expensive hotel.'

Jackie opened her mouth, but no words came out. She then caught sight of Raj, he had just entered the bar and spotted her and Ryan, the look on his face a mix of anger and jealousy and hurt. Jackie watched as he turned and rushed out of the bar. Fuck, that was all she needed. She hurried after Raj.

'I'm here all week,' Ryan said after her.

What a jerk, she thought. What a drop dead gorgeous sexy hunk of a jerk.

Chapter Seven

Kenwood House, set on the fringes of Hampstead Heath, had been closed off as the cast of *Kismet India* descended on it. Raj had decided to shoot the wedding sequence that ended the movie there, with the entire cast present. He was feeling anxious, Zara noticed him rubbing his stomach a lot.

'IBS,' he told her. 'Irritable bowel syndrome,' he explained to her blank expression.

'You need some medication?' she offered, although not sure what exactly she could give him. He shook his head.

'How are you feeling?' he asked her. She shrugged, what could she say to him? The events of the previous night would shake up the best, and who was she not to be affected? 'I wish you'd let me cancel the shoot.'

'Come on, Raj, I know it takes a lot to book out a place like this. Money and contacts and strings. James Kapoor might struggle to get you this again. I don't know what's happening, Raj, I don't know how anyone could access my room like that. But I won't be beaten. I didn't let a fucking bomb beat me, I will not let something like this do that to me.'

'Where's your bodyguard?'

Zara looked around the grounds and saw Dan not too far from her. He nodded, and she smiled back. There was definitely a thawing in their relationship, in the way he had taken charge and started to look into how her safety could be improved. He seemed to take it personally that her room had been accessed, it was more than just a job. He actually seemed to care about her. Or was she just assuming things?

Zara was dressed in her wedding outfit for the shot, with the bright sun shining down on her. The sky was a clear, deep blue and as she breathed in, she didn't want to think about the threats she was facing. Raj was making this movie that could break his production house if things went wrong, and she wasn't going to be the one to ruin that. Zara could also do loyalty.

'You look beautiful,' said Sasha, who had come on set.

'Thank you. It's probably the closest I'll ever get to tying the knot,' she said.

Sasha was dressed in a sleeveless purple kurta and shalwar, her hair loose. In contrast Zara was dressed in the showstopper outfit of the movie. Sabyasachi had created an elaborate pink, red, gold, and aquamarine *lengha* for her. The skirt was made from the finest organza and silk, covered in intricate decorative work of semi-precious stones and gold threads, glistening as the sun shone down on her. The matching *choli* top was made from the same, her midriff on display, with a gold and ruby gemstone in her belly button. It would be the wedding outfit every Asian girl in the world would be copying if things went right, she thought. The beautiful *lengha choli* was finished off with a heavy *dupatta* that sat carefully on her head, exposing one arm, while falling softly around one side of her. She was wearing real heavy gold, diamond, and ruby jewellery, mostly brought over from Malabar Jewellers, but her centrepiece necklace worth millions had been loaned by Van Cleef & Arpels for the day. There were extra security guards on set just for that.

'Today's going to be fun,' Zara said. 'Everyone is here.'

'Yes,' Sasha agreed. 'I promise I won't look upset if you have to kiss Imran again.'

'No kissing today. Ironic really as in this scene we are actually married.'

'I was thinking...' Sasha seemed unsure at first, then carried on. 'Can we have lunch or dinner one day?'

Zara was physically shocked by the invite. In all her years in Mumbai she was yet to be invited out by someone like Sasha. The wives usually sneered at her.

'I know you have a lot on, obviously. But if you find yourself at a loose end, it would be good to spend some time together.'

'Not to sound rude, but what brought this on?'

'Imran's kissed about two dozen heroines in his movies. You're the first one that actually thought to ask me how I feel about it. I mean I know in Hollywood it's the norm, but it's still a thing in our movies and our culture, isn't it?'

'Yes, I know what you mean.'

'I still don't get it. We're ok now for women to wear skimpy outfits on-screen, to even feign rabid lovemaking, but kissing is just a step too far.'

'It's the intimacy of it. The sex scenes are never explicit, just two people cavorting around under the sheets. The skimpy outfits, I guess everyone is used to that now. Kissing though, it's just too erotic.'

'Yes, although I noticed it's usually all the non-Asian extras they put in the most revealing clothes for songs. When did that become a thing?'

Zara laughed, it was true. Mumbai was now full of women dancers from the UK, America, and Australia, all white, who were being put up in shared flats and given the moves and outfits producers and directors didn't ask Indian women to do and wear for songs. The girls loved it; it was an exotic holiday while being paid top dollar to be in dance videos, almost like a gap year. Zara thought it was exploitation, also reinforcing the stereotype that white women did things Indian women wouldn't. Which was bullshit in her experience of the Bollywood set. They did everything and worse, only behind closed doors usually. Although with social media that was becoming difficult. You couldn't date if you were a Bollywood star, or go clubbing and get drunk any more without being pictured. Luckily, society wasn't as judgemental as it had been before, as the next generation was doing exactly the same in the big cities. What offended the conservative pockets were the big things. Like offending historical icons or religious ones.

'At least Raj doesn't indulge in that. He's in London, he could have a whole army of white women in bikinis twerking in the background if he wanted, but he's keeping it classy, not exploitative.'

'Yes, they're twerking in dresses,' laughed Zara. 'I think to really make a difference we need more women behind the camera.'

Sasha looked thoughtful. 'Yes, I agree, but it's not an easy task. Not even in Hollywood. Anyway, I appreciated what you did. Also, I know from my husband that you have issues with your family. I know how that feels. I have parents who are alive but don't see me. Sometimes it might help to talk to someone who understands that pain.'

Zara knew from Imran too about Sasha's own parental situation. The Rathores had cut off their daughter, much like Zara's own parents had.

'No rush, whenever you have time,' said Sasha.

Zara watched her walk away, and for once, couldn't find an emotion to display.

—

Jackie had dressed quickly, deciding to give the filming a miss and take in some galleries instead. Sasha was being boring and watching the day's shoot, probably making sure Imran didn't snog the face off that tart Zara. Jackie still didn't get Raj coming to London for her. On top of the issues that Jackie and Raj were having, it just added to her confusion and suspicion of him.

Jackie's phone rang, and she immediately felt the tension in her veins. She picked it up after letting it ring a few times; the voice on the other end was never one that brought good news.

'Where are you?'

'Just getting ready to go out. Is everything ok?' asked Jackie.

'Yeah, just checking you haven't left town after our little meeting yesterday.'

'I'm not going anywhere. This is far too important for me.'

'Yeah, I know it is. I was thinking, it's probably worth a bit more than you've given me as well.'

'Really? Is this what things have come to?' Jackie sighed.

'You came to me, remember.'

'Don't you feel any compassion for my situation at all?'

'Don't lecture me. I wanna see you. Now.'

'I have plans.'

'Well cancel them, baby doll, I said I wanna see you, so you make sure you're here within an hour and we can talk.'

-

Jackie took a cab to Oxford Circus and walked from there. She had kept the woman close to Selfridges and close to the clinic on Harley Street. She was hoping the whole thing would be over in hours, but now felt it might drag on for a few days. She wanted everything done, and the woman gone before anyone found out what she was up to.

The hotel she had kept the woman in wasn't shoddy by any standards; it was one of the best four-star hotels in London, but Jackie had been cagey about the fact she was staying in a seven-star one.

Oxford Street was busy in the heat, something she hadn't been prepared for. Everyone had filled her head with the stereotype of the British weather, the summers that lasted a week if that. Her own previous visits to London had reinforced those clichés. This year though there was a heatwave, and the city was sweltering. Unprepared and sweltering.

Jackie was glad she could walk around wearing her summer clothes without being conscious of guys looking at her as though they were seeing her naked. It wasn't so much what she wore – the Mumbai circle she was part of were all the upwardly mobile jetsetters of the city – it was more who she was. India was still mainly full of Indians. With her Mediterranean skin, auburn hair, and bright blue eyes, Jackie stood out wherever she went. Most people thought she was a tourist, but in her head, she was a Mumbaiker. She had adopted the city after her marriage to Raj.

As Jackie pushed her way through the crowds, she thought how strange life and fate could be. You could spend a lifetime looking for love, not knowing that it was waiting for you in another land.

Outside the hotel, Jackie took a swig on the miniature vodka bottle she had taken out of the Mirage minibar. She felt she needed it.

-

Zara watched as Ruby came towards her on the arm of a rather well built and good-looking man, with a structured face and a carefully cut beard.

'This is Salman Rana,' she announced. At first, Zara thought it might be Ruby's boyfriend. 'He's playing my on-screen husband.'

Of course, Raj did say he'd cast a British Pakistani actor to play the role of Collins in the movie, after his original choice got stuck at immigration. In the books Collins was a rather foolish character, but Raj had turned him into a himbo instead. Initially he was making a play for Zara's Elizabeth, but on her refusal, he would end up with Ruby's Charlotte. It was a statement: the character had everything in *Kismet India*, looks and money, but he couldn't engage Zara's character mentally. It was saying something different at least, that women didn't want handsome, tall, rich men coming into their lives. Unless they had some substance.

'An honour to meet you,' Salman said, offering Zara his hand. 'It's a dream come true to star with you.'

'Steady on, jock-face, you're my flirtation for the movie, not hers,' said Ruby. 'This place is gorgeous, isn't it? I've never been in all the time I've lived in London.'

'Not as beautiful as you though,' Salman said.

'That's better, he's a quick learner,' said Ruby. Zara threw her a look, one that was intended to remind Ruby that she had a boyfriend and maybe she should focus on that. 'Wow, check out that. Who hired the stripper?'

Zara looked over to see Minnie emerge from one of the side doors to the stately home where the changing and make-up rooms were. She was wearing a purple *ghagra*, split up both sides revealing lots of leg, with a silver-beaded brassiere, her entire torso on display, and a thin purple *dupatta* over her shoulder.

'As if she'd wear that to a real wedding,' said Ruby.

'I wouldn't put it past her,' said Zara.

'Oh, look she's just Insta'd. *When you upstage the bride #canthelpit*. Please, Zara, post something classless and bitchy. I'm so bored with her going unchallenged.'

'She's a messed-up brat, leave her be, Ruby. I'm playing the long game and will win where it actually matters.'

'Hell no, I'm going to start a fight with her for you.'

'There's her mother,' said Salman.

Zara saw Laila Chopra walking towards them across the freshly cut lawn, dressed in a full saree, purple and silver as well. It was heavily embroidered, and finished off with silver jewellery, her hair pulled back into a chignon. She looked classier and more stunning than her daughter. Zara saw the look on Minnie's face as she stormed off.

Zara had met Laila briefly at the soirée but they had only ever been passing acquaintances on Mumbai's social scene. Laila was Bollywood royalty, a living legend, who had retained her star status by shrouding herself in mystery, and it was a template that Zara admired. Keep the world out while still letting them love the surface.

'You look stunning,' Laila said, coming up to Zara.

'Hardly. I may be the bride, but you are the most beautiful woman here,' said Zara.

'I just Insta'd,' said Ruby. 'How to *really* upstage the bride. With a picture of you Laila*ji*.'

Laila nodded but didn't say anything. She didn't use social media: her fame was mythological, and she kept it alive with her aloofness.

'That is very kind of you, but I've had my heyday. It's now time for you youngsters to take the mantle.'

'No one could hope to take anything from you,' Salman said, oozing the sort of charm that actors were expert at. Ruby made vomiting motions behind his back to Zara, who got the giggles.

'I see you are still flirting with me,' Laila said. 'He was doing that all day when we filmed together. Young man, I am old enough to be your mother, but please do carry on.'

'Old enough to be his grandmother,' Ruby mouthed at Zara.

Fear and terror seemed a million miles away from Zara as she stood in the warmth, surrounded by people dressed in their bling for a wedding. The *lenghas*, sarees, *shalwar kameezes*, and *sherwanis* had all burned up Mumbai's finest designer's bank balances, as the Kapoor billions were lavishly spent. And emerging in his *sherwani* was the boy that was responsible for all of it; Rocky Kapoor.

Zara was yet to meet him and had to admit that Kapoor Jnr cut quite an entrance. He was built and handsome with designer facial hair as standard but had an arrogance in the way he moved. He was almost strutting, wearing tight jeans which were packed and on view with his wedding *sherwani* jacket buttons opened. His eyes were behind shades, as he casually sauntered up to them, with nothing about his demeanour to suggest that he knew he was in the presence of stars like Zara and Laila. She supposed he didn't have to care – his daddy was there to act as his safety net.

'We have a heavy day of filming tomorrow,' he said, by way of greeting. Despite his shades, Zara could clearly tell he was checking her out. And it wasn't bad meeting a sexy young man for the first time when you were dressed as a bride. 'And I can't wait,' he added lasciviously.

Zara laughed despite herself, plus it didn't hurt to be nice to the producer's son. Ruby pushed herself forward, shaking

Rocky's hand and going in for an air kiss, making sure to press her breasts against him. Salman looked on, slightly put out, but Rocky only seemed to have eyes for Zara.

'Where's your groom? If you fancy a quickie before you tie the knot, just say,' Rocky winked.

'In this *lengha*? I think they must create them to avoid such nonsense.'

'The desi version of the chastity belt,' said Ruby.

Rocky seemed to notice Ruby properly for the first time, and Zara felt a momentary stab of jealousy that the attention had been taken away from her. Ruby was only meeting him because of her, because Zara had wanted someone on set who might be on her side. Truth was, Ruby hardly kept in touch when they were in different cities, usually only messaging to get a quote or the lowdown on Zara's latest drama. Even when calling to see if Zara was ok after the bomb blast, it seemed Ruby was more interested in the inside salacious details she could use. Zara felt like a bitch for having the thought and pushed it away.

She looked around at the marigolds garlanding the Georgian stone, at the lawns decorated with *rangoli* patterns, a temporary *mandap* erected in the centre of the grounds, its pillars and canopy gold and red, numerous extras in bling clothes and jewels, and some of the most famous Asian faces on the planet milling around. She felt as though she was in the middle of a circus, as though she didn't belong, and felt her breath catch in her throat. She was about to make a retreat to her make-up room, scared her anxiety would engulf her, when she caught sight of Dan watching her. It seemed to steady her, give her comfort. She hated that this man who had judged her so harshly was the one person right now who she needed.

–

Sasha watched from the sidelines as Raj put his scenes together. While the audience watched, they would see a seamless cut of a wedding; Imran and Zara finally getting together for their happily ever after. There would be close-ups of parents, siblings, and guests, random drops of people dancing, eating, and purporting the myth that nothing else in the world could make you happier than a big fat Indian wedding, where the women were blinged up to their eyeballs, and the men looked sturdy enough to father the next generation.

Sasha's own wedding had been a small affair. Six people had attended, none of them relatives, two complete strangers. It had been over in a matter of minutes. Imran pushed her regularly for them to have a marriage renewal ceremony, something grand and opulent where she would get to wear the sort of outfit Zara was rocking today, where they could invite hundreds of guests and feed them until they burst.

Sasha had refused. However her parents had reacted to her marriage, she wouldn't insult them further by hosting a party she knew they wouldn't come to. Sasha's parents had been broken by their daughter marrying a Muslim, even worse, a boy from the slums, the son of their maid. When they found out she had undergone a conversion ceremony to take part in her *nikaah*, changing her name from Anita Rathore to Sasha Khan, that was it. They didn't stop to ask her why or care that Imran had carried out the seven *pheras* circling the sacred fire central to the Hindu wedding ceremony for her. He was no more Hindu than she was Muslim, but they had done that for each other, hoping the families would be okay.

Sasha's mother was a middle-class housewife who had spent her time ensuring her husband's world ran smoothly, overseeing the cook, the cleaner, the maid and making sure she was part of every local initiative for every festival and holiday. She did everything for everyone but had left her own children to the care of Imran's mother, who they called Amma. Why she even employed Amma in the first place, Sasha never understood. Her mother despised Muslims, and the fact she would give the care of her children to one spoke volumes about the importance she put on them. Then again, her mother had grown up being told daughters were second best. And she had failed as a human, producing four.

Sasha was close to her sisters, even after her scandalous marriage to Imran. They were Mumbaikers, they were used to such things. Plus, they loved how Imran treated their sister.

Imran's mother had also been great. She didn't really have a choice, Imran was her only child. Still, she had welcomed Sasha into her life, saying she was gaining a daughter at last. So, Sasha had forever dropped her birth name, and Anita Rathore became as silent as her parents' love.

Even that morning, as Sasha had Facetimed her children, watching them on the screen as they filled her head with their nonsense, Amma had moved her to tears.

'We miss you, Mummy,' her son Yash, named after her father, had said.

'I miss you more, Mom, Yash is so naughty when you are not here.' Nadia, her daughter, named after Imran's mother, had been quick to outwit her younger brother.

Amma had shushed them both and reassured Sasha that everything was ok, and she shouldn't worry and enjoy the break.

'For years now, I've watched you give everything to your children, and to my child. This is your time, my daughter. Let Imran shoot his movie. I want you to shop, go and spend my son's money. You've worked just as hard as he has to earn it.'

Sasha had ended the call before they all saw her tears. Amma had meant well, she genuinely cared for Sasha. Yet she too thought that Sasha should simply do what the other Bollywood Wives did, just like Imran.

As the camera rolled, and Raj directed his actors, Sasha went over her own script in her head, the images of how her movie would look sharp in her head. She imagined Imran mouthing dialogue she had written, imagined Deepika Padukone, Alia Bhatt or Kareena Kapoor playing the female lead.

She knew Imran's words were from a good place. He believed Sasha had saved him and his mother and wanted to give her the world. He wanted her to be the happiest woman alive, and for everything she wanted to be hers. But it was his version of contentment, not hers.

Sasha didn't want to live in a gilded cage; she wanted to make waves. It was almost as though Imran didn't want her doing anything for herself because it meant she didn't need him. However he dressed it up, Sasha felt trapped and empty. No, she was more determined than ever to get her movie made. Jackie was right, if Sasha wanted this to happen, she would make it happen. Even if it meant losing Imran in the process.

–

The room was thick with smoke, and Jackie coughed despite herself. It was a four-star hotel, but the woman, Melody, had made it look like some cheap motel. The bedcover had been bunched into a corner of the room, there was ash on the white bedsheets, and some stains that looked like spilt wine and grease from takeaway food. Clothes were scattered across the room, bags of Primark merchandise lined up against one wall.

Melody was in her mid-thirties, but looked much older, thanks to decades of neglect. Her skin was haggard, hanging loose off her bony frame, her hair short and coloured an odd magenta shade. Jackie stared at her, looking at the half empty whisky glass on the side cabinet, next to a completely empty bottle. Jackie was never model beautiful, but she was attractive in a different way. She had good skin and hair, and a warm smile. It made her more stunning than half the fake beauties out there. That's what the women at Temple had told her, as they tried to fix Jackie up with every eligible Jewish bachelor on the scene. And it was what Raj had told her when their paths had crossed.

'You want to join me?' Melody rasped, laughing as she took a swig and then another drag on her cigarette.

'Hardly,' said Jackie. 'I'm here. So, come on, what do you want?'

Melody narrowed her eyes. 'I can see the judgement on your face. Looking down on me. Who the fuck do you think you are?'

Jackie turned to leave, unable to engage with this woman any longer. It wasn't worth it. No, she chided herself, some things were.

'I don't have time to argue. Are you going to help me or not? And if you weren't going to help me, why did you come here? For a free holiday?'

'You owe me, you little cunt. Look at you, living the life I wish I had. Growing up in that Jewboy's mansion, and now some film star's wife.'

'He's a film director, and that Jewish man and his wife gave me a home and a future when our mother chose to abandon us as children. It's not my fault you ended up where you did. I didn't even know about you.'

'You were too young to remember what the bitch did to us. Me? I will never forget. The things I had to see, the men she brought back, screwing them in front of us.'

Jackie tried to picture what Melody was describing, but she couldn't. She had been two when she had been placed in foster care and was adopted a few months later. Melody had been eight, too old to be adopted easily, and yet old enough to remember the years of neglect they had suffered.

'She didn't have a clue who our fathers were, did you know that? I remember she loved putting her cigarettes out on you when you were a baby. Yeah, she loved doing that. To stop you fucking crying.'

Melody laughed, as Jackie fought back the tears, thinking of their younger selves. She had read the report from the private detective she had hired. It wasn't easy, any of it. Melody had been abused by her foster father's best friend, getting pregnant twice in two years. There had been regular beatings, drug abuse. Of the two sisters, Melody didn't have a chance, and it was true, Jackie had gotten the better deal. Melody might have been better off staying with their batshit crazy mother. Things had been easy for Jackie growing up, she knew that. The Newmans had given her stability, a future, a community.

'Anyway, I dealt with the dumb cunt,' Melody said bitterly. 'She's not laughing now, is she?'

Melody had tracked their mother down when she was in her late teens, given her heroin, and then set fire to her trailer.

'You were out of your mind. You'd just lost your second child.'

Melody had given birth to two stillborn babies. Jackie couldn't even imagine how that must have screwed her up.

'I found her though. I found out all about her, and then I watched as she burned alive. You know at the end she was screaming? The fire must have scared the bitch down from her high, and she knew she was gonna burn. Fuck, that made up for everything. Almost. I was lucky my lawyer was good, put it all down to the dead babies. But I knew what I was doing. And given the chance, I would do it all over again.'

There was silence in the room, heavy, sad, painful. A lifetime and a world away from the Mirage and Bollywood. And while she would never feel the pain Melody had, Jackie had her own demons. The emptiness of her marriage clawed at her, which Jackie filled with the worst of things: she called it her *Valley of the Dolls* phase. Her inability to have children hadn't mattered before Raj. Now, she wanted nothing more.

Jackie had never been tempted to find out about her birth family when her mother had first told her about the adoption. It was when she was eighteen and heading to college. Her mother had reluctantly accepted her daughter was an adult now and had a right to know. Jackie had simply turned around and told the Newmans that she knew who her parents were, she didn't need to find the woman that had given her up. She was curious about her sister, and often wondered where she was, but thought it would be a betrayal to go hankering after the past. And what would it do to her life with her parents if she suddenly introduced her sister to the mix? She also had to accept the fact that her sister had never come looking for her.

That all changed one summer when Melody turned up in New Jersey. Jackie was still in college, but home between semesters. The adoption agency had contacted Jackie's parents, saying her sister wanted to make contact. Jackie's parents had left the decision to her, and Jackie had agreed. Melody had turned up a mess – a junkie, looking trashy, and swearing. They'd met at a coffee shop and Jackie was immediately sure she would never see Melody again. Melody had asked Jackie for money, and Jackie had agreed, shutting that part of her life off.

And then, fate had intervened. Jackie had been forced to go back and dig up the past, so she could try to have a future. Using a private detective to trace Melody, she had discovered the past was an absolute nightmare, so much worse than she could even imagine.

'We have an appointment tomorrow morning. I need to be sure you will be there. So tell me, Melody, what do you want from me to make that happen?'

Melody licked her lips, swigging her whisky again. Jackie knew the price would be high, but she was willing to pay it. And in a way, Jackie was trying to make amends. She would pay above and beyond, because Melody had suffered so much more so that Jackie didn't have to. Melody had also gotten a revenge on their mother that Jackie didn't believe in, but somewhere she was glad it had happened.

–

VJ wandered down the Edgware Road away from the flyover. He resented being away from the cast, in their posh hotel, but at least he had made it to London. Stupid cunt Zara didn't bother with the fine print so VJ always managed to add clauses to screw her over.

VJ lit a cigarette, the first drag hitting his lungs hard, the *money shot*, he liked to call it. All this nonsense about not smoking inside in this crazy city, when the pollution was far worse, although nothing compared to Mumbai. The air there was something special, tinged with the bittersweet taste of failure and hope. Zara had been caught in that race, and it was VJ that had made her. She was just another beautiful girl in a country teeming with them; it was VJ that had made sure she took the best route to success.

He spat on the pavement, causing a passer-by to give him an angry look. VJ didn't care. He was beyond caring about very much now.

The internet café was the sort of place he needed, tucked down an alley off the main road, near one of the social housing buildings. They called it 'council flats' here, he had no idea what that meant. The café owner was black and spoke Arabic. He looked bored and didn't clock VJ as he took his cash and gave him a token. The token meant VJ could access any machine for an hour and there would be no central trace on him, and there was no CCTV.

VJ picked the terminal at the furthest end of the café and inserted his token. He had already set up a fake email account and in the drafts folder he had kept the files he needed attached to new messages he had never sent. He checked the file size to make sure it was the correct one and entered the email address he had on his smartphone screen. Once done, he sat back and stared at it for five minutes. Once he hit send, things would never be the same again. Not for him, and especially not for Zara.

VJ scratched himself, stretched his arms and shoulders back, and hit send. It was done. And he was ready for the fallout.

Chapter Eight

Raj had chosen to film the scene at the OXO Tower restaurant, with its panoramic views across London. Zara was seated at a table with Rocky as extras milled around them playing diners and staff. There was always so much time in between shoots, when directors blocked shots and went into discussions with their crew. Imran always huddled with Raj to have those discussions, but Rocky wasn't interested. He had been flirting with Zara throughout the day when the camera wasn't rolling, and carrying it on when it was. She could feel their chemistry, and knew that despite this being his first movie, Rocky would make an impact.

Rocky was definitely hot, with his gym body, broad shoulders, his biceps and pecs clearly discernible under his shirt, a narrow waist, and thick thighs. He had the face of a model, with his Roman nose, olive skin, thick black eyelashes around almond-shaped eyes, and lips that were full and just called to be kissed. His cut-glass English accent was roughened by the slang he peppered his conversation with, but it couldn't hide his posh British schooling.

'It's beautiful, isn't it?' Zara said, looking out into the oil painting sky from the big open windows of the restaurant. The sun was beginning its descent, and the sky was tinged with grapefruit red in places.

'Yeah, it's the pollution,' Rocky told her. 'It's what gives us amazing sunsets and sunrises.'

'Mumbai is the same.'

'I remember, I been Mumbai a few times. Dad has a house in Malabar.'

Zara wasn't surprised, she expected someone like James Kapoor to own a villa in the most expensive part of Mumbai.

'Would you move there, do you think?' she asked. 'If your career takes off?'

She couldn't really see Rocky having a long career. He would work well in the metro-movies, catering for the new middle class, but he didn't have superstar charisma about him. There were thousands of pretty boys and girls with perfect bodies trying to make it, but you needed something else to get to the top.

'Yeah, of course. I really wanna do this. I wanna be a film star. No, more than that, I want to be an actor.'

'I thought this might just be a fantasy for you? Something to tick off, like a sports car?' Zara arched an eyebrow and smiled so her words didn't come over as offensive.

'I'm not going to lie, that was definitely me, not even that long ago. But I just know this is meant to be mine. I felt good when I saw the dailies, and finally I feel like I can do something worthwhile.'

'Why, what have you been doing until now? You're hardly a child.'

'I was a cliché. People see me as this spoilt dick, with no problems. And it's true, I was always party central, with the cash of my billionaire father, and no limits. I attracted the other billionaire sons who were just like me, and together we surfed the world going from one hedonistic orgy to the next.'

Zara thought of her own upbringing, and worse than that, she thought of those early years in Mumbai. Rocky didn't really appreciate the words coming from his mouth; his life was so untouched by problems.

'You know, my mother died when I was a child, I was only nine.' *The same age Dev was when he disappeared*, thought Zara. She knew how trauma at that age could change you for life.

'Dad waited two months after Mum died before he got married again. And to a woman who was his mistress while Mum was still alive. And then he wonders why I went off the rails.'

'And did you? Let me guess, she was an evil stepmother?' It seemed Rocky was really bothered about her opinion, he was trying to justify himself to her.

'No, she was just indifferent. She had her own kids, my half-sisters, but I got cared for by the same nannies they did. Until I was old enough for Eton. Dad just picked up my bills until one night when I totalled his Maserati in Leicester Square.' Zara saw Rocky's face darken. 'I injured three people. Luckily it wasn't serious, but it really got to me. It's all fun and games until you hurt other people.'

Zara looked away. She thought about her own car exploding, about the children left destitute because she had led to their mother being hurt. She really needed to do more for them. Housing and schooling was fine, but she needed to give them a proper future. Yes there were millions of children like them in the world, but the universe had sent that family into her life.

'What happened?' Zara asked.

'Dad fixed it, obviously. Thing is, even in London, if you have money the law can be manipulated. I didn't face any charges, and he paid out compensation to stop the people I injured from going to the press. He was proper mad, and said I'd better sort myself out, stand on my own two feet, all the usual bullshit. When he asked what I wanted to do, I said acting. So he got me lessons.'

'And then he got you a movie. Way to go standing on your own two feet.'

'Brutal,' he said. 'Dad didn't force Raj to take me. I had to screen-test like everyone else.'

Zara smiled at him, taken by his naivety. *Daddy bought you this role, but how many films will he bankroll if they keep failing at the box office?* she thought. And Rocky would never know what screen-testing meant for some people, especially girls like her.

He was typical of a certain type of entitled rich brat, thinking he could be a star on-screen because money had made him a star by birth on the social scene. He would come to Mumbai, drink and fuck his way through some minor movies for a few years, and then end his career washed up, living off his father's handouts for years.

'You definitely have presence,' she said seriously. After all, you didn't piss off a billionaire's son, not even when you were Zara Das. 'I think you're going to be a huge star. I bet Imran is having nightmares already.' She laughed.

'Please, the guy has no sense of style and hams it up in his movies. I don't get why he's so popular.'

Zara didn't reply, she didn't want to irritate Rocky or risk him dropping something salacious to the reigning actor in Bollywood. She felt like putting Rocky in his place, though. Imran had worked his way up the hard way, just like her, and he was dynamite on-screen. It was why audiences and the box office loved him.

'Well when you have to act opposite him, you can try to work out just what it is that makes him so popular.'

'I'm gonna act him off the screen, just you watch.'

–

Dan checked Zara's rooms before allowing her to enter. After the bloody rose incident, he now refused to let her in until he'd thoroughly examined the rooms, no matter how much she complained. He still didn't understand how anyone could have gotten into her suite, and was working with the hotel security, and had his own team investigating. They were now carrying out stealth missions, in plain clothes, hanging around the lobby to collect soft intelligence. There hadn't been any more messages sent to Zara, and there hadn't been any other incidents. His contact in MI6 was still working on testing the make-up, and Dan had sent over the remnants of the bloodied gift that had been left in Zara's room as well.

Zara walked into the suite once he had given her the ok and collapsed on her sofa. She looked at him, her eyes apprehensive, as though she wasn't allowed to be so raw anywhere else. He had watched her all day with Rocky, and seen her with the cast on other filming days, and saw how unaffected she seemed with them. Except for moments when he saw a frightened young woman, lost and crying out.

'You're handling it very well,' he said to her. 'I can't imagine what's going on inside your head, but you are holding yourself together out there.'

'I don't have a choice,' she said softly. 'I'm here to do a job. If I break down now, it will be over. Raj can easily replace me, that's the truth. I'm sure Minnie would love to step into my role – she's probably waiting for someone to kill me just so she can. I need this movie though. Back home I'm untouchable, and not in a good way. Raj is the only filmmaker who was willing to risk working with me after the car bomb. If I mess this up, nobody else will.'

'I understand,' Dan said. He really did. 'Still, is it worth risking your life over?'

'Yes,' she said. 'I have nothing else.'

'That's a bit extreme.'

'You know, Dan, to the world I am the dream. I made it, I am on top. The reality? There is no one in my life. I have no friends, my family have disowned me and everyone that is nice to me is either on my payroll or someone else's payroll.'

'I genuinely am concerned, I'm not asking you because James Kapoor is paying me.'

'I didn't mean you,' she said quickly. 'I mean everyone around me.'

Dan saw a bottle of her signature drink in the centre of the coffee table.

'Shall I pour you some? You look like you might need something hard to take your mind off things.'

Zara looked at him carefully, and then at the silver bottle. It was a sleek design, with Zara D in elaborate letters on it. She nodded, and he opened the drink, pouring some of it into a glass for her.

'It's the new packaging. A drinks company want to launch it in Europe and America. I don't know why, I don't like the taste particularly. Collette sent me this as a sampler.'

Dan handed her the glass, and she sipped it slowly. He refused her invitation to have one himself.

'Always on duty.'

'I have to be. I still don't understand how someone got into your room and into your vanity van to tamper with your make-up. It's impossible.'

'Yet somebody did,' she said, putting her glass down.

'Aren't you afraid?' he asked her. 'You seem so calm all the time.'

'Honestly? There are moments when I'm so scared I can't breathe. I look around me, and I see so many faces and I think, any one of them could hurt me. Then in those moments I can't breathe.'

Dan took a seat opposite her. She was still wearing her clothes from the shoot; a stylish jacket with a feathery collar and a tight skirt that fell above her knees, exposing her toned legs in boots. He kept his eyes away from them, but her face was even more distracting. She had the most amazing green eyes, and they glowed like fire against her skin and hair. He had watched videos of her movies as research, and he could say she was just as beautiful off screen as she was on. More so in some ways, as on-screen she was never as exposed as she was now. Zara picked up her drink and sipped at it again, the alcohol giving her confidence in him.

'The thing is, you get used to it. The first time is the worst. The first messages I got, the death threats, the burning effigies… I was terrified. I thought at any moment it was over, that someone would find me and butcher me to death. Then, when they didn't, the hatred just became words, pictures, videos. Yes I panicked, but I also became immune to it. And then one day, they hit you so hard it takes it to the next level, and someone is dead because of you. What did my driver ever do to them? Why was she the one to pay the ultimate price? And then, even that becomes the norm. Someone died. What else is there? Am I making sense?'

Dan nodded. She was making more sense than she even knew. Dan had seen the same. When he had first joined MI6, his own missions had been terrifying, thrilling, and life-threatening. Dan still remembered the first time he had killed a man. He had felt the guilt, despite knowing he had just saved hundreds of lives. Still, it was horrendous.

'When I was in the military, the first time one of my comrades fell... I can't tell you...' It was always the cover he gave. He was in the army. In truth, Sabrina was his colleague from MI6. She was an accountant who had done a secondment into a field role because she wanted to experience first-hand the sort of adventures she only ever got to pay the invoices for. Only her first experience was deadly. Dan had been the one to rescue her from an ISIS stronghold in Raqah, but he had been too late. 'Her body... the state it was in. I will never forget that. I still have nightmares. But after that, nothing was quite as bad. Everything else was difficult yes, but I also became immune to it. It's a shit way to be, and I wish I could go back and undo it, not be so scarred.'

'You can't though, that's the thing. Once it's happened, it's there forever. So you live every day, and you find a purpose for living, and you ignore it all.'

Zara came close to him and squeezed his hand.

'I'm sorry about your colleague, I really am. I know what it's like.'

'And what's your purpose?' he asked, staring into her eyes which were softened now with emotion.

'To be Zara Das. When I was going through this, I realised that there wasn't a single person who could help me, or that I could turn to. So I decided I needed to be as tough as I could, to inhabit the woman I've created, so that I wouldn't need anybody else.' She looked away from him as she said it, embarrassed by her candidness. 'What about you?'

Dan knew what his purpose was, but he didn't want to share that with anyone. He was tempted to tell her just then, but stayed silent.

'I don't know about before, but I'm here now. Anytime you need someone to be there for you.'

'You forgive me for what I did to that woman in Tristan's then?'

'No, but nobody's perfect,' he said, seriously.

'I won't do it again. I can promise you that. I mean I will still act like a fucking diva, because that's who Zara Das is. But I won't do that again.'

Dan left the room as Kasim came in to bring Zara a light meal and some hot chocolate, but his head was full of Zara as he did. He had seen the real her, the person she kept hidden under layers of make-up and designer clothes. Underneath it all, Zara was just a scared lonely young woman, and he wanted to protect her, to be there for her when she needed a break from fighting the world.

–

Zara lay naked under her sheets, unable to settle. Dan's words had affected her deeply, seeing his vulnerability had endeared him to her. There had been genuine concern in his eyes when he promised to be there for her. Maybe it was all words, empty and repeated, but she wanted so badly to believe them. For the first time in a long time, she wanted to believe in someone. She wanted to believe in Dan Rourke more than anything in the world.

–

With Dev's disappearance, Pari's life was thrown so far away from normal she didn't think it would ever centre again. Her parents were broken, as each day turned into weeks and months, with no sign or news of him. They couldn't mourn their son, but they knew that there were fates far worse than death that could have happened to their boy. Her father would go to Delhi nearly every weekend, searching the streets, desperately trying to get information from strangers and authorities, a picture of Dev in his hands, while her mother would spend her days silently weeping. They kept Dev's room as a shrine to him, and Pari was all but forgotten. They forgot that she had lost her twin, that she was halved in an instant. She wished she could feel him, have some premonition of where he was, or if he was ok. There was nothing, though. Just her emptiness and her loneliness.

There was no one there for her to watch movies with, no one to offer her salve for her pain. Just Pari, alone, with her broken parents. As she grew older, the accusations then began. Somehow it was her fault, for surviving, for still being there. Every time she made a mistake, no matter how small, her father would curse her and ask why she hadn't been the one to have gotten lost. Dev had been their future, and instead they had been left with Pari. And she was their nothing. Her parents at least had each other, but Pari had nobody. They couldn't see that the person who had lost the most was her. She, more than anyone, wanted Dev home again.

Only he never came back.

As time passed, Pari withdrew into such a dark place she thought she would go crazy, that she would forget how to exist. The world had pushed her into a corner to forget about her. And then, one day when she was out shopping in a mall with her mother, a talent scout had spotted her. He said she had 'something'. Could she act or dance? No? No problem. She could stand in front of a camera, right?

The man was VJ. He had charmed her, filling her head with dreams of Mumbai. Of fame, wealth, happiness. Her parents had threatened him to stay away, but it was too late; Pari had the bug. For the first time someone had said she was worth something, that she was not nothing, that she didn't have to stay in that corner.

VJ gave her enough money for a bus ticket to Mumbai, and there he arranged for her to stay at a women's hostel. It was run by a Mrs Fernandez, a Goan Christian widow. She was strict but had a soft heart, treating her guests like wayward daughters rather than tenants. It was where she had first met Shanti, too. She had escaped a violent, abusive marriage. Born mute, she had put up with her treatment for years, not feeling like she had any other way to survive. But one day it got too much for her, and she had walked out. Learning sign language through the help of an NGO in Mumbai, she had managed to get work as a cleaner and maid, and finally through the movements of her hands she had shared her painful story. Pari had read it one day when Shanti had written her a letter explaining her past, and she had decided then that Shanti was the first person she would help if she ever made it.

VJ was an almost daily visitor to the hostel, paying for her to attend acting and dance classes, and even paying for a gym membership for her. He didn't want anything in return, but made her sign a contract saying he would be entitled to twenty percent of future earnings. After a few weeks, VJ set her up with a number of client meetings, for modelling shoots, ads and even TV serials. It was all bullshit though. VJ would make deals with the men she was meeting. They were expecting favours in return before signing her. When she complained to VJ, he had simply told her to get with the programme, this was the only way she would make it. If she didn't do what they wanted, then she could rot at the bottom of the pole and he wasn't to blame.

She had confided in Mrs Fernandez, who told her to go home. She said it wasn't worth it, the little fame she would get wasn't worth the price she would pay. She also banned VJ from coming to the hostel any more.

Pari though had already come too far. She knew her family wouldn't let her just walk back into their lives; she had shamed them by running away. And what would be waiting for her? She also wanted this, she felt she was born to do it. She was afflicted by the same lunacy she knew millions suffered from, most of them never getting even a glance of success let alone attaining it. She had no money and felt she had no option. So she went along with what VJ wanted.

The sleazy sexually charged sessions for a few pictures in a glossy magazine, or a few minutes screen time advertising tampons, toothpaste, and even haemorrhoid cream. The disgusting men she had to accommodate so they would give her a break. Sitting stupefied and helpless as they touched her in places she washed afterwards with bleach and Dettol, making her do things to them she didn't even like to remember any more. Always she would say no, hope that the man would come to his senses, but they all expected it.

It seemed so easy for other actresses. They would win Miss India competitions or be spotted by top modelling touts and then land up in starring roles in TV and film. VJ told her that was only a few, and that unless you had star parents, you had to do this.

Each new opportunity brought with it another man wanting to use her. VJ was pimping her out, and she wasn't the only one. What she hadn't known at the time was that he was also taking pictures and secretly filming some of these sessions. Later he used their existence to threaten her, telling her they would ruin her if they were seen. As far as the press and the rest of the world knew, she had simply gone from modelling to ads to film. No one except VJ and the sleazebags that had used her knew about her real struggle to the top.

For her break into films, she ended up having to do the one thing she had sworn never to do but her head was so fogged, she had passed out, waking up in the morning sore and bloody, knowing what the bastard producer had taken from her. Pari had broken down, her first time not some fantasy experience with a man she loved and had married, but forced from her by a man who wanted to use her in return for a role in his movie. She wanted to kill him and kill herself, but VJ told her she had just made the most powerful man in Bollywood very happy; that it was worth it. She hated VJ then, what did he understand about the price she had been paying since she was a child? All the years of being hated and used, when would it all end? And she knew the producer would be back for more.

Luckily for her, the movie had been a huge success, and the press lauded how overnight a star was born. She had been renamed Zara Das for the films, and just like that her past had been written away. But *none of them could erase it. And now she was about to lose everything she had achieved.*

Chapter Nine

James Kapoor's wife, Penny – real name Pramila – had missed the soirée in his suites at the Mirage, so had instead organised a lunch at their St John's Wood mansion. The Bollywood Wives, Sasha, Rani, and Jackie were all in attendance, along with what looked like Penny's friends from her committees, charities, and social contacts. There were fifteen women seated in her tastefully decorated sunroom, which looked out over the expansive swimming pool and manicured gardens, all with drinks and plates of Indian appetisers in their hands. The air was thick with the smell of hot samosas, pakoras, bhajia, chaat, and gossip.

'I thought I would make you ladies feel at home. Usually I only serve the best hors d'oeuvres, caviar, and champagne. But today I thought we would go Indian.'

Cue false tinkling laugh as though she had somehow cheapened herself by doing just that. Jackie couldn't stand her. She spotted Sheikh Walid's formidable daughter, Emel, having a whispered conversation with one of the other guests as Penny Kapoor held everyone hostage. Penny was in her late thirties, with long black hair falling over her shoulders. She had chosen to wear a white sleeveless dress, showing off her ex-model figure to its full extent, and had the air of a woman who had just spent hours at a salon, but acted as though she had rolled out of bed and looked that fabulous.

'Such an honour you are all here. I personally don't really watch Bollywood movies, aren't they ridiculous, Kam?'

She turned to a woman to her right, her bestie no doubt, who seemed to have had as much if not more filler and Botox as Penny. The room was full of bad facelifts and Jackie realised the only real breasts in the room were probably the meat in the chicken pakoras.

'Yes, darling, I mean no offence, ladies, but really, some of the storylines! All those lost twins reuniting, all the forbidden love stories and the copious amount of action. I mean really, they give me such a headache. Not to mention the gawdy outfits and songs. My MIL, *the bitch* as we know her, loves them, of course.'

'She would, Kam. No offence is meant to you ladies, of course.'

Jackie looked at Penny, trying not to throw her second-rate champagne into her fake tits. Drenching that Versace dress would be fun just to see her reaction.

'They give such a bad reputation to our people, we are held back by the clichés of Bollywood. Where is the sophistication, the modernity?' Penny continued.

Jackie looked over at Sasha, muted into silence by the onslaught, looking uncomfortable. Jackie didn't know if she had the energy to deal with Penny, who looked more like a candidate for the *Real Housewives of Mumbai* than the wife of a billionaire tycoon.

She had had a few tough days, dealing with Melody and the tests they had to carry out. Luckily Melody's grubbiness was predictable, so Jackie had paid her off easily. She was now on a plane back to America, ready to spend the money she had been given. Jackie hoped she drank herself to death on cheap alcohol. Then felt cruel for wishing that. She would do something for her. They were half-sisters after all.

Now the wait had begun. Jackie was anxious about what the tests would reveal, and what she would say to Raj. He didn't have a clue what she was doing or about her past. Jackie scanned the room, nodding at Emel, and then her breath caught as her eyes focused on the woman she was whispering to. She hadn't recognised her at first without her white coat and glasses, but it was definitely Dr Madhu from the clinic. The doctor didn't acknowledge Jackie in any way, but carried on talking to Emel. Both ladies were turning their eyes in her direction. No, Jackie thought, it's just paranoia, she can't possibly be breaking the Hippocratic oath. Still her throat went dry.

'And some of the actresses these days, what do they look like? Porn stars, that's what,' said another woman. 'You were so classy in your day, Rani,' she added.

Rani Kumar nodded her head to accept the compliment, but didn't engage. Sasha noticed Jackie had gone suddenly quiet and was casting glances her way. Not that she had been saying much anyway, but Jackie had an effervescence about her, and when her mood changed the energy around her seemed to.

'Even in your day though, remember Laila?' The same woman who had called her classy was directing her comments to Rani again. Sasha had met Rani a number of times in Mumbai, but they weren't friends, particularly. She was a legend, and it was difficult to hold conversations with legends. Sasha didn't know what was appropriate to say when you seemed to know everything about someone from their press cuttings.

Rani's thoughts were obviously elsewhere and the name of her husband's first wife and supposed great love rival caught her off-guard. There was a gentle hush in the room, just for a couple of seconds. For a room of ladies that didn't indulge in Bollywood movies, they seemed to all know Laila would be an uncomfortable topic for her, Sasha thought.

'Laila was such a tramp,' said Kam. 'And I hear her daughter is in this one? She's just as cheap.'

Rani didn't comment, but looked embarrassed by the conversation. Sasha had met Minnie a few times on the social scene, and the young girl was sweet enough, although she seemed to be having an identity crisis. She always looked the part, but her bratty behaviour, quick drinking and loose morals, all were a clichéd cry for help, as far as Sasha was concerned.

'I thought you didn't watch Bollywood movies?' said Sasha, trying to take attention away from Rani.

Kam was flustered and looked embarrassed. 'I told you, *the bitch* does, I catch glimpses now and then.'

'So what movies do you watch?' Sasha went on.

'Oh you know, French ones, so artistic, and some Italian and Spanish ones.'

'She wasn't asking about the nationality of your lovers, darling,' Jackie said, laughing into an empty and shocked room. Sasha gave her a grateful smile for coming to her aid in protecting Rani. 'Do you speak French? Or Italian?'

'Well not exactly,' said Kam, who was now as red as the polish on her nails. Penny edged away slightly from her friend as though she had started to go off. 'I read the subtitles,' mumbled Kam, as she guzzled her champagne for courage.

'Well I happen to love Bollywood movies,' Jackie went on. 'Not just because my husband makes them. Actually, all our husbands make them. And now, so does yours, Penny.'

'Oh that's just a hobby thing for his son Rocky, you understand how we parents are; we will do anything for our children.'

Jackie felt the sucker punch hit her hard. She caught Dr Madhu's eye and saw a reaction at last. It was concern more than anything.

'Really, this food is so greasy, there's a reason I don't eat Indian.' Penny pressed a button on her phone and a young white woman in a maid's outfit appeared. 'Kristina, get me some caviar please. In fact caviar for everyone. And more champagne. I'm sure you ladies haven't had the best caviar that I'll be serving.'

'Actually, Rani is the face of caviar in India. She gets a lifetime supply of Beluga,' said Jackie. Penny's mouth opened involuntarily, and Kristina smirked at Jackie as she curtsied and wandered off.

'Such good workers these Eastern Europeans, better than my Filipino ones,' whispered Penny so loudly the whole room could hear. 'Don't know what I'll do after Brexit.'

'I know, it's so difficult to get help now, dear, they have visa restrictions for everyone that's cheap,' said another woman sadly.

'Can you point me to the nearest bathroom please?' Jackie said, and then looking pointedly at Penny added, 'I think I'm going to throw up. Must be all the cheap greasy Indian food.'

—

Jackie splashed water on her face, staring at her reflection in the mirror. The stress was showing, she knew, and the real terror was inside. As everyone guzzled champagne around her, she had asked for water. She knew one sip was always too much, and she needed to be sober to make this happen.

Exiting the bathroom, Dr Madhu was waiting for her.

'Are you all right? These things can get so tedious,' she said.

'I'm surprised to see you here, doc,' said Jackie.

'I saw on your face. Don't worry, I am a professional, what happens at the clinic is not for discussion when I leave the premises.'

'Thank you, I don't think I could cope if word got out.'

Dr Madhu squeezed her arm. 'It won't, not from our side.'

'Why are you here, anyway? I didn't think these moneyed airheads would be your type?'

'They're not. But they have clout. Penny Kapoor helps my business through her contacts. This is me guzzling free champagne from the hand that feeds me too.'

Jackie laughed. Then felt her stomach tighten as she asked what she really wanted to know.

'Any idea about my results yet?'

Dr Madhu softened the look on her face. She had probably been through this dozens of times with different women over the years.

'It's all looking promising. We need your husband though. Have you spoken to him about it yet?'

Jackie's silence was enough for the doctor.

'Jackie, unless he's involved, we can't progress this. You need to tell your husband as quickly as possible.'

If only it was that easy, Jackie thought.

—

'It's a very expensive hobby,' Sasha said gently. 'Mounting the most expensive production outside of India.' She was normally so placid, but Penny was everything she hated in people. Narcissistic and entitled.

'Well money is nothing to him, and it is his only son,' Penny said bitterly. 'I gave him two daughters, and he dotes on them, but Rocky is his first born, so he feels differently about him. You know how our men are. It must be difficult being the wives of such famous husbands,' Penny carried on. 'I know, of course, James is such a celebrity now, thanks to the *Sunday Times* Rich List. It's such a burden and such a danger, having everyone know you are worth ten billion.'

'I know, and you had to call and correct them, didn't you, when they got his net worth wrong?' Kam said, as though it had been such an inconvenience.

'Yes, journalists, such a pain. Always wanting to interview me, take pictures of my home, talk about my style. I'm sure you ladies are the same. So tiresome.'

Sasha kept quiet as the room looked over for confirmation or denial.

'What do you do with all your spare time?' Penny asked, while doling caviar into her mouth, so her smile became all black teeth. 'I mean, while your husbands are working.'

'You make it sound as though we sit around idle,' said Rani jovially.

'What else is there to do? You must have servants galore to do all the housework and chores. I mean, I do and I live in London most of the time. My homes in Delhi and Mumbai are crawling with them, they are so cheap to hire.'

'I stare at the TV mostly, waiting for Raj to come home,' Jackie said, sarcasm dripping from her every word as she came back into the room. 'Don't you two?' Rani and Sasha could barely suppress their giggles.

'We fill the time,' Rani said diplomatically. 'I have my charities, Jackie makes documentaries, and Sasha...' She stopped suddenly. Sasha held her breath. There it was: in the realm of Bollywood, she had no purpose. Rani couldn't come up with anything.

'Sasha has young children, and unlike a lot of people she doesn't leave it to the nanny to raise them,' Jackie intervened.

'Yes, they can be so demanding, I had to hire help just to cope,' said Penny. 'Are they back at the hotel?' She addressed this to Sasha who was turning crimson with the focus.

'No,' she said croakily, 'I left them in Mumbai with their grandmother.'

There was a hush across the room.

'Quite,' said Penny.

'Sasha's a screenwriter, and a bloody amazing one,' Jackie said suddenly. 'And she's going to produce her script. Watch this space, ladies, but please don't put that on your Insta accounts, it's not public knowledge.'

Sasha felt gratitude for the support, mixed with embarrassment and irritation because it wasn't true, not really. If she wasn't looking after her children, what was she doing, really? And she did have nannies, two of them. What was she? Imran Khan's wife, the woman he had sex with, his companion on his foreign shoots, the woman that accompanied him to premieres and parties. And without him? What if he left her, or God forbid, he died? Sasha felt her breath catch in her chest, the room close around her.

'I need some air,' she said rushing from the room.

–

Jackie found her a few minutes later in the downstairs cloakroom, staring at herself in the mirror.

'This is surreal, they have a dressing room for guests. I'm sorry, Sasha, but she was being such a bitch. Saying you're nothing.'

'She didn't say I was.'

'She was implying you didn't do anything, though.'

'She's right, Jackie. What do I do with my life? I'm a spoilt housewife, whose only job is to shop and look pretty for my husband. And I can't even get that second bit right. Look at me, I still haven't shifted all this baby fat.'

'Oh, come on, you have less fat on you than one of my thighs. Stop this. You're gorgeous, more than most of the Bollywood tarts and definitely more than the Botox brigade in there.'

'What am I though, Jackie? Rani is an actress, a former superstar, and a philanthropist. You are an award-winning documentary maker. What about me? I'm a footnote in Imran Khan's life. That's it.'

Jackie rubbed her back, her eyes locked on Sasha's face in the mirror.

'You are a film maker in waiting. And I swear to you on Penny's fake boobs, one day Imran Khan will beg you to cast him in your movie. And then, darling, if you don't tell him to go do one, I will slap you in the face with those very same silicon breasts. You hear me?'

Sasha nodded, knowing it meant nothing. Her movie was not going to happen, and as the months and years passed, she would lose every sense of herself. It happened to millions of women around the world all the time, why would she be any different? The thought terrified her.

–

As they were leaving, Penny asked for a picture to be taken.

'I have no interest, but James has that seven-star iceberg to advertise, and every little helps,' she added, while standing with her arms locked around Sasha and Rani, as though she was with her best friends.

'Be careful there, you wouldn't want to attract the wrong sort of clientele, you know, the type that watch those rubbish Bollywood movies,' said Jackie.

'It's fine, darling. People with more money than taste are welcome to stay if it keeps that place afloat,' said Penny icily.

Penny's friends took their cue from her and started to take selfies, a couple even asked for autographs, making sure they couldn't be seen. One woman came up to Rani afterwards, gushing about how big a fan she was.

'I watched all your movies, Rani*ji*, you were the best. I was so excited to meet you today, but this is how it is. You come to Penny's and it's her court.'

'Thank you,' Rani said graciously.

'I must say, it's very brave of you to let your husband act opposite Laila again. They were quite the item back then.'

'I think a thirty-year marriage is worth more than a brief mistake, don't you?' she said politely. The woman laughed, embarrassed at least. Rani said she was going to visit the bathroom.

–

Sasha knocked on the door, but there was no answer. She knocked again, and the door opened slightly.

'Rani*ji*, please let me come in.'

Rani opened the door, and Sasha found her dabbing her face with toilet roll, to mop up the tears. She had seen the look of despair on Rani's face as she had rushed to the bathroom, and while she was still acutely aware of the difference in their status, she knew a woman in crisis when she saw one. Having seen one in the mirror on a daily basis of late.

Sasha took some better quality Kleenex from her purse, and gave them to Rani to use.

'Ignore those women, Rani*ji*, you must come across them all the time.'

'It's not about that my dear. I just…'

'I'm guessing it's the situation with Ajay*ji*?' Sasha was hesitant as she spoke. Was it her place to ask such a thing? Still it was done now. She felt sick waiting for Rani's backlash.

'Thirty years, Sasha. Thirty years I made that man the centre of my universe, gave him four children, eight grandchildren, nurtured his superstar status, and gave up my own career. And for what? So that after thirty years he could do this to me?'

Sasha stayed silent, unsure of what she could say. She hadn't exchanged more than a hello with Rani before, and now this woman was about to reveal her innermost turmoil to her? Turmoil related to the legendary Ajay.

'When I saw them at the soirée, together, I didn't know what to do. So I pretended everything was ok, and we were all getting on fine. Everyone was watching, what else could I do? Still, it cuts me up inside, really deeply. Today look at them, on-screen again, as if their marriage break-up never happened. He was an absolute mess because of the way she treated him, and I was there when she took that country bumpkin for a ride.'

Sasha had heard the story of course, like most Indians who watched movies. The great Ajay-Rani-Laila love triangle was legendary. Ajay had made a splash at the box office and married the siren Laila, who was ruling Bollywood in the late seventies and early eighties. Only she had been a nightmare, and he had left her six months later, when Rani had finally gotten the man she had been in love with years. What the reality was nobody knew, but from the outside it seemed as though Ajay had been in lust with Laila, but found true love with Rani. That was the Bollywood fairy tale, anyway.

'I picked up the pieces, and I spent my life with him,' Rani was saying. 'Knowing he would never love me with the same intensity that he loved her. She was the woman he had grown up fantasising about, and then there she was. Fate had happened, and he became a star and she was in his arms. Laila knew what she was doing, manipulating him like a lap dog. And when she threw him away, I didn't care. Because I could see the decent man he was and always had been, and besides, I was getting the marriage, the kids, and the life. And then, he agrees to do this movie with her. Does he not understand how that would have impacted on me? It feels like he's gone back to her. How can I compare to her?'

'Raniji, please, don't do this to yourself. You are still the most beautiful woman in any room you walk into, you still have legions of fans. You and Ajayji are one of the couples that Bollywood holds up as being an example of true love. Hema Malini and Dharmendra; Dilip Kumar and Saira Banu; Amitabh and Jaya Bachchan; and yourself and Ajayji. You made it work.'

Rani wiped her face, bits of tissue stuck to it. She caught sight of how she looked at the same time as Sasha did, and they both laughed at the ludicrous nature of what they were doing.

'I'm sorry for breaking down on you, dear. I just... it was suffocating me. I'm sure you understand what it's like, being a superstar's wife. It's so lonely, and there doesn't seem anyone you can turn to.'

'Imran is hardly in Ajayji's league. But yes, I do understand. I felt as though I didn't have anyone for years. Thank God for Jackie, she's been a life saver. She came with no notions of who she should and shouldn't be friends with. I find people still look down on us a bit.'

'Yes, that whole *Slumdog Superstar* nonsense. It's pure envy, you do know that, don't you? Back in my day it was so much easier to be given a chance. Now it seems to be about who you know, or for women, which beauty contests they won. I came from a theatrical background. That would be unheard of now. Sorry, I must be boring you with my "things used to be so much better" speech. They weren't. Not in everything.'

Sasha helped Rani touch up her make-up, and then invited her to lunch with Jackie.

'You'll like her. Now, let's go back out there, and show them what Bollywood Wives are made of.'

Chapter Ten

Raj had decided to turn the opening Netherfield Ball of the novel into a typical Bollywood extravaganza. The scene where his lead actors met for the first time was being turned into an exclusive party set against music, and would include the entire cast. Zara was slightly nervous that she wouldn't be dancing, but instead it would be Minnie's set piece.

'You'll be in the song, and don't worry, I'll make sure there are lots of close-ups of you looking stunning,' Raj had assured her.

'Minnie will get all the YouTube views, though. These things matter nowadays.'

'What really matters is that the film is a success and you're the lead heroine.'

The choreographer Raj wanted and Zara's favourite, the renowned Chandni, had sent him the steps via video the night before. She was meant to be onset in London but had feigned an illness that meant she couldn't travel.

'I heard she's being paid a fortune to choreograph someone else's movie,' Raj fumed to Zara.

'That's how Bollywood works, Raj, it's fine.'

'I'm going to send her a memo to be here for the other songs.'

'You don't need her for the other songs, they're all pretty romantic. Maybe throw in another song at the end? A club-based number over the credits featuring me and Imran?'

'I might just do that and hire Chandni's biggest rival.'

Zara secretly was glad Chandni wasn't there. If Minnie was going to get all the dance moves, no way should they be done by her go-to dance genius.

'So who have we got?' Zara asked.

'Right on fucking time,' Raj said as a young man in skinny jeans came their way. He looked emaciated, and Raj looked put out. 'EZ, this is Zara.'

EZ had never done an actual Bollywood movie but had put together a few live events with Bollywood stars, apparently.

'I also do, like, weddings and clubs, innit,' he told them both, an unlit cigarette hanging out of his mouth which Zara was convinced was covered in lipstick. He was wearing a clinging T-shirt with his jeans, showing off his boyish frame. He was fair with dark hair and stubble.

'This is a different thing,' Raj said, his voice clipped. 'This movie isn't a wedding or a nightclub.'

'Have you seen weddings these days? Check out YouTube and all the wedding dances up there. They are slick, proper professional set pieces.'

'Still hardly cinema level,' said Raj.

'Relax, boss, I can handle this. I did a couple of Hollywood movies and a British Asian flick too. Chill.'

'Yes because Hollywood is renowned for its big budget dance extravaganzas isn't it?'

They were standing in the hotel lobby. The crew had already departed to the location of the shoot, a mansion in Regent's Park that was being loaned by the production unit.

'Everyone needs to start somewhere. Here, check this out, boss.'

EZ showed Raj and Zara a video on his phone of a girl in a *ghagra choli* dancing with a man in jeans and T-shirt to a song from one of Raj's earlier movies.

'What's that?'

'It was opening night for London's hottest Gaysian club, innit? I did that. That girl's a dude, a drag queen, she's good though, eh?'

Raj watched the drag queen dancing to his song, and Zara had to admit she had some grace, but there was a heaviness to her steps which gave her away.

'Listen, today I'm desperate,' Raj said, as he watched EZ stroke his flat stomach, and pull on his jeans, which must have had a twenty-eight inch waist. 'Chandni has stitched me up, so you will do.'

Zara couldn't hide her smile as she thought how laid-back EZ seemed, and what a shock he would have when he had to work with the nightmare that was Minnie.

'Don't worry, Raj, just let it be,' she said, seeing the look of frustration and despair on the director's face.

-

Raj was busy blocking the scene they were going to shoot, with both Imran and Ajay 'helping' him. How he would cope with both these perfectionists/control freaks through the movie was anyone's guess. It was only the end of the first week of filming and they were already trying his patience. They had been busy all morning, and into the afternoon, leaving the rest of the cast to their own devices. The stars had been given rooms in the house to double as their dressing rooms while others were being used for sets. The mansion block in Regent's Park belonged to a friend of James Kapoor, who had leased the house to him for the duration of the film's shooting. Raj wasn't paying a penny for it. It was just another perk that was paying for Rocky Kapoor's big launch.

Zara was busy doing her hair and make-up, her hands already painted with elaborate fake henna patterns. It was a sequence that would allow her to show off her curves in a traditional *ghagra choli* outfit, so she had gone for a lemon yellow Manish Malhotra ensemble, with lots of gold brocade on the blouse and skirt, set off with ornate traditional gold jewellery encrusted with semi-precious stones around her neck, ears, and a *tikah* on her forehead. Zara was at the top, and it was her star power that attracted the best designers to make her outfits, and gave her the power to choose her own looks rather than leave it to wardrobe. It was heavy to wear, would be even heavier to move in. Luckily she wasn't expected to do any dance moves in it. In fact, she wasn't doing any dance moves in the entire movie, which was a first for her. She had protested when Raj had first told her, but he had convinced her, reminding her it was her dance moves that had caused the Jhansi controversy. She would be the acting powerhouse in *Kismet India*, and nothing was going to distract from her performance. Zara had bitten down her panic, trusting him to do the right thing.

'You look gorgeous. Very traditional. Some would say old-fashioned, even. Not me though.'

Zara looked up in the mirror she was sitting in front of to see Minnie. The girl was already dressed and ready, wearing a figure-hugging shimmering gold dress. Zara recognised it as Elie Saab.

'Thank you, Minnie. And when are you planning on getting ready?'

Minnie smirked at her, rather than being offended by the barb.

'They wanted me to look my age for this movie, so I'm dressed the way a twenty-three-year-old should be. It's odd we are only a couple of years apart in the movie.'

'Odd why?'

'Just strange. Although I suppose it's easy for them to make me look older than make someone look younger, I guess.'

Zara stared at Minnie in the mirror, unflinching.

'Did they tell you to look cheap as well as young, my dear?'

'It's designer, darling, but I suppose you can be forgiven for not knowing that. You probably grew up wearing made by mum or hand me down from sister rather than Chanel or Prada.'

Zara narrowed her eyes at Minnie. She remembered how when she had first got to Mumbai back in the day, Zara had followed Minnie and a host of other Bollywood personalities on social media. Minnie had always flaunted her wealth and her fashion accessories; her latest designer handbag, being first in Mumbai usually to get the latest iPhone. Minnie and her group were always jetting off around the world for each other's birthdays or for shopping sprees. She remembered a particularly difficult post showing Minnie saying she craved macaroons, so she had swanned off to Paris to get them. Did they not have any sense? Despite their wealth, India still had millions of people with literally nothing. Zara had promised herself that if she ever made it, she would not be so oblivious. She couldn't be, she knew.

'You know, Minnie, your arrogance would look so much better if you had earned it. Just like your dress, everything you are is because of your mother. If you walked in off the street, you wouldn't even be hired as an extra. And trust me, darling, a Chanel handbag can't buy you a brain. Or class.'

'At least my mother paid for my Gucci without needing some sugar daddy to stick his cock in her mouth in return.'

Zara felt the anger deep inside her as Minnie repeated back the rumours that plagued her. There was no way someone like Zara could get to the top without sleeping her way up; that was what they all thought. They made it sound like she had had a choice, that she was in control. None of them would ever know the desperation that had clouded her mind, or the decisions that were taken for her.

And yet promiscuous women like Minnie and her crowd acted without impunity, screwing their way through life by choice and with nothing to gain.

'Well at least I don't do it for free,' Zara said coolly, hiding her turmoil.

Minnie gave her the finger and walked off.

Zara bristled, again thinking how unfair life could be. While stuck-up arrogant bitches like Minnie could get the world without paying a price, the universe had extracted everything from Zara. As she looked at herself in the mirror, she saw nothing, except images of her past.

—

The item song they were filming had been recorded by the latest winner of *Indian Idol*. Bollywood tunes were always recorded in the voices of real singers, with the stars lip syncing on camera. Zara was finding it difficult to be in the scene as a spectator; she was sure the song would be a huge hit and Minnie would end up with the wolf whistles and the YouTube views. Raj had promised Zara every other song in the movie, but still she felt this would be the most popular tune.

The music started and Zara watched behind the scenes as Minnie began to gyrate to the song, feeling the hatred hit the back of her throat.

'She lacks your grace.' The voice was smooth and close to her ear. Zara turned to see Laila, dressed for her part in the audience, playing their glamorous mother.

'Laila*ji*, no, not at all. She is definitely your daughter, she has your beauty and screen presence.' Zara hoped she had hidden the thrill she got from having Minnie's own mother support her.

'Star quality can't be taught, Zara, dear, and it's not the birth right of the children of stars. It's something that's given to you. Some have it, most don't.'

'You have it in spades, ma'am.'

'I've been watching you for a while now, Zara, not just the Jhansi bomb drama, but your career for the last few years. You have star quality, you always did. Women like us, only we understand the personal sacrifices needed to make it in this industry.'

Minnie shouted, 'Cut!', interrupting them.

'There's too much smoke,' she screamed at Raj. 'I'm choking here. It's not Halloween, it's meant to be a fun party.'

Raj sent his technicians over to control the scene, while Minnie called for make-up.

'Ok, let's do some reaction shots while we wait for the smoke to clear on the stage. Zara and Imran in twenty minutes please.'

Laila squeezed her hand as she walked past, and Zara felt grateful to the woman. She probably understood more than anyone what Zara was going through.

Twenty minutes later Zara walked to the side of the ballroom for a close-up of her leaning against a pillar. The idea was that the refrain of the music would capture the moment when she would make eye contact with Imran for the first time across the room. She was going to walk into the centre of the room, and the space would be cleared, so that it was just her and Imran facing each other, an inserted dream moment that was pure Bollywood.

Raj called for action, and Zara looked into the camera trained on her. Raj called the shot to cut.

'Zara, I'm not getting that sense, that first attraction you feel for someone. And it's not a physical one only, she sees something in him she can't explain. And action!'

Zara counted herself in and faced the camera again, but failed to get the right look she wanted. On the fourth take, she saw Minnie on the sidelines, the same smirk from earlier on her face. Zara was determined to get this next shot right. She tried to remember the first time she had been attracted to anyone when she had felt more than just physical longing. She couldn't picture anyone. Except for Dan. She walked with the camera to the centre of the ballroom. Imran would film the opposite and then they would stand together in the same scene.

As Zara came to a stop, she lowered her eyes, and then looked into the camera. Raj shouted cut and told her it was perfect. Before she could move, Zara saw Dan running towards her. In a flash he had pushed her out of the way. Zara landed on the floor with Dan's body pressed solidly on top of her, and then heard the crash. Where she had been standing only seconds earlier, were the remnants of a smashed chandelier.

Chapter Eleven

Raj was pacing the room that had been given over to Zara. He was talking into his mobile phone, scratching his head under his baseball cap as he did so. Zara could see scratches on his legs; he had been helping out with building the set and behind the scenes as usual. Her first meeting with Raj had been on her debut movie his father had produced, where Raj was the assistant director, earning his stripes. And now here he was, India's most successful director, having saved his father's fading production house.

'Are you sure?' Raj was saying, still pacing. 'How? Did we not check? This can't happen again. Every day I want a full inspection, I will do it myself. This is ridiculous.'

He ended the call and stood in front of her. Zara was portraying calm at least. She hadn't said much since Dan had saved her from the falling chandelier, allowing everyone around her to take care of her. She was sitting drinking black tea with sugar, Ruby by her side, as Raj was apologising for the accident.

'You say accident, Raj, but do you really think so?' Ruby said.

Zara looked at Raj. He knew what had been left in her room, why was he being so stubborn about this? Did he genuinely think it was a coincidence? She needed Dan, at least he would believe her, but he had gone to check on the fallen chandelier. He was in fact the only one that knew everything: the message, the make-up, the rose, and now this. He would know this was deliberate.

'Zara, we could easily become paranoid. It was an accident, the cables holding it up seem to have been worn away. These old buildings attract mice, they said.'

'Killer mice. Are you winding me up?' Ruby said.

Zara stared into space and wrapped herself tightly with the shawl she had been given. The rest of the cast had already left for the day but Ruby refused to go until she had some answers.

'I think, maybe I should let you make this movie with someone else,' Zara said. 'Obviously somebody doesn't want me to act anymore.'

'No fucking way,' Ruby shouted. 'Zara Das doesn't give in to cowards. When I find who did this, I will drill their skull with my Jimmy Choos.' 'You can't let them win,' Raj agreed. 'You fucked up, Zara. But you don't deserve to be killed for it. Your *chutiya* director should have had more sense. I know what that idiot was thinking. He thought he was making a historical epic which was going to get him an Oscar nomination. He took his eye off the ball in his arrogance.'

'He's too busy playing with his assistant's balls, according to the grapevine,' Ruby said.

'I forced him to include that song. I was scared, I thought my audience would want it. He wanted to get someone else in to do it. Truth is, Raj, my ego couldn't take it.'

'You didn't kill anyone. It was a song. People can choose to watch it or not. And this was an accident.'

'Dumb ass men with their dumb ass too much time on their hands.'

'You know that's not how things work over there, Ruby. I will have to be made to pay for that video. Until I do, they won't leave me alone. They even made Sita walk through flames to prove herself. What am I?'

'Steady on, love, I adore you and all, but let's not get carried away, yeah? Comparing yourself to Sita is a bit of a leap. You're an actress, not a goddess.'

Raj came over and put his arm around her.

'I won't let anyone hurt you, Zara. Not this time. I wish…' Raj stopped, then carried on. 'I won't let anything happen to you, I promise you. Now come on, let's go back to the hotel, and we can reconvene tomorrow and start again. We will do this movie together, even if it kills us.'

'Be careful what you wish for,' Ruby said.

–

Dan was in the heavens, the platforms that had been set up around the ballroom to reflect the right sort of lighting down onto the film set. Up close he could see the painted Renaissance figurines in the ceiling, lavishly and minutely decorated to bring to life a Bacchanalian feast with such realism that would mirror the one below, they hoped. *Crazy rich people*, he thought. Money and sense really didn't go well together.

He had already looked at the broken crystals of the fallen chandelier and the cable it had been attached to. It had definitely been hacked at, he could see that clearly. Mice? Not unless the mice in London had suddenly started sprouting metallic teeth. There was a discreet door leading up to the room where the cables and electricity metres were also kept. Dan had checked the room earlier, the door to it was locked, and nothing had seemed untoward. Pushing the door now, it opened to his touch. Someone had forced it through, this was not mice. Or was it one of the crew who had come to investigate earlier? Dan would have to check. He really needed to get his head in gear, this was turning into a major security operation. James Kapoor had assured Dan that the people who had tried to blow Zara up were behind bars; that it was just notional security. That's not what it seemed like to him: someone was out there deliberately trying to hurt the woman.

Dan was going to have to run a check on the gangsters that had targeted Zara, see if they had any links to anyone in the UK, or if any of their members had come to London recently.

He looked at the bit of cable remaining on the floor that the chandelier had been attached to, and he could clearly see the first cut. And Dan had enough experience to know when a knife had been used to say with certainty what had happened. The chandelier was meant to fall at precisely the moment Zara had been on set. It was no accident, this was attempted murder.

–

Minnie was pissed off that the shoot had been cancelled because of Zara. Stupid bitch would milk the falling chandelier forever. Despite the closed set, stories were already leaking online. Someone had told Miss X and the vicious gossip was running with it. Zara's face was plastered everywhere. That wasn't meant to happen. She should have died. That would have been a better story.

Minnie didn't understand her hatred of Zara. The woman just irked her. Minnie was the one who had put up with a bitch of a mother all her life; she was the one who should have been rewarded with the number one position in Bollywood. So what if she had only made a handful of movies compared to that tramp's two dozen cheap flicks? Minnie was Bollywood royalty, not that jumped-up little whore.

Truth was, Minnie wanted to be free of her mother. No matter how much she loathed Laila, it was her mother's money Minnie was addicted to most of all. The endless shopping, the trips abroad, the best Swiss finishing schools. Minnie was used to having the freedom from sixteen of clubbing all night, and sleeping with anyone she wanted to. Initially she had been hoping Laila would react to her bad behaviour, scandalised by her loose sexual mores, but when she didn't, Minnie became more and more extreme. And now she was sick of her mother, sick of living in her shadow. Minnie wanted freedom, but she also wanted to keep her life as it was.

And that meant getting rid of Zara. That cow was commanding the box office, and in Minnie's head, if she wasn't around, the movies would be hers for the taking. She could have her own apartment, not be beholden to her mother.

Minnie made her way to the magnificent hotel pool, which was surprisingly empty. It had been decorated with faux rock formations, giving it the effect of being under a waterfall or somewhere exotic. The walls and ceiling were glass and aquamarine, the lighting soft to add to the exoticism.

Minnie lowered herself into the pool, which was barely over a metre deep, and swam rapid lengths to relieve her tension. She really needed to fuck Rocky again, he could easily afford the life she wanted. Only he seemed to be bored with her. Bastard, she would show him.

As she emerged from the water she was surprised to see Ajay Kumar walk in. He was wearing shorts and a dressing robe, which he took off. He waved at her, and she looked him over. He might be sixty, but he was still a hunk, with a toned hairy body. There was grey in his chest hair, but she found herself aroused by him and what he represented. Minnie had inherited her mother's looks and her sultry appeal, she knew that, and wondered if Ajay was being reminded of better days. Minnie pulled herself out of the water, her bikini clinging to her, revealing her nipples clearly, and Ajay couldn't take his eyes off her.

–

The room was bright as soon as Dan walked in. The light sensors had kicked in, and he surveyed the cavernous suite, checking it for intruders. He couldn't help being paranoid, thinking of all the incidents that had led up to that point. He walked to the bedroom, pushing the door open lightly. Empty. Next he checked the bathroom. Reassured, he ok'd Zara entering the room.

'I've asked security to be stationed outside your suite permanently, even when you're not here. The hotel won't let us put up CCTV cameras, saying their exclusive guests don't appreciate it. The rich and their dodgy goings-on, obviously. Anyway, I'm vetting everyone at this place and on the crew myself. And I've told Kasim to only use two members of staff I pick to clean your room under his supervision constantly.'

'Dan, stop please. You're scaring me more than the falling chandelier.'

'I won't let anything happen to you on my watch.' He didn't have to say that this was about the past, about him failing somebody else. What Zara didn't know was that it was also very much about his present. He needed to do this job, he needed James Kapoor to be happy with his services.

'I trust you,' she said. 'In fact, I trust you more than anyone else at the moment.'

For a moment they locked eyes, and Dan felt something inside stir. He had always been expert at separating his professional and personal lives. For the first time though he was feeling himself cross those lines inside. He was developing feelings for Zara that he didn't want.

Dan made a hasty exit, unable to stay around her much longer. Great, he thought, that was all he needed to complicate matters. She was already so vulnerable, the last thing she needed was him messing up on her.

–

Zara took her time to undress, carefully folding her Vetements jacket. She hadn't needed it, London was sweltering, but the Mercedes air con had been so strong on her way back she had used it to warm herself.

The chandelier incident had rattled her; mainly though because of the assumption that it was an accident rather than sabotage. Why had it fallen at the precise moment she was standing there, didn't the bastards ask themselves that? Maybe they would only take her seriously when something really bad happened. Zara had been livid at Raj's acceptance that it was an accident. For the first time she had seen in his eyes the fear that the movie might get delayed, and that there might be a cost implication. Zara had discreetly asked Collette to leak the story of a threat to her life to Miss X instead, and the internet and Indian news channels had gone crazy.

That had been the right thing to do, she thought. Accident, as if. Zara knew that the best way for her to come back was to try to gain sympathy. And if she was going to be the victim of these acts, people had better know about it.

When she was in her night wear, Kasim brought her some hot chocolate again. It was a ritual her mother had instilled in her and her brother from childhood. It was a special treat, and one they loved.

Zara asked Kasim to bring one for himself, too.

'Please, I don't feel like being alone tonight,' she said.

Kasim obliged, and they sat in companionable silence, both lost in their thoughts. Zara's mind always turned to Dev when she was with Kasim. It was the eyes, the same uncanny colour. She liked to fantasise sometimes about Dev being alive still, of having a life unknown to her.

'You seem sad, ma'am,' Kasim said, breaking the silence between them.

'I was just thinking about my brother,' she said.

'Is he unwell?'

'I don't know.' Kasim looked confused. 'He disappeared when I was a child. When he was a child, too.'

'I'm sorry to hear that, ma'am. Where did he go?'

'We don't know. We were at Independence Day celebrations, and he just vanished. Maybe somebody took him, maybe he met with an accident. I don't know. He was my twin.'

'I am sorry, ma'am, that is extremely sad.'

'I suppose it is. Sad, I mean. Now I'm just used to it, and still I miss him every day.'

'He is your twin, that is most natural.'

Zara took a gulp of her cooling drink, wishing again that she could feel something from Dev. A sign that he was alive at least.

'I never tell people about that, but you remind of him. He had eyes the same colour as yours.'

Kasim didn't respond, just smiled wanly. What could he say?

'I tried to find him, so many times. Especially when I became famous and had the money. I hired private detectives, and we even found some men pretending to be Dev. But they weren't. Just fraudsters after money.'

'People are very evil sometimes.'

'Yes, yes they are.' She wondered what Dev would make of her. 'Do you think it's bad, what I do? Acting, doing my dance numbers? Being Zara?'

'Not at all, ma'am. It is not for me to judge, but also think of the happiness you bring to people. You give them some break from their daily life, and some of your films, the messages in them are so strong.'

That was true. Zara loved making hard-hitting movies with social messages, but dressing them up with her sexy outfits and sultry dance routines. It was how to get men into the cinema hall, so that she could then tell them why beating their wives was a fucking crime. Her women were never pushovers. Zara had been beaten too many times in real life, right from childhood. Her movies were a big fuck you to everyone that had tormented her and used her.

'I hope one day you find your brother,' Kasim said, wishing her goodnight.

Alone in her bed, Zara thought of Dan and felt secure knowing he was just metres away from her. James Kapoor had given him a room in the basement where emergency accommodation for staff was kept. She felt like calling him, asking him to keep her company. Only she knew that would be a mistake. Whatever she was beginning to feel, there was something much bigger that she needed to focus on. And Dan would not play a part in that.

Chapter Twelve

They were back at the mansion in Regent's Park, the tension on set palpable. Raj tried to focus on the scenes he was going to shoot that day, but his entire cast seemed to be locked away in corners skulking. The only one not party to the mood was the actor he had roped in at the last minute to play the role of Collins. Salman was a meathead, all muscles and swarthy good looks, but the main issue for Raj was that Salman was Pakistani. Born in Lahore, he had recently relocated to the UK, playing bit parts on British television, mainly terrorists and honour killers. Raj had already been lambasted online for hiring an actor from Pakistan. It wasn't as bad as it had been years before, and he was just glad the two nations weren't at loggerheads over Kashmir and exchanging gunfire this week. Salman was available, he was convenient and if the film did get a release in Pakistan, then Salman's name might help draw in the crowds there, as he had played roles in Pakistani TV dramas over the years.

'Don't mind, Raj, sir, but you should consider filming a song in Bath. Jane Austen loved that place, it would play right into the whole *Pride and Prejudice* angle. It's a beautiful little city, too.'

'I haven't got the time, Salman, to shoot anywhere else. I was planning a song sequence in Istanbul, but logistics won't allow it. I only have these guys for a few days, and I am so behind schedule.'

'Yeah, I heard. Is Zara on set? We have some scenes to shoot later, I thought maybe she wouldn't come? Is it true about the chandelier?'

Raj busied himself blocking the shot and liaising with his lighting and camera guys, not willing to indulge Salman's curiosity. Bollywood operated in the currency of gossip more than most industries. It was always the way stars avoided negative attention, by calling out the failings of their rivals.

Zara had recovered well from the incident, and seemed to think she was doing Raj a favour, letting her commitment to his movie override her own safety, but Raj was concerned for her. Dan had stepped up his team, adding another four men to the security detail to go undercover in the hotel to see if they could recognise any hostile reconnaissance taking place. Dan kept repeating that it was nearly impossible to get into Zara's room without someone having access through one of the adjoining rooms. Raj had tacitly broached it with Minnie, but she had been tart in her reply. 'I'd gladly let anyone use my room to bring down that bitch.'

-

They were all seated at the mock dinner table, another room in the mansion posing as the Bennett family residence. In the movie they were called the Banerjees, a sprawling Bengali family. Laila and Ajay were seated at the table, with both Zara and Minnie. Three British Asian actresses were cast with them, including Anjali Goyal playing the role of Jane. Anjali was the most famous brown face on British television, and Raj had cast her for the audience she would bring with her, not to mention the British press who still didn't really care that there were a whole load of Bollywood A-listers in town.

The atmosphere was unbearable in between scenes. The lead actors didn't exchange a single word until Raj shouted action.

Zara looked past Minnie, unable to meet the eyes of the vicious tramp. Every time Zara accidentally looked her way she had a knowing smile on her face. It was lucky they weren't particularly close even in the movie, as Zara would have struggled to come up with any sort of familial emotion for Minnie.

Ajay tried to break the ice when Raj shouted cut, as the half dozen make-up artists stormed around them, touching up their faces and hair. Zara had a mirror brought to her by a spot boy as she did her own.

'I feel so vain in comparison, Zara dear, you sure you wouldn't like some help from my assistant?' Ajay winked at her as he spoke.

'No, Ajay sir, it's fine, honestly. I'm used to it.'

'Used to looking like crap,' muttered Minnie. Everyone ignored her comment.

'I wish I had your skill,' Laila added kindly, throwing daggers at her daughter which Minnie was oblivious to. 'I shudder sometimes when I look back at some of the get-ups I was forced into. I think they copied the Alexis Colby school of make-up all through the eighties with me.'

'What do you mean, Laila*ji*? You always looked stunning. I don't think any of us can match the glamour you brought back then.'

'We used to think that about the heroines from the sixties and seventies. It's strange, isn't it? I think the way you all dress today is so sophisticated.'

Minnie yawned exaggeratedly. Laila pinned her with a heavily kohled stare, but she didn't notice.

'And you have such better roles now too. I think I did too many movies where all I did was shout *bachao* and dance in tight *cholis*.'

'Please, Mom, your *cholis* weren't just tight, the stitches had come apart by the end of your dance numbers,' said Minnie. 'And it was all so tacky, with the pipe cleaner backing dancers, I mean, seriously?'

'The audience was different then, India wasn't the booming powerhouse it is now,' Ajay said gallantly. 'We were catering to the front benchers, the masses that worked so hard and needed us. We were the only entertainment they had, this was pre satellite and pre Internet.'

'There's no excuse for crudeness. Then again, some actresses today look pretty shoddy,' said Minnie, looking at Zara. 'No class.'

'You think you guys had it bad, you should check out some of our heroines from the eighties,' said Salman.

'I remember there was talk of an Indian-Pakistani co-production back then. Me starring opposite Anjuman. Alas, it never materialised. As ever, politics got in the way.'

'You ever think how successful our nations might be if we weren't spending so much on military and defence?' said Salman.

'I think India's doing just fine,' smiled Ajay.

'Do we have to talk politics?' whined Minnie.

'Worried your one brain cell might combust?' said Zara.

'The only bust you're familiar with is your fake one, so keep your comments to yourself.'

'Where's the fun in that?' Zara retorted.

'I don't know why Raj cast me in this role though,' Salman said, changing the subject blatantly. 'I mean, this guy is an absolute weirdo, and a bit fugly in the novel.'

'It takes all sorts to make the world turn,' said Ajay, wisely.

'I'm just saying it's bad casting, surely?'

'You can always walk out of the movie if you want to, Salman,' said Minnie. 'No one will miss you.'

'This is Raj's interpretation, remember. He is renowned for his love of beautiful things,' said Anjali, trying to act as though she too belonged with the Bollywood superstars. 'Your character is different in his interpretation. His heroines always look the best in his movies, his sets are always the most opulent.'

'Oh the irony,' Minnie said, looking at the very far from attractive Anjali.

'His stories are simple,' Anjali went on, 'but he mounts them so well.'

'I wonder how well he mounts Jackie,' muttered Minnie.

'Don't be vulgar,' said Laila.

'Says the woman who let Ajay*ji* drink water running down her neck. Was that before or after you were married?' said Minnie. Ajay blushed and averted his eyes. Salman looked between Ajay, Laila, and Minnie. Zara looked to see where Dan was. He hadn't come on set and she hadn't seen him that morning either, instead she had been protected by his team.

'So tell me, how are you both finding working together?' Anjali asked Laila and Ajay. Again Salman looked between the principal players, wondering how they would respond.

'It's been one of the best shoots of my life,' Ajay said, graciously. Laila smiled at him, but Zara noticed that Ajay's eyes as he spoke were clearly on Minnie.

–

'I'm really feeling Salman,' said Ruby. She was on set now as she was about to play out a scene between herself and Zara with Salman before she acted out scenes alone with him. 'He's right up my street.'

'He is a beautiful thing apparently, according to that Anjali,' said Zara.

'That woman, I don't get it. She's the darling of British TV and media, can barely act and looks like the sort of woman that would play the housemaid's mum in a Bollywood movie.'

'*Kismet*,' said Zara. 'It's not about how you look or your talent always, sometimes it's just meant to be.'

'Allow it, Zee, she's been ticking a diversity box for years. I see it everywhere, especially now. Oh, let's get an ethnic face in just so we can't be accused of being racist. That's not the point or the way to do it. Get the talent in, not just the right colour.'

'Steady on, Ruby, you're sounding like you're on a soapbox.'

'I know, I'm boring myself. Let's get drunk tonight. Sorry, I forgot your health regime won't allow it. Let me rephrase that. I'll get drunk on the free champers Kapoor has put on tap for you, while you eat celery dipped in tomato juice or whatever it is that you class as food these days.'

'Don't be facetious, it takes effort, you know. For every Zara Das, there are a million girls that are younger, thinner, and more talented than me. I'm not so arrogant I can't see it.'

'Candid confessions one-oh-one. Yes, but you forget, none of them have that x-factor. It takes something special to make it.'

'Hard work and not drinking.'

'No wonder I never made it. I'm a lazy alkie.'

'You're looking pretty good for anyone indulging in those vices,' said Salman, coming up to join them.

'Thanks, bud, you're not so bad yourself,' said Ruby.

Zara saw the pupil-dilating flirtatious stance both Salman and Ruby took and immediately felt like a spare part.

'I need to go and touch up something,' she said, leaving them alone for a few minutes.

-

Ajay was in the room given over to him for his make-up and wardrobe. The converted Georgian mansion was like a palace, with more rooms and annexes than he could count. Set among two acres of gardens, the realty value must be beyond the reach of even most millionaires. He had heard it was owned by a non-domicile friend of James Kapoor, who needed to put the mansion to use when he wasn't resident for tax avoidance. The mansion was used for filming period dramas, movies that required grand sets and movies like *Kismet India* where the people were all a bit posh. He thought how it was so different from his heyday. They'd needed films to distract from the poverty back then. They'd wanted men like him to fight the rich, or to make it big by hard work. Now, they wanted aspirational movies for the middle classes. When money was flowing, they wanted to know how to dress, love, and spend money.

There was a knock on his door, and Ajay expected it to be make-up or one of the crew. Instead it was Minnie. She had changed into shorts and a top that showed off her midriff, accentuated her breasts, and yet kept her looking sophisticated. It was quite a skill, and he remembered how her mother had been able to do the same for years; look sexy but not cheap.

'I had to get away, and I know you are the one person she won't come near,' said Minnie, slumping into the empty chair next to Ajay's. 'Honestly, I don't know why you married her, she has such a stick up her ass.'

'Minnie, darling, that's no way to talk about your mother. Show her some respect, at least.'

'The same respect you showed her when you re-married her biggest competition and had four kids and a stable happy family life you paraded under her nose? While she lived out a complete car crash of a life?'

'I didn't do anything deliberately. That's just the way things worked out for me. And car crash or not, she had you.'

'Yes, to use like an accessory. She's been so cold to me, she doesn't have a maternal bone in her body. Honestly, what did you see in her?'

Ajay shrugged. 'We all make our mistakes in life. You are young, you will hopefully learn from yours.'

'Please, mistakes are when you do things you regret later. You can't call going off with a tramp like that a mistake, your brain must have gone for a vacation to the moon and then some. No one is that stupid, surely?'

'Your father married her as well,' said Ajay a bit too quickly, regretting it as he saw the look that crossed Minnie's face. 'Apologies, I shouldn't judge a man I've never met.'

'It's ok, he was a coward. He should have stood up to her, instead of running away and leaving Miss Haver-shame to raise me.'

'She loves you. Look at what she's done for you. Acting opposite me so that you can be in a Raj Dillon movie. Bollywood is a massive game of who blinks first. Raj took a chance on you, and that means every A-list producer, director, and actor will too. Otherwise, being the daughter of a star can only get you so far.'

'Come on, Ajay*ji*, she's only acting in this movie to try to prove she still looks hotter than me even at her age and to raise her own profile. Someone needs to tell her she's like an exhibit in a museum, curated to near death.'

'Do you mind if we talk about something other than my ex-wife?'

'Sorry, it's just very few people know the real dragon. You saw through her I know, and you understand what I'm saying. To everyone else she's this untouchable legend.'

'Even legends can be hollow. Haven't you seen *The Wizard of Oz*?'

'Judy Garland. Another legend with messed-up kids.'

'How are you enjoying London?'

'I studied here, so it's like a second home to me, I come here all the time. It's fine. I wish Raj had picked somewhere more exotic for us.'

'Maybe the idea is that you bring the exotic to London this time?'

Minnie locked eyes with Ajay in the make-up mirror that had been set up for him. 'Tell me honestly, am I more beautiful than her?'

Ajay smiled, but didn't answer. He didn't want to admit to Minnie that she was stirring feelings in him he hadn't felt since he had first met her mother. Rani was different, she was the sort of woman you married; beautiful, faithful, and fun to be with. She was the sane sort of individual you wanted to have kids with.

Women like Laila and Minnie were different. They were like shots in human form. You did them occasionally with the sole intention of forgetting reality. And then in the morning you could wake up to the familiarity of Rani. And Ajay was planning on doing just that.

'You know who else is a sort?' said Ruby. 'That bodyguard of yours. He can guard my body any time he wants.'

They were taking a walk in the gardens, exploring the maze. Dan was a safe distance from them as they walked arm-in-arm.

'Come on, sleeping with the help? Isn't that a bit old school?'

'Not when the help looks that hot. He's so brooding and sexy, and you know he will protect you in those sturdy arms of his.'

'I don't need protecting,' said Zara.

'I think you do, Zee. Anyway, what plays in London stays in London. No one needs to know. He barely knows who you are and there's no papz or gossip mags around that care enough. You are free, that's the best thing about shooting overseas.'

'Ruby, stop this nonsense, I'm not interested.'

'I think you're protesting a bit too much, Zee. What about the butler then? Those eyes. If he was my butler, I'd be ordering room service all night.'

'Kasim is sweet, he's been through so much.'

'And?'

'Come on, Ruby, leave this subject now.'

'I'm not talking about Mr Right darling, just Mr Right Now. You need to get laid. It will solve all your problems.'

Zara smiled thinly, but didn't believe it. The great myth that sex was the key to happiness or resolving issues was just that – a myth. Zara had seen the dark side of sex for too long, she didn't want someone who was going to enjoy screwing her for a few weeks or months. Inside, there was a gaping emotional space, just waiting for someone to make a connection with her. She didn't want a man to look after her, or provide for her, or because it was what people did. She felt so alone, and the only thing she wanted was for someone to love her for herself.

And that was a problem because Zara never let anyone see the real her any more. She had played the part of a diva for so long she didn't quite know how to switch it off. As she looked into her future, Zara could only see emptiness, and once again felt anger. She had run away from home to get away from a nightmare, had been forced to follow a path she would never have chosen, and had kept running and climbing to save herself. And now what was she left with? She had reached the top, but there was no one left to catch her. And she could already feel herself begin to crash and fall.

Chapter Thirteen

The day was going to be a complicated one as Zara and Rocky were scheduled to do tourist shots for a song. It was the equivalent of Elizabeth and Wickham bonding in the novel, but in Bollywood style, Raj had decided to replace the tedious chats with snapshots interlaid against a soft breezy romance number. They were going to aim to shoot a whole week of 'dates' in a couple of days, with seven outfit changes and seven different locations for each segment of the song. The idea would be to showcase all the London tourist hotspots so that moviegoers, the vast majority of whom could never afford to travel to London, would get a sense of the city. James Kapoor had pulled strings with the Mayor of London to get them permission to close off landmarks like Waterloo Bridge and film at places like the London Eye. In fact, all their shooting locations had been greenlit through Kapoor's contacts. This included an entire London underground tube train, and the hiring of dozens of local extras so the scenes they shot would look natural among the crowds of Londoners.

EZ was on hand again to do the actual shoot, and Raj was feeling the stress from having him so close. As EZ ran his fingers through his thick hair, Raj felt the searing jealousy inside his brain, imagining Jackie reacting to him, preferring his lithe figure to Raj's own. Raj couldn't stand to be near EZ any longer so told him to leave. The hotel lobby became empty, and thoughts of Jackie and the man she had been drinking with in the hotel bar started to haunt him. The man had looked like he had just stepped out of a magazine like *GQ*. Jackie had said it was just some random man who had been making small talk. But Raj was no fool, he knew what happened in hotel bars late at night when people were away from home.

Raj opened his WhatsApp and started a tirade to his wife, his anger banging out in every letter he typed to her. How fucking dare she talk to that guy, and if she hadn't wanted to be with him, she should just have left. He knew he wasn't skinny or hot himself so why was she with him? When he wasn't her type at all? Raj felt his anger dissipate as he sent the messages. But they were gone. He checked the phone, everything had two ticks, indicating that the messages had been sent, but they weren't blue yet so Jackie hadn't read them. He went through and deleted every hate-filled word.

This wasn't her problem. Her exes being the way they were in Raj's head wasn't Jackie's problem. He needed help, this couldn't go on. He had to deal with this. Or he had to let Jackie go.

–

Dan had thought the idea was insane when Raj told him about the shoot. Here was a woman who people were out to kill, who had had a couple of close shaves already, and the director wanted to expose her to an open environment where she was a free for all? Dan was used to expert security in closed situations. He made sure his clients were in places with plenty of exit points if needed, and where he could monitor entry points. He made sure he did a full stakeout of any location before his client would have to be there, in his head mapping the layout and ensuring he was comfortable that there were no significant risks.

London, though? There was no way he could protect Zara in such an open space, even knowing the locations they were going to shoot at: Westminster Abbey, Buckingham Palace, Trafalgar Square, the London Eye, Tower Bridge, St Paul's Cathedral and the Shard. Not to mention shots on Waterloo Bridge and in the different main royal parks. Raj had even managed to arrange permission to shoot down Billionaire's Row in Kensington.

The only concessions Raj had made were to keep the crew small: a cameraman with a handful of technicians, one person to do hair and make-up and one to do outfit changes, plus that bookmark choreographer EZ. They would travel in a minivan, and would try to cause as little disruption as possible.

'And where do you expect the stars to change and have their make-up done?' Raj had protested.

Dan had relented and agreed to a mobile vanity van to meet them at each location.

'You think Zara will share with Rocky?' Raj had looked incredulous when he said it. Dan had to stop dismissing Zara when he was dealing with her, he needed to remember that she was the Angelina Jolie or Jennifer Lawrence of Bollywood. Just because he had never heard of her before James Kapoor asked him to be her security didn't mean anything.

'Ok, fine, two vanity vans. They meet us at each location, they do not form an entourage. Once they've done their changes, the vanity vans can head off to the next location while you shoot.'

'You expect me to mount a big-budget movie with a crew that consists of less than ten people? I need more, Dan.'

'Tough. I need to make sure we are low-key so your leading lady doesn't end up dead.'

Dan had left Raj open-mouthed in the bar of the Mirage and headed off to explain the day's arrangements to his team. Dan didn't like the way he was feeling about Zara; she was definitely affecting him more than any client had in the past. He was aware of his own feelings, aware of just what she was waking up in him. It was a risk, too big a risk for him to take. Dan had decided the only option was to keep his distance from Zara, to avoid being physically near her. He was starting with this shoot, leaving it to the men and women he trusted on his team to secure Zara's safety. For both their sakes, he wouldn't be going.

Rani, Sasha, and Jackie had risen for a late breakfast, then decided to hit London for some retail therapy, and enjoy the unusually hot weather. Jackie had been sceptical at first when Sasha told her.

'Rani Kumar? Come on, what have we got in common with her?'

'She's having a hard time, and she's sweet.'

'She's one of them, the women we hate. The establishment.'

'I think she's lonely. It's only lunch.'

'Yeah well, you also invited that bitch Zara to lunch. I mean, what were you thinking? I hate her.'

'I'll meet her on my own, don't worry. Don't judge her though. You don't know her.'

'Yes we do. What's happened to you in London? It was me and you against the Bollywood Wives.'

'Newsflash, Jackie, we *are* the Bollywood Wives. Now come on, be nice, Rani's sweet.'

Jackie had put on her best 'have a nice day' American fake face, but through the day Sasha could see she too was warming towards Rani.

The biggest problem they faced when shopping wasn't their inability to get on with each other, but the pricing. In Mumbai, the ladies pretty much got given most things, especially Rani, or were able to bargain prices down to supplier level. In London no one was offering them that luxury, so they spent their time trying to work out what everything cost in rupees.

'My head's whacked,' said Jackie. 'I'm so used to thinking how cheap everything is compared to how much it would cost in dollars, I can't compute this. I'm now thinking how much this costs in dollars, and how many rupees is that, and then realising just how much it is.'

'The quality will be good, though,' said Sasha. 'I think I might purchase some cosmetic sets for my sisters and Amma.'

'What happened to tacky tops with *my friend went to London and all I got was this lousy fucking T-shirt* – which was made in a sweatshop in Bangladesh, anyway?'

'Isn't that what your last documentary was about?' said Sasha.

All three of them were wearing designer shades against the sun. Rani was wearing a simple indigo Ritu Kumar saree, while Sasha had opted for a long off-white Anita Dongre kurta over Versace jeans. Jackie was wearing Target shorts with a sleeveless Gucci top. Despite their clashing outfits, the three women were giving off an undeniable chemistry.

'I do love your documentaries,' Rani said.

'Cut the shit, you watch my docs?'

'Of course. Why wouldn't I?'

'Most of your set think I'm a hippie troublemaker.'

'If you think I sit comfortably with the Penny Kapoors of this world, then think again. I especially loved the one about the logos.'

'Yes, how we pay for luxury goods in Mumbai and Delhi because they have a western logo emblazoned on them, while the stitching is done down the road. I had a lot of flak for that, mainly from the fashion houses themselves.'

'No one likes an exposé,' Rani said thoughtfully.

'Come on let's go to Knightsbridge and then wander through Harrods and then we need to do lunch. There's a new sushi bar with views across London near Hyde Park I want to try out.'

'What I don't understand is that for someone who loathes consumerism, you are hell bent on indulging today,' said Rani.

Jackie threw Sasha a look.

'I don't loathe consumerism, there's nothing wrong with doing both things. Shopping but also being aware.'

–

'Ok, darling, so I want you to hold him like this, right, your arms around his neck, your hair like floating away from you, so tilt your head up to him. And you, babe, I want you to put your hands on her lower back, and then touch your forehead to hers. Shall I show you, guys?'

Zara and Rocky shook their heads, locking eyes and trying not to giggle. EZ was taking things far too seriously; they could manage an embrace on a bridge without so much direction.

Zara was wearing a Balenciaga crimson-burgundy coat, her hair softly curled loose. Rocky was dressed in jeans and a brown Armani shirt, as they both stood against a sky with a rising sun casting beautiful shades of violet, cerise and gold to frame them. London was spread out along the glistening river behind them. Raj counted them in, hearing the music in his headset, watching the monitor as the camera panned in, then walked around them and zoomed out again. The shot had taken about half an hour to set up, and they managed about five seconds of usable footage.

Zara looked for Dan, seeing him sulking but alert. When he had told her he wasn't going to be doing her personal security any more, she had panicked.

'I don't want a member of your team, I want you. What's the problem?'

'I'll still be overseeing your security detail, but the personal detail will be done by someone else.'

'That's not fair, I haven't done anything to deserve that. I want you.'

Zara hadn't accepted his decision and had put in a call to James Kapoor. Within thirty minutes Dan had arrived on set to look after her. He barely acknowledged her, and she wondered what had happened to him to make him behave so coldly to her.

'Well I guess you have me on your payroll after all,' he had said to her when she had first seen him. She didn't get time to ask him why he was being so aloof and felt shattered that he was.

Hitting the tourist spots was a mistake, and Dan could see Raj's realisation dawn on him slowly. It was July, London was in the grip of a heatwave that made just manoeuvring around the city tedious, plus tourist season was hitting its stride. And lots of those tourists were Indian, all going to the same locations Raj would hit. On top of which were the London-resident Asian population, all with smartphones and social media. By the time they got to lunchtime and the London Eye, they had a crowd.

Luckily for Dan it was only Zara who was drawing them. If it had been a combined shoot between her and Imran, he would have needed a bigger team. Still, as they disembarked, there was a scrum of people taking pictures and calling out Zara's name. Zara graciously waved at them all, but Dan was feeling the tension and the sweat rolled down his back. There were dozens of faces, mainly brown, all focusing in on Zara. He scanned them, trying to identify a threat, but it was difficult, not knowing who he was looking for. His team had formed a human line of markers between Zara and the crowd, pillars that everyone knew were not to be passed. Zara rushed into the mobile vanity van that had parked up. Raj had managed to get parking and filming permits from the mayor, Sadiq Khan's, office. Dan had worked for him on occasion in the past as well during his time at MI6 when the MP and London Mayor had made trips abroad.

When Zara emerged, she was wearing a sunflower-yellow summer dress, looking sensational. The crowd, which he saw was mainly families, got excited and started to swell forward. Zara broke with the protocol Dan had taught her and went up to meet them. He moved quickly, and was by her side in a flash, as his team stepped in to keep the baying crowd back. He had to keep his distance from her, but the pressure James Kapoor could apply was immense. And Dan needed his bonus desperately. Reluctantly, he had agreed to come and protect

Zara personally again, but now he was glad. The situation was too precarious to leave to anyone else.

'Zara ma'am, we love you!'

'Autograph please!'

'I love your movies!'

'You are so beautiful!'

'OhmygawdIcantbelieveitsyouI'msuchabigfanIloveyousom-uchohmygawd!' The crowd was screaming and shouting, as hands and smartphones were thrust into Zara's face. Dan pushed aside any that got too close, while Zara casually took selfies with people and signed bits of paper, napkins, and even one boy's arm.

The people seemed pleasant enough, but they were too close to her, and Dan didn't see fans, he saw potential attackers, all with easy access to his client. He watched every single interaction, making sure no one was moving into a threatening angle, using force on the more excited fans, who were so caught up in the Zara buzz they didn't care. And then they were surrounded, literally. Zara was in a thick circle of people. As realisation dawned on her, she looked at Dan, and he saw the flicker of panic on her face. Meanwhile, the crowd was gathering attention, and more and more people were coming to join it, even people who had no clue who she was. There were no gaps being left between Zara and the people trying to get close to her. She tried to maintain some sort of composure, but Dan could feel the sheer heat and intensity from the gathered people who were now adopting crowd mentality. His phone buzzed; Zara had pressed the emergency app on her phone.

He grabbed her around the waist and pulled her close to him. She took the cue, and leaned in to him, curling her body into his grip, as Dan started to push at the people around her. They resisted, some even pushed back, but he exerted more force, shouting at them to move back. He comm'd his team, asking them to clear a path, and within seconds there was a gap. Dan pushed his way through, making sure Zara was with him, and eventually led her out of the throng and into the safety of her vanity van.

-

The sushi bar, Fugu's, was on top of a car showroom selling Ferraris. It all seemed a little kitsch to Jackie as she took Sasha and Rani through a side entrance. There was a good selection available, so the ladies ordered quickly and sipped on their water until the food came.

'How's the script coming along?' Jackie asked Sasha. 'Did the rewrites work?'

'I like them, it definitely makes the movie more commercial.'

'And Imran, what did he think? Is he on board?'

Sasha didn't make eye contact, instead looking out across the expanse of Hyde Park, which was being reflected in her shades.

'Fuck him. You don't need him,' said Jackie.

'You know what they say,' Rani added. 'The only things that seem to work at the box office these days are sex and Imran Khan.'

'Send me the script, boo, I'll write so much sex into it you won't need your jerk of a husband. Men.' Jackie shook her head as she spoke.

The waiter brought their food over. They were sharing teriyaki salmon, California rolls and an assortment of bento. Rani was on a vegetarian day so was sticking to the avocado maki.

'Listen Sasha, there are so many ways to make a film now,' Rani said. 'With Netflix and Amazon, the market has really opened up. And cinema-going isn't the same any more. Intelligent films can work in the metros, we have both the cinemas now and the audience. The educated middle classes and student brigade started frequenting movie halls years back. There are always options.'

'I already told her all this,' drawled Jackie. Sasha could tell Rani was irritating her a bit.

'I know, Rani*ji*, but I had a dream. I wanted to make something big, something that would really make my mark. I don't want people to think Imran Khan's wife made that chick-flick or that award-winning movie. I want them to say *Imran Khan's wife made history at the box office*.'

'By casting Imran Khan?' Jackie arched an eyebrow as she said it. 'It's bullshit, Sasha darling. You want to make a blockbuster, fine, but don't do it with your husband.'

'You make it sound as though I can't see beyond him. You're here with Raj as well.'

Jackie was taciturn now, filling her mouth with sushi instead. There were reasons for her to be in London. Reasons she wasn't ready to share with these women yet. Even Raj didn't know.

'I think we might be making headway, though. Imran and I spent yesterday just relaxing. He took me on a canal cruise, just the two of us, then lunch at the Ritz, followed by a visit to Cartier.'

'Aww, how cute, he got diamonds for his little babymama,' said Jackie.

'We talked about the movie over dinner at Nobu. He said he would think about reading the script. That's further than we've got before in terms of discussing this project.'

'He agreed to think about reading the script? Yeah, Sasha, I can see the finish line already. Right next to pigs that fly and not smelling the coffee.'

They ate in silence for a few minutes, time needed to let the tension between the two women to calm down. Rani broke their mood.

'I love London, I think it's my favourite city now. It used to be New York, but I think I've taken to this place more. I needed a break, and some time to relax. Just think – nobody really knows who we are here,' said Rani. On cue a middle-aged man came up to their table. He was a type, in a business suit with grey facial hair, and spoke with trepidation.

'Are you Rani Kumar, ma'am?' Jackie wanted to laugh as this man who was probably the same age as Rani calling her 'ma'am'. She didn't get this nonsense respect thing her adopted homeland had going on. Even journalists would ask some twisted questions and still add 'ma'am' and 'sir'.

Rani smiled and nodded, she was a professional all right.

'I thought so, you still look the same. You are so beautiful and were always my favourite actress. I tell my kids and grandkids, today's actresses with their nothing-on clothes and dirty moves, they have no class. I can't even watch the films nowadays.'

'That's so sweet of you, thank you,' Rani said, smiling sweetly. The man asked for her autograph and took a selfie.

'What are you doing in London, ma'am? Is Ajay sir with you?'

'Yes, he is. My husband is here shooting a movie: it's Raj Dillon's new one.'

'I blame Raj Dillon and his generation for the downturn of our movie industry. They have no vision, no style. It's all about costumes and locations. Not like when Ajay sir and you, ma'am, were making movies.'

Everyone's a critic, thought Jackie.

'I'll be sure to pass on your comments to my husband,' she quipped. 'Jackie Dillon, pleasure to meet you.'

The man turned crimson and left them quickly.

'What was that about not being recognised?' said Sasha.

'You know what I mean. We'll just stick to the areas where there are only white people.'

'This is London, good luck with that,' said Jackie.

-

Zara was trembling, as the make-up artist touched up her face, and Raj came in with a thermos of something.

'It's Irish coffee,' he said, making Zara gulp it down. 'That was insane. It's what we expect in Mumbai, I didn't think they would get so crazy here.'

'I did say it was a huge risk. You need to shut these areas down if you want to film here,' Dan said. She could tell he was angry. She had felt the onslaught of a panic attack earlier, she had felt so trapped and for a moment thought the crowd might topple her over and smother her.

'We can't close off these areas, they're London's top spots for visitors. We have help from the venues in filming, but that's all we can expect. I've never seen an outdoor shoot abroad descend into chaos like that. Normally people are well-behaved.'

'You underestimate the power of frenzy,' Dan said.

'Shall we go back to the hotel?'

'No,' Zara said firmly. 'I'm fine, nothing happened, let's carry on.'

'I recommend we go back...'

'Dan, please, I've faced worse than this. I'm fine, honestly. It's part of the territory. Now come on, let's go film on the London Eye.'

—

The shots on the Eye were more secure than some of the other locations they had filmed at. They had been given a pod to themselves, so it was easy to feel secure inside it. Dan had his team guarding an exit point and the minivan, and the vanity vans had headed off already to Westminster where the next segments would be shot in Westminster Abbey and Parliament Square. Dan had insisted the Met be alerted and they send some officers to help in case of crowd trouble.

EZ seemed to be buzzing off the drama as he told Zara and Rocky how to pose.

'My lord, I thought you were a goner for sure. I was just watching and thinking, *bas*, she isn't going to survive this. I tell you, my heart is still racing like, feel it.'

He touched Rocky's hand to his chest, the Kapoor scion clearly uncomfortable with the intimacy of the action.

'Seems fine to me,' Rocky drawled. Zara giggled. She seemed to have put it all behind her, or maybe she was just pretending. It was her profession, after all.

'I nearly fainted like, it was so intense.'

'Can we get on and shoot, please, we need to get out of here,' Raj said.

EZ breathed in deeply. 'Yes, the art must always come first. You look great though, darling. I always say if you're going to be trampled on by a crowd of the unwashed, at least look hot.'

Zara and Rocky shared a fake laugh and joke for the camera, staring out across London for another segment, and then filmed individual reaction shots where their eyes were smouldering for each other. As Zara filmed hers, she looked directly at Dan who was poised behind the camera. When Raj shouted cut, she mouthed the words 'Thank you' to Dan. He tilted his head slightly, feeling something he didn't like inside.

–

Sasha, Jackie, and Rani ended the afternoon with massages in the hotel spa. The three of them lay naked under towels, as Thai masseurs pummelled and pushed their skin. Meditation music floated around them.

'I could get used to this,' Jackie mumbled, her voice sleepy. 'A whole month of being pampered and no worries.'

'It feels like a waste,' said Sasha. 'I miss the kids.'

'Listen, Mother Teresa, no one's buying that bullshit. I know how stressed you always are. Take this well-earned break. The kids aren't going anywhere.'

'I think, technically, Mother Teresa didn't have children,' said Sasha. 'Anyway, when is it your turn?' Jackie and Raj had been married for two years now, and neither of them had said they didn't want to have kids. Sasha had never followed through her suspicions, but Jackie going so quiet after her comment made her realise maybe she had said something she shouldn't.

'It was good of Raj to mount such a lavish production and invite us all along,' Rani said, sensing a change of subject was needed. 'Why did he feel he had to move the shoot to London though?'

'No idea, some bullshit about his father. Said his father had given Zara her first role in films, and he felt an affinity towards her. After she truly messed up with that stupid song, I think he wanted to help her. I don't know what hold that tramp has over my husband, but I don't like it. Makes me question his integrity when he's so protective of trash like her.'

'Protective is one thing, but making such an expensive movie? In London?' Rani added.

'It was too dangerous in Mumbai. Raj got death threats after he said he was going to put Zara in this movie. He felt he had no option if he wanted to cast her. He knows it's risky, but that's why he has all the big guns on board. Imran, Laila, Ajay. The little Bratz doll Minnie.'

'You're such a bitch,' Sasha laughed.

'It's true, though. I think she's a fan of all those reality TV stars and doesn't realise this is real life not reality life. Have you ever spoken to her? It's like she's not there. All she does is pose for selfies, tweet, and Instagram. A conversation with her is the human equivalent of sucking on ice cubes.'

'Zara is sweet though,' Rani said.

'Yes she is, isn't she? I totally misjudged her,' Sasha agreed.

'Please, Zara's the biggest bitch of them all,' said Jackie. 'She's just behaving because she knows that if this movie tanks, she's finished. If it hits big, the diva will be back bigtime.'

—

Dan noticed the changing dynamics by the second day of filming. Most of the scenes were close to the hotel, so it was easier to navigate in terms of security, and Raj had insisted that more crew members be involved. Dan thought there might be something to safety in numbers, plus they had been assigned a couple of bored-looking police constables to help.

They were shooting in Trafalgar Square, with Zara and Rocky pulling the usual poses that tourists did by the lions on the plinths, on the steps to the National Gallery and walking around the fountains. It was difficult for Dan to imagine how this could be of interest to any moviegoer. Raj showed him a rough cut on his phone, with the music playing. Dan liked the tune even though he couldn't understand a word, and despite the vocal tones he wasn't used to. He saw then how the shots they had done were set against the music, making it look as though Rocky and Zara were involved in a relationship across London.

He felt a stab of jealousy seeing her like that, with Rocky so close to her, touching her and sharing so much laughter with her. Even now, they were seated by the fountain, off camera, and Rocky was making her laugh.

–

'You are so bad,' Zara was saying. 'I thought you liked Minnie?'

'I'm terrified of her; she uses her pussy like a bear trap. She's crazy, seriously.'

'You'd better be careful then, she can't stand me. When she finds out we spent two days filming, it will make her livid.'

'She twisted my balls when she caught me in bed with another woman. And stuck a stiletto up my ass.'

Zara burst out laughing in shock and surprise.

'She really is crazy.'

'You know what would really annoy her? If I took you to dinner. What do you think?'

Zara didn't know why, but she looked over at Dan, who was watching them both. This was nonsense. Dan had been so standoffish for the last two days, why was she even thinking about him? She was single, Rocky wasn't bad looking, so why shouldn't she? Especially given how she imagined Minnie would react. There was no way she would ever fall for someone like Rocky, though, he seemed to have a bedroom rota.

'I'd love to. Shall we go tomorrow night?'

'Great. I'll take you to my favourite French bistro, and then we are going to Naked.'

'That's being presumptuous, isn't it?'

'We're not getting naked, we're going to the club. It's the hottest place in London, even the VIP room has a VIP section it's so full of celebs and royalty. It's on the King's Road, trust me, you will love it.'

'Can't wait.'

'And well, anytime you want to get naked, I'm not going to say no.'

Zara laughed, admiring the sheer front and cockiness of the young man. And why not lap up the compliments of a man in his sexual prime? There was nothing wrong in that. She wouldn't cross a line with him though. No, she didn't want to settle down long term with a billionaire's son. She wanted a stable long term future with someone. Dan came to mind again, and she thought she saw irritation on his face. Maybe she was just imagining it. She hoped for some reason she wasn't.

Chapter Fourteen

Jackie had sense enough of Raj by now to understand when something was about to break. They were in their hotel suite, Jackie on the lounge sofa, flicking through *The Economist*. It was trailing an article on the super-rich of Asia, about how the Chinese and Indians were now more powerful economically in terms of individual wealth than America. Jackie scoffed at the idea, having seen it all first hand. Sure, you had more millionaires and billionaires than ever, but the sheer level of poverty she faced in India and on her trips to China, you rarely got that in America and Western Europe. Even trailer-park trash like her sister lived like royalty compared to the slum kids she tried to help through her foundation work.

Raj was flitting around the suite, on his phone, arranging details for the next day's shoot. He wouldn't look at her, and he had been silent since he had come back. The previous night she had been asleep by the time Raj returned and found him sleeping on the sofa in the morning. Jackie had started drinking too early, and she was knocked out so didn't hear him come in. She really needed to cut back. Even now she was craving a drink, but wanted a clear head while speaking to Raj. Despite what everyone said, she was not an alkie. She knew she drank too much, and that was the sign that she was in control, right?

Raj's moods always had a pattern to them. He would not say much to her, act sullen. Then the WhatsApp messages would start, an absolute tirade. She preferred those, because he got his poison out of himself, so by the time they met he was almost back to normal. When he had her on communication silence, like the last two days, she knew the argument would be face to face and it would be ugly and personal. Fuck it, she thought, and headed to the side cabinet to pour herself a gin. She swallowed it too quickly, and choked, some of it pouring down her chin.

'Classy,' she muttered to herself, wiping it away with her Hermes sleeve, another free gift. Raj carried on ignoring her, shouting into his phone, so she poured herself another one and sat back down. She flicked through her magazine, but the words were blurred as she waited.

'That's right, get drunk as usual,' he muttered. It was his signal that the argument had begun. Jackie waited to see what this would be about. 'What did you do today? Who were you with? Let me guess, that guy from the bar, right? He's right up your street, isn't he? All model good looks.'

Jackie felt like smacking her palm to her forehead, not this again.

'I just spent two days with that EZ joker. Maybe you should hit on him, he's got a six-pack like your exes as well.'

Jackie counted inside her head, therapy techniques via Google.

'I don't know why you're even with me.'

'Probably for the great sex.' Jackie couldn't help herself; the second glass of neat gin she had drained was doing its job of loosening her tongue. She felt idiotic as soon as she had said it. She needed Raj on side tonight, she needed him to attend the clinic. Dr Madhu had called and reminded her that afternoon.

'What the hell does that mean? Go on, say it, why don't you? I bet none of your exes had a fucking problem getting it up, did they? How did it feel with them? I bet you did fucking bedroom gymnastics with each other.'

'For God's sake, Raj, why is it an issue?'

Jackie felt tears burning her eyes as the same old arguments came at her. Raj and his insane jealousy about her past, about her exes. She didn't understand it, Raj had plenty of experience before her. She knew this was all related to his inability to have sex with her. When they had met in New York, it had all been great, and even in the early days in Mumbai it was good. But just a couple of months into the marriage, the problems had started in the bedroom. Raj had been unable to sustain his hardness during sex, and couldn't come inside her. She didn't berate him for it, in fact she tried to support him, knowing it was probably a temporary thing. Only as time went on, Raj's inability to fuck her had led to an insane jealousy of every man she had been with or even spoken to.

'Raj, please. I can't keep doing this.'

'Then leave me. Go and fuck bar guy. He's just the way you like them. Do you even understand what I feel like around you all the time? Every time I see a guy with a good body I immediately think of you and your exes. Every time you call me baby or tell me you love me, I remember those very words you wrote to others on your fucking Facebook and I think how empty your words are to me. You say I love you like it means nothing; you've said the same thing to boyfriend after boyfriend. So what am I? Just another guy you say it to? And then what? You will find someone else to say the same things to?'

Jackie felt the tears crawl down her cheeks now. She looked at this man, the man she loved most in the world, and she hated what he was doing to her and to himself. The hurt he was causing her, and the distress he was in, caused a physical pain she could feel.

'What do you want me to say? I did everything you asked me to. I deleted every picture of my ex boyfriends, I tore up every card, and letter. I don't keep in touch with any of them. I've written you more social media posts saying how I feel about you than any of them. We've been together longer than I was with any of them. I love you, Raj, it's you I want to be with for the rest of my life. But not like this. Tell me, what can I do?'

'You could not whore yourself to any random stranger you meet in the hotel bar, for a start.'

'We were talking, Raj, that's all.'

'Talking, is that what you call it? Why don't we *talk* any more?'

Jackie jumped off the couch and poured herself another gin. She had tried to make love to Raj on numerous occasions, always instigating it. He responded usually, but even though he could fuck her, he couldn't come and she felt the humiliation of him becoming limp while his dick was still inside her. The only way he could come was by wanking himself off. Who he was imagining while doing that she had no clue. Maybe that's why she was so pissed off about his obsession with Zara Das and making this big budget relaunch for her.

Jackie swallowed big gulps of the gin, as Raj started to pace behind her.

'I can't stand this anymore, Jackie. I can't cope.'

'I love you, isn't that enough?' Her voice was measured as she spoke to him.

'I wish it was, but it isn't. It's not my fault you were such a whore before you met me.'

'Yes, I apologise I slept with so many men before you, Raj. Maybe the issue is that you wish you had, instead.'

He threw his phone across the room, storming into the bedroom as it smashed into the drinks cabinet. Jackie sat down calmly, drinking her gin, her tears falling freely as she silently sobbed.

–

It felt clandestine, secretive, as though she was on a date. Sasha's heart was hammering her ribcage, and she felt adrenaline rush through her as she made her way to the Café Paris, situated on the roof of the hotel. It was split into two halves; one a bar with rooftop views across London and the other a more low-key café. In the midst of the July heatwave, the doors were open onto the terrace, allowing the scant breeze to flow through. Sasha looked around and saw Emel Walid seated in a corner table, a phone to her ear and a tablet in front of her, as she typed and talked. As usual, Emel's make-up was subtle but flawless, and she was dressed in a burgundy Chanel suit, her hair pulled back smoothly.

Sasha felt over-casual, wearing a pashmina shawl over her Sonia Rykiel dress, her feet in mirrored slippers she had picked up from Fashion Street in Mumbai.

Emel caught her eye and smiled, nodding her head to gesture Sasha into the seat opposite her. About to sit down, Sasha felt the seat pulled back for her as a waiter appeared to help her. He looked like an out of work actor, as did most of the Mirage staff.

'I took the liberty of ordering us some food,' Emel said in her exotically accented English. Most of the women around Sasha in Mumbai had faux American accents, apart from old school actresses like Laila and Rani who seemed to emulate the queen of England. 'I thought it would distract from our conversation and you did say you were short on time.'

'Thank you, I appreciate the kindness. I have to say, I was surprised to hear from you, and wasn't sure what you wanted from me. To be honest, most people usually want my husband. They see me as the easy way in as he's always too busy to be approached directly.' Sasha blushed at the candid words coming from her mouth. She barely knew Emel and here she was using her as a therapist. The waiter brought them cocktails, brightly coloured in oranges and reds. Emel clinked glasses with Sasha.

'I don't drink but I ordered you one with a kick,' Emel said.

'Thank you, I don't really drink myself. Since the children especially. It's always such a PR incident when I do. Imran's Muslim, and the media pick up on it and make an issue out of it.'

'Did you convert?' Emel asked, her glossy lips pouting as she drank.

'Nominally. I did for the ceremony, for his mother. We don't really let it interfere in our lives. I believe in the gods I grew up with, he believes in his own. Although, I don't know, I think I'm more spiritual than anything.'

'And the children?'

'We bring them up with both faiths. That's the plan, they are only four at the moment, though.'

Emel looked concerned for an instant, then relaxed as the waiter unfolded linen napkins into their laps and put down plates of lobster thermidor, the lobster claw sticking out of the top, a fine drizzle of oil around the plate. Sasha hadn't eaten properly all day, the heat had been too prickly, different from the heat she was used to in Mumbai. Now she felt famished and started to eat with relish.

'Delicious,' she said after the first mouthful.

'It's a speciality here, I thought you might appreciate it.'

They ate in silence for a few moments, Sasha still unsure why she was there. Had her earlier tirade put Emel off asking about a favour she needed from her husband?

'Are the children with you?' Emel asked.

'No, they are back home with their grandmother and the two nannies we hired.'

'They will survive a month without you?'

'Yes, I hope. There have been some emotional Facetime tantrums, but generally they seem to be having a great time. Probably being spoilt by Imran's mother.'

'It must be difficult leaving them behind? Apologies, I don't intend to judge you.' Sasha felt pretty judged as Emel looked at her; why should she have to defend herself? Did anyone ever ask Imran where his kids were when he went on his outdoor shoots, when he spent twenty-hours a day filming, or editing or generally being a star?

'My children are more important to me than anything, I wouldn't be here if I thought it was a problem and affecting them negatively.'

'I didn't mean anything by it. You see, Sasha, actually I just wanted to be sure that you were ok about it.'

'Why wouldn't I be? And not to be rude, Emel, but I don't see how this is any of your business.'

Emel smiled at her, hoping to defuse Sasha's anger, no doubt. Sasha took a gulp of the cocktail to remove the slick creamy taste in her mouth and to steady her nerves. It was an odd choice to serve the fruity mix with the sophisticated food. She let herself relax, and faced Emel squarely. Sasha knew that part of the reason for her instant anger was her own guilt at leaving her children behind. She felt like she was missing part of her, the most important part. She knew she cared for them more than she did for Imran. Still she had given in to him, putting him before them. And then she knew what was really driving her guilt; it was the fact that she was actually enjoying the break away from her parenting duties. She bit her lip, feeling awful for having that thought.

'I would like to make it my business,' said Emel carefully. Sasha didn't understand what she was saying, or where this conversation was going. 'I heard what was said at Penny Kapoor's lunch, about you being a scriptwriter and producer. It intrigued me. Superstar Imran Khan's wife wants to make movies, and yet she doesn't. I thought it would be easy for you. So I came up with my own assumptions and thought maybe the problem was *because* you are superstar Imran Khan's wife.' Emel arched an eyebrow subtly.

'You are an astute observer,' Sasha admitted after a pause. She still felt under attack though and still didn't understand what Emel's interest in her private world was.

'Indeed. Can I ask, when you all met me at James Kapoor's soirée, what did you all think of me? Honestly?'

'That you were intelligent, articulate, a very interesting woman.'

'A slut, hired by my father for the evening? The colour rising to your face is answer enough, but it is a common misconception. You see, Sasha, my father, and I do love him, is… how they say? Yes, my father is a dick. He is old school from

178

a lost generation. He is ignorant, and was brought up with tribal values in a way, with nothing to occupy him and all the money oil can bring. His generation, they gambled, whored, and partied their way through life and the world, and lived up to the closed cliché of what it means to be a Gulf Arab with wealth.' Emel stopped as the waiter came back to clear their plates and bring them dessert. A citrus sorbet.

'It is difficult to fight tradition,' Sasha meekly countered. 'I know how difficult it was for myself and Imran. If he hadn't become who he was, I dread to think of the half existence I would have faced.'

'Tradition is powerful, I agree. My father was not following any tradition, though, apart from trying to emulate the worst playboys in the West.'

Sasha thought it was ironic that Emel was talking about her father and the West's playboys, when she could clearly see a table with a couple of Russian oligarchs she recognised plying women who did not look like their wives with Moët. Sasha wondered what stunning women like that wanted from life. They surely wanted to be more than a man's shadow or plaything? She had the dream these women were craving. The designer dresses, the diamonds, the champagne, the flash cars. It all lost its allure after a while.

'Still, this isn't a session to bash my father,' Emel said, cutting into her thoughts. 'He has lived his life how he wishes to. This is about the future. My future, my brother's future, and the future of my nation.'

'And what does that future entail?'

'You see, my brother and me, we are a new generation of Emiratis. We are educated, we are travelled, we don't believe in excess for the sake of showing off.'

Sasha didn't comment on the Buccellati diamond and ruby cuff bracelets Emel was wearing. Maybe when your worth was in oil billions, bracelets that cost a hundred thousand were nothing. Emel absent-mindedly twisted them as she spoke.

'We want to invest in our nation, to build strong foundations under the magnificent towers the world sees. I want to educate my people, put in infrastructure and bureaucracy that is the envy of the world. I want to inspire a generation, and generations to come. And most of all, I want the world to see that we have changed.'

Sasha loved the zeal in Emel's eyes, the belief in what she was saying. She didn't comment on how it was the bondage of her own countrymen, working for next to nothing, and in horrendous conditions that had built the gleaming towers Emel was so proud of.

'And, Sasha, I want you to help me tell the world what the future for my nation is.'

'Me? How?'

'You are a film producer, a script writer?'

Sasha nodded, as realisation finally dawned on her. She felt her insides squeeze, and anticipation flow like bubbles through her. 'I want to finance your movie, Sasha. I want you to make the movie of your dreams. And in return, I want you to show-case my country and show it off to the world. I want you to help me inspire a generation. Mine is the most populated Emirate, and the least well known. We are lost in the shadow of Dubai, Sharjah, and Abu Dhabi, and our oil reserves will run out. I want to make my nation the film capital of the region, set up a production house and studios that will be the envy of the world.'

Sasha let the words sink in, barely able to believe that her dream was a step closer to reality.

–

Jackie switched off the air con and lay on the sofa in the hotel suite. She knew she and Raj would sleep separately again, so she parked the gin bottle near her and closed her eyes, hoping it would kick in.

The initial weeks and months of their relationship had been full of passion; they hadn't been able to keep their hands off each other. They would make love whenever they got the chance. Raj was like a randy teenager experiencing his first time, even making her leave the table at the Russian Tea Room so they could fuck in the bathroom.

It was in those heady first days that she had told him about her past, about her lovers, and Raj too had told her about the women he had dated when he was younger. They had shared Facebook posts and pictures of each other's exes, laughing drunkenly, and rating them out of ten, telling each other how crap they were in every sense. It was true Raj had dated the way high school students would, whereas Jackie had been in long term serious relationships, but still, he hadn't seemed to care.

Only then he had developed his erection issues, and an unhealthy obsessive jealousy. The Facebook pictures she had shown Raj came back to haunt her as he quoted comments she had made back to her in bitterness. Jackie didn't understand it, shocked by his outbursts at first, then devastated. And she didn't understand how he could be so jealous of the dickheads she had dated. They had been fun, sure, and yes, some were beautiful, but so what? They had treated her like trash in the end, cheating on her and denting her confidence so severely she hadn't thought she would trust a man ever again. Was that what Raj was jealous over? Men who had the morals of a slug? They weren't worth even the paper Raj would use to wipe his ass – if he wasn't Indian, as they did the whole bidet stuff.

And to confound issues, when she had found the one man who had finally undone the damage her exes had inflicted on her, not only was he struggling to get it up, but she then found out she wouldn't be able to have children, her body physically unable to bring them to term. Jackie had thought that was it, that she and Raj were on some doomed war march, and that eventually they would have to face the enemy and their relationship would come to an end. That was until she found out there might be a way she could have a child with Raj, a child that would be as close to her biologically as possible. A child that would hopefully bring them together. Jackie had reached out to her sister, and she had agreed – at a very high price – to give Jackie some of her eggs to try to create a child with Raj's sperm that could then be carried by a surrogate. They needed this, she thought, it was the only way to fix this marriage.

Although the way she was feeling now, she didn't know if bringing a baby into this disaster zone was such a good idea.

–

Excitement coursed through Sasha as she made her way back to her suite. Imran was sprawled on their couch, barefoot and in jeans only. His skin was taut over his abs and his biceps, the definition clear all over him. Sasha felt herself wanting to touch the small down of hair that went from his belly button and disappeared into his jeans. The elation of her meeting with Emel seemed to have woken her libido too.

'That's bullshit, Fernandes, I'm here shooting for a movie. What do they expect?' Imran bellowed into the phone clasped to his ear while rolling his dark eyes at Sasha. Fernandes was Imran's secretary and manager, and it was his team that had helped manage Imran's day to day professional life for years. Like most star-secretary relationships, Fernandes had started off small with wannabes, but as Imran's star had risen, so had his.

Imran's hair was damp and flopping over his face and he was freshly shaved, his facial hair trimmed and neat. Sasha sat down on the couch and started to massage his feet. He loved the sensation of her fingers rubbing against his arches, and almost instantly she saw his jeans stir.

'So? I'm not beholden to them forever. I don't give a shit, dude. You tell them they can pay an appearance fee if they're that desperate, but I'm not handing out freebies. Why do *desis* think they own you and always want something for nothing?'

Imran ended the call and pushed his smartphone across the coffee table, while undoing his belt.

'Problem?' Sasha asked, still moving her hands against Imran's feet.

'No,' he said, moaning. 'Fernandes trying to get me to do an appearance at an Indian restaurant in East London somewhere. Apparently, they sponsored the PR for one of my earlier films, and now want me to do a free appearance. It's so difficult focusing when all this stuff is going on, you know? Today I wasn't needed for filming so thought I could just chill. Instead what happens? Wardrobe called me for fittings, they said I've put on muscle so some of the fitted shirts are too tight around the chest and shoulders. Then I had five interviews with British papers, another eight interviews for magazines back home. I then had to read the answers Fernando wrote for loads of online blogs, and do a Facetime interview with Miss X, that nasty piece of work.'

Miss X, despite her gutter journalism, was a fan of Imran's, so had been relatively kind to him over the years.

'It comes with the territory, *jaan*, you always tell me that. Relax, we have the evening to ourselves.'

Sasha moved her hands up Imran's legs, his erection now straining painfully against his jeans. He opened his button and unzipped his fly, pushing them down to his thighs. In his red boxers, she could see his hardness clearly now, and felt herself react. She wanted it inside her. Sasha was amazed at the reactions taking place in her body. It seemed something had been released during her meeting with Emel. Her dreams were within reach, and it was making Sasha feel alive.

She undressed herself quickly, and straddled Imran, kissing him deeply as he played with her nipples, enlarging them, sending electricity through her body. She rubbed herself against him, and couldn't help vocalise the pleasure she was feeling when his fingers found her clitoris. Sasha wanted him so badly right then, she pulled down his boxers, and guided him into her, riding him in a way she hadn't for years. She felt every stroke deep inside herself, her body and soul moving to make love to this man who she loved. This man who even now was looking at her with the same undisguised lust and passion as he had when he had turned up aged eighteen to whisk her away. He never seemed to tire of her, and as he sucked on her breast, Sasha felt herself trembling as she came for the first time in too long. Imran sensed her orgasm, and fucked her harder, turned on by the effect he was finally having on his wife, his mouth finding hers. Imran pushed her back on the couch, his hands cupping her rear, as he moved with her rhythm. As Sasha came again, she felt Imran tense and shout out her name as he did too, falling on top of her and kissing her as they both felt their hearts battering their ribcages.

Chapter Fifteen

Dinner had been awkward for Zara, not so much because of the food or ambience, she loved the French bistro in Marylebone Rocky had chosen, more because of Dan. He had insisted on occupying a bar stool, his eyes on her all evening, while he checked out the other diners and anyone that might be a threat outside. Zara noticed the crowd was white, and probably didn't have a clue who she and Rocky were; it was an evening of anonymity ruined by the presence of burly Dan drawing attention to them.

Zara was dressed in an Oscar de la Renta sea-coloured sparkling dress, which accentuated her green eyes. The cut was figure-hugging, long enough for a classy dinner but short enough to be sexy for the club later. She would use the bathroom after dinner to put glitter in her hair, and sharpen her make-up so it withstood the dim lighting of Naked.

Rocky was dressed in an Armani leather jacket and Boss jeans, his hair slicked back revealing the angles of his face and his dark eyes, with their almost girlish lashes, and full mouth. He looked good, in that well-groomed no cares in the world rich boy way, with the confident swagger that was the result of a lifetime of privilege. He was surprisingly normal though, relatively. When the wine was brought to the table, he was very adult about it, tasting it first and then approving it to be poured into their empty glasses.

'Cheers,' Zara said, but he wasn't having any of that.

He linked arms with her and said, 'Salut,' before locking eyes deeply on hers. 'To prevent seven years of bad sex,' he said with

185

a wink, releasing her arm. Zara caught the look on Dan's face as she relaxed back into her chair. He seemed to be annoyed, which irritated her. Who did he think he was, judging her? He was only her bodyguard for crying out loud. Zara tried to dismiss him and thoughts of him and focused in on Rocky instead.

'You're stunning in real life,' he said suddenly. 'Even more than on-screen and in magazines.'

'Thank you,' Zara said without emotion. She was used to the compliments. She wanted to tell people just how many hours a day she spent in the gym, having facial treatments, watching what she ate and drank, the supplements she took, the fillers, and Botox she used on days she didn't quite look fresh and the sheer effort she took to look after every inch of her body from her luxurious black hair to her pedicured toenails. So when people told her she looked good it was vindication not of any freak of nature, but of the sheer hours of hard work it took her to maintain herself. 'You're not so bad yourself,' she said graciously.

'Better looking than Imran Khan?'

'Of course, but don't tell him that. Fragile ego, easily bruised. You know how these actors are.' Zara had barely taken a few sips of her wine, she couldn't be so open. She had seen the selfies and phone pictures and social media posts of their shoot and their social trips already. The same had happened to Rocky and Zara when they did their outdoor shoots. Damn the phone camera, it had destroyed privacy, but also excitement. Zara wanted her female fans to see her carefully chosen outfits on-screen, to see the look she had created for this movie amplified. She wanted to be unattainable, someone they aspired to be, so they bought her products and watched her YouTube tutorials on how to recreate her look. Candid shots of her in everyday situations while filming, or chugging a coffee between takes, made her all too human.

Beyond that though, was the fact that Zara wanted to shield herself. She didn't want to let anyone into her inner self, or get so close they could see the hurt she was carrying. She didn't want them to know the sense of loss for Dev that made her feel like half a person all the time, or even worse, see the bad choices that she had been forced to make to keep the wolf from her door. Only, she'd had to make a deal with the wolves themselves to do just that.

No more though. The time when she was at the mercy of other people was over; she was no longer in need of their help. She would not be controlled by anyone again. Except, maybe was she now dependent on Raj to save her career again? No. Zara was still in control. Nobody would know just how much.

Only Dan had been able to see beyond all of that. He had seen the vulnerable woman inside her, and he had reached out to her. She hadn't known just how much she needed him until he was there, as though she had been looking for something since the night Dev had disappeared. Someone to be by her side the way he had when the world turned on her.

Rocky winked at her, pulling her back into the restaurant, into the luxurious fittings and sensual lighting.

'Every man in this place is staring at us,' he said lasciviously.

'I think you'll find they're staring at me. Even the gay ones.' She winked at him, he smirked at her.

'What's it like being you? Knowing everyone wants you? Do you ever just want to be invisible?'

'All the time. And then I stand on my terrace and look out at the view of the sea, and remember how lucky I am, how much the gods have blessed me and I remind myself it's a price worth paying. How are things with you and Minnie now? Has she assaulted you again?'

'No, haven't been near her. She seems to have gotten the message, she hasn't been calling or knocking on my door of late. She's probably found someone else.'

'Really? She's like a succubus.'

'You have no idea.' Rocky smirked again.

'I think I can guess. I suppose if I ever had children they would end up like her. It must be difficult growing up in the limelight, there can't be any normality.'

'I don't know. Ajay and Rani Kumar managed it. Their kids stayed away from the movie business, all seem to be normal. Minnie's crazy on a whole other level.'

'We're all a bit crazy,' Zara said knowingly. 'Some of us just hide it really well.'

The waiter arrived with their starters. Zara had ordered asparagus drenched in honey and mustard seeds while Rocky had gone for bruschetta with tomatoes and rocket. Rocky cut his bread pieces, and insisted she take one, pulling a face at the asparagus as he tasted it from her plate. Zara's eyes darted towards Dan again, he looked impassive, but as though he was trying hard to be. Zara took a large sip of her wine. She wasn't a big drinker, alcohol played havoc with her skin and figure, but tonight she felt like letting loose. Maybe it was the trauma of the crowd incident, or just everything else that had built up over the last few months. Living with the stress of death threats wasn't easy. Tonight Zara just wanted to be a woman dressed up and out with a sexy young man, having fun. Fuck Dan and his judgement.

'Have you thought about what you'll do next? After *Kismet India*?' Rocky asked.

'No, not yet. Everyone is still a little scared, I'm hoping it will all calm down by the time this movie is released. I need it to work at the box office though, that will bring everyone back. The audience is forgiving, and producers don't care as long as they can bank on me. I have a lot riding on this.'

'I'm sorry if I mess things up for you.'

'Why would you?' Zara was surprised at this rare vulnerability from Rocky.

'Come on, we both know Dad got me this film. But honestly, I want to do well, I really want this to work. You see, my mum was a huge Bollywood fan. That's what I remember most about her. Dad was always so busy building his empire, and Mum was always alone. She would watch a Hindi movie almost every day, and on special days she would let me watch. Always the black and white ones, curled up in her arms on a sofa, we would eat freshly made samosas and popcorn. I grew up watching Dilip Kumar, Raj Kapoor, Guru Dutt. They were her favourites. And Meena Kumari, Madhubala, and Nargis. You look a bit like Meena Kumari, has anyone ever told you that? Mum looked like Waheeda Rehman. She was so beautiful, but always so sad. And she would cry at those movies, and even though I was so young, maybe four or five, I knew it was Dad who the tears were for. His being away, and later I found out he was also playing away. Still, I remember the way Mum smelled, that mix of face cream with her Joy perfume, and the way she held me so close. And this, well I wanted to do this for her. I pretend she's with me on set, and she's so excited, to think her little Rocky Baba is going to be in a movie.'

Zara reached across the table and covered his hand with hers. In truth there was no sexual chemistry with Rocky, he wasn't her type and Zara was so messed up by intimacy she didn't know how to be attracted to anyone under normal circumstances. Still, she felt for this young man, who to the world was nothing more than a spoilt, rich, playboy. Yet inside he was a man yearning for a mother he had lost as a child, and a father he had lost in some senses even earlier.

'Listen, Rocky, I've seen so many actors and actresses try to make it in the last ten years. And in truth there is no reason why I made it over anyone else. Except *kismet*. So you just do your best, work as hard as you can every time, and the rest is out of your hands. Honestly, from what I've seen so far, your mother would have been so proud of you in this film.'

Rocky smiled, his eyes heavy with pain. The waiter came with their main courses, interrupting their moment. Rocky had ordered a rare steak – lamb not beef she noticed – with seasonal veg. It made Zara hungry as she delved into the rather sad side salad she was having as her main dish. They ate in relative silence and then got ready for Naked. Zara felt the anger emanating from Dan as they left the restaurant.

–

Rani and Ajay were dozing in an evening slump in front of the TV. It was a comfort thing, watching series and movies, or historical documentaries that Ajay loved so much, while eating fruit and relaxing. They had so many social commitments back in Mumbai it was always a luxury when they managed these evenings. In London Rani was hoping to make the most of them.

Ajay started to snore lightly. Rani stroked his hair and then checked her phone. Bobby had texted her to say he would be coming to the hotel as a surprise. Rani checked Ajay's face to make sure he wasn't awake and reading her messages, smiling to herself at the thought of seeing Bobby again.

There was a knock on the door. Rani started, she hoped Bobby hadn't just come to the room directly. She gently eased Ajay's head off her shoulder and placed a pillow under it. He stirred but didn't wake up.

Opening the door, Rani was surprised to see Minnie. She was dressed in a short red dress, wearing high heeled black shoes, which Rani recognised as Louboutin from the red soles, her hair piled on top of her head with enticing ringlets falling from it. Her face was made up perfectly, with red lipstick and sharp rose and gold tones on the rest of it, ruby earrings finishing it off. She looked stunning, and Rani thought how Minnie was like a poor man's version of her mother, Laila, then felt cruel for having the thought.

'Rani Aunty, really sorry for disturbing you.'

'That's ok, are you all right? Would you like to come in?'

'Yes, if you don't mind. I have a huge favour to ask of you.'

Minnie walked in confidently without a single misstep on her heels. Ajay had woken up, their voices probably waking him, rubbing his eyes and smiling genially at Minnie.

'Minnie dear, how are you?'

'Ajay*ji*, apologies for just turning up. I have a favour to ask of you both though please.'

'Of course, what can we do for you?' Ajay said, as Rani joined him on the couch.

'I need you both to come clubbing with me tonight,' she said. Rani arched an eyebrow. She wasn't expecting that.

'Clubbing isn't really our thing any more,' Rani began.

'Please, I wouldn't ask but I don't know who else I can trust. You see it's meant to be London's hottest club, and I want to go desperately. Only Mum won't go, she's a right cow sometimes. Imran and Sasha are having a date night, and Jackie and Raj aren't answering. So that just leaves you both. I don't want to go alone. Please.'

'Minnie dearest, honestly, my clubbing days are too far behind me, I really can't.' Rani was thinking of Bobby. 'You must have friends your own age you can go with, surely?'

'They all seem to be out of town for some reason. Please, Aunty, come.'

'Dearest, I really don't have the inclination,' Rani said, amused at how childish Minnie was being. It reminded her of her own daughters at that age.

'Ajay*ji*, what about you? Rani Aunty, please make him come. I need someone to look after me, and I understand if you don't want to. But Ajay*ji* will be fine there I'm sure, and having a male presence will help me in case anyone gets too fresh.'

Rani looked at Ajay, not taking it personally that Minnie had dismissed her so quickly. The fact was, Rani was definitely less of a clubbing prospect than her husband, who still managed to look suave and sexy despite the grey in his hair. The unfair advantage men seemed to have over women. They could get away with being slimy pervs at any age. Actually they could keep that. Minnie looked so earnest that Rani found herself encouraging Ajay to go as well.

'Are you sure?' he said. 'We had plans this evening.'

'Yes, to doze in front of the TV and eat fruit,' said Rani. 'We have a damsel in distress, it's classic Bollywood. She needs a hero and you are it.'

'Thank you so much, Aunty, I really appreciate it. I wish you would come too though.'

'Not tonight, dear, maybe another time,' Rani said. While Ajay got changed, she texted Bobby and told him she would meet him at his place. Yes, tonight could work out very well indeed.

–

Naked, like most celeb hangouts, was a mess. The main part of the club was full of girls in short dresses and guys in designer shirts, all vying to see and be seen by the elite that were in the other rooms. The minor celebs, reality TV stars, popstars, and YouTube stars were all in the VIP room, standing around drinking, looking sultry and taking selfies for their social media groupies. The VVIP room was further into the venue, and was more like an old man's club than a nightclub.

The décor was still stylish, all metal floors and walls with mood lighting, chandeliers instead of glitter balls, and the weirdest-shaped sofas Zara had seen. They were like modern art installations all twisted up, and she managed to perch her body on one of them. There was a private bar in the room, and a line of bouncers stopping anyone from getting in. Zara observed a number of drunk rather crassly dressed women screaming at someone they knew in the VVIP room, begging to be let in. The woman they were screaming at was all excitement and smiles, but didn't ok their entry.

'That's the most famous celeb from reality TV, only she's allowed in this room. And she loves it, keeping everyone else out. It's like marking her territory, telling them all she's the one that's on top.'

Zara nodded as Rocky explained to her what was going on, accepting another glass of Dom Perignon. She had lost count of how much she had drunk and was beginning to feel her head spin. Being so close to Rocky, she felt something buzz inside her for him. Dan was standing with the bouncers, his eyes darting around, and coming to land on Zara a lot.

'That guy in the multi-coloured Joseph technicolour dream coat, he's actually the cool face of physics. Typical isn't it, most famous Asian TV presenter, and he's all about the science. He's gay though and snorts cocaine with me on a regular basis, so all good.'

Zara smiled at the candid confession. She wasn't shocked, she'd seen enough of that behaviour on the Bollywood party and awards circuit.

'Most of these celebs are from our daily soap operas though, like your dramas. That over there is one of the royal family.'

Zara couldn't help be curious, but was disappointed by the plainness. It seemed it was the outsiders like Kate and Meghan that brought the real glamour to the British royal family. Still, it was funny to see the fair hair disappear into a bucket of champagne, surrounded by scantily clad models. Very classy.

'Listen, dickweed, in about ten seconds you are gonna regret acting like such an asshole, so just move and let me in.'

Zara looked over to see Ruby tussling with one of the giant bouncers, her body wrapped in a tight red strapless number, breasts pushed out, with matching lips.

'Someone had better let her in,' Zara told Rocky, who immediately got up and spoke to the bouncer. The man reluctantly waved Ruby in while others in the VIP room screamed to be allowed to follow.

'What the actual fuck?' said Ruby, accepting a glass of champagne from Rocky. 'I mean, I think I know how you felt at immigration now, Zee. I tell you, if I wasn't a journalist I would have decked that guy.'

'Bit extreme,' Rocky said, introducing himself.

'I know who you are, darling, we've done coke off a toilet seat together. I'm guessing you don't remember.'

'What do you do?'

'Journalist for the *Asian Eye*. This place is rife to be written about.' Rocky looked worried for a moment.

'It's ok, Rocky, Ruby is also in the movie,' Zara reassured him.

'Yeah, so you're safe. But if I see you again, I will expose your ass to the world. I bet you've got a nice ass.'

'Rubes, come on, leave him alone.' Rocky went to greet some of his friends, leaving them alone.

'You need to jump on that,' Ruby said, when he was out of earshot. 'I hear he's a legend in the bedroom, got the best tongue action in London.'

'That's ok, he's been sleeping with Minnie Chopra. I don't think… what do you call it, seconds…'

'Sloppy seconds…'

'Yes, Minnie's sloppy seconds aren't for me.'

'That Minnie is such a bitch though, and a randy little madam as well from all accounts. Rich, spoilt, and slutty. Actually she and I should be besties.'

'You try to replace me with her, Ruby and see what I do to you.'

'Chill, Zee, just joking. Where is Rocky? I need to get my A game on, and get some of that coke inside me to spice up these bubbles.'

'I don't believe it,' Zara said. 'Look who just turned up.'

Trailing Ajay Kumar on her arm, was Minnie Chopra, wearing a dress so short Zara was sure she could see her lack of underwear.

'Someone should tell her you're meant to wear the skirt not just the belt,' Ruby said.

They lay in each other's arms, feasting on the free goodies in the minibar. Imran sucked chocolate off Sasha's fingers, and she felt herself quivering inside. It wasn't going through the motions any more, she was feeling the emotions she had been bottling up inside her. Imran poured himself a still water, the health obsessed gym junkie never leaving him, while he poured Sasha a Coke Zero. He dropped salted nuts into her mouth and brought the fizzy drink in a wine glass to her lips.

'Thank you, *jaan*,' he said, stroking her hair.

'For what?'

'For saving me so many times. And for letting me love you.'

Again that conflict between gratitude and love. Did he just see her as his saviour?

When Imran was eight, his mother had fallen ill and was unable to come to work. The child Imran had come to Sasha's mother to tell her, and ask for help, saying his mother had a fever and she couldn't move. Imran was so meek, so quiet, so fragile, he looked about four rather than eight. But Sasha's mother hadn't cared, she had thrown him out of the house and told him to tell his mother that she was fired.

Sasha had watched from her bedroom as the child Imran had wandered away hopelessly, head bowed so low. He had sat by the kerbside, his face covered in tears. Cars were rushing past him, and people were jostling around him. Sasha thought he would break, and she hated her mother for being so cruel to Amma.

Sasha had acted quickly, grabbing any food she could that wouldn't be missed, and raiding the medicine cabinet. She had been thirteen at the time, hardly a child, and had packed her stolen goods in a plastic bag. She had then raided her piggy bank, and sneaked out of the house, asking one of her sisters to keep watch.

Imran had never met Sasha before and didn't understand what was happening. She grabbed his hand and hired a rikshaw.

She found Amma in a delirious state in her hovel, a room smaller than her mother's closet. Sasha made her take the tablets she had brought with her, and force fed her some food, too. She told Imran to keep giving his mother water. He had looked at her blankly, and she'd realised there wasn't any beyond the bottle she had smuggled from home. It was getting late though, and she would be missed. She told Imran she would be back the next day, and for a week she did the same routine, eventually borrowing money from her sisters to pay for the rikshaws to and from the slums.

Imran had turned up a decade later, grown-up, a man — a very attractive one at that — and told Sasha he had loved her all his life and wanted to marry her. Sasha had laughed in his face, still thinking of him as the eight-year-old she had given medicine and food to. Imran had been persuasive though, turning up outside the office where she was working as a junior writer for online content on a daily basis, until she had agreed to have lunch with him. Sasha found him funny and endearing as he slowly broke her down. He was so grown-up, with a head on his shoulders that belonged to a much older man. He wanted a future beyond what he had been assigned by his birth, and he wanted Sasha to be a part of it. He was so infectious, and in truth no one had ever loved Sasha so completely before. It was that more than anything that had led her to marry him, despite knowing the risk of her parents abandoning her if she did, a risk that proved well-founded.

That Imran loved her, she had no doubt. But beyond the love, Sasha always questioned whether he was also paying her back for when she had saved his mother's life.

Sasha put her doubts aside, letting herself enjoy the good mood between them. She felt so relaxed and was too happy to care or second guess anything. Emel had been in touch, saying she loved the script.

'Is everything ok? You seem... different,' Imran said.

'Different good?' she said, wrapping his arms around her.

'Different very good,' he smirked. 'Yesterday and today, I've noticed you really enjoying our adult time. I thought I'd put you off sex for life these last few months.'

'Oh, darling, no it's not that at all,' she reassured him, kissing the back of his hand. 'I was just tired and recovering I think, after the twins. Thank you for being patient and not leaving me.'

'I would never leave you.'

'And thank you for not cheating on me either.'

'Come on, Sasha, you know me better than that. So, what happened? Why the sudden change?'

Sasha sat up opposite Imran and held both his hands in hers. He looked so expectant, and she thought for a moment he might be thinking she was pregnant again.

'I met Emel Walid yesterday,' she said. Imran looked confused. 'Sheikh Walid's daughter. She was at James Kapoor's soirée, the pretty girl with the sheikh we all thought was his latest mistress? Anyway I met her again at Penny Kapoor's lunch, and she said she had a proposition for me.'

'She propositioned you? Sexy.'

'No, she had an offer for me. I didn't want to say, didn't know what she was after.'

'What did she say? Is she launching a fashion label and wants you to model?'

'Come on, I'm hardly a model.'

'You, Sasha Khan, are the most beautiful woman in the world for me. If I get to heaven, I will hope that you are there with me for eternity. Forget all the *hoors* on offer, I will demand to have you.'

Sasha was used to these mixed compliments from her husband. On one hand he was forsaking heaven's beauties for her, on the other he was demanding her as though she was an object and belonged to him.

'Who knows, I might get to heaven instead of you. I might ask for Aamir Khan instead.'

197

'Mean,' he said, mock-hurt displaying on his face as he fake stabbed his chest. 'Anyway, you believe in reincarnation. And for what you did for me, in the next life you are going to be born as Bill Gates. Or Kim Kardashian.'

Sasha laughed and threw a chocolate at him.

'So come on, what did the sheikh's daughter have to say?'

Sasha breathed deeply, her eyes on her husband. She actually felt as excited as she had when she told him about her pregnancy.

'She wants to finance my movie. She said Jackie mentioned at Penny Kapoor's how I had a script and wanted to produce a film, and how she thought it would be great. Her only condition is that I shoot it in in her Emirate. I can't believe it, my movie might actually happen.'

Sasha saw Imran's face change as she finished speaking. His eyes became darker, and there was a look of absolute irritation on his face, his jaw tightening.

'Isn't it great?' Sasha said, trying to enthuse him.

'Has she read the script?'

'Yes, I emailed it to her after the meeting. She said she loves it. She said she wanted to work with me, to help change the perception of her nation. To launch their film industry to rival that of Dubai and Abu Dhabi.'

'And she actually read the script? What did she say exactly? Is she thinking about it or has she committed to you?'

'She said she wants to finance my movie, but she wants it filmed in her country. That's all.'

'And that's enough for you, is it? For you to get so excited and build your fantasies around?'

'*Jaan*, I can work out the details later, but can't you see what a big deal this is? Someone finally wants to finance me.'

'Great, and what then? What do you really know about producing a movie? Have you got any experience at all? Writing scripts is easy, being a producer is fucking difficult. And that too in a country where you don't even speak the language or know anyone.'

'I'll know Emel.'

'And what does she know about films? Do they even have a film industry there? All I see is beaches, skyscrapers, and shopping malls. You haven't thought this through at all.'

'I thought you would be excited for me. I thought you could star in it, we could go to the Emirates for a few weeks while we film.'

'And dump the kids on Amma again, I suppose? I mean, your mother's not going to help, is she?'

Sasha felt winded as the poison hit her, the words like rocks coming from his mouth. What had happened to him?

'She's managing fine while we are here,' Sasha mumbled.

'And what? You think now she can raise our kids for us? Is that who we are?'

'It will only be for a few weeks. She's doing it now, isn't she, while you film this movie?'

Imran jumped off the couch, put on his boxers and jeans again. He went into the bedroom, came back with a tight T-shirt, and made for the door.

'Where are you going?'

'East London. For that fucking appearance. I'd rather do that than stay here and indulge your nonsense.'

'Nonsense? These are my dreams, *jaan*.'

'Dreams? You are living the fucking dream. Millions of women would love to be who you are. They would do anything to be my wife, and that's not enough for you?'

'I can't be those women. I need more.'

'Enough now, Sasha. You either be one of those women or it's over. Then you can do what the fuck you want.'

He left her confused and hurt, unsure of what had happened. For years he had supported her, saying she would make a great producer and that as soon as the script was right it would get made. And now when it finally was beginning to happen, he was behaving like this?

Through her tears, Sasha read the WhatsApp message that had just come through. It was from Emel.

So excited!

Sasha stared at the message. Just hours before it would have made her whole being dance with joy. Instead she was sitting naked, cold, and crying, once again feeling nothing inside.

Chapter Sixteen

Zara was in the VVIP bathroom touching up her make-up. The night was going ok, the music house/trance/world mixed to create an exotic ambience. Rocky had done his best to explain who people were, but they were all minor British celebrities, no film stars, and she was struggling to remember or be interested. It was evident that despite the price tag and exclusivity factor, Naked was all about the drugs, alcohol, and sleazy sex.

Zara took some hand tissue and blotted her lips and as she did so, Minnie walked in. She was sweating from all the dancing she was doing, dabbing at her face. She totally blanked Zara and took out some wipes for her face instead.

'You're here with Ajay?' Zara said. It was curiosity really, she wasn't bothered.

'And you're here with Rocky,' Minnie said bitterly.

'Yes, I am. He's lovely, isn't he?' Zara said, locking eyes with Minnie in the bathroom mirror. 'Although a bit damaged, must be the low-rent people he's been playing with.'

Minnie narrowed her eyes at Zara.

'Well, I suppose people with your upbringing are used to second-hand goods, aren't they?' she retorted.

'You're the one here with someone else's husband. In fact, isn't he your own mother's ex-husband? Isn't that tantamount to incest?'

'Obviously you were too poor to go to school so don't understand the concept of incest.'

'You were sent to a Swiss boarding school, weren't you? All the money on a foreign education and you still end up a cheap little tramp.'

'You're calling me a tramp? The woman who supposedly sucked every dick in Mumbai to get to the top?'

'At least I was on a mission. What's your excuse?'

'Fuck you.'

'No thanks, I know where you've been.'

Zara washed her hands and shook the water deliberately in a wide circle so it landed on Minnie's bare legs.

'You bitch!' she shrieked, as the cold water soaked her.

'Probably a strange sensation, water trickling down your legs rather than the copious amounts of come you normally expel.'

'I suppose water's a luxury for you anyway, growing up in the slum you did.'

'Check your facts, you little cow. I grew up in a house, I'm not the *Slumdog Superstar*. And guess what, I'd rather grow up the way I did and retain some dignity, than grow up in a fucking mansion and end up with none like you.'

'Dignity? The woman who couldn't even keep her clothes on in a historical epic? What class. Then again, you probably have generations of whores in your family, difficult to fight against your genes.'

'Yes because your mother is a nun, isn't she?'

'She's a messed-up bitch, but she's a fucking legend. What's your mum? A streetwalker?'

'Don't fucking bring my mother into this.'

'That's rich, since you just mentioned mine.'

'I have to mention your mother. She's the only reason you have a career. In fact no one gives a damn about you without her.'

'Don't be bitter just because I'm about to knock you off your throne.'

'You can try, many better women than you have over the years. They're all playing housewives on TV now. You should

202

check them out sometime, it will give you an inkling of what awaits you. Although actually a career in porn might be more up your well-used alley.'

Minnie laughed, loud, fake, sardonic.

'That's rich. I guess you haven't seen the latest social media headlines have you?'

'What bullshit are you spreading now?'

'I'm not the one spreading anything. You are. Your fucking legs.'

Minnie took her phone out of her purse, and within a couple of clicks, the bathroom was echoing with sounds of a man grunting. Minnie turned the phone around. It was only a five second clip, the man's face wasn't visible, neither was the woman's. But Zara recognised the woman face down, her hair open, and hanging off the bed, as the man on top of her fucked her from behind. She remembered the taste of the mattress the morning after, the damp smell, and the feeling of her tears as they covered her face. She felt the colour drain from her, and her legs begin to give way.

'This is just a trailer darling, apparently the full video is going to be available pay-per-view via a private link very soon. The headline claims it's you.'

With that Minnie walked out of the bathroom, so she missed seeing Zara's legs fold under her as she crashed to the bathroom floor.

-

Jackie was in the middle of dreams where she couldn't breathe, trapped under water by shapes resembling her ex boyfriends. She was pushing against them trying to call Raj's name, but no sound came out, and she felt her body grow limp and herself start to fall, jerking awake as her dream-self hit a rocky floor.

'I'm sorry,' Raj said, his voice catching in his throat. Jackie rubbed her eyes awake, and saw his were red, the telltale post crying look. He reached out for her hand, and despite the anger at him that was still glowing like embers in her core, she took his fingers in her own.

Raj had been ignoring her all day after their row the previous night, and now he wanted to reconcile?

'Come on, I can't sleep without you, please,' he said, not waiting for her answer, instead lifting her up from the chaise lounge, and wrapping his arms around her, walking her to the bedroom. He pulled the covers back, and laid her down, sitting on the edge of the bed. 'I hate myself for how I behave. I don't know how I can control this, *jaan*. You mean the world to me, I think I might die if you leave me.'

'Steady on, love, no one died from breaking up. We'd both be six feet under by now if they did. I'm not going anywhere, babe. I said for better or worse and until death do us part.'

'I'm sure we didn't in that civil ceremony.'

'Whatever, it's implied, ok?'

'Yes, in Christian weddings. You're Jewish, I'm Hindu.' He stroked her cheek, Jackie enjoying the sensation of his fingers caressing her skin, then pushing her hair behind her ear.

'Point is, I'm here, Raj, forever.'

'We met in New York, you need to be more cynical about love.'

'You make Bollywood movies, love always wins.'

'I'm thinking of putting a twist in *Kismet India*. Have Elizabeth and Darcy die at the end. Or maybe just Darcy. He can knock Lizzie up and leave her as a single mother. Cue sequel.'

'I love you,' she said, kissing his fingers. He reached down and kissed her forehead, then her eyes, then her cheeks and finally her lips.

'I love you more,' he said. 'And I promise you, tomorrow I'm going to deal with this, I'm going to get help.'

'Maybe wait until after you make your expensive movie?'

'No.' He was firm. 'I have to do it now. I won't hurt you any more.'

Jackie needed to tell Raj about the clinic, about her sister, about needing him to create the baby. The words folded in her mouth and then were lost, as Raj started to kiss her mouth more passionately, gently parting her lips with his tongue. Jackie responded, tasting him and running her fingers through his hair. Raj started to kiss her neck, gently, sending shivers through her. This was the bit she loved the most, the first touches, her skin sensitive to his hands, currents running through her as Raj slowly made his way through soft dry kisses from her throat to her breasts. He pulled up her kurta, bunching it on her chest, and started to kiss her breasts slowly, tracing them with his fingers as he did so. He slipped one of her nipples from her bra, and rubbed his short beard against it. Jackie's body tensed with the sheer pain/pleasure mix, as Raj gently traced the outline with his tongue. He was still seated on the edge of the bed, and Jackie traced her own fingers up his strong thigh, rubbing his crotch through his jeans, feeling the hardness inside strain against the material. Raj pushed her hands away. He didn't want to spoil it. He was aware he wouldn't be able to come, so this was all about Jackie. Raj pulled Jackie's kurta over her head, leaving her in her underwear, and slowly ran his fingers under the straps of her bra and the edges of the cups. Jackie felt herself respond to the gentle teasing before he pushed back the second cup and started to run his tongue over her other nipple. He kissed her slowly, moving down, flicking his tongue into her belly button, which tickled her. She didn't dare laugh, instead guided his head downwards. Raj kissed her mound through her Victoria's Secret underwear, and she felt sensations run through her. He slowly peeled the lace back, and she felt her insides heighten at the anticipation of what was going to happen next. Raj gently brushed his face against her, and then kissed her down there, before letting his tongue take Jackie on a journey. As Raj tasted her, biting and toying with her clitoris, using his tongue and his fingers, Jackie felt herself come, the wetness exciting Raj even more. Her body shuddered as she orgasmed three times, Raj undeterred and never tiring of using his tongue and fingers to pleasure her. After the third time, Raj took his clothes off, and held her naked, breathing softly against the side of her face. She could never kiss him after he had been down there until he had brushed his teeth at least, but this she could do.

And she felt confidence from the intimacy and what they had shared. The confidence to start at the beginning and tell Raj what she had been hiding for so many years. She didn't want to look at him, so as the words came out of her mouth, she stared at the far wall, dimly lit by the emergency lighting in the suite. She hadn't worked out how to switch it off, and Raj liked to sleep with some light.

As her story spilled out about her being adopted, about the car crash of a birth mother she had, Raj's hands simply tightened around her body, and he pulled himself closer to her. His head rested against her hair, and she felt his warm breath on her neck.

'So there you go. You actually married trailer trash pretending to be the New Jersey dream.'

Raj turned her around carefully in the bed, kissing her forehead and her mouth.

'I love you, Jackie. This changes nothing. I just wish you had trusted me enough to tell me a long time ago.'

'It's not about trust, I just pretended it wasn't real for so long. I know who my family is, who my real parents are. I had no Damascene moment where I wanted to go and find my birth family or find my roots. I'm quite happy being Jackie Newman.'

'Jackie Dillon now.'

'Yes. I'm sorry. I should have told you before. It's such a big part of my life, and I thought if I told you, it would end badly. I was terrified you wouldn't be able to accept me. No matter how I grew up, Raj, when I saw you in your element here, you don't understand how different that was. In New York you were just the amazing man I fell in love with. In Mumbai, all of a sudden I became Spielberg's wife. You grew up in this world, with the fame and the money. I felt like Cinderella; as though I would be found out and thrown out of your party.'

'Do you know how ludicrous that sounds?'

'To you, yes, but to me it was a real fear. And if I added my crazy birth family to the mix, I thought you would be the one asking me to leave. That you might be embarrassed by me.'

'I know now, and I think I have even more respect for you.'

'Even knowing everything my mother was and did?'

There was a beat of silence between them. She was thinking about how her mother's addictions may have been the reasons for her own alcohol problem, and in that moment she knew Raj was thinking the same.

'You are not her, Jackie. Just like I am not my father. We can fight our natures. Trust me, I have spent a lifetime doing just that.'

'Your father isn't so bad.'

'I spend every day trying to not be like him.'

'I love him, but if it makes you feel better, you are nothing like him. Plus, the films you make are so much classier.'

Raj leant in for a kiss, and rubbed her lips tenderly with his fingers.

'I'm sorry,' he muttered. 'For everything I put you through. And for...'

Jackie kissed him to stop him speaking.

'It doesn't matter.'

'How can you say that? Everyone has needs, how can we survive a relationship where I can't get it up long enough to do anything?'

'We've done it before, we will do it again. It's not the only thing in a marriage, and I told you, I love you. A little bit of erectile dysfunction isn't going to scare me away.'

Raj stiffened as she spoke. 'Don't mock me. I hate myself for it.'

'We need to laugh about it, make it a non-thing. I don't want you stressing out about it. I will survive. And if I get really horny, I'll buy a dildo.'

'Any excuse,' Raj said lightly.

'Sex is so cheap and available. I can get drunk and get laid in a heartbeat, anywhere. What we have, this intimacy, me and you, here and now. You can't buy that, my love. It's precious, and it's worth so much more than a quick fuck. I wish I could make you believe what I'm saying.'

Raj touched his forehead against hers, his fingers tracing her face, then moving down to her lower back, and pulling her close to him. They didn't talk about Raj's sexual problems, because he usually had bursts of self-loathing fit for any Colors or Star Plus drama. It shut down any time or space for a meaningful conversation between them, and Jackie felt he had done it on purpose since the problem had started. Despite his privilege, Raj was still a man and an Indian man at that. He wouldn't casually just discuss this with her, she knew, still she hoped he might once he saw she wanted to. His inability to get it up usually resulted in him storming into another bedroom in the mansion they shared with his parents, or going out to stay with friends. He would shout at her, blame her for her past, accuse her of phantom infidelities, anything so that she became the issue, not him.

At first Jackie had blamed herself, thinking that he just didn't fancy her any more, and couldn't even get it up enough to make love to her. In her weaker moments she had told him he would be fine when he found someone who he was actually attracted to. This had set him off even more as he accused her of wanting to leave him and of having someone else. On other occasions he had said he was leaving her. No wonder he resented her exes, he probably felt like a lesser man in comparison to them, she knew how men were; thinking their dicks defined them. She had told him repeatedly, her exes were absolute shits, or she would still be with them. It didn't seem to matter to him. Raj was fixated on the physical act of sex, and she could understand why. Still, his assurance that he would get help urgently was a positive move, and hopefully dealing with the physical issues would help him mentally as well.

Jackie felt the heat from his body against hers, and felt as though tonight was a night for confessions.

'Raj,' she began, 'there's a reason I told you all this tonight. I need to tell you something else. Please let me finish before you say anything.'

—

Ajay was engrossed in conversation with Rocky when Minnie went back to the VVIP room. She looked at the two men, so different, at opposite ends of the male spectrum. Rocky was young, built, fresh-faced, and cocky as hell. Ajay was a silver fox, with a tight body, and rugged features that age had simply enhanced. Minnie couldn't decide who was more her type. And then the answer was easy. The man that would piss off her mother the most was Ajay.

Minnie pinched the inside of her arm, and bit the inside of her mouth. It caused a reaction of tears to form in her eyes against the pain, a learned trick she had perfected as a teenager. She then pictured the day her father had left, pictured the girl in pigtails aged five sitting on the veranda steps clasping her teddy bear and crying because he had gone. Looking down on herself, Minnie felt the pain open up inside her and she began sobbing.

She walked over to Rocky and Ajay.

'Darling girl, what is the matter?' Ajay said, immediately putting his arms around her. Strong, safe arms, his fingers lingering on her shoulder.

'That bitch Zara just threw water all over me,' sobbed Minnie.

'Why?' Ajay said, wiping the tears from Minnie's face.

'She's jealous of me after that article said I'm going to dethrone her.'

'Such immaturity, shall I go and speak to her?'

'No, Ajay*ji*, please just take me home.'

Ajay wrapped his arms around Minnie and guided her to the cloakroom, then asked his security detail to arrange transport back to the hotel. Minnie put an arm delicately around Ajay's waist as she walked with him, the other hand folded around his. She leaned into him, making sure her breasts were pressed against him, and felt him lean back.

–

Rani Kumar was reeling after her meeting with Bobby. He insisted she take an Uber back to the Mirage and wanted to come with her. She said she needed some time to let her mind settle.

The taxi was making its way through the London traffic, from Bobby's flat in St John's Wood back to Charing Cross and Trafalgar Square. Rani leaned her head against the side window and closed her eyes.

She wondered if it was her fault somehow. She didn't have an issue with what had transpired, it was common enough in Bollywood. And then she wondered how Ajay would react when he found out. That was the part that worried her the most. She loved Bobby intensely, and that would never change. Ajay though, he was different. He was typical of too many men in India who held a certain attitude, and she was frightened for Bobby.

Rani's phone buzzed. It was Bobby.

'I'm coming to the hotel. I need to speak to him.'

'No, Bobby please, let me speak to him first.'

'No, I can't let you take the heat for this. I might lose my nerve. I'm in a cab right behind you. Wait for me at the entrance. Please.'

'This is a bad idea.'

'I know, but I'm feeling reckless tonight.'

Rani felt her insides tighten with apprehension. She just hoped Ajay would stay calm through this, but knew he wouldn't.

Minnie liked to think he made the first move, but she couldn't swear to it. She had been crying, so Ajay had taken her to her room, and comforted her. He had asked the butler assigned to her to bring her strong coffee, and had added whisky from the minibar, before holding the cup to her lips and making her drink. She coughed, and he rubbed her back, which was naked to his touch.

And then they had been kissing, Ajay ripping her clothes off. He was an expert at getting her undressed, he had probably had enough experience. She closed her mind off to the fact that that experience included her own mother. He didn't bother undressing himself, just pulled his erection out of his trousers, and thrust it inside her.

'I can't wait,' he said, groaning.

Minnie felt the waves come and go as Ajay inserted himself inside her then pulled out and then pushed himself in again. She was begging him to stay in, desperate for him. She didn't understand why this was turning her on so much, but knew deep down it was because this was the holy grail. As Ajay came inside her, she felt her body shudder to orgasm, turned on more than she had been in her whole life. This, she knew, was the one. The revenge fuck, the one that would kill her mother. It was how to fuck two birds with one cock and she had just done it.

–

Raj sat on the edge of the bed, his head in his hands, the room flooded with lights now. Jackie felt the chill goose her skin and pulled the sheets close to her. She felt like a fool. It was too much in one night, she should have stopped at the revelation about her family, about her crackhead whore mother, and her screwed up sister. Instead, she had taken courage from his calm reaction to all of that to tell him about Dr Madhu and the clinic and the surrogacy arrangements.

'So what, there is some slum woman back in Mumbai who knows about this? Who is going to carry Raj Dillon's baby? Are you stupid? You think something like that stays secret?'

Jackie felt stung by the return of the vitriol, so quick and so hurtful.

'It's an agency, a lot of women from America and Europe use it. The women are poor, yes, but they are supported during the pregnancy by the agency, and at the time of birth they are taken to one of the best maternity clinics in Mumbai. It's where they have the baby. The women never know whose baby it is. Nobody does, apart from the clinic's medical directors.'

'And they won't tell the press, will they?' he said sarcastically.

'They swore an oath.'

'And yet are hell bent on making money from other people's misery.'

'They give hope. The lead director went through the same thing; she had her children by surrogacy. She understands.'

'So why didn't you do all this in Mumbai? Why come to a clinic here in London?'

'Melody, my sister, she wouldn't travel there. London, she agreed to. It took a lot of research and planning on my part, and Dr Madhu liaised with Dr Deol back home. The eggs have been collected from Melody. We need your input now. And then the rest will be handled. We then just have to wait nine months. All we will know about is a financial transaction to the clinic in Mumbai every month, and then a final fee after the baby is born.'

'My input. What is that? Jerking off into a plastic cup because I can't come in my wife?'

'We've had this conversation before; it's both of us that can't conceive.'

'And what did I say to you? I don't want a family. I don't want to have children. I don't need the responsibility of fucking up someone else. I will not do to someone else what my father did to me.'

Jackie looked at his back, hairless and smooth. She wanted to run her fingers down his spine, but stayed seated where she was, scared of moving.

'I do,' she said softly. 'I think I want to prove I'm not my mother and show that I can do this. I mean, I'm the biggest feminist around, I stand by every decision a woman makes. Have children, don't have children. I always thought I wouldn't care about it, that I was happy as we were. It's just something inside me, it's making this feel so important. I really want this, Raj. Please.'

'Do you realise how fucked up this is? That you would plan all this behind my back? Finding your birth sister, bringing her here, all these conversations with doctors? You have it all planned out, don't you? Do you even need me to raise this baby? Or do I just come in a cup and then that's it, you walk off?'

Jackie moved across the bed on her knees, resting her naked body against the back of his, her arms folded around his shoulders and neck.

'This child will need its father. It needs you. I need you. I don't want to do this alone.' She didn't say that she could if it came to it, though. 'I want to give this child a stable home, the sort of home my parents gave me. It will be like paying back to the universe for my lucky break, by giving it to another human being.'

'I need some time, Jackie.'

'Ok. It's just, we will need to do this before we leave London.'

'Stop pressuring me. You know what? Why don't you just go and ask that blonde asshole from the bar for his sperm? I'm sure he'd be willing to give you a sample.'

Raj threw her arms off him and stood up.

'Where are you going?' she said, as he threw on his jeans and a jumper, heading out the door. 'Raj, please, we need to talk about this.'

'Talk about what? How you are so unhappy you need to have a child just so you can stay in this marriage? I need space.'

Jackie felt his words wind her. He had held up a mirror to her feelings, and he was right. Was she doing what too many couples had done, using children to mask the gaps between them? She loved him and she wanted to be with him. Could she do that if there wasn't a child?

Raj left her alone, her own thoughts so loud in her head she was unable to move.

–

Ajay was feeling decades younger, his hips actually thrusting with confidence as he walked back to his hotel suite. He may be hitting sixty, but he still had it. Minnie had been gagging for it, and she was even better than he had imagined. For all her screen siren reputation, Minnie's mother Laila was too in love with herself to be very giving in the bedroom. His wife Rani was old-school Indian housewife, they only ever did missionary position. After thirty years that got pretty boring, and with the kids and grandkids, sex had dried up anyway with her. Minnie though, she was dynamite. No inhibitions; she had used her tight, young body to do things to him that he had only ever fantasised about. This was the new Bollywood, the younger generation were on heat.

Ajay smelled his fingers, traces of Minnie on them, and smiled at his own moves. He had surprised himself, the daily jogging and weight sessions paying off. He had enough stamina to keep up with a twenty-three-year-old. He still had it. Fuck Imran Khan and Rocky Kapoor, Ajay Kumar was the real stud in this movie.

He still had a smile plastered over his face as he let himself into his suite, only for it to freeze. Rani was sitting on the couch in the lounge area with a young man, who had his face covered with his hands. As he removed them to reveal his chiselled features, his amber eyes, and short dark hair, Ajay thought how good he looked. A younger version of himself.

'Bobby, you rascal, why didn't you tell me you were in town?'

Ajay rushed forward and took his son in his arms, hugging him tightly. Bobby, his youngest son, lived in London and New York, working in investment banking. He hardly came to Mumbai any more, only at Diwali and Ganpati, so it was good to see him. Ajay felt guilt flush through him as he caught sight of Rani watching them, her eyes full at their display of father-son affection.

Ajay kissed Bobby on the cheek, pushing back the guilty thought that he had just been kissing Minnie with those same lips barely minutes before, and led him to the sofa.

'Where have you been?' Bobby asked, but Ajay saw there was something clouding his light eyes. He noticed the circles around them, too. The boy was obviously working too hard.

'Clubbing. That's right, the old man still has it in him. Listen, let me go and freshen up. Pour me a scotch, and one for yourself. And then we will talk properly, ok?'

Ajay hastily washed his face with the Bulgari lotion on the sink, and wiped a damp towel over as much of his skin as he could. He needed a shower really, his cock felt sticky after being in Minnie, and sweat had dried all over his body from their acrobatics. He smiled at his reflection and then felt the familiar pricks of guilt as he thought of his wife.

Back in the lounge he took a big gulp of the drink his son gave him, patting him on the back and rubbing his shoulder.

'Why didn't you tell me you were in London?'

'I wanted it to be a surprise. I told Mum, she met me earlier today.'

'I see, mother and son secrets. You two always had surprises even when you were young. How are you? How is work?'

'All good, Pops, tough but I'm doing well.'

'I can see, you look like you haven't slept in a week. What you need is a wife. We get so many proposals for you every week, you are a real eligible bachelor. I think you should tie yourself down. Look at me and your mother, look how happy we are.'

There was a silence between them as Bobby and Rani exchanged looks. She turned her eyes away and stared at the floor.

'What is it? The pair of you aren't concealing this very well. What's the issue? Bobby?'

Bobby drained his glass and steadied himself. Rani still avoided eye contact with either of them. Ajay felt light-headed, the scotch mixing with the drinks from the bar. He felt tiredness overcome him suddenly, maybe Minnie had taken too much out of him.

'Bobby? Son, are you in some sort of trouble? Is it a girl?'

'No, Pops... it's a boy.'

Ajay looked at him, not registering what he meant.

'At work? Have you made a loss or something?'

'No, Pops, work is great. What I'm trying to tell you, Pops... fuck... I'm sorry, I... Pops, I'm gay.'

Ajay looked at his son. His son who reminded him of himself. This virile young man, with the matinee idol looks and his interest in cricket and helicopters.

'Very funny. Is this a new surprise or prank you and your mother have dreamt up? Very good. Now tell me, what is wrong really?'

'Pops, I told Mum today. And I wanted to tell you too. I can't do this anymore. I feel so alone. I live my life here and in New York, and then I'm with you both and I pretend to be the typical good Indian boy. I guess I got your acting genes, and Mum's too. But I'm sick of pretending, Pops. I can't. I want to be honest about...'

Ajay didn't remember every step that led to it, or even deciding he was going to do it, but it happened. He crossed the room and slapped Bobby hard across the face.

'You listen to me. No son of Ajay Kumar is going to be a dirty little queer. I won't allow it. Do you understand? It's all this being away from Mumbai, being away from us. Your brain has been poisoned by all these Western ideas. You aren't gay. Look at you, you're tough, a man, you're not some queer fairy type. I won't hear this nonsense again.'

'Pops, it's not nonsense. This is who I am.' Bobby had tears in his eyes, his face red and smarting from the slap. Rani had also stood up and was staring at him. *This couldn't be happening*, thought Ajay. His son was not going to be gay, he would not allow people to question Ajay's blood and think it weak because he had produced some *hijra*. The scandal, it would be too much.

'Ajay, please,' Rani said, her voice pleading. 'He is our son.'

'Not if he does this. No son of mine is going to shame me like this. I'd rather he were dead.'

Bobby straightened his back and shoulders, facing him. Ajay felt like knocking him across the room. Rani came and stood between them.

'How can you behave like this? Half of Bollywood is in an open closet. Your make-up artists, your clothes designers, your backing dancers, directors, producers, co-stars. You manage to treat them with love and respect. And yet for your son it's an issue? For once think beyond your public image and think of your children. He is not a commodity. This is his choice, and we will support him.'

'Have you lost your mind? Do you know what people will say? Do you know how these perverts live their lives? Preying on innocent kids and indulging in every filth there is. I won't allow it. Not in my family.'

Ajay was bellowing now, the rage and alcohol mixing in his brain to make him crazy. And Rani was taking his son's side? Yes, there were enough gay men and women in Bollywood, and he tolerated them, the way he tolerated every kink in the creatives around him. This though, his own son?

'Preying on kids? What the actual fuck, Pops?' Bobby tried to push his mother aside, but she stood firm. 'I'm not a paedophile. Gay men aren't paedophiles any more than straight

217

men are. I'm gay, I love men. Grown men, not boys. I want to be open about who I am in a relationship with, I want to be able to marry and…'

'Relationship? You're in a relationship? I will kill him. And you. This is not happening.'

'No I'm not, but when I am, I am not going to hide it. I don't need you, Pops. I don't need your money or your name. I came to tell you because it was the right thing to do. If you don't accept it, that's not my problem.'

Ajay felt the darkness descend on him and felt like ripping Bobby apart. Instead, he left the room and headed down the corridor. Minnie opened the door within moments.

'Can I spend the night?' he said. She didn't ask any questions, letting him in, allowing her flimsy negligee to drop to the floor as she followed him into her bedroom.

Chapter Seventeen

They were in Dan's flat in North West London. Zara had changed out of her clubbing outfit into sweatpants and a shirt. Dan didn't dwell on the fact she still looked stunning, freshly showered with no make-up. She folded her legs under her on his couch, looking at ease despite the difference in accommodation from what she was used to. Dan was in his tiny kitchen, making her a hot chocolate, aware all the time of the tension that was between them.

His phone buzzed, he checked the message. Shit, he had forgotten to check in, with all the commotion and events of the evening. He had been so lost in watching Zara flirt with Rocky, trying to make sense of his confused emotions, trying to justify the feelings she was arousing in him. He was protecting her, that was all; it was his job to look out for her. There was nothing else to it. Over and over again, as each action of hers made him jealous, he was trying to lecture himself.

By the time they'd got to Naked he was feeling physically sick and was tempted to call in one of his team to look after Zara instead. He was thinking about giving up the assignment totally. And then he remembered why he needed the job so badly. The ache so real and familiar, jolting him back to reality.

He couldn't let himself feel something for this spoilt, arrogant piece of work of an actress. She was a star, and she knew it, and the way she had purposefully gone after the sales assistant in Tristan's, he couldn't forget that. And yet, there was something about her. It was his job to watch her all the time and watch everyone around her. He could see in her eyes, there was a vulnerability there. She was afraid of something, but more than that, she was lonely for something. And when she had collapsed in the club, the way she lost all sense of herself in the hotel room. Dan's heart went out to her, she was so lost.

Dan hastily sent a message on his phone, thinking of the money and what it would do for him. He had to shut off how he felt about Zara, or he wouldn't be able to finish the job.

When she had collapsed in the club toilet, she had called Dan, asking him for help. He had helped her out of the bathroom, and taken her out of the club to where Rocky's Ferrari was waiting.

'He's still inside,' she had said breathlessly. 'Can you take me home? Please?'

Dan dialled one of his team and asked them to bring round a vehicle for him.

'No,' Zara insisted. 'Can we just go? Get a cab?'

Dan used his Uber app, but Zara insisted on checking who was picking up the job. She cancelled on the first few as they were all Asian, and settled for a man with an Eastern European name. When he arrived, Zara got in quickly, the cab driver blatantly eyeing her up. Dan gave him a warning look, and seeing Dan's obvious size and strength, the driver soon got back to what he was doing.

'You go Mirage?' he said, in thickly accented English.

'Yes,' Dan said.

'No,' Zara said, almost hysterical. 'Not there. I need to be normal, Dan. Just for a while. Take me home, please?'

'The hotel?'

'No, I mean your home. I can't be in that fake place tonight. Please.'

Dan felt reluctant, but Zara looked so vulnerable and lost that he decided to comply.

'Is it ok? I mean, is someone there? Will they mind?'

'I live alone,' he said, and immediately sensed her relax.

Dan and the driver argued for a couple of minutes, as Dan changed the destination of the trip, and looked out of the window in silence as London at night passed him by. Zara texted Kasim to say she wouldn't be back, so he could relax for the night, and didn't say a single word all the way to Willesden Green, where Dan was occupying a top floor one-bedroom. It was one of a number of flats in a converted house which belonged to his uncle who had relocated to Canada. Dan got a good deal on the rent as long as he vetted and kept an eye on the other tenants.

Dan didn't know how long Zara planned on staying, but he informed his team about her location. It felt less secretive when he had. Everyone knew where she was, it was no big deal. He could handle this.

–

Zara had taken a long time to undress and put on the too-big clothes Dan had given her, her hands were shaking so much. They smelled fresh, of laundry detergent, and the extra material almost felt like a blanket as she sat folded on Dan's couch. Maybe it was his military background, but the flat was immaculate. She wouldn't have expected it from a man living on his own, but there were OCD levels of neatness, she thought. Yet it was so neat it felt unlived in. Dan had been staying at the Mirage most of the time, so maybe that was it. She couldn't see any signs of a female touch, not even something casually left behind or the sort of odd piece a girlfriend would leave.

Zara felt she should cry or worry or feel something. Seeing the video had really hit her hard. She didn't though, she just felt an empty coldness. Was this it, she wondered. Was this how it ended?

Zara pulled herself up sharply and dialled VJ's phone. He didn't pick up. She tried again and again, the last few calls going straight through to voicemail. He had seen her missed calls and switched it off, no doubt. She felt even colder, realising he had sent her a clear message. There was no room for bargaining. He was playing his hand and she couldn't stop him.

Dan came in carrying her drink and set it down on a coaster on the coffee table. He had made himself a coffee. There was only one sofa, made for two, but there was a padded cushion on the floor. Dan took up position on this, cross-legged.

Zara stared into the TV, at herself and Dan reflected back against the blank screen. She bit back the slight that he hadn't sat next to her. What was that about?

'What's with the hot chocolate fascination? I know Kasim makes it for you every night too.'

'I didn't grow up with much money, we weren't slum poor, but you can't imagine what life was like for me. I didn't know any different really, though, only when I got to Mumbai and saw how much wealth there was for some people. Then I realised exactly what I had been, how low down on the economic scale me and my family were. Yet, despite all the financial restraints, I remember my mother held on to a tin of cocoa powder that had been imported from Belgium. I still don't know where she got it from, but whenever I was ill, she would make me hot chocolate as a treat to make me feel better.'

'And now you drink it every night? Are things really that bad?'

Zara felt an emotional punch to her chest. Yes, they really were. As if the scandal of her movie wasn't enough, people were trying to kill her and now there would be the humiliation of a sex tape. Zara knew what had happened that night, and she felt disgusting for having gone along with it. It was ironic; she had done that for her break into movies because she was so desperate never to be in that situation again. It didn't make any sense. None of what she did made sense to her.

'What happened tonight? Can I ask?'

Zara considered Dan. Would coming clean help her? What could he do? No, he would judge her, just like the rest of the world.

'What do you mean?'

'Something brought you here tonight. There must be a reason you left the club in that state. It's my job to protect you, remember. Let me help you if I can.'

Zara took a sip of the drink, and burnt her mouth, wincing. Dan stood up almost instinctually and then looked awkward.

'Are you ok? Sorry, it's very hot, I should have warned you.'

'No, it's fine.'

Zara stared at him, this tall, built man with the beautiful blue eyes and the aura of comfort around him. The look of concern on his face just now, the fact he had helped her tonight. And she felt secure that she could tell him anything. Dan listened to her, still standing, his face expressionless, as with each word Zara felt her insides curl up and die of shame. She was shivering as she finished, and felt tears in her eyes. Real tears, so unexpected, and a relief, almost. She could cry without faking it after all. It had been a while.

Dan sat down next to her, still in the black trousers and white shirt of his uniform, but he had removed his shoes. Hesitantly, he put an arm around her.

'Are you sure this is real?' he said. 'You said yourself there have been fake videos before.'

Zara wiped her eyes, unable to stop the tears falling. She hated being like this, she had spent years being strong. She hated having to turn to anyone for advice or help, everyone let her down in the end. And yet, there was something about Dan, there was honesty in his eyes. Whatever else, she rarely found that in Bollywood.

'I recognise this one, the setting, the man in the video. I remember exactly when it happened and why. It's me, Dan, and I don't know what to do about it.'

'Can't you just laugh it off, say it's another fake?'

'That's just it, the man who is posting these, he may have more. A lot more. And he may be able to verify them, show a journalist that he filmed them. I don't know, I just don't want this one out there.'

'Who is posting these?'

Zara took a sip of her drink which was much cooler now, swallowing hard, both from nervousness and a need for comfort. 'VJ,' she whispered.

Dan stared into nothingness for a few seconds, his arm still around her. Zara felt his closeness and could smell him, a mixture of leather, sweat and the aftershave he wore. She had a desire to kiss him, and he caught her staring at him.

'The problem is, this isn't the past where only one copy might exist. He could have made numerous digital copies by now. What does he want from you?'

'He won't answer his phone. What he wanted was to control me for as long as I was making money for him. Only, for the last few months, I've been breaking away from him. And I think he knows I won't go back to him and this is his way of destroying me.'

Dan ran his fingers over his head, holding Zara's hand, without looking at her. 'Men like that always want something. They can always be bargained with. Leave it with me, let me deal with it. In the meantime, I think you should let Colette know, from the PR agency. Let her prepare for the shitstorm in case I can't handle this. She's good, I've seen her work with other clients I've looked after, if anyone can turn this around, she can.'

'Thank you,' Zara muttered, feeling how inadequate those words were, for what he had done. Zara had been feeling as though someone had buried her alive since Minnie had shown her the video. Dan had given her hope, no matter how flimsy it felt, she clung on to it desperately.

'No promises, but I will try,' he said simply.

He made a move to get up, but she held onto him. He locked eyes with her, and slowly she pulled him towards her, until their lips were almost touching. She wouldn't be the one to kiss him first, he had to want this. And he did.

He kissed her lips gently at first, as though he was navigating his own conscience, unsure if he should continue. Zara kissed him back harder, opening her mouth slightly as she did. Dan responded, gently pushing her back onto the couch, and lying on top of her. The bulk of his body felt good on her, as he let his tongue enter her mouth, and explore, all the while gently rocking himself on top of her. They lay there for interminable minutes, as Zara became more and more excited, her body coming up to meet his. She hadn't made love to anyone for years now. She didn't have to, and if truth be told, she had never made love to anyone. There hadn't been anyone she had let in; every man had simply used her.

This, for the first time, felt real. She wanted Dan, for all the right reasons. And he seemed to sense that this meant something, he wasn't trying to rip off her clothes or stick his dick into her. He was taking his time, stroking her face and her hair, kissing her lips, her throat. She moved his hand down to her breasts, and he gently squeezed them through the material of his own shirt. She gasped, as she pushed herself up into his cupped hands, his mouth still on hers. Slowly, he lifted his head, his eyes on hers, sending shivers through her, as he unbuttoned the shirt, just enough to reach in. There was no rush, as he enjoyed giving her pleasure, sensuous and intimate and body shattering. Zara was the one who wanted him badly; she took one of his hands and moved it between her legs. She pushed herself up and pulled down the jogger bottoms he had given her. They laughed as they caught on her ankles, but she was soon gasping again, as his long thick fingers found her clitoris, and were circling it, rubbing against her sex. She arched her back, feeling herself come under his touch.

Dan stood her up, holding her by the hand, walking her to his bedroom.

'You look hot in my shirt,' he whispered, as he stopped her taking it off.

On the bed, he carried on massaging her, kissing her, using his hands to explore every inch of her body, undoing all the tension and fear she had knotted in her. He went into his bathroom and got a bottle of baby oil, which he used to massage her between her legs, until she was writhing with pleasure.

'I need you,' she gasped, as she felt herself close to climaxing again.

Dan removed his clothes, revealing a body she had only imagined until now. He was hard and lean, his body all muscles and skin, but thick. He had hair on his pecs, and a trail down to his underwear. There were random scars on his torso, which added to his allure.

Zara giggled when he removed his underwear, showing his hardness.

'Just the reaction any man wants,' he said, smirking, confident that he didn't have any issues down there.

He gently mounted the bed, resting his hard, naked body against hers, gripping her fingers with his, and pulling her arms and hands above her head as he entered her slowly, until he was completely inside, all the time kissing her and staring into her eyes. That was the difference, she thought. All the other times the men had never looked into her eyes, too ashamed and aware of what they were doing to her, and she had rarely looked into theirs. With Dan, he moved her somewhere deep inside, telling her with every second this meant something.

He took it slowly, and then he picked up his pace, thrusting harder and harder, as Zara felt herself open up to him, physically and emotionally, wanting him so badly and letting him know she did. Zara thought her body would break she was so ready, when finally Dan shuddered to a climax, her own body reacting the same way. They both fell back, sweating, breathing heavily, and laughing.

Zara didn't think she had been happier than in that moment, as Dan held her in his arms, still inside her, kissing her gently.

–

Zara felt aches in her body, but didn't care when she woke. She felt so light inside, as though she had the answer to everything and no worries or cares at all. She rubbed her eyes in the darkness, and reached out for Dan. The bed was empty, and she sat up rigid. She checked her phone. It was 4 a.m. He must have gone to the bathroom or to make a drink. Zara stretched, feeling the pleasure in her muscles she normally got when she did a hard session at the gym, or had had a particularly rigorous ayurvedic wrap treatment or massage. She was still wearing Dan's shirt, and no underwear, feeling free and also sexy at the thought.

She got out of bed, thirsty, and padded to the door in the darkness she broke with the feeble light from her phone. She was about to exit the room when she heard Dan's voice. He was in the lounge, one of the lamps sending a shard of light into the bedroom. She looked through the slightly open bedroom door, her heart catching as she saw him sitting on the sofa, naked apart from boxers. That beautiful, muscled body, that had been all over her. She felt desire for him again, to make languorous love, as though every part of her he kissed and touched erased every bad memory of her past.

She was about to open the door when his words stopped her.

'You know I love her, she is all I think about. There are no other priorities, this job is only for her. She shouldn't worry. You shouldn't let her worry. Amy is my universe. I know mothers-in-law are supposed to be battleaxes, but I honestly believed you would be on my side, at least.'

Zara retreated carefully, not wanting him to know she had heard. Her heart dropped, and she felt sick, as she collapsed onto the edge of the bed. Her mind was full of darkness, and everything she believed about Dan disappeared in an instant. Mother-in-law? Amy? She had never asked him outright if he was single, but why would he sleep with her if he was married? *Come on, Zara, you fool*, she chided herself. *Married men do this all the time, they've done it with you. Dan's just another cock that wanted a piece of you. Grow up.*

How could she have been so naïve? Why had she let herself think for even a moment that Dan was different? She had fooled herself, thinking he wasn't awed by her star status, and he wasn't after a 'compromise' for her starring in a project of his. Yet all the time he had been protecting her, and now he had taken his pound of flesh. One made up of her heart.

She felt the tears threatening, tears that she had thought he might stop from falling ever again. She had gone to sleep thinking Dan would protect her from the world; that she no longer cared about her movies, her status or the threat from VJ. She had given her all to him so quickly, and now she felt like a hard-done-by virgin from an eighteenth-century English novel. Why would Dan be any different? Had any man she'd met been different?

Zara called herself a cab on her phone, thankfully her location tracker making it so easy now. In reality, she didn't have a clue where she was. She found the jogging bottoms he had loaned her, and some flip flops. There she was, one of the most renowned beauties in the world, looking like a dishevelled reject.

Confidently, she strode into the lounge. Dan ended his call, surprised to see her.

'Hey, gorgeous,' he said, standing up with his strong arms open and a smile on his face. *No guile or shame at all*, she thought. He was too much.

'My cab will be here in ten minutes, I just need to change.'

'What's wrong?' he asked, but she brushed past him to the bathroom and changed into her dress from the night before. She waited until the cab was nearly there before going back into the lounge. Dan was sitting on the couch, worried and unsure. 'Zara, what's happened? Last night...'

'Was great. I was really horny, and it's so difficult to find someone to screw me in London. I have a whole list of fuck-buddies back in Mumbai. Did you have fun? Sorry, my cab is here. Listen, I hope I can trust you not to do a kiss and tell on

228

me? I am Indian, it's still a bit scandalous for a woman to do this sort of stuff.'

She left him silent and aghast, probably pissed off because he'd wanted another go at her before she left. Zara sat in the back of the cab and silently cried all the way back to Mirage. She rushed through the main lobby, not making eye contact with any of the staff. She hoped they didn't alert Kasim, and he didn't end up trying to provide her with a midnight snack. She was so hurt and confused, she just needed to be alone for a few hours.

Taking the private elevator up to her room, she kept checking her phone, hoping Dan would apologise or explain or make some sort of contact. He messaged her as she was about to use her key card, asking if she got back ok. Nothing else. She noticed none of his team were in place watching her door. He must have tipped them off. *Don't worry, I'm bedding her tonight.*

Zara threw her purse and phone into the empty hotel suite, switching on the lights. She was so angry, but more than that, she was feeling devastated. Finally she had let someone in, and he had returned her affections in the worst possible way.

She was about to go to her bedroom, but froze as she caught sight of the sofa, her heart starting to hammer in her chest. She felt the hairs stand up on her arms and the back of her neck. It took her a few moments to adjust and focus on what she was seeing. And then she did, and she saw him and went cold.

He was lying on her couch, unmoving, his face contorted and a stream of blood and froth rolling down his chin. Next to him was an upturned glass, and her complimentary bottle of Zara D.

Zara screamed.

Chapter Eighteen

She couldn't breathe; his face was looming at her from all angles. It was like a mask of *The Scream*, unnatural and terrifying. Her heart was hammering at her ribcage, so hard she thought it would burst through. She was walking into her suite, again and again, and each time he was in different places. Behind the curtains, on the coffee table, in her bed. Always the same expression; stupefied in death. And the empty glass, and the bottle. Her name emblazoned across it, telling her that it was meant for her.

Zara turned to her side, hoping air would come in, but nothing did. She was drowning, the terror coursing through her. It was just like before, just like Mumbai. After the bomb, Zara had been a wreck, unable to function. It had been the thought of her driver's children that had spurred her to action then. Now it seemed nothing could move her.

And all through it, she knew one thing. That drink, it was meant for her. Whatever poison was in it, it was meant for her. Her name emblazoned across it. Zara D. Toxic.

Her phone had been ringing all night and into the afternoon, but she wasn't answering. The events of the previous night were like scenes from one of her movies, surreal and devastating. She had screamed and collapsed, unable to go near the grotesque dead body, unable to get help. Her mobile was in her hands, but they were trembling to such an extent she couldn't even enter her PIN. She only had the strength to press the emergency alarm, the one that connected her to Dan.

Within minutes, the night manager and Kasim were in her room. She didn't know until afterwards that Dan had stood down his security team for the night because she was with him, and he didn't want anyone to know she wasn't in her room at night. So chivalrous for such a betrayal.

The night manager and Kasim had sprung into action. Kasim had checked for a pulse while his boss called James Kapoor. As Zara sat staring and devastated, their plans kicked in to curtail the situation. It had to be contained, managed. Zara watched in horror as they started to speak to elite departments in the police; as James Kapoor called to say he had spoken to people of influence who would take charge. Zara looked at the dead man, his face so tortured, and wondered who was going to care about him. More than that, who was going to protect her?

The poison was meant for her; she knew it. That should have been her. Dead. Would they have cared, then? Or would they have carried on, trying to manage her death?

'Call an ambulance, do something,' she had screamed at them. Kasim had the decency to look embarrassed, but the night manager just told her it was pointless. The man was already dead.

What was he even doing in her room? How did he get in? Zara's mind was racing.

'I'm not safe,' she said. 'I'm not safe. Do you understand? That should have been me. I'm not safe.'

Dan arrived later and assessed the situation. She was paralysed with fear, and despite his betrayal, she felt a sense of relief when he took charge. He organised a different room for her, got his team back to the hotel and had the decency to cover the dead body with a sheet from her bed.

Zara had been taken into her bedroom by Kasim on Dan's orders, and she waited there until her room was ready. Kasim then walked her quickly past the covered corpse, and through the empty corridors to the new suite, which had two members of Dan's team posted outside. Still she couldn't stop shaking, her mouth dry and her head full of images of death.

She had been petrified of being left alone, so made Kasim sit with her. He gave her the sleeping tablets she had brought with her, and ordered hot chocolates for her. Eventually she had drifted off, only to be woken by screaming, realising as she did, that the screams were her own.

–

'The room should have been safe, locked down, how did anyone get in?' Dan was fuming, absolutely livid that the hotel had failed so completely. 'You assured me that nobody could make an extra key to the room. But look, your systems show an unregistered key was used to open the door. Your security is flawed.'

Gareth Jones didn't drop his guard or let his patrician attitude fall.

'We are looking into it, let's not jump to conclusions just yet. And my security team are still trying to ascertain what exactly went on. The police are now involved.'

'The police? The PDP, you mean.' Dan knew the diplomatic branch of the Met had been drafted in at the say-so of the Indian Ambassador, a friend of James Kapoor, no doubt. The PDP would be under pressure to use the same opaque techniques that all cases involving foreign diplomats did. They had already started, removing the body discreetly through the basement, using a team of only two forensic technicians. The officers in charge of the investigation asked for absolute discretion, and there were no reports of the death to the other guests or hotel staff.

Dan had the feeling that the death was going to be PR'd out of existence, all to save the billions that were propping up the Mirage.

'I will find out who did this, and when I do they will be sorry,' he shouted at the hotel manager.

The day had dawned over London, the sun crawling into the skyline out of her window, but Zara had insisted Kasim keep the blackout curtains closed. She couldn't face the world, didn't care about the film or anything. She just wanted Kasim with her, and for the outside to stay there. Away from her. So she could hide and be safe in this little space she had created.

'Would you like me to get you some food?' Kasim asked. 'Something light, maybe? Yoghurt and fruit or toast?'

She didn't answer him, and he took it as a refusal.

'I am here if you need anything, please just ask,' he said.

Zara felt as though she had been awake forever. Her dinner with Rocky, her run-in with Minnie, and the knowledge that the video would be released seemed a lifetime ago. And amid all of that fakery and the impending storm, there was Dan. Never in her life had she felt so safe or content than when lying in his arms last night. She didn't know anything about him, he didn't know anything about her. Zara felt reborn almost, as if a fresh start had been handed to her, with a man who she had come to rely on. And in the end, Dan too had betrayed her. And then she had come back to a nightmare. She had thought it was over, that the bomb was a one-off, it would never happen again. But no, someone had gotten so close to killing her again. How many chances would Zara get to live? Next time it would be over, she was sure.

Again she wondered what the man was doing there. Why was Salman Rana in her hotel suite last night, and who had poisoned the drink that had killed him?

-

Dan was asked to help the police with their enquiries. He was supposedly the name that James Kapoor had given to them, the man with the detail. Dan appraised the two officers from the

PDP, trying to work out what their orders had been from the top.

DI Natasha Mace and DS Nick Pride looked young and inexperienced, the sort of new recruits that might easily conform. Although Natasha had made Inspector, never easy for a woman, and Nick was black, so maybe he shouldn't dismiss them.

'How well did you know the deceased?' Natasha was asking.

'Not at all,' Dan said. Gareth Jones was also with them, he said the same.

'And you have no idea what he was doing here?' Natasha said. Dan shook his head. He went on to explain the entry system; that only one lift operated on the floor, which could be accessed via the ground floor or the basement. 'So someone had a key card and let Salman onto the floor and into this room.'

'That's the most likely scenario,' Dan said. 'Only the drink that killed him wasn't meant for him.'

'What do you mean?'

'That bottle was a prototype. It was especially sent to Zara Das, the actress, as a sample before its launch.'

'Are you saying that Miss Das was the intended victim?'

Dan nodded. 'It definitely seems that way.' He went on to explain the other incidents that had happened. Gareth Jones looked embarrassed when Natasha asked why they hadn't been reported to the police.

'She was the victim of an attempted bombing back in Mumbai as well,' said Nick.

'You seem to know a lot,' said Dan.

'I did a gap year in India, fell in love with Bollywood films.'

Great, Dan thought. A fan, he was really going to handle things objectively.

–

Zara was shivering when the police came to speak to her. She had dressed too quickly, throwing on a chiffon Ritu Kumar top and Balmain jeans, her feet bare. She caught the male cop looking at her, actually ogling her. She rubbed her arms under his scrutiny. The female cop seemed too pretty to be an officer. Zara wondered if she had a brain in her blonde head. Then she felt guilty – people often dismissed her too, because she was an actress.

'I barely know Salman,' Zara was saying. 'I met him only a handful of times, always while we were filming. I have no idea why he was in my room, and I don't know who let him onto the floor even. The drink, though…' She trailed off, and felt tears spring to her eyes. She didn't want to be here, speaking to these people. She wanted to be in her room, safe, with Kasim there to comfort her. Just like Dev would have done. She had even started watching movies with Kasim. Just the two of them.

'And in these interactions you had with him, what did you make of him?' said Natasha.

'Not much.'

'And so there's no reason for him to be in your room that you can think of?'

'None at all.'

'You didn't invite him?'

Zara stared at the police woman, shocked that she was being serious. She didn't reply, the look on her face enough of an answer, she hoped.

'Miss Das, I read reports about threats to your life back in Mumbai. Can you tell me more?'

'It's all online. All I can say is that those threats have followed me here. Salman was just unfortunate. He drank something that was meant for me.'

'Who wants you dead, Zara?'

'Who doesn't?' she said.

–

Imran hadn't spoken to her properly since their argument the night before. He had disappeared and only materialised at breakfast, his eyes red and his whole demeanour telling her that he hadn't slept all night. She suspected he had been drinking as well, but he wouldn't get close to her or engage her in conversation so she couldn't be sure. Heading straight for the shower, he had finally broken his silence when he got a call from the hotel manager saying there had been an incident and the police needed to speak to them both.

Sasha had started worrying that the incident might involve Imran, her mind reeling from all the things he might have done that could warrant police intervention. There were years in Imran's life that only she knew about, when he was just a slum boy trying to hustle in Mumbai. Nothing is off limits when you are trying to survive. Luckily for Imran, no one pays attention to the invisible poor, so his secrets stayed with him.

Her heart softened for a moment as she remembered how she had taught him to read properly after their marriage. Education was lower down the list than available toilets in the slums, and without the ability to read, Imran would have struggled with his scripts. He was a quick learner, super intelligent, but she had to rehearse and go over his lines constantly in his earlier movies. Even when he started to become successful, he was too embarrassed about his ignorance to seek professional help, so Sasha had stepped in. Thinking about that vulnerable young man, the vulnerable young boy, she understood why he felt so indebted to her. Only that didn't mean he could control her now and stop her from breathing.

Before the police came, he simply told her to say he was with her all night. Sasha didn't even have time to register that fact before the cops were there. She had no idea what had happened. They were interested in Zara though, asking Imran about the threats to her life.

'The explosion rocked us as an industry. We are a country used to terrorists, Mumbai itself was targeted by fundamentalists. It saddens me as a Muslim that people twist my faith in such a way,' Imran told them.

'You think the attack on Zara Das was terrorism related?' said the female officer, Natasha.

'Did it not cause terror? Of course it was. Maybe not in the sense you think. All terrorists are only terrorists if they are Muslim, correct?'

Natasha arched an eyebrow. 'I am not so ignorant.'

'Glad to hear this. I think there are people with sensitivities everywhere, and they can easily be offended and moved to action.' Imran ran his figures through his thick, glossy hair, and sat back on the sofa, stretching his arms over it. The action exposed his chest, showing the definition to his pecs and a silver chain with a silver amulet sitting against his skin. Sasha thought how vulgar he was, trying to flirt with a police officer in such a way. She still didn't know what had happened, but if it was serious enough for the police, maybe it wasn't wise to lie for Imran. But she knew she would, if asked.

'And these sensitivities, Zara has offended them? Were you offended by her film?'

'Not at all. I was amazed that both Zara and her director didn't realise what they were doing, but I have a high threshold of offence. I had to develop it. People are very passionate in my country, and you need more than a *thick skin* as you say, to cope with this. Plus me and Sasha had our own battles.'

'Oh?'

'Her family are Hindu, mine are Muslim. The marriage was hardly loved by them. And when I started to act, it seemed lots of people had an opinion on the legitimacy of the marriage. The thing is, we also received plenty of death threats. Luckily no one seriously made an effort to carry out their threats. I have always had security, we need to. Mumbai is so small, I am never far away from my well-wishers.'

'So why are the threats against Zara being carried out, do you think?'

Imran looked into the distance, rubbed at his temples. Sasha saw her husband in a light that made her skin crawl. Here he was, the consummate professional. Every act was so studied, as though he never switched off, always performing, even when being interviewed by the police. She felt the disgust bubble in her throat.

'Honestly? I think it's because she is a single woman. However far we have progressed in my country, when you have a billion and a half people, you will always have certain attitudes deep in some areas.'

Sasha bit her lip when he said this, crossing her hands in her lap, hoping these gestures would at least portray calm.

'And last night, can I ask where you both were?'

'We were here, asleep,' Imran said quickly. Sasha looked away, scared her eyes would give away his game.

'Did you hear anything unusual? Or see anything?'

'No. Can I ask what has happened? We were only told that the police needed to speak to everyone on the floor urgently this morning. I thought it might be related to Zara. Is she ok? I have called her and sent her messages, but she hasn't responded.'

'She is fine, we are just investigating an incident that happened in the early hours. And you, Mrs Khan? Did you hear or see anything last night?'

Sasha shook her head, but her whole body felt tense, still dismayed by the lies that Imran was so easily telling the police.

'Can I ask how well you both know Salman Rana?'

'I've met him a few times with Raj, and he's been on set with me. We did a couple of scenes, but nothing else. Can I ask why?'

'Just part of the investigation. And you, Mrs Khan, did you know him at all?'

Sasha shook her head again.

When the police officers left, Sasha turned on Imran and demanded answers from him.

'Where were you? I messaged you and called you so many times, but your phone was switched off. Who were you with?'

He turned eyes ablaze with fury and hurt at her.

'That's right, jump to conclusions, let the voice in your head tell you the worst! Where I was is my business. And look at you, one night away and you're questioning my whereabouts. How will you cope being away from me for so long?'

'I'll survive,' she said bitterly. 'And how dare you tell me it's none of my business? I'm your wife, I have every right to know what my husband is doing. Why did you lie to the police? And worse than that, made me lie too?'

He didn't answer her though, instead heading to the bedroom.

'I'm tired, I need to sleep. Raj has cancelled filming today.'

With that he was gone. She felt like following him into the bedroom and screaming at him, but she knew she wouldn't get a different answer. Well fine, she thought. If he can be an asshole, then so can I. She grabbed her purse and left the hotel room.

Chapter Nineteen

Alone in their room, Rani and Ajay carried on the détente they had established since the morning. Ajay had called her and told her they needed to meet the police, and met her in the lobby of their floor. Rani didn't ask him where he had spent the night, and when Ajay told her he had slept on Minnie's couch, she was nonplussed.

The police only seemed interested in Zara, and the threats to her life. Rani wondered if something had happened to her and asked Ajay to message her and to call Raj to see if there was anything they could do. Raj had sent messages to the cast cancelling shooting, but he hadn't elaborated beyond that.

Rani went to do her *puja*, hoping for divine intervention to heal the rift between her husband and son. Ajay started to read the newspapers, with CNN playing in the background. Rani emerged after her prayers, dressed casually, her hair tied back, yoga mat under her arm. She stopped by Ajay before she was about to leave.

'Are we going to discuss Bobby?'

'No.'

'So what, will you just cut him out of your life?'

'Our lives. I forbid you to see him.'

'Has that ever worked?'

'I can try, at least. Aren't you terrified for him? What sort of life has he chosen for himself? Aids, loneliness, casual sex.'

'He's not Freddie Mercury. Things are different now.'

'Just because the law is changing in India, doesn't mean attitudes have. He's a fool, living in his little bubble. The real world will not accept him. He should try going to the Asian areas of London, walk hand in hand down those high streets with his boyfriend. And if the British Asians can't accept him, how will people back home?'

'I don't care about the real world. He's my son. I want him to be happy and I will support him in this. I wish you would too.'

'If my father was still alive, my mother, what would they make of it?'

Rani knew he was right, they would barely understand it and definitely wouldn't accept it. She wasn't expecting the world to embrace Bobby, but she also knew he could live his life safely if he chose to. But he would never be happy, knowing his father had disowned him.

'Tell me, no matter what you did, all that drama with Laila, did they ever disown you? You were a national scandal. They still loved you and let you make your mistakes. Give our son that chance too.'

Ajay's face contorted in hatred and disgust.

'Oh and let me know what Minnie likes, I'll send her a gift for us inconveniencing her last night. Did she ask why you needed to stay with her?'

'No, don't worry, your son's sordid secret is safe.'

'It's not sordid, and it's not going to be a secret for long. He's done a YouTube video and is going to post on Instagram to tell the world. Please, Ajay. Support him, or it will make everything so much worse.'

Ajay was red in the face, his anger palpable as she left him. She understood what Bobby was doing, but wished he would give everyone more time to adjust before announcing it on social media. Rani knew that once he did, she would have to choose between her husband and her son.

–

Laila didn't wait until they were alone, but started her onslaught in the corridor after their police interview. The police had asked to speak to both Laila and Minnie together, and when it came to Zara, Minnie didn't hold back. She gladly told them that Zara was a narcissistic egomaniac, and capable of anything. Laila had been kinder in her estimation, but the shock revelation was what Minnie had told them. When asked where they both were the previous night, Laila had been honest enough and told them.

'I was alone in my room asleep. So whatever incident took place I can't help you I'm afraid. I sleep with ear plugs and an oxygen face mask, so I wouldn't hear, anyway.'

'Oxygen? As if. It's bolts of electricity shocking the skin all night,' Minnie had added. 'I don't need that shit.'

'Yet,' Laila had said, still smiling, but her eyes were showing her irritation.

'As for me, well, I was in my room too. I wasn't alone though.' Minnie had looked directly at her mother as she said the next words. 'Ajay Kumar spent the night with me, so he can vouch for my whereabouts.'

Laila was unable to keep her composure at the revelation, her face betraying her feelings clearly. Once in the corridor alone, Laila's anger escaped the dam she had been building for years to stem her growing resentment against her daughter.

'You pathetic little girl, what exactly was Ajay doing in your room last night?'

'None of your business. He needed a place to stay and so I gave him one.'

'Why you?'

'What's wrong? Jealous? Did you think he might be pining after your decaying body still? Maybe he can't stand the smell of formaldehyde. The one you use to preserve your carcass.'

'Do not speak to me like that, I am your mother.'

'You are a selfish cow, you wouldn't know what it means to be a mother if the manual whacked you in the face.'

'You think it's easy raising someone as difficult as you? I did my best.'

'Your best? Driving my father away? Not touching me when I hurt myself in case your make-up or nails got ruined? Leaving me to the hired help? Those illiterate maids you had were more maternal than you. Thinking that the latest fashion accessory or tablet or phone or piece of jewellery would make up for everything. You are deluded.'

'Your father left for his own reasons. That had nothing to do with me. He isn't this saintly figure you've imagined, he only married me for my money and fame, and when that wasn't enough, he left us. What was I supposed to do then? I was a single mother. I had to work bloody hard to keep afloat. The money you spend like water, it took my blood, sweat, and tears to give you.'

'Bullshit. You are the shrewdest bitch in Bollywood. I know all about your property investments, you never had to work so much. You chose to keep going after you forced my father to leave because you are like a vampire. You crave the fame like blood.'

'Your father left me for another woman, an industrialist's spoilt little daughter. Another fool who would pay his bills for him. Do you ever wonder why he doesn't keep in touch? Because he had his own children with the harlot he ran off with. She refuses to let him near us. Yes, that's the truth I've shielded you from all these years.'

Minnie felt shocked at the revelations from her mother. It wasn't true, it couldn't be. She had spent her life thinking her father had been scared off by her mother's lawyers, forced to stay away and make no contact. That he was probably living a normal life somewhere, thinking about his daughter. She used social media so much partly because she was hoping he was watching, that she was sharing her life with her father. That he would get in touch. No, Laila was lying. It wasn't true.

'You're a liar, I don't believe you, you evil bitch. And who are you, calling someone else a harlot? Pot and fucking kettle, Mother. You gross me out.'

'Then go and live with your father if you really want to. See if he and his wife welcome you with open arms. Although he's hardly wanted you back all these years, so why would he now?'

'He only stays away because you were such a massive whore he probably can't even be sure I'm his.'

Laila raised her hand to slap Minnie, but Minnie caught her mother's wrist in time and stopped the slap mid-flow.

'No, you don't. When we get back to Mumbai I am moving out and I never want anything to do with you for the rest of my life.'

'Good, well don't, finally you're standing on your own two feet instead of living off my hard work. And I'd like to see how well you do when you are no longer trading under my name, when I am no longer calling in favours so people cast you in their movies.'

'I don't need you,' Minnie said. 'By the way, Mother, you didn't tell me just how good Ajay is in bed. That's right, I fucked him all night. And you know what? It wasn't the first time.'

'You spiteful little madam, I don't believe a word you say.'

'Oh really? Well I'm sure you remember how he likes his balls squeezed when he's about to come. And I'm sure you remember the black beauty mark on his cock. Now tell me I'm making that up, too.'

Minnie watched in satisfied joy as Laila reacted just as she had hoped she would. Her face drained of colour, her mouth open in absolute shock, her eyes wide as though Minnie had just slapped her. There was pain written all over her features, as she clutched her stomach, as though winded. Minnie laughed maniacally as she turned to go to her room, but then stopped short. Standing behind her, yoga mat under her arm, dressed in her casual gym gear, and a look of devastation on her face, was Rani Kumar.

Jackie opened her eyes to her phone buzzing. She was naked and stretched herself, her body aching in ways that she hadn't experienced for a while. Raj was breathing heavily next to her, and she tried to make sense of where she was. Her head pounded as soon as she raised it, and she knew she must have got drunk after their argument. In fact, she remembered going down to the hotel bar to get drunk. She couldn't remember coming back to her room or reconciling with Raj though. And then the night before hit her like a flash.

She had gone to the bar and ordered herself a number of drinks, and then… fuck. She looked over and saw it wasn't Raj lying next to her, and this wasn't her room. His eyes still closed, his blonde hair tousled, but his hard, studly torso exposed, was Ryan. Seeing him reminded her exactly what they had done.

He had bought her drinks, and she had bitched about Raj to him, telling him everything about herself. She was so angry and past it that her adoption, her birth parents, and the whole surrogacy drama had come out of her mouth. Ryan had been sympathetic, had listened. When it became late, she'd said she didn't want to go back to her room, couldn't face an argument with Raj over her drinking on top of everything else. Ryan had been gentlemanly and offered her his bed, saying he would sleep on the sofa. It wasn't a suite, it was a normal room. Jackie let him do that for about half an hour, but had woken up and found him still awake.

She remembered climbing on top of him, and encouraged by his immediate hardness, she had given way to any inhibitions the alcohol hadn't managed to remove and spent the rest of the night making love to him. She hadn't had a man inside her for so long, given Raj's problems, that she had forgotten how much she enjoyed it.

But now, the guilt was pricking her. Jackie picked up the phone that was causing hot pokers in her head from the hangover and saw it was Raj calling. That was the last thing she needed, so she switched it off. She was too tired, and not in any state to have a meaningful conversation with him.

Ryan must have been disturbed by the call, and smiled at her.

'Morning, beautiful,' he said, and came over to kiss her. She averted her face, aware of morning breath, but he didn't seem to care. Kissing her roughly, she found her legs opening for his hands, as they nimbly found her pleasure points, and felt his body on top of hers. He didn't give her much foreplay, but was inside her quickly, and once again, Jackie was taken to brinks she hadn't experienced for a long time. Caught up in the moment, she let her body take over. She could deal with the guilt much later.

—

'I have to apologise,' Raj said, after failing to reach his wife again. 'I will ask her to contact you when I can.'

The police had been trying to contact him all morning, but he had deliberately stalled meeting them, letting them interview his cast members first. He needed to speak to Jackie, to get things in order before they spoke to him. Raj appraised the two cops, the strong female lead, Natasha, and her young sidekick, Nick, who seemed to have been given the job of interviewing him.

'I'm in shock,' Raj said. 'I just spoke to him yesterday. He called me about 10 p.m. I think. He wanted to know how the schedule was shaping up, and if he could improve.'

James Kapoor had called Raj earlier, telling him what had happened. He asked for the news of Salman's death not to be shared with any of the other cast or crew, not until the police saw fit to do so.

'He didn't say he was coming to the Mirage?' Nick said.

'No, nothing. I would have met him if he was.'

'How close were you?'

'Not very, but I think he latched on to me as the other stars are a bit different to him. The Indian stars are obviously familiar with each other from Mumbai, and the British actors all know each other too. Salman felt a bit of an outsider if I'm honest, not fitting in with either camp. Yes, he's settled here now, but he's from Pakistan originally.'

'Do you know where he lives?'

'Yes, there's an address I have on my contact card for him in Stepney Green. And his agent will know more details.'

'Thank you, we will check it out. Do you have any idea who would have a motive to do this to him?'

'Not at all. I didn't know him too well, but in any case he was an actor, not a gangster. I don't know why he would be a target for anyone, really.'

'And you have no idea why he was in the hotel? Or even how he got here?'

Raj shook his head.

'If anything does come to light, please let us know.'

'I will. I shouldn't say, but luckily he's filmed all the scenes I needed from him. His swan song, how macabre, no?'

'Yes. And your whereabouts last night?'

'I wasn't even at the hotel. I had an argument with my wife, so went to stay with a friend.'

'Can we have their details to verify that please?'

'Yes of course. I was with Bharat Kumar. He's Rani and Ajay's son. We all call him Bobby, though.'

–

It was midday by the time Jackie had extricated herself from Ryan's arms. She showered in his room, not wanting to risk meeting Raj post coital. Fuck, why had she done it? She had risked everything in those moments, her marriage and her chance to have a child with Raj. She hoped he wouldn't find out and had made it clear to Ryan it was just a one-off. A desperate housewife losing the plot sort of thing.

Walking into their suite, she saw Raj on his laptop, with his phone in one hand. She took the opportunity of his distraction to rush into the bedroom and change her clothes, setting aside her bar/Ryan ones for laundry, so they could remove all traces of the previous night.

Raj came in just as she finished changing. She expected a full flow Raj in meltdown routine, but instead he held her hands and sat her down on the bed.

'I'm sorry I didn't come home last night,' he said.

Jackie didn't react. So he hadn't realised she was gone, he had simply come back and assumed she had left their suite in the morning. No wonder he was being so calm about things.

'The police were here just now. Salman Rana, the guy playing the Collins character, they found him dead in Zara's room last night.'

Jackie couldn't hide her shock.

'How did he die? Did she kill him? I mean, I always thought she was a stuck-up asshole, but a murderer?'

'No, she wasn't there. She found the body. They didn't say how he died, but James Kapoor called me this morning. His hotel manager told him it looks like poison. They're saying it's an overdose or something, already spinning this. These people remind me never to get into bed with billionaire scum again.'

Jackie avoided his eyes at the mention of beds and who you shared them with. She felt sick as she thought of last night. The police would probably want to know where she was.

'The police and James asked this not to be shared with any of the others. So please, don't tell Sasha.'

'Of course. What was he doing in Zara's room?'

'Nobody seems to know. They can't even work out who let him onto our floor, never mind into her room.'

'Poor kid. Have his family been told?'

'No idea, I've told his agent. It's all hush hush at the moment. The hotel are trying to protect themselves, bastards. They covered up all the stuff with Zara but I'd like to see how they cover this up.'

Jackie felt for Salman even though she didn't know him very well. He was so young.

'I told them you were here last night, but they probably just want you to confirm it.'

At least Jackie could be honest with the cops without Raj there.

'And also, I called Dr Madhu. I'm going over there a bit later, to give her a sample. Let's do this, Jackie. Let's have a baby.'

Jackie couldn't speak, and just stared at him, winded by what she had done.

'I went to Bobby's last night, you remember Ajay and Rani's son? He's an investment banker now, got a swish place in St John's Wood. Although I think it's Ajay's flat he stays in. Anyway, he let me sleep in his spare room, and we had a good talk. I told him about all this, and he made me realise what a tool I've been.'

'Yes, you have, but it's ok.' Fuck, she thought, the guilt was making her nauseous.

'I'm sorry I didn't call you,' he said. 'I was just so mad. And I knew if I did I would say things that would break us both completely.'

'Raj, please it's fine. I'm sorry too, I should have told you everything much earlier on.'

'The way I react to things? No, it's ok, I understand why you didn't. Anyway, I have an appointment this afternoon at a private clinic in Knightsbridge. They deal with men's problems.'

'Raj...'

'Come on, Jackie, we both know what's wrong with me. I looked it up online and you're not dumb. Erectile dysfunction. It's why I can't... you know. And I think we need to deal with it. I need to deal with it. They say it's temporary, so hopefully I can get to the reasons behind it.'

Jackie felt like crying. Raj was saying everything she had wanted him to for months. He was going to get help to try to save their marriage, just as she had gone and royally fucked it up.

And – oh, fuck – she hadn't even used a condom, Ryan could have infected her with anything. She felt sick, the headache and hangover mixing with guilt, and she ran into the bathroom just in time to empty out her guts. It was mainly vodka that came out. She flushed it away quickly before Raj came in and saw just what she had been consuming. How could she have been so stupid? It was alcohol and anger and revenge and just self-loathing. She had read the ED websites, they always said not to blame yourself, that this is something going on in the man's head. And yet in the list of possible causes there was always the one that winded her: he's just not that into you anymore.

She had wanted to feel desired, and sexy and alive. So she had gone with Ryan to make herself feel better. Only now she felt like a complete shit.

'Are you ok? Can I get you anything?'

Raj was all concern and love when she went back into the bedroom.

'No I'm fine, think I ate something off last night.' *Yeah, Ryan's dick.* 'Listen, let's just put it behind us. I'm sorry for lying to you as well. I should have been honest. And I should have involved you from the start. I just wanted a baby so badly.'

'It's ok, you don't have to explain.'

Jackie looked at Raj, as he became the man she was desperate for, had been craving for so long. And in return, Jackie had become everything she hated.

Chapter Twenty

Dan was still angry from the previous night. The hotel didn't seem bothered by what had happened, or worse, they were only bothered by what the events would do to their reputation. His team had told him that Zara was still locked away in her room, none of them aware what had really happened. How long was the Mirage going to try to hide this? he wondered. How could they? It was murder after all. And attempted murder of Zara.

Alone in his flat, Dan had tried to sleep, but away from the intensity of the investigation, his mind wandered back to the events of the night with Zara.

Dan didn't know what he had done wrong and had slept confused and woken up just as confused. Everything seemed to have fallen into place, he and Zara were having a great time. He'd thought he could tell a player, could tell when someone was faking it. He'd thought Zara had real feelings for him. No, he'd let himself believe she did. When she had walked out of his flat so coldly, he'd questioned everything about himself. How could he have got it so wrong?

He didn't feel he could abandon her now. She needed him, no matter what she had done. So she had used him, big deal. Men did it all the time to women. He couldn't equate the scared young woman he had seen with the cold, callous bitch that had left his apartment. Something was wrong, he was sure. Either way, he needed to help her now. Someone had laid a trap for her, a deadly trap. Salman Rana had paid the price ultimately, but Zara would not be safe until whoever was behind it was found.

Before she had left his apartment, Dan had come up with a plan to help Zara. When she left he had decided to let her go to hell, but his conscience was getting the better of him. He had seen her real self, behind the fake glamour and the designer brands, the image that she fabricated for the world. He had seen the vulnerable young girl, the one that had been so hurt for so long and by so many people, and it was for her that he would do this. Zara had gotten into his system so badly that he was willing to forget the arrogant woman that had left his apartment in such a cold way, and help the girl that she had been. Whatever Zara had done to him, he wouldn't abandon her.

Reluctantly Dan switched on his laptop. He wasn't done with Zara Das just yet, and despite everything telling him not to pursue this, Dan had to. He had always been a crap spy because of this; because he could never quite switch off his sense of right and wrong. Even if it meant helping the enemy. And at that moment that's exactly what Zara was.

–

Sasha had spent the morning at the Bulgari spa in Knightsbridge, being pampered into nirvana, needing to get away from the Mirage and Imran. A facial and revitalising mask had followed a mani and pedi, which had been preceded by a full body massage after a sauna session. She was now considering the vaginal rejuvenation treatments, ready to spend more of Imran's money. If that's what he wanted her to be then she would show him. Her treatments that morning had already cost close to two thousand pounds, and when he worked that out in Indian rupees he would realise just what having a typical Bollywood wife would mean.

Leaving the salon, Sasha hit New Bond Street and managed to rack up another ten thousand pounds in shoes and clothes at Louboutin, Jimmy Choo, Bulgari, Dior, and Victoria's Secret. When she used Imran's card at Harry Winston, he called her.

'What?' she demanded.

'Don't you think you've done enough damage to me for one day?'

'Not really. It's nowhere near the sort of damage I want to do. And this is just one day, Imran, imagine what I will do to you when this is my life. Every weekend I'll be at the DLF Emporio in Delhi, and every day in Mumbai I will visit every store that even has a whiff of designer about it. Is that what you want?'

'Come back please, we need to discuss this.'

'There's nothing to discuss.'

'Sasha, we can compromise, please. Don't do this, *jaan*. Please.'

'You're making me do this.'

'What do you want from me?'

'You see why this is all so painful. Because it's your money that I'm spending.'

'No, *jaan*, you're wrong, every penny I have is yours. Spend it as you want. Not like this though, not in anger to hurt me.'

'If it was my own money, it wouldn't matter to you, and that's what you don't get. I want to be making my own way in life. I want to buy something that I earnt.'

'You paid your dues a hundred times over to deserve the success I have. Without you, Sasha, none of this would have happened. Please don't do this.'

Sasha became aware of herself, standing on New Bond Street shouting into her phone, surreptitious looks from passers-by making her feel self-conscious. She lowered her voice as she continued.

'Well you asked me to be a Bollywood wife, so I will become your dream Bollywood wife and I will bankrupt the hell out of you.'

'That's not what I meant.'

'Then what did you mean? Stop living in the eighties. Look at women like Twinkle Khanna or Gauri Khan. They're successful in their own right. I want to be known as more than

253

just Imran Khan's wife. You gave me an ultimatum, Imran, so now listen to mine. I am making this movie, and either you support me, or I will leave you and take your children with me. Do you understand?'

Sasha ended the call and hailed a cab to take her back to the hotel. In the back of the taxi she messaged Emel Walid telling her that come hell or high water, she would make her movie. If in the process she lost Imran, then maybe he wasn't worth keeping, anyway.

–

James Kapoor had spared no expense to make the Mirage the finest hotel in London, and part of that included an indoor land-scaped Oriental garden. It was set around a small lake populated with colourful koi fish in oranges and red, with an intricate red stone bridge over it. A Buddhist temple stood to one side, a multi-level pagoda at another, while the most beautiful and exotic flowers were everywhere with finely carved jade statues placed strategically. To keep the flowers in bloom, a light mist was ever present, controlled by the temperature gauge, the only sound that of the wind chimes.

Rani stood on the bridge, looking at the fish and the greenery, and tried to anchor herself. She hoped the peace around her would invade her own senses, which were hurtling at a million miles. In her head she replayed the scene with Laila and Minnie. It was the craziest irony that Rani had been waiting for the argument to finish because she felt for Minnie and wanted to comfort the poor girl. Imagine your own mother being so cold. Only, in the end, to be faced with the same horror and realisation that had been on Laila's face. They both knew what Ajay liked in bed, and the mark on his penis. They had exchanged a look that said it all: Minnie knows because what she is saying isn't just hurtful words to get at Laila, but the truth.

Rani lowered herself onto the bridge, folding her legs, and covered her face. She let her body wrack with sobs, and felt the hurt and betrayal pour out of her. Thirty years she had loved that man, and he had done this. There had always been rumours right from the start, but she had ignored them, because none of them ever came to anything. There was never any proof. She had gone through a stage when Bobby was born of trying to catch Ajay out, carrying out low-level espionage, checking his pockets, receipts, bank statements. She was terrified of Ajay leaving her with four children to raise. The paranoia had subsided over time and she hadn't let it raise its head again.

Now, hearing the proof from the little slut's mouth, Rani questioned every rumour she had heard over the years. Her insides were so painful she wanted to rip them out, wanted to beat herself for being so naïve. And so she let herself cry, in the silence of the serene garden where she was alone. Because once she was done crying, Rani was going to break everything. Starting with Ajay Kumar.

–

Jackie was desperately trying to stay calm, despite her previous night's drinking and burning guilt at her infidelity playing havoc with her system. It had been a mistake, she knew that, she had to move on from it. Raj had gone to meet Dr Madhu already, and later he was going to see the clinic about his bedroom issues. Why couldn't he have done it all just twenty-four hours ago? Then she wouldn't be in such a mess now. She had to see Ryan and tell him to keep quiet. Or was that playing with danger? Could she even trust herself to be alone with him? Yes, of course, there was no alcohol involved, and he had already scratched the itch she had inside.

To her shame she couldn't remember which room he was in, so had to ask reception. She didn't even know his surname. In fact she wasn't sure he had ever told her and they hadn't exchanged numbers. Body fluids, but no numbers. She felt like she was in a sorority in college again, and felt ashamed.

Just as she was about to give up, she suddenly remembered. Ryan Matthews. Yes, that was it. She tried the receptionist again who reluctantly gave her his room number.

Ryan opened the door in a towel, fresh from the shower. *Great timing*, she thought, not trying to look.

'I need to talk to you, doll,' she said, walking in as casually as she could. *Yeah, you're naked but, meh! I've been there, done that, definitely will not be doing it again*. She didn't sit down despite him offering because that would block an easy escape and suggest she was here more than just fleetingly. Ryan sat down, his towel opening at just the right place to show a lot of thigh and inside leg. Jackie recalled exactly what the towel was covering up.

'Last night,' she began.

'Was amazing,' he said.

'Thanks. And a one-off.'

'Really?'

'Yes. I'm a married woman. A happily married woman.'

'You were all of those things last night as well.'

'I was also drunk.'

'Not so drunk you didn't know what you were doing. You started it all, remember?'

'Yes, I do remember, thank you, no need to get smart. Anyhow, the point is, I'm married, and it can't happen again. Ever. In fact, it never happened, erase it from your memory.'

'I wish I could. It was one of the most intense nights of my life, Jackie. Seriously. I really like you.'

Jackie opened her mouth, but no words came out. Was he crazy, was he not listening to her? She couldn't help feeling flattered though that this Adonis was telling her that she was a highlight of his life. She was human, after all. She compared him in that moment to Raj. Miserable, highly strung, impotent Raj, who went into rages about her past because he couldn't get it up. Then she felt bad. He was the man who loved her, told her she was his for life, and was right now jerking off into a plastic cup somewhere trying to create a baby because she wanted it.

Although what was that about? Was the baby like a piece of jewellery to apologise or keep the peace? Did he even want a child? He had been so against it and now in one night he had changed his mind? And when he realised this gift for Jackie was for life, not just for the last night of Chanukah...?

'You're thinking about it too, aren't you?' Ryan said, and shamelessly he opened his towel, showing her that whatever she was thinking, he most certainly had other things on his mind. His erection was pointing right at her.

'Enough, put your clothes on. This is over.'

'We just started.'

'Ryan...'

'Jackie...'

She turned to leave, but he sprung from the bed and turned her around so she was facing him. He held her face in his hands and she could smell his freshly washed body and remembered how it had felt and tasted the night before.

'Look in my eyes and tell me you don't want me again,' he said.

'You cocky asshole, I'm not some adolescent drip who's going to fall for that.'

She removed his hands and with all the strength she could muster, left his room. Before she could, he shouted after her.

'I'm not giving you up that easily, Jackie.'

Fuck, she thought, trust her to not only cheat on her husband but cheat with a bloody stalker. This was not going to end well at all.

–

Zara was feeling restless, unable to sleep, her mind full of nightmares and her anxiety levels heightened. It had been two days now since she had left her room, and despite the presence of

Dan's team outside her door, she missed the comfort she got from knowing he was nearby. He still hadn't contacted her, not even to ask why she had left his apartment the way she did. He probably didn't care, Zara was probably just another of his clients that he screwed. Maybe that's what he did to all of them. It all seemed a world away from where she had been at that moment. Which part had happened and which she had dreamed, she wasn't sure any more.

Her phone was switched off, anyway. The only interaction she had was with Kasim and the police giving her updates. They hadn't found any leads on anything, didn't know why Salman was in her room, or who had killed him.

Zara watched her favourite Bollywood movie *Pakeezah*. It was a classic from the early seventies, starring Meena Kumari, probably her favourite actress. She had lived a tragic life, which ended when she drank herself to death. Zara used her as an example always, not to go down that road, to keep control of her world. Zara had a shrewd business head, she thought that like Laila, she would have a career that never ended if she played it right.

Now it all seemed so pointless. She had no get-out clause. What use was Zara X or Zara D, her millions of Instagram followers? What she needed most was people who loved her, cared for her. Her parents, where were they? Maybe she should call them, tell them? Surely they weren't so cold-hearted that they wouldn't care that someone was trying to kill her? Only she knew her father was though. Her mother had called after the bomb, only to check she was still alive. Her father hadn't been moved then so why would he care now? She could have given her parents a life that was so much better. She knew her father had retired early on a meagre pension, Dev's disappearance ageing him prematurely. She knew her mother had become his carer while nursing her own broken heart. Zara could have brought happiness into their lives if they had let her. She needed them. She wanted to rest her head in her mother's lap again, have her sing *loris* to her and oil her hair and tell her stories about princes and demons, and the victory of good over evil.

Zara had always thought the key to freedom and safety was money. She could buy herself a gilded cage to keep the danger away. Instead, she had built herself a prison. The only ray of light was Kasim. The man she kept thinking of as her substitute for Dev. He was watching the movie with her, but his head was dropping. He was probably knackered, sleeping in the chair in her room.

'Thank you, Kasim. You don't know what you've done for me.'

'It is nothing, ma'am. Can I get you anything?'

Zara shook her head.

'Can I ask you something?' she said.

'Yes, of course.'

'Don't you want more? Don't you get sick of answering to the whims of rich bitches like me? Don't you want to be in control of your own destiny?'

She wanted Kasim to fly. He was so decent, and he was stuck with her, because that's what his bosses demanded of him.

'Forgive me, ma'am, but who is in control of anything? Are any of us? I believe in God and the destiny that is written for us.'

'I find that belief so fatalistic. Why bother doing anything then if it's all written anyway? You might as well just fill your short life with everything you can, have as much fun as you can! It's all written anyway, right? And if death is the end, then at least you had a great time, right?'

'It is complicated, I think. You do your best always, and the rewards come. In this life or the next.'

'I see millions of people every day in Mumbai, all struggling and working really hard for little or no reward. I hope you are right, Kasim, I hope there is a universal equalisation somewhere, otherwise it would just be too painful.'

He nodded at her and smiled, but it lacked its usual openness.

'Are you ok?'

'Yes, ma'am, I am well.'

'You seem a little sadder than normal. You know you can talk to me in confidence. I'm guessing it must be a lonely existence you have?'

'Lonely?'

'Being away from your family?'

'It is hard, yes. There are lots of people like me though. I have met a lot of people who have left their families behind too. Many of them are also like me, in that they are running away.'

'Can I ask you, what you were running away from?'

He was quiet, looking down at his hands, determining what he should say. Whether he should trust her or not. Eventually he decided to.

'I was being abused. From when I was just a child. Not just by one person. There was a gang of them, and they were… they did things to me that I am ashamed even of repeating. And they threatened me, said if I told anyone it would end badly for me and my family. They made videos of everything. And told me they would show the world, to shame me and my family. And I believed them, because the men involved, they are rich and powerful. And in Pakistan when you are a rich and powerful man, you can get away with anything.'

Zara was stunned into silence, her heart going out to him. Every word he said, she could relate to.

'I understand, Kasim,' she said. 'I went through something similar. And I want you to know, you are brave for still being here. They wanted to destroy you, make you feel like nothing. But you didn't let them. So for me, I want you to keep looking at the stars and I want you to keep bettering yourself. Make your life the best it can be because that is the greatest revenge you will have.'

He nodded silently, unable to hide the pain that she had brought to the surface in him. Pain that she knew all too well.

She had sworn she would never let another man use her again. And Dan had done just that.

But for the first time since she had seen Salman's lifeless damaged body, Zara began thinking of something other than her own darkness. She looked at Kasim, the poor broken soul, and she realised she would have to start living again. Because he had, after everything he had been through. And whoever was trying to destroy her, they had failed. Zara would keep going until someone stopped her.

Chapter Twenty-One

Ajay was in Minnie's arms, their bodies locked together, naked, sweaty, and satiated. Rani had come back earlier from her yoga to tell him she was going to stay the night with Bobby. Ajay had assumed it was a ruse to try to break him, get him to accept his freak of a son. He had barely acknowledged her and hadn't even cared when she left without saying goodbye to him.

Instead, he had messaged Minnie, saying his wife had gone for the night to stay with their son, and asking if she was free. Minnie had taken a while to respond, but eventually did so. And that had led to an evening of raw sex and room service food which was delivered while he was in the shower.

Ajay loved how vigorous and young Minnie made him feel, rekindling sensations he hadn't felt for years with his wife, sensations he had only really felt with Laila, if he was honest. There had been other women occasionally, his leading ladies, wives of politicians and industrialists, women with as much to lose as him if the affair was revealed, but they were all like Rani in a way. Women that commanded a level of respect. Minnie, like Laila, was different, wilder in bed definitely, doing things no self-respecting Indian woman would. He felt as though he was taking in Minnie's youthful energy every time they made love.

He kissed the top of her head and asked her what she was thinking.

'I was thinking how great it would be if we could be together.'

'Yes, I think it would be. Unfortunately I don't think that can happen.'

'Why not?'

'Are you asking me seriously?'

'Yes.'

He felt a little nervous then. Was she really unaware that this couldn't be? No, she was just tired, he was sure of it.

'I'm married, for a start, I can't just leave Rani. And as for you, trust me, young madam, you don't want to end up being my carer. This is what it is. A moment in time. Enjoy it.'

'None of that bothers me. I've always felt as though I was looking for something, for someone. I know this is such a cliché, I totally have daddy issues, but really, Ajay, I love you. No man has even come close to making me feel like this.'

Ajay felt actual panic now, and pulled away from Minnie.

'You must not think like this, my child, it is dangerous. What has happened? Did you row with your harridan mother again?' Minnie nodded. 'I see. We discussed this. When you go back to Mumbai you need to move out. I have an apartment you can stay in for a while until you find your own.' He didn't add how he would then be able to see her as much as he liked, and when he was bored with her, she could move out.

'The fight with my mother got ugly. Really ugly.'

'What did you say to her?'

'I told her about us.'

Ajay was sitting up now, the shock running through him. 'How could you be so stupid?'

'I didn't mean to, it just came out,' Minnie said in a little-girl-lost voice.

'You did it on purpose, I bet you couldn't wait to rub it in her face. Is that the only reason you slept with me? To get back at her?'

'No, not at all. I really want you, I'm falling in love with you.' Minnie's face was wet with tears now. Ajay didn't feel any sympathy, the stupid girl had ruined everything by telling Laila.

God only knew what she would do with the information, but it wouldn't be good. 'That's not all,' Minnie said in a smaller voice. 'When I was fighting with her, I didn't realise, but Rani*ji* was standing there. She heard all of it.'

Ajay felt his heart crash into his throat and his world go black.

'You silly, silly little girl. What have you done?'

–

Dan had spent his day trying to put to rest his final responsibility to Zara. He was going to do one last thing for her then forget she even existed. His first job was to track down VJ, but the man had simply vanished. He had been staying with the rest of the Indian crew at the Hilton London Metropole, but when Dan checked, it was confirmed that he hadn't been seen there for days. Dan had asked one of his contacts there in the security team to check if the room had been occupied at all recently and got the confirmation that it hadn't.

Dan was at a loss trying to figure out how best to hunt down this man who had disappeared into London. He decided to put that part of his plan on hold while he set in motion the next part of what he needed to do. He had a friend in RAW, the Indian secret service, Ravi Gupta, who he contacted. Ravi and Dan had been on a joint mission into Afghanistan once, and had struck up a friendship when Dan had helped save Ravi's life. Spies didn't make good friends, there was always a limit to just how much you could trust them in Dan's mind, still, he had to believe Ravi would come through with this.

It took him four hours to find out the information that Dan needed.

'You were right to be suspicious, we found copies on his hard drive. It seems he made more copies onto a USB as well. He probably has that with him.'

'Did you do what I asked?' said Dan.

'Yes I did. I'm sending you the link now.'

Dan watched the video on his phone and thanked Ravi for his help.

'You can run, VJ, and you can hide, but when I find you, it's over.'

The question was, would Dan be able to track him down before he was able to carry out his threat of unleashing Zara's videos into the ether? Once they were out there, it would be impossible to stop people accessing them to watch. In preparation for that eventuality, Dan took the executive decision to contact Colette. If the worst happened, there had to be a back-up plan in place, and Colette was it. Dan just hoped he didn't have to use it.

It was late at night, and Dan was dozing in front of the TV. He had decided to hand over Zara's remaining security detail to his team, and would not be involved personally. Still, all he could think about was Zara and what nearly was. He flipped to YouTube, where he had created a playlist of Zara's songs from her various movies, and he spent the night watching her lip sync to numerous songs he had to read the subtitles for.

When he did eventually sleep, it was Zara who danced in his head and he thought again just how much he cared about her still. She had gotten to him in ways that he didn't like to admit.

–

The news was out first thing in the morning. Actor Salman Rana had died of a suspected overdose, having taken a mix of alcohol and cocaine while partying with friends at the Mirage. Staff had called for an ambulance and Salman's body was rushed to hospital, but he had died on his way there. Police were still investigating, but they weren't looking for anyone else in the case and didn't suspect foul play.

It was the best and the cleanest headline that money would buy for James Kapoor, that much was clear. A murder was a scandal. A celebrity overdose was almost sexy. Raj was livid as he read the online reports shredding Salman's character. Miss X reported how close friends of the deceased said they had warned him numerous times about his addictions, and how he had been forced to leave Pakistan because of his behaviour.

There had been further reports leaked about his character, saying he was a dancer at Asian gay clubs under the name of Maran, and also worked as an escort for both men and women. The gossip mags and online film rags were having a field day. Ironically as Raj got more and more angry with the dissection of Salman's life, the stock and interest in *Kismet India* was going through the roof.

'That's a bit much,' Raj said in disgust, closing down an online article claiming that Salman was not only an escort and exotic dancer but also a rogue landlord. 'It says he rented out some dingy flats in Stepney Green to huge Bengali families for friends of his. He lived in one and was an asshole to the families there, but he loved his cat. Fuck's sake. His poor family. What are the police doing leaking this information?'

'Don't worry, you know what these gossip rags are like. You've been the victim of their attention enough times. I think they've linked you with all of your leading heroines.'

Jackie was being as calm and nice as she could. She felt so guilty for what she had done, and Raj was being so nice to her. Dr Madhu had said everything was good to go, and she was ready to fertilise the eggs Melody had donated to try to create a healthy embryo for the surrogate back in India. Transportation had also been arranged for the frozen embryo to be taken safely so there would be no damage in transit. Jackie couldn't believe her plan was all falling into place. If only she hadn't wrecked it by straying with Ryan. Still, he was keeping his distance so far, so maybe she could pretend it hadn't happened.

'What happened at the ED clinic?' she asked Raj. She refused to say erectile dysfunction. It sounded like a taunt in her mouth.

'They took some blood tests and will take it from there. They said I'll probably need some counselling, so I think this might take longer than I hoped.'

'Are you ok with that?'

'Yes, of course, for you my love, anything is ok.'

Fuck, Jackie thought. What was he doing to her?

'What I don't get is if you can get an erection, and come while pleasuring yourself, why can't you have sex?'

'They're just different things, I guess. I don't know. The doc said everything is in working order, because I can wank. But I need some help to get over the barrier to actually doing the other stuff.'

Jackie felt like such a bitch. All this time she had been thinking of her own needs when it was her husband who really needed the help and support. She would be a better wife, she really had to step up. She felt like she owed Raj now for the rest of her life. Although a voice in her head also said how that wasn't exactly a healthy way to exist, either.

'So what are you going to do about the movie?' she asked him.

'I don't know. Zara hasn't left her room in days, and I don't feel like carrying on. But James Kapoor is showing his true colours. I'm telling you these people, they have coins for hearts. He has billions, Jackie, and he's still worried about the money we're losing by not filming. I've told him, until Zara is ready we don't film. And I don't think she will ever be ready. Someone tried to kill her.'

'We leave in ten days,' Jackie said. 'You might have to finish this movie in Mumbai after all.' Ten days, she thought, to avoid Ryan and keep her secrets safe. Just ten days and she was ok to go and live out her future.

—

It had been three days but Rani hadn't budged. She was holed up in Bobby's flat, refusing to speak to her husband. Ajay had tried calling numerous times, and had even turned up, buzzing the apartment to be let in. He hadn't relented and called his son, but had called the other children and asked them to make their mother speak to him.

'He's a fucking hypocrite,' Bobby had fumed when Rani told him what had happened. 'All the stuff he said to me, and he's the one knocking off his ex-wife's daughter? Isn't that close to incest?'

Rani hadn't said anything beyond the facts to Bobby, hadn't given her opinion, hadn't broken down or cried. She had made a decision on that bridge and she was sticking to it.

'What did Aunty Kaneez say?' Bobby asked, coming over to give his mother a tea. He sat down next to her. Kaneez was a friend of Rani's, one of Mumbai's hottest lawyers and an expert at family law.

'She asked if I was sure, and when I said yes, she said she will put everything into motion for my return. I've got my Juhu flat to move into, and I am entitled to half of everything that man has earned.'

'Mum, don't go back. Stay here. At least until the divorce is done. Please?' Bobby's phone buzzed. 'Fucking asshole,' he said, checking it.

'What's wrong?'

'He's asked me to vacate the flat within twenty-four hours or he will have me evicted. I'd like to see him try.'

Rani breathed deeply, she had seen this coming.

'It's ok, it's time you found a place of your own.'

'Mum, I might be an investment banker but you need to be a billionaire to buy property in London these days.'

'Find a flat to rent by the end of the day, and I will help you buy your own place.'

Bobby studied his mother, impressed and worried about just how stoic she was being. He wanted her to react and break down or get angry. Something, but she was so in control of herself, it was scary.

'He's bluffing,' Bobby said.

'I don't care. We've taken advantage of his hospitality enough. I don't want anything from him anymore. I will have

268

my day in court and I will get my recompense for the last thirty years. For now, please, I need to be free of him.'

Bobby would support his mother completely, she had done the same for him all her life. Still, he had to ask, for her sake.

'Are you absolutely sure you want to do this, Mum? You don't want to give him a chance or hear his side of things?'

'Not really. He will probably deny it, lie, say I'm overreacting. And well, if I had small children or couldn't support myself financially I might consider it. But I have nothing left to lose now, and however many years I have left, I want to focus on myself.'

'Ok. Just know I'm here for you. And you know the others will also support you once they find out?'

'I don't want them to find out, Bobby. He is still their father, their grandfather. I don't want them to suffer. Nobody needs to know why I'm doing this. Please?'

'He doesn't deserve it, but ok, for you.'

'Thank you.'

Rani hadn't returned any messages from Jackie or Sasha for the last few days either, she didn't want to have to explain to anyone what had happened. It wasn't embarrassment or shame; she just wanted to get her head around everything first and make her plans for freedom. Now they were done, Rani was ready to speak to them. She sent them both a message asking them to lunch. Ajay had kept her trapped for long enough.

Chapter Twenty-Two

'Where the hell have you been? Make-over island?' said Jackie, blunt as always. They had chosen to meet at The Ivy in Covent Garden, Sasha and Jackie arriving early. Rani had made her entrance minutes later, and Jackie's mouth had dropped open.

Rani, who was usually wearing sarees or classic Indian outfits by the likes of Tarun Tahiliani and Ritu Kumar, seemed to have been given a makeover by someone from the *Real Housewives* franchise. Her hair had been coloured with blonde highlights, her face made up in palettes of pinks and honey, and she was wearing jeans with a kaftan style top, and very tall heels. She was struggling to walk quickly and sat down fast.

'Gucci jeans, Dior top, and Manolo Blahnik shoes,' she said, giggling, while ordering Dom Perignon from the waiter. 'Bobby's friend took me shopping. He said I needed some fun, so I was at the behest of one of those rich spoilt brats I loathe. And this is the result.'

'Ajay won't recognise you. I mean you were always gorgeous, but you now look like you stepped off Rodeo Drive rather than Marine Drive.'

'Thank you, I think,' Rani said.

'Where have you been?' said Sasha, who was wearing her own recent purchases from Hermes and a diamond pendant she had picked up from Harry Winston's. 'I've been trying for days to get in touch with you. Ajay*ji* said you were staying with family, but nothing else. Did you hear about Salman? So shocking.'

'Don't believe all the gossip on that one,' Jackie said, mysteriously. She was far more subtly dressed in her Abu Jani-Sandeep Khosla kurta with jeans she had picked up from Primark, and sandals from Foot Locker.

'What do you mean?' Sasha asked, as the waiter brought their drinks over. Champagne for Rani, a vodka orange for Jackie, and a fruit juice cocktail for Sasha. The three women cheered, looking each other in the eye. 'To avoid bad sex for seven years,' Sasha said.

'I've been having bad sex for seventeen years, so forget that bullshit,' said Jackie.

'I've been having bad sex for thirty years, so I win,' said Rani.

'What is wrong with you?' Jackie said, laughing. 'You've been drinking all morning, haven't you?'

'Maybe a little,' said Rani, giggling again. They ordered lunch and then Jackie asked what had been happening.

'Not a lot. The usual. Found out my husband has been cheating on me with his ex-wife's daughter. All in a day's work in Bollywood.'

Jackie and Sasha looked dumbfounded. Rani, aided by gulps of champagne and nervous laughter, told them the whole story. And that she was leaving Ajay. That, in fact, she had left him, and she and Bobby were in a rented apartment in Chelsea for the time being.

'I don't even know what to say, which for me, is a first,' Jackie said.

'Rani*ji*, are you ok? That's awful,' Sasha said, reaching out to fold Rani's hands in hers.

'Awful? I think it's fucking disgusting. What the fuck was he thinking? Eugh, I actually feel sick thinking about it.' Jackie made retching noises to illustrate the fact.

'It's fine, I think it's been building for years. There were always rumours, but there always are. I dismissed them, but now I believe all of them. So rather than stay and put up with it, I've decided to move on. Start again. As I'm heading towards sixty.' She emptied her champagne glass and ordered more for herself.

'That's not the way to go, trust me, you're speaking to a proper lush here,' said Jackie.

'Oh, Jackie, I haven't got a problem, I'm just in need of medication today. My life of thirty years is over, it hurts, you know? Really hurts. That bastard. I don't want to make you feel bad, but I'm just glad I have my children. If I didn't, those years with him would have been a waste. I'm sorry, I'm drunk, I know I shouldn't say it to you, but it's true. And the way he reacted to Bobby while all the time he was…'

'What's wrong with Bobby?' Sasha asked.

'Nothing. He came out to us. As being gay.'

'What? Hold up? Bobby is gay?' Jackie thought of Raj staying over at his house on the night of Salman's death. Is that why Raj told him about their issues, had Bobby told him? Being gay was the worst kept secret in Bollywood, the glamorous world of films providing protection for young men and women escaping their small worlds to live openly. 'Is Bobby even old enough to have sex?' Jackie added, remembering the young chubby teenager she had seen years ago.

'Oh God, how much did I drink? It's ok, it's going to go public soon anyway. When he's ready, Bobby will come out and tell the world. It's what started my fight with Ajay, and why he left that night when he stayed with that tramp. I haven't seen him so angry for a long time. He was even threatening to cut Bobby out of his will. Said he didn't want some queer lover of his to get his hands on his money.'

'Your husband, sorry, soon to be *ex*-husband, needs to wake up and smell the repeal of the law criminalising homosexuality in India. Blatant hypocrisy if you ask me, the amount of screwing around these guys do on their wives.' Jackie stopped abruptly.

'It's ok, I'm not so naïve. I used to read *Stardust*, *Filmfare*, *Movie*, and *CineBlitz* back in the day. I saw the stories. I didn't believe them, or maybe I was in denial. But now I know there was truth to them.'

'Come on, Rani, those magazines are full of bullshit. Peering inside the bedrooms of the famous, only when they find nothing, they just make shit up. I don't think he was as bad as they probably made out.'

'Smoke and fire,' Rani said, bitterly.

'Listen, you tell Ajay this is not 1958. Bobby is allowed to love whoever he wants to. It's none of his business. And if he wants to lose his son over his ego and what he thinks people might think, then I'll adopt him. As it is, I'm fucking struggling to have my own.'

There it was, dropped into the space between the women. They had always suspected, but neither of them had ever asked Jackie.

'I'm so sorry,' said Sasha.

'Hey, hold the sympathy, it's fine. I came to terms with it. In fact, part of the reason I came to London was to get treatment. There's a clinic on Harley Street. You remember Dr Madhu from Penny Kapoor's lunch? She's a specialist and well, there's a way. Raj has always been so funny about kids, but he's agreed. We've been having problems for a long time, there's so much tension between us.'

'Why? Sorry I shouldn't pry,' said Sasha.

'Hey, we're sharing today, don't worry yourself. To be honest, I don't know. He just has issues with the men I've slept with, keeps bringing them up.'

'I don't know why, I saw him grow up, I know just how busy he was,' said Rani. 'He wasn't a monk.'

'I know. I keep thinking this might heal things though.'

Rani didn't say anything, but didn't think bringing a child in to try to heal a marriage was a good idea.

'Sorry, I know this is about you, Rani, but well, Raj and I are having a baby.' She told them about the surrogacy, about Raj's sperm being used to fertilise a donated egg, but again held back on sharing any details about her birth family.

'That's amazing,' Sasha said, actually squealing.

'Steady on, doll, everyone's looking.'

'That's brilliant, so the child will be Raj's at least?' said Rani.

'Yes, I guess,' said Jackie.

'You'll be the baby's mother,' Sasha said, consolingly.

'Yes, you will,' Rani said quickly. 'It doesn't matter, all that genetic bio thingy, it's just nonsense. You are going to be a mother. I am so happy for you.'

'Thanks,' Jackie said, her eyes darkening though. 'Although I suppose it will be his baby and not mine.'

'Jackie, don't think like that. Are things still tense with him?' Sasha asked.

'No, on the contrary, he's being so nice to me of late. Like *super* nice. I can't even describe it. He was so sure he didn't want kids, and then he agreed. Actually we had a row, and he stayed the night at Bobby's. The night Salman... you know. And in the morning he was all, *I'm sorting this out*. Only...' Jackie hesitated. She knew she shouldn't tell, secrets always got out, but she was dying inside. 'I slept with someone else that night.'

'You did what?' Rani said loudly, slamming her glass down.

'I know you don't want to hear it, given your situation. I feel like such a bitch for doing it to him. I was drunk, and we had had a massive row and he just left. And this guy in the bar...'

'How could you, Jackie? Look at me. Look at what's happened to me, and you did this to him? Raj is the sweetest man, he's never cheated on you, I'm sure of it. I can't believe it. You have to tell him.'

'What? No,' said Sasha.

'She has to. Lies will always come out, and the longer you wait, the more devastating their effects.'

'Seriously, I can't. He's being so nice about everything, he's like a changed man after that night with Bobby. I don't know what your son said to him but... look, please don't repeat this, but things haven't been all that in the bedroom department for a while. He's been having some issues getting... it... up...'

'Poor you,' Rani quipped. 'I know how that feels. Ajay hasn't been near me for so long I can't even remember. No wonder though when he's all over that little tramp.'

'It happens, to lots of men,' said Sasha.

'Imran?' said Rani.

'No, but sometimes when he's tired he can't. Other times he can't stop doing it. It's just not unusual, that's all I'm saying to you.'

'I know, I did all the Google searching. Still, I can't help but take it personally, that he just doesn't fancy me anymore. Maybe he never did? And with that guy from the bar, I just... I don't know. I just wanted to feel desired. It was stupid and I swear to you, Rani, I haven't done it before and I won't do it again. It was a mistake. They happen, right?'

'Yes they do,' said Sasha. 'Trust me, Jackie, don't tell him. Focus on your baby and your future.'

'You're making trouble for yourself by not telling him. He has the right to know, and to decide whether he wants to stay with you after he knows the truth. He might forgive you if it's a one-off.'

'The way you're going to forgive your husband?'

'That's different. I've had a lifetime of this, and I've had enough.'

'You have your children, like you said. I don't.'

'Well don't say I didn't warn you,' said Rani.

The lunch came and they ate in silence for a while.

'Come on guys, let's not fall out,' said Sasha.

'Ok, Miss Congeniality. Now spill. You keep looking like someone cut off the head off your Barbie when you think we're not looking. What's happening?'

Sasha told them both about the script and Emel Walid's offer.

'That's such good news,' said Rani.

Sasha then told them of Imran's response.

'Fuckety-fucking bullshit men. What is wrong with all these Indian men? Have they not heard of modernity? India is a global superpower now, it's time they moved with the new wave. Give them some Chetan Bhagat books to read, or make them watch some Karan Johar movies. Or better yet, that racy *Hate Story* series. I feel like punching both your husbands. At least Raj doesn't see me as less of a woman for not having children, he definitely got that memo.'

'It's difficult to go against generations of thought and belief,' said Rani.

'Bullcrap. No it's not. And not for men like our husbands, they don't answer to anyone, they are so rich and powerful they don't need to. Their celebrity status is enough clout to help them stand up to any politician or billionaire business tycoon.'

'So what do I do? I don't want to lose him,' said Sasha.

'If you lose him because of this, then quite frankly, darling, he wasn't worth having in the first place. And it's better to lose him than lose yourself.'

'I told him that if he didn't support me on this, then I would leave him and take the kids with me.'

Jackie wolf-whistled and Rani started clapping.

'That's the right answer, babe.'

'Yes, I agree. Why should he be the one to threaten to end the marriage? Play him at his own game. Obviously he thinks you can't cope. Well, show him, by making the best movie anyone has seen in years. And Jackie, you know I can't condone your cheating, not after what I've been through. But you are going to be a brilliant mother if that's what you want to be. No matter who you have your child with.'

'Thanks, I think.'

'And me, I'm going to be fucking amazing. Watch this space, Ajay Kumar, because my son and I don't need you.'

The three clinked glasses, excited by the futures that were waiting for them. All of them unaware how different those futures would end up being to the ones they were imagining in that moment.

The light had held and the warmth of the heatwave almost reminded him of filming back in Mumbai. Raj stood on the balcony, surveying London, and thinking how things had gotten so complicated so quickly. His mind turned to Salman. What a tragedy. Then he thought about the pressure he was under from James Kapoor.

The door to the suite buzzed, and on opening it he was surprised to see DI Natasha Mace and DS Nick Pride. Maybe they had an update for him?

'How are you both?' he said, amiably.

'We need to speak to you,' Natasha said. 'It's urgent.'

Raj felt apprehension, but told them to come in.

'How can I help you?' he said, as they were all seated in his lounge.

'Mr Dillon, you said that on the night Salman died, you were staying with a friend of yours? A Bharat, aka Bobby, Kumar?'

'That's right,' said Raj, feeling himself grow tense.

'We were checking Salman Rana's phone records. On the night of his death, he called you.'

'I told you he did.'

'We also did a check to see where you were when he did so. Mr Dillon, are you still insisting you were staying with Bobby Kumar?'

'Yes, you can ask him,' said Raj, feeling the sweat on his back now, as the nerves were sending his heart into overdrive.

'In St John's Wood, right?'

'Yes.'

'Then can you explain why, according to your mobile phone, you and Bobby were both in the Mirage hotel all night? At the same time as Salman Rana was murdered?'

Raj felt his heart burst in his head, it was beating so fast, as he pictured his life about to fall to pieces.

It was a dingy bedsit off Green Street in Upton Park. Dan walked past shops full of clothes, jewellery, and food. His stomach rumbled as he passed one South Asian restaurant after another and picked out one he would go to later. They promised the best biryani in London. It was probably crap but he would call their bluff. As he looked past the shop windows full of bright, gaudy clothes, he saw that many of them had posters of Zara Das in the windows. Dressed in bridal gear, or other fashionable pieces, she was everywhere. Each time he caught her image staring out at him, beautiful, untouchable, he felt a stab to his heart. The way she had so callously used him and walked out of his apartment. Still, after today, he would hopefully have no more to do with her.

Dan walked down towards the end of Green Street, where the retail stores thinned out, and the houses began. He turned off into a side street, Kitchener Lane, and walked down about halfway. The terraced houses all looked the same, cramped and in need of repair, with the ornate gates and windows on some still unable to mask what was there. His contacts told him prices had shot up as with everywhere in London, and even a place like this that used to be seen as a dump was beyond most Londoners' reach. The Pakistani community had settled here decades before, and Dan definitely felt out of place, as every face apart from his was brown.

Dan checked the number on the front of the door he had stopped at and confirmed that the target hadn't moved on his phone. He discreetly tried the front door, found it was a series of flats and buzzed them all until someone answered and let him in without even asking who it was. It was that sort of place. Everyone came here last minute and for short periods, mainly illegal immigrants and failed asylum seekers running from immigration. The landlord didn't seem to care from what Dan had found out, fleecing his desperate clientele.

Dan made his way to the top floor and knocked. There was no answer, but the distinct sound of movement travelled through the flimsy door. Dan knocked again, then stepped away. He waited five minutes, and the door opened, the man's gaze travelling around the landing to see who had been there. Dan took advantage of the moment, and rushed at the door, pushing the occupant backwards, making him fall to the floor.

Dan closed the door behind him and stood over the fallen form.

'Hello, VJ,' he said. 'We need to talk.'

–

The bedsit was cramped, with nothing more than a single bed opposite a sink which had a microwave on top of it. There was a wardrobe and a desk, on which sat an unlocked laptop. The room stank of damp and mice droppings, and the stale sweat and breath of a man that hadn't left it for hours on end.

VJ was sitting on his bed, while Dan rested on the side of the desk, idly flicking the laptop so it wouldn't lock and need a password. VJ had tried to escape and fight Dan, but the low-level thug who intimidated Mumbai's bright-eyed girls with dreams of stardom in their eyes, was no match for someone who had MI6 training. Dan had subdued him in a neck lock, punched him a couple of times, and threatened to do much worse if he bolted.

'I just want to talk,' Dan said, and when VJ had nodded in pain, Dan had released him. He gave him a few moments to calm down before telling him just what was going to happen. 'This video, in fact this series of videos you have showing Zara: I need to know how many copies you have and who you've sent them to.'

VJ stared at him mute. Dan made to get up and saw the man flinch.

'What is it to you? This is my business, not yours.'

'If it affects my client, then it's my business too. So I will ask you again, how many copies have you made and who have you sent them to?'

VJ stayed silent, so Dan walked towards him. VJ physically jumped away and moaned when Dan sat down next to him. Dan took his phone from his pocket and played a clip for VJ to see. VJ's face visibly drained of colour and he tried to snatch the phone from Dan.

'That won't make a difference. You see, I think you dismissed me as not being able to do anything to stop you. But let me tell you, the world is different, it's a lot smaller, than you think. And I know people, even in India, people who can make your life very difficult. So talk to me. You want revenge against Zara, you want to hurt her for your own twisted reasons. Is it worth risking your life over? And not just your life, but that of your family, too?'

VJ stared at Dan, actual emotion in his eyes. Dan had thought the pantomime villain act VJ put on was too good to be true, and in his experience everyone had a weakness. It just had to be found. VJ's was his family. Hailing from a tiny village outside Hyderabad, VJ was one of eight children, his parents now old and frail, but still very much alive. VJ was the oldest and had set off to make a better life for his clan, heading to Mumbai and through his work sending money back home to educate his siblings.

'Two of my brothers are engineers now,' he said to Dan. 'They are in Silicon Valley in America. I paid the dowry for five sisters.'

'By whoring out other people's sisters and daughters?'

'It is a hard place. You live or you die, there is no in between.'

'There is always a fucking in between, you were just too lazy to see it. Still, you now have a choice again. You can choose to live, by giving up this campaign against Zara. Or you can choose to die, trying to ruin her.'

VJ considered his options and looked at the phone in Dan's hand again. Dan had played him an interview that Ravi Gupta, his RAW contact, had carried out with VJ's parents and his siblings, including shots of his nieces and nephews. He had also played him a clip of his flat in Mumbai being ransacked and his laptop there being destroyed.

'What do you want me to do?' VJ finally said, and Dan let himself breathe.

Chapter Twenty-Three

After her lunch with the girls, Rani was feeling so tipsy, she asked Sasha to take her back to the Mirage so she could sleep off the alcohol, while Jackie went to an exhibition at the British Museum. Rani was too far gone to think of the possibility of bumping into Ajay at the hotel and instead welcomed the feel of the quality of sheets in Sasha's room.

'I do miss this absolute luxury,' she mumbled sleepily, before her eyes shut.

It was hours later when she woke, at first disorientated, and then positively nauseous. She hadn't consumed that much alcohol for years, in fact, not since the children had come along. How did people do it every day? She wondered. Rani made her way to the bathroom, and on her return found a note from Sasha to say she had gone to meet with Emel Walid. Rani checked the time, it was nearly seven o'clock. Looking at her phone, she saw that she had no messages from Bobby asking where she was either.

Rani washed her face in the bathroom, appreciative of the expensive make-up that didn't simply disappear with water, and ran one of Sasha's brushes through her hair. She smoothed down her clothes, and used one of the hotel dental kits, walking through a burst of Sasha's Jo Malone Pomegranate Noir scent.

She messaged Sasha to say she was off, then realised she didn't have a key card to operate the lift. She had already locked Sasha's door, and she had left her key cards back at Bobby's. Stuck, Rani stood there and messaged Sasha. She didn't reply, probably busy discussing schedules and details with Emel. Rani sat down on one of the chairs that broke up the corridors of the exec floors, praying that Ajay wouldn't turn up.

The lift came to life, and Rani's heart sank when the doors opened. It was Laila. The two women eyed each other before Laila asked Rani to join her.

'You have me at a difficult moment,' Rani said. 'I have no key so am trapped.'

'Serendipity,' Laila said, and led them both to her room.

—
.

DI Natasha Mace was interviewing Raj Dillon under caution, his lawyer sitting with him. She was a young Asian woman with immaculate make-up and a designer suit. A friend of the family apparently, Dia Sharma had advised Raj to cooperate fully.

'Raj, so tell me, why did you lie to us about your where-abouts on the night of Salman Rana's murder?'

Raj looked shaken, his face betraying his anxiety and stress clearly, sweat stains under his armpits.

'It didn't seem important at the time. I was with Bobby, I didn't think it was important to say where we were. I thought if I was in the hotel, well Jackie, my wife, she might have got upset I didn't go back to the room.'

'You didn't think it was important to tell me you were at the same location someone was murdered? Someone you had a meeting with?'

'There were a lot of guests at the hotel at the same time,' said Dia.

'All of them with meetings with the deceased?' asked Natasha.

'I didn't want you to think I was involved.'

'So you met with Salman the night of his death, then?'

'Yes I did.'

'Where exactly did you meet him?'

'He came to the room I was in.'

'What room?'

'Bobby rented a room for me, through his work. I needed somewhere to crash, and we needed to talk.'

'Why didn't you ask your pal James Kapoor for a room?'

'People talk. I trust Bobby, I wanted to keep my private life to myself.'

'What time did Salman come to see you?'

'I think it was ten, no, just after eleven.'

'And this room it wasn't on the executive suite?'

'No, it was on the third floor.'

'How did Salman seem when you met him?'

'He was agitated. Something had happened that had rattled him.'

'Did he say what?'

'Yes, he said he'd received death threats from a group in Pakistan. For starring in a Bollywood movie.'

'Do you know who from?'

'No. I told him to ignore them, that this always happens. When actors from either country cross the borders to star in movies, there are always incidents like this. They are hoaxes mainly, nothing ever happens. I told Salman this, reassured him not to worry. He also wanted some tips on the shoot we had in the morning. There were some scenes I wanted to redo with him; they didn't quite fit right when I watched the dailies back. I guess now I'll have to just use the footage I have.'

'And why did you hide all this from us?'

'I didn't want to implicate myself. I have a multi-million dollar film to finish. I wanted to avoid this because I haven't done anything wrong.'

'How well did you know Salman?'

'I told you, not that well. He was a last minute addition to the cast.'

'So you don't know he was an escort?'

'No of course not.'

'You didn't hire him for that reason?'

'No, what are you implying? That I hired him for sex? I'm a married man.'

'You're a married man with erection issues. We received a report from a clinic in Knightsbridge you recently visited. On top of that you were holed up with your friend, Bobby Kumar, who just recently has come out of the closet.'

Raj looked at Dia, who was trying to hide her surprise about what she was hearing. Raj was sweating profusely now.

'Bobby and I were friends back in Mumbai, until he left to study abroad. We kept in touch, and we met up again while I was in London. I was having issues in my marriage, and I needed someone to talk to. He happened to be there. And he in turn wanted to tell me about his sexuality. Look, I don't care if he's gay or straight and I told him that. And just because he's gay, doesn't mean he infected me and turned me gay when I spent the night with him. What do you think this is? Bobby and I had an orgy with Salman and to keep him quiet, we killed him?'

'We found hard drugs and liquor near the body. Maybe you were both wired?'

'Feel free to test us, I never touch the stuff and I don't think Bobby does either.'

Natasha felt frustrated. This was the downside of being in the PDP and running secret operations, she just didn't have the resources to deal with a full-fledged murder investigation. In the Met she would have verified Raj's alibis and got his phone mast results a lot more quickly. The real tricky cases the PDP dealt with always had secret service help because of their diplomatic involvement. This case just wasn't up there. She didn't know what to make of Raj, he seemed to be earnest. But the lies he had told made her question everything he was saying.

'We didn't do this, detective, don't waste your time with us.'

'So tell me then, was Bobby with you when Salman came to visit?'

'No. He came afterwards. He was with his mother on the exec floor at first. When his father came back, he had a massive blowout with him when he told him he was gay. Bobby wasn't meant to stay the night, but I asked him to. I said we both needed a friend to talk to. And that's all we did.'

'So before Bobby was with you, he was on the exec floor?'

Natasha narrowed her eyes. Maybe then Raj wasn't involved, maybe he was a convenient decoy for Bobby who had been quick to book the room for him, while he himself was on the exec floor. Where Salman's body was found.

–

'Well this is a first,' said Laila, as she took a seat beside Rani in the lounge of her hotel suite. Rani had refused anything to drink except for mineral water, and Laila had taken the same. She had summoned the butler the Mirage had supplied her. It wasn't Kasim, the butler that had been looking after Zara and herself and Ajay. Maybe each butler only got two rooms, she thought.

'Don't you remember the old days?' Rani said, taking a sip of the room temperature water, her throat dry from sleep and alcohol. 'We used to hang out all the time at Filmistan and RK studios, the outdoors in Ooty and Shimla. When Switzerland was just being discovered by Yash Chopra. Now there was a legend. It's funny neither of us ever got to work with him. They were crazy days though.'

'Yes, doing back to back schedules, rushing from one studio to another, barely having time to change clothes and wigs. I hardly remembered which dialogues belonged to which movie then, learning our dance steps just before the camera was rolling. Shooting for sometimes three different films a day, keeping the producers and directors waiting because one film's shooting overran. Can you believe how we used to work back then?'

'It does feel surreal. When I see today's artists complain I really want to just punch them. They have it so good. Air-conditioned vanity rooms, shooting for one movie at a time, everything so professional and organised. No mafia money propping up the industry.'

'They just don't have our work ethic,' said Laila. 'Halcyon days.'

'Yes, quite. It was busy but I don't think I felt so alive as I did back then or worked so hard either.'

'And the awards ceremonies and functions. There were so few of them they actually meant something.'

'Exactly,' agreed Rani. 'Now you so much as sneeze on screen and someone invents an award for you, and then a ceremony to give it to you. It's all become so commercial, it's all about brands and advertising. Where is the glamour, the mystery, and the art?'

'Yes, I hate how bitchy actresses always get with each other these days. In our day there was a rivalry but also a common respect. Nowadays a generation of actors and actresses love going on *Koffee with Karan* and spilling their bedroom secrets and calling each other out. It feels so juvenile.'

'Yes. Though the industry is so much better now in so many ways. It's definitely safer, and cleaner, so much more slick. But still, I miss that layer of grime that we worked in.'

'Apart from the pervert producers and directors and actors.'

'Yes, apart from them. Honestly, when I think of the situations I found myself in, the sort of propositions I got, and the things we were expected to do. I can't believe it sometimes. How did they get away with it?'

'I think they still do in some places,' Rani said.

'Yes. Apart from the lecherous men, I miss that time. Remember when a cover shoot on *Stardust* or *Filmfare* would be a thing? People would buy the magazines and talk about how great we looked. They didn't much care for the articles. And now, everything is online. The buzz is gone. When Madhuri Dixit broke, people flocked to the cinema to see her dances, even then in the late eighties and early nineties. And now, it's all videos watched online. There is a lot to miss, Rani. And you know what I miss most of all?'

'The free clothes?'

'No. You.' Rani choked on her water at Laila's words. 'Before Ajay, you and I were friends. You were practically the only one of the actresses at the time who genuinely spoke to me.'

'Well can you blame them? You had the reputation of being a man-eater, and on top of that, you really were a bitch to all the new girls.'

'I know,' agreed Laila. 'It was just a shield I created, to protect myself in a way. And then it became who I was. It's who I still am: Laila, the impenetrable diva. The eternal mystery. Still, you didn't put up with my nonsense. You always treated me so normally.'

'I was too excited to be acting to have an attitude. I really loved it.'

'I could tell. I envied you your innocent passion for the movies. I'm not making excuses, but you know I made it the hard way.'

'Yes I do. I was fortunate to have a mentor who wasn't a perv.'

'I think he was gay, so you were safe.'

'He treated me like his daughter, really shielded me from the worst.'

'Yes. I was so messed up in those days, I really was playing a part on and off screen. When I look at Zara now, she reminds me of myself. I can see the same scars in her eyes.'

The two women sat in silence for a few moments. Rani took in the classy brocaded *saree* that Laila was wearing, lime green with emerald threading.

'That's Sabyasachi, right?' she said. Laila nodded. 'It's beautiful. I really do admire how you've managed to stay so gorgeous all this time.'

'This is the face of a very selfish woman. I only care for it and myself, as you can tell from my crashed life.'

'Your life isn't that bad from the outside. You're still making movies forty years after your first film. That's an achievement.'

'Is it? And what about the rest? Two failed marriages, and a child that loathes me.'

'Hey, I'm halfway there now, thanks to that child of yours. And I don't look half as good.'

'You were always like this, unaware of just how much the camera loved you. Why did they say you would be the next Sridevi or Rekha? Because you had it all. The looks and the acting ability. They even said you had the potential to match Hema Malini's box office record. Still, you chose to give it up for him. Was he worth it, Rani?'

Rani paused before answering. 'Honestly? I don't know. If you ask me now, then not at all. But we had thirty years together, and he gave me my four children and my grandchildren. I was also happy for most of that time.'

'Isn't that enough to forgive him?' Laila said. 'I wish he had forgiven me. If we hadn't broken up so badly, maybe I could have been happy too.'

'I can't forgive him, because I forgave him so much already. This was one step too far for me.'

'I'm sorry for what she did. It was my fault. She was trying to hurt me.'

'And did she?' asked Rani.

'Honestly, I still love Ajay in my own way. Not the man he is now, not your husband. But the man he was, and what he represented at the time. If I hadn't treated him so badly, I could have made a future with that man.'

'I suppose you can take comfort from knowing that man thirty years later turned into the man I am leaving,' said Rani softly. 'I think I'd better go, it's getting late.'

'Yes. I hope you are going to be ok.'

'When I'm in Mumbai again, would you mind if I came to visit you?' Rani said. 'I don't think anybody else will really understand what I need to say.'

'I'd like that. It's funny. I create this image of the aloof untouchable diva. And now? I really am all alone. I could do with a friend. Maybe we should do a *Koffee with Karan* special or get Simi Garewal or Neha Dupia to do one.'

Laila walked Rani to the lift, but as they were about to enter it, Ajay came out of it. He stared at both women, but rather than looking embarrassed or ashamed, his face turned red with anger.

'What is this? The Ajay Kumar ex's society? Did you have a good time discussing me? Pathetic.'

Both women looked at each other and burst into hysterical laughter, which wound Ajay up even more. They could still hear him shouting as the lift descended to the ground floor.

—

Bobby Kumar had inherited his mother's looks and his father's physique, thought Detective Sergeant Nick Pride. He was finding it surreal that he was interviewing a star son, and one born of two legends. But he had put his professional hat on, and could manage this. Bobby's lawyer was from the same firm as Raj's, a Mark Chambers. He was watching Nick shrewdly. Bobby, an investment banker by trade, wasn't even breaking a sweat. Nick thought of *American Psycho*.

'Bobby, we know you were at the hotel at the same time that Salman Rana was murdered. In your initial statement to the police you corroborated Raj Dillon's story that you were both at your flat in St John's Wood. Can I ask why you would do that?'

'Raj said we were, so I went along with it. He was with me most of the night, from about midnight onwards I think, so what did it matter where we were? He didn't do it.'

'So you thought it was ok to lie to the police to protect your friend?'

'My client didn't say that,' said Mark.

'Not in so many words.'

'His words are important so please don't twist them,' said Mark.

'Fine. So you lied about your whereabouts so Raj wasn't caught out in a lie that night?'

'Yes.'

'What else have you been lying about? Did you know Salman Rana?'

'Not at all, I never even met the guy.'

'And yet his last known movements before he ended up dead were in the same room in the Mirage in which you and Raj spent the night together?'

'If he was there, he left before I arrived. Raj called me up and said he and Jackie had had an argument and he needed to stay with me. I told him I was at the hotel, but I could get him a room if he needed his space. Booking the room under his own name, well I didn't think it would be a good idea. Hotel staff gossip just like everyone else, so I booked it through my company. I sent Raj the e-key card, and he went there directly. I waited with my mother for my father's return, and when he did, we spoke and then I went to Raj's room.'

'Why didn't you go home?'

'I intended to, but it was late, so Raj said there was no point and I should just stay with him. He said he needed to talk to someone. And to be honest I needed someone to speak to as well. Raj and I, well we come from the same circles in Mumbai. We both grew up in filmi families, and we know that world.'

'What did you speak to him about?'

'I told him about my personal situation.'

'Which is?'

'Not relevant,' said Mark.

'I think it is. You see, we found a video on your laptop, one where you announce to the world that you are coming out. It's not been posted anywhere yet, I take it?'

'Why is this relevant?' said Mark.

'It becomes relevant when I tell you that Salman Rana was also an escort, and we believe that he was on the exec floor at the same time as your client. So tell me, Bobby, what time did you leave your parents' room, and what time did you get to Raj?'

'I can't remember, not exactly. It was a while back.'

'It was a few days ago. Surely you can remember, especially when something so serious depends on it?'

'It was maybe midnight when I left my parents, and then I was with Raj a few minutes later.'

'How did you get to him?'

'The lift.'

'And how did you operate the lift on the exec floor?'

'I had a key card...' Bobby's voice trailed off.

'So you had access to the floor, and you were there at the same time a gay escort ended up murdered?'

'It was my mother's key card and you can check with her what time I left and you can check with Raj what time I got to him. I did not do anything to this Salman dude, because I don't even know who he is.'

'So you want me to ask your friend Raj to verify your timings, when you have both lied already? Tell me, Mr Kumar, what is your relationship like with Mr Dillon? Are you both just friends or is there more to your relationship?'

Bobby laughed. 'So because I'm gay every man I'm friends with must be gay too? Is that what you're suggesting?'

'I am asking you about this man, not all the men in your life.'

'Raj is my friend, that's it. He's straight, I'm gay, and for your information, not that it is any of your business, but Raj isn't my type at all. Who knows, officer, you might be though.'

Nick actually felt himself blush. Mark was smirking at him.

Nick's phone buzzed, and he left the room, meeting Natasha in the corridor. She looked livid.

'The Mirage just sent me security footage from the main lobby. It shows the times that both Raj and Bobby used the non-exec lifts to access the third floor. And also shows Salman Rana go up to the non-exec lift at 11 p.m. and leave again forty minutes later, which must have been when he met Raj.

Bobby took the non-exec lift at five minutes to midnight. If Rani Kumar confirms the time her son left her room matches the time he took the non-exec lift, then it's unlikely he made contact with Salman at all. Fuck, fuck, fuck. I think our case is blown against these two. Which means the real killer is still out there.'

–

This wasn't how this day was meant to end, Jackie thought. She had spent a nice day with Rani and Sasha, and despite Rani's lecture, lunch had been fun. This was followed by a trip to the British Museum after which she wandered around Covent Garden. After treating herself to a solo Dinner by Heston Blumenthal at the Mandarin Oriental Hyde Park, which she had cheekily asked her Mirage butler to book for her, Jackie had a nice long soak in the bath while she waited for Raj to come back. She decided to have a drink in the bath, thinking how she could actually drink all through the pregnancy, then decided she would give up. She was so excited at this decision, it spurred her on to get out of the bath and get dressed quickly, needing to tell Raj. She was highly strung by the time Raj came back.

When he did, he was a mess. He was hot, tired, and sweaty, and just collapsed into the sofa. And then told her where he had been and what had happened.

'They think you committed murder? After an orgy? I was wondering why everything looked a bit odd in the room today, it felt as though someone had been through it. And I was right. Why would they suspect you?'

'They have it in their heads that Bobby and I are lovers. They found out I went to the ED clinic. The doc, by the way, confirmed I don't have anything medically wrong with me, so I think it's all in here.' He tapped his finger against his head.

'What does that mean? Or is it like I said, if you find someone hot and young you won't have this issue. Or should I say someone hot, young, and male?'

Raj put his head in his hands and wiped away the day. He looked imploringly at Jackie, who was feeling terrified but also questioning herself. Is that why he was having problems? She knew gay men and women stayed in straight marriages for years. Had Raj simply hit a brick wall now? Could he no longer fake it, was that why he was struggling?

'I'm not gay, Jackie, please. Let's not do this. There are other things that are in the way.'

'Like what? The fact I don't have a penis?'

'Jackie, please. Try to understand.'

'How can I, when you won't tell me? So did you and Bobby have sex that night? Oh my God, is this your way of having children with your gay lover? By going through the surrogacy with me? Is that why you've been so different since that night with Bobby?'

Jackie felt nauseous, her day evaporating in seconds. Had Raj played her? It all made sense to her now.

'You're jumping to conclusions, crazy ones.'

'Yes, that's right I'm the crazy one, while you're carrying on with him and then expecting to take my baby from me.'

She was shocked by the shrill tone her voice had taken and turned away from him. Looking at him made her angrier.

'Jackie, there is nothing between Bobby and me. Or any man and me.'

'Is that why you are always so jealous of everyone from my past? Because secretly you wish you had slept with them?'

'Stop, please. You're hurting me now.'

'I'm hurting you? And how do you think I feel?'

'Jackie, please sit down. I need to talk to you. I wanted to wait until tomorrow, but I can see tonight will be unbearable for you if I don't. Please.'

Jackie trudged to the sofa as though she was being dragged, and sat at the edge, as far away from him as possible.

'Go on then, Mr Movie Maker, sell me another lie.'

When he was finished, Jackie was left reeling. She hadn't expected to hear anything like this at all.

Chapter Twenty-Four

Zara didn't feel like attending, but Colette had instructed her to, it was non-negotiable. She had been in her room for a week, with just Kasim for company for most of it. After some persuasion from him, Zara had gotten dressed and taken a walk to the Oriental gardens. He then persuaded her to go for dinner in one of the hotel's restaurants. Finally he had invited Ruby over.

Zara had trusted Kasim in a way she hadn't trusted anyone. Always friendless and alone, she felt that in this man who had come to her through such a twisted route, she finally had someone who didn't want anything from her. It made her sad to think Kasim was the only friend she'd probably ever had, and yet she felt grateful that at least she had him. He wasn't just doing what he was paid to, but had gone beyond that for her.

Calling Ruby was the right thing to do, she thought. Zara felt like she had been in mourning. Even if it was fake, Zara could escape into Ruby's self-absorbed nonsense.

'Come on, Zee, what's going on? There is so much security in this place now I got frisked about four times before they let me in here. And not the voluntary frisking I normally enjoy, either.'

'I've missed you,' Zara said, before telling her what had really happened to Salman.

'You know I'm a journalist, don't you?'

'I'm telling you as a friend, Ruby. Please don't print that.'

Here it was, the moment when Zara would discover if she really did have a friend in the world. Here was a story that could make Ruby's career.

'I swear to you, I won't say a word. Unless someone else reports it first, in which case you are giving me an exclusive. Poor Salman, though. He was so hot. Poor you. Who the fuck wants you dead that much? I know you can be a bitch sometimes, but really?'

Zara laughed along with Ruby and felt the darkness pushing into corners.

When Collette told her about the event, Zara had flatly refused no matter how important it was. But Kasim again persuaded her that it would be a good thing to do.

'It is the Ambassador, they will surely have the best security available. You will be safe. I promise to you.'

Kasim's earnestness and his being there for her had been enough to make her get ready. Every second was filled with terror and fear, but she was determined to do it, for his sake if no one else's. And in his eyes she saw Dev, and that was really why she was willing to go.

Collette had agreed.

'Zara, it will do you the world of good to get out and mingle with the vacuous rich. Security is tighter than the queen's arsehole, and you will have a team of bodyguards with you all night. I can't emphasise enough how much publicity this event gets in the media. They like to tick their diversity boxes by covering it, and if you are missing it will look odd. Not to mention annoying the Indian Ambassador.'

'I don't even know who he is, I'm sure he won't miss me. Not with Imran and Ajay there.'

'It's a she, Nirmala Devi, and she's a huge fan of yours. So yes, she will. You keep forgetting, you may not know who watches you, but they all know who you are.'

–

The party was a dinner and drinks event hosted by the Indian Ambassador at the Dorchester hotel on Park Lane. Every A-list British Asian would be there, and Zara was expected to be one of the guests of honour with Ajay, Imran, and Laila. Tickets had been sold at a thousand pounds per head for charity, and the event was one of the hottest tickets in town.

Zara was still feeling unsettled by the unsolved death of Salman and had been shocked when she learned that suspicion had fallen on Raj and Bobby. She couldn't imagine Raj killing anyone.

Zara felt her heart in her throat all day and into the evening before the event. The unknown person who hated her was out there somewhere. And after VJ released his videos, then what? The trailer had been taken down from YouTube, but she had no doubt it was all over the internet by now. She couldn't bring herself to search for it. VJ had gone dark, his phone switched off, and no communication. Zara was terrified, and didn't know who she could trust. Maybe if she warned Colette, she could do something about it? But do what? Nobody could stop this from happening. As usual, Zara would deal with it herself.

After her ten-step beauty regime, influenced by the latest K-beauty trend from Korea, Zara applied her own make-up with a shaking hand, layering and contouring her face carefully. The result was the trademark Zara look, her heavily kohled eyes a throwback to the heroines of the sixties, her hair bouffant à la Sophia Loren in her heyday. She chose to wear long diamond earrings from Mouawad studded with rubies, her long thin neck naked down to the plunging neck line of her Sabyasachi dress in magenta and silver filigree. It was made from silk and taffeta, with a tight bodice on a long Ottoman princess style jacket, and layers of red material making up the swollen skirt, with Anita Dongre heels.

Zara studied herself in the mirror; every inch of her looked like it had been painted and placed into perfection. The beautiful, glamorous veneer that would be copied and transported around the world, the one that concealed the turmoil inside. She was reminded of Swiss lakes, so still and calm and ethereal on the surface, hiding the depths below. She shuddered, and said a prayer. It was the same one her mother used to mutter to ward off evil.

-

The press were all inside the hotel, in a makeshift area with giant billboards showing a happy child drinking clean water. There were logos from every major corporation and brand in India including Aditya Birla's Peter England, Café Coffee Day, Tata, Titan, Bharti Airtel, Godrej, Lakme, Louis Philippe, Jet Airways, and Jaguar, all sponsoring the event. Guests were being asked to pose in front of the billboard, and as Zara stood there, the digicams freezing her image thousands of times, she wondered how long this would last. When the video of her leaked, what would the reaction be? Probably the same that had resulted from her item number in the Jhansi movie. Men jerking off to it, enjoying her being forced to carry out the despicable acts she had, and then publicly burning effigies of her. She was already a huge risk for producers; once her sex video was released, she would be untouchable.

Inside she was dying, but Zara didn't allow her face to betray any of it. She smiled, looked sultry, and threw her trademark poses for the cameras. Whatever tomorrow brought, Zara Das would at least look like the reigning queen of Bollywood in the images that would circulate the globe in minutes. She couldn't let anyone know how she felt, there were a thousand girls watching her, hungry to dethrone her, waiting to see her falter so they could take their chance.

As if on cue, Minnie arrived, dressed in less material than Zara's pillowcase. She was wearing a Mui Mui dress Zara recognised, and had even considered wearing, but decided was too slutty for her. Minnie obviously didn't think so, and as the press clamoured for Minnie, Zara could see it all so clearly. Here was the one person who would most benefit from her demise.

She felt bile trap her breath, and turned panicked eyes away from Minnie, to where Imran was standing. He tuned into her mood, and came up to guide her to the green room, where they would wait with the other stars.

'You look stunning,' he said, kissing her hand. 'It's crazy inside, I had a look earlier. It's like a car crash of money and bad taste.'

'Great, sounds like my kind of night,' she said drily.

—

In the green room Zara sat in a corner next to Imran, who was wearing a tux with satin lapels and a maroon bow and cummerbund.

'Hugo Boss,' he told her when she asked.

'It's very smart. Did Sasha pick it out?' she asked with an arched eyebrow. Imran's face darkened. 'Trouble in paradise?'

'Something like that.'

'I like her. She's not as fake as some of the other star wives, and at least she's never a bitch to my face. So tell me, what's wrong? Maybe I can help?'

Zara liked being with Imran. Sitting here she felt Salman, and the poisoned cocktails were in another dimension. She was reminded instead how they had both had risen up from absolutely nothing. She was feeling the defiance return to her. The way it had slowly but surely after the car bomb.

'Yes, because you do so well at relationships, Miss Chronically Single. How is your imaginary husband?' Imran said it with a smirk, and Zara took it as the joke it was meant to be.

'Ouch, but that's ok. I am a woman, maybe I can explain what's going on in her head.'

Imran told Zara about Sasha's script and the offer of finance and production that Emel Walid had made.

'But that's wonderful! Imagine the looks on all the other wives' faces when they see Sasha actually get off her rear and do something more than shopping or gossiping, or interior design – which is just code for shopping and gossiping. Why are your balls getting so twisted about it?'

'I hate the fact that she wants to do anything. I want to give her the world. I *want* her to be one of those wives who does nothing but shop and gossip. Occasionally shops – I saw how much damage she can do in a day when she's pissed. But after what that woman did for me, Zara. She not only saved my life but also my mother's.'

'And for that you are going to punish her for the rest of her life?'

'What do you mean?'

'Don't you get it? The girl who went against her own mother and her own middle-class upbringing, the girl you fell in love with, who had a conscience and a backbone, you expect her to give up who she is?'

'It's not like that. I want her to be so happy she will be the envy of everyone, I want to treat her like a queen.'

'Maybe she doesn't want to be treated like a queen, but as the woman she is?'

'I don't want her to feel like she has to work, that she hasn't got a right over what I earn. And what about the kids?'

'Oh yes, your kids that you bring with you to your outdoor shoots and your foreign stage shows?'

'Come on, that's not fair.'

'It's funny how they become an issue when she wants to do this movie, but before that you were fine just to leave them to nannies and your mother. Imran, the nineteen-fifties are over. Even in Mumbai.'

'Come on, Zara, you know what our industry is like. The men will eat her alive for daring to invade their territory. How can I knowingly send her into that space? It cuts me up inside. I can't let anyone hurt her.'

Zara sighed, closed her eyes, and rested her head back.

'I know more than anyone what a nasty world this is. Bollywood is so big, bold, colourful, and glamorous, we are the touchstone for magic and entertainment. We have something in our movies that no one else does, and we cast a spell on our audiences. Yet the darkness… I know it, Imran, you know it too. Its taste lingers and suffocates. But things are changing, and Sasha has you. No matter how bleak it gets for her, you will be her shoulder to cry on.'

'I don't want her to suffer.'

'So you are going to lock her up and deny her the dreams she's carried for always? If you do this, if you push her like this, I promise you one thing, Imran. You will lose her.'

Imran looked into Zara's eyes and smiled.

'And you? Are you going to stay single forever?' he asked.

'I was hoping the Jhansi movie would be my big moment, when box office and career-defining role meet. Then like everyone else I was going to marry a rich NRI businessman or doctor and live happily ever after as a housewife far away from Mumbai.'

'There are other options,' he laughed.

'I'm only joking, you of all people know that. I don't think I could ever leave Mumbai. I made it my home, and if I rise or fall, I will do in that city. And when I find a man I can trust, I will marry him.' She didn't tell Imran how Dan had been that man for an instant. He had seen past her façade when she had acted like a bitch to the retail woman in Tristan's; he had seen past the bling and designer clothes to see the confused and scared woman acting out her life. She had told him about the choices she had been forced to make, about the ready abuse that the world had handed out to her. Zara had confided to Dan in a way that she had never been able to before, shown him the vulnerable little girl that hid behind the mantle of the Bollywood queen she portrayed. And still, in the end, he too had gone the way of everyone else.

'You'll be fine, Zara Das,' Imran said. 'We both will.'

'Well unless you sort out your ego, you won't be. With Sasha gone, you will be the target of every wannabe and gold-digger east of Kabul. You won't ever know again if the woman you are with loves you, or loves Imran Khan the movie star. Sasha knew you before all of that, she loved you. And if you throw that away, seriously, I think it will make you Bollywood's biggest fool.'

'You're awful sometimes,' he said, laughing.

'Talking of awful,' she said, as Minnie came in.

'This looks cosy,' she said, seeing Imran clasping Zara's hand. He moved it away quickly and stood up to greet her. 'Don't let me interrupt,' Minnie added.

'You are so cheeky,' Imran said, kissing Minnie on the cheek.

'Very,' said Zara, 'in fact we can see most of her cheeks tonight.'

'Envy isn't in fashion this season,' said Minnie, grabbing a flute of champagne.

'Did you run out of pocket money, darling?' Zara said. 'Is that why you couldn't afford the full outfit?'

'It's Mui Mui, from Paris. Where did you get your dress from? Did you steal the curtains from the Mirage?'

'I didn't have to shop in a store to get my outfit like everybody else. Sabyasachi created it for me especially. Then again, I wouldn't expect you to spot an original. Are those breasts from your last visit to Palm Springs? Or did you go cheap and get them done in Hungary?'

Ajay came in next, wearing a black *sherwani*. He deliberately avoided sitting next to Minnie for some reason and instead perched next to Zara. Minnie looked put out.

'It's so busy out there,' he said. 'I think Raj wants to break the box office records for Bollywood films released in the UK with *Kismet India*.'

'He's apprehensive about the response in India I think, so wants to capitalise on the diaspora,' added Imran. 'Plus he doesn't know when he'll be able to finish filming.'

'I think we have, what, four days left? He can probably film most scenes in studios back home.'

Zara didn't say anything. If there was danger to her life in London, how could they expect her to film in Mumbai? Maybe she should speak to Raj, get him to start filming again and quickly wrap up anything that needed doing?

'I don't know why he's nervous,' said Ajay. 'The film has everything to make it a hit. A love story, family politics, the class divide, great sets, and the songs are already being well received.'

'The soundtrack is out?' asked Imran.

'Raj said the music company have released the audio for two songs on YouTube. The views are going up daily. He just needs to finish the filming.'

'He'd better enjoy the attention while he can,' said Minnie, 'I've got a feeling a new video is going to be released soon that will really get the viewers up.'

Zara narrowed her eyes at Minnie while her insides clenched and she felt apprehension run through her.

'I'm glad a hoax has got you so excited,' said Zara. 'Minnie's seen some bullshit trailer, apparently it's a sex film involving me.'

'Something tells me this one's real,' said Minnie.

'People are always putting up fake pictures and videos,' said Imran. 'My face has been doctored on so many porn images, Caucasian men's bodies with my face. It's laughable.'

'We will see,' said Minnie. 'In fact we will see more than we want to, I'm sure.'

Zara felt anger rise in her at the gloating expression on Minnie's face. She stood up and excused herself, going to the bathroom.

–

Imran asked Sasha to meet him outside the green room. They had been like strangers really for the last few days, silently occupying each other's space, but pretending the other didn't exist. Imran and Sasha weren't really given to rows, her personality was too sweet-tempered. Imran often had outbursts about other people to her, and she would just laugh off the nonsense that others did. It helped him relax, and she loved hearing the gossip he brought back about people she didn't necessarily want to spend time with.

The last few days had been a killer though, she felt so alone. Even speaking to her children without Imran had been painful. His mother seemed to know something was up and kept telling her she was praying for them both. They hadn't done a group Facetime chat for a while now. She missed that link, her family all together, for those precious moments.

'Sasha, *jaan*. Am I that bad a person that you can't even bear to look at me anymore?'

When she did, she saw his beautiful dark eyes with their long lashes against his creamy complexion, his pink mouth, the neat beard, and the earnestness in his expression. She felt a bout of longing for him and felt the pain that this argument had caused. Imran held his hands out to her, but she didn't take them.

'I understand I've been acting like a bastard,' he said. 'It took me a while to realise. This is me saying I'm sorry.'

Sasha stayed silent. She was surprised by this sudden change. It wasn't enough though, she needed to hear that he understood what he was apologising for. And more than that, she needed to know he was actually going to support her.

'I love you more than anything on this earth. And if I got to heaven, and you weren't there, I'd ask them to make me leave.'

Sasha started laughing, she couldn't help it. It was a cheesy line from one of his movies, and he grinned at her as he said it.

'I've missed your smile, baby, so much,' he said. 'Please forgive me. I want to give you everything, and I forgot that there are some things which only you can do for yourself. If you want to make this movie, I promise I will let you.'

'Let me?' Sasha said, her tone rising. 'Get one thing straight, Mr Imran Khan, I don't need your permission to do this. I am telling you I'm doing this.'

'Okay, okay, I'm sorry. That came out all wrong. What I mean to say is, you have been there for me and you have helped me all through my life practically. From that little boy you saved, to the star I became. You were always there for me. And I promise you this, *jaan*, I am here for you. Whatever you want to do, I will be there in any way that you need me or want me to be.'

'And you won't cause dramas when I leave for two months to the Emirates?'

'No, I'll come with you if I can and if I can't I'll help Amma look after the kids so you can focus on your movie. I am going to be the best Bollywood husband in town. Now please, will you come here? I've been walking around with a raging boner all week.'

Sasha fell into his arms laughing and he kissed her deeply, as though it was the first time they had ever kissed. His touch was rough, showing how hungry he was for her. Imran led her by the hands into the disabled toilets, and despite her initial protests, she let him half undress her, leaving her kameez on top. He didn't bother undressing himself, pushing her against the toilet door, making her wet with his fingers and mouth, then unzipped himself and thrust inside her. He came quickly, panting against her.

'I'm sorry, but it's been a few days, and I was so horny. I love you, Sasha.'

Sasha pulled her kameez down, and checked her reflection in the mirror while washing her hands. She touched up her make-up, and felt something shift inside her. It was excitement, a feeling she hadn't experienced in too long, and she liked how it felt. She wasn't so naïve to think life would be perfect, nothing ever was. Still, in that moment, with her children, her career and a husband willing to support her dreams, Sasha felt that it was.

'I love you too,' she said, stroking Imran's face. 'And thanks for supporting me. Although you didn't have much choice.'

They both laughed, holding each other, knowing how lucky they were to have found someone they might last the distance with.

Chapter Twenty-Five

Jackie was seated in the ballroom of the Dorchester hotel, at a table with Rani and Sasha. She was wearing a Christian La Croix tailored dress in aubergine, showing off her curves to their fullest advantage. She wanted to feel sexy tonight, and she had gone out of her way to make sure she did. She had borrowed one of the make-up artists and hair stylists from the movie to create her look for the evening.

Sasha was dressed in a Manish Malhotra sky blue shalwar kameez, studded with blue stones. Her face was made up subtly, her hair loose, and looking a bit rough after her trip the bathroom. Her eyes though, were sparkling.

'Are you pregnant again?' Jackie intoned.

'In a way,' Sasha said, mysteriously.

If Jackie and Sasha had gone glam, Rani had outdone both of them. She seemed to be channelling some sort of goddess, dressed in a heavy gold saree with more semi-precious stones and gold thread than Jackie had ever seen up close. She was sparkling in the lights from the ballroom, her face made up to perfection.

'Did you steal Tiffany's?' asked Jackie.

'It's Abu Jani-SK if you must know. I love that colour on you, by the way. In fact I'm going to tweet it.'

'Hold the press, since when do you tweet? I thought that was your husband's forte?' said Jackie, throwing back champagne as if it was free, then laughing as she realised it was. 'Sorry, ex-husband.'

'Since today. Why should I avoid social media? I have spent too long playing this *sati savitri* matriarch. I was once the hottest actress in Bollywood, you know. Even more desirable than that cheap tramp Laila.' Jackie spat out her drink, wiping furiously with a napkin as it spilt down her chin.

'Rani*ji*, are you ok?' said Sasha, concerned.

'Sorry, that was mean of me. She's not so bad. We had a heart to heart and I think we might be on the way to friendship.'

'Seriously, what is wrong with you?' said Jackie.

'Nothing, forget me, what's going on with you, Sasha? You look like you're expecting.'

'Well I was waiting for you to get here before I said anything. Imran came on board. He apologised and said he's going to support me making the movie.'

'That's amazing! In fact, that's better than getting pregnant again,' said Jackie.

'And listen, I spoke to Emel. And I asked if you can direct.'

'Me?' said Jackie. 'Are you kidding me?'

'Not at all.'

'I make documentaries; my husband's the director.'

'I thought you might want a break,' said Sasha, looking hurt now. 'Sorry.'

'Send me the script. I'll think about it.'

'Oh, Jackie, it will be amazing.'

'I said I'll think about it.'

'There you go, Jackie, I just tweeted about you,' said Rani. 'Follow me, will you.'

'Fuck, you're making me check Twitter when there's caviar, champagne, and Penny Kapoor dressed like a Christmas tree to bitch about.'

The three women turned to see Penny walk by, wearing a bright green saree with enough stones and gold to blind anyone that stared at her for too long.

'I think Ali Baba's online cave threw up on her,' said Jackie, scrolling through her phone looking for Rani's tweet. She then burst into hysterics. 'What the actual fuck, Rani?'

Sasha took the phone from Jackie who was collapsing with laughter and started giggling too.

'What is so funny?' Rani asked, put out that her tweet was having this reaction on the women. Jackie couldn't breathe she was laughing so much, which encouraged Sasha to lose herself.

'What is wrong with you both? Oh look, Bobby's here.'

Rani felt the tension in her stomach watching her handsome son walk across the ballroom, dressed in a tux but with a sparkling ruby bow tie. Bobby was perplexed by the giggling women sitting with his mother. He kissed her on the cheek.

'This is my son,' said Rani. 'You remember Bobby, don't you?'

'Bobby? Little, shy, tubby Bobby Kumar? What the hell happened to you?' Jackie said. 'You look like a model.'

Bobby blushed, as he kissed Jackie on the cheek, and waved at Sasha.

'Hi, again,' he said shyly.

'Jackie's right, Bobby, you look gorgeous. Although I did like squeezing your cheeks before. What did university do to you? You look like a polo player.' Sasha was awed by the change in him. He had a feline face with long lashes, bordering on pretty, with a well-toned, slim body. He really did look like he should be on a fashion ramp, a big change from the spoilt chubby teenager she had last seen.

Bobby sat down next to his mother, uncomfortable at the scrutiny.

'Now I've seen you I can definitely say nothing's going on between you and my husband,' Jackie said. Sasha looked confused. 'You are so out of his league. You should be a movie star.'

'Let's not talk about that,' Rani said. 'You arrived in good time. These girls were having hysterics.'

At the reminder, Jackie started laughing again while Sasha tried to shush her. She didn't want Bobby to see what his mother had put on Twitter. Too late. Rani handed her phone to Bobby, whose face went bright red.

'Oh, Mum,' he said, and then started laughing too.

'What? I don't get it?' said a perplexed Rani.

'Mum, you didn't type the word aubergine to describe Jackie's dress. You've used the aubergine emoji.'

'And?'

'Rani, darling,' Jackie said to spare him, 'what your son is trying to say is that the aubergine emoji is the international symbol for a man's cock. Sorry, Bobby.'

Bobby was now sweating in embarrassment as Rani stared at her tweet.

'Oh my God,' said Rani, reading her tweet in the light of what she'd just been told.

> *I love the aubergine @JackieDillonDirector is wearing. I do love aubergines, in fact I could have giant aubergines all day, every day, I just can't get enough aubergines.*

'Best. Tweet. Ever,' Jackie added, collapsing into laughter again.

–

Back in the green room, Rocky and Laila had also joined the ensemble. Rocky had gone off centre and was wearing jeans with rips at the knees, topped with what looked like a Spanish bullfighter's jacket, and boots. Zara again thought how hot he was, totally not her type, but definitely he might get the female audience on side. It would be a tough ask, given that Ajay and Imran had most of the audience creaming for them.

Laila was as tasteful as her daughter was tasteless. She was wearing a gold saree, with heavy embroidery, glittering with gemstones and filigree. Her neck was wrapped by a gold choker studded with rubies, with matching earrings and bangles, and a ring on every finger. Ajay avoided looking at her.

'Zara, dearest, you look like the belle of the ball, absolutely gorgeous and so classy,' Laila said, standing to air kiss the younger woman. They both knew how much time their flawless make-up took so didn't want it smudged.

'Thank you, Laila*ji*, but still you are the most beautiful woman in any room. You look like a Maharani.'

'Thank you, dearest. I heard what happened the other night, I do hope you are feeling better. I would be a mess if it was me.'

'You are a mess anyway,' Minnie said icily.

'These things happen,' Zara said, ignoring Minnie. 'When you have faced death like I have, everything else seems so inconsequential.'

'Faced death?' Minnie started to laugh mockingly. 'You hardly went to the border to fight the enemy.'

'Her car exploded, I think that's probably a big deal,' drawled Rocky.

'Yet she miraculously survived,' said Minnie. 'Funny that.'

'You are such a bitch, Minnie,' said Rocky.

'You didn't think that when you were fucking me,' she said tartly, her eyes on Ajay.

—

The evening was standard. Which was dull and tedious and boring. Jackie watched as her husband was introduced by the Ambassador, and listened as Raj thanked the Indian High Commission and the Dorchester for inviting him and the cast. This was then followed by the cast all assembling on stage, saying a few superlatives and then Raj interviewing them.

'I miss bread sticks,' Jackie said to Sasha. 'I could use them to force my eyes open. Do these lot know how up themselves they sound?'

Behind the cast was the first poster of *Kismet India* to be revealed to the public. It would mean the charity event got a lot of publicity and hopefully more donations while also associating the movie with a good cause. In the centre of the poster were Imran and Zara, her head thrown back as Imran's lips caressed her throat. On either side of them were Laila and Ajay, with

Minnie and Rocky in smaller images. None of the British cast were on the poster, nor Salman and Ruby.

'I'm sure they don't mind,' Jackie said, knowing full well they would. In her experience, all actors had egos. They were laid bare on social media. One of the actors playing the role of Bingley had just released a video of himself coked up to the eyeballs gangsta-rapping and trailing a fake gun down his abs. In typical fashion he was lambasted then had to apologise, and in the space of a day went from villain to contrite, all of it desperate publicity seeking, she thought. 'Sasha, let's go. I need the bathroom. Come on, Rani, you too.'

On stage, Raj was making a speech about Salman, and how his death was such a sad loss, before asking a group of assembled journalists if they had any questions.

'Can you tell me, Zara, ma'am, what has it been like to work with Jasmine and Laila? Is it odd working with a mother-daughter team?'

Zara was subdued in her answers, feeling nervous on stage. 'It's been an absolute pleasure. Laila has adopted me I think as a second daughter, and Minnie has been so loving and warm. Rather than making me feel an outsider, they have both been so supportive. We share everything.'

Minnie smiled broadly. 'So sweet, Zara, I too feel like I've gained a much older sister to help advise me.'

'What about rumours of the rivalry between you both?'

'I find it so embarrassing,' said Minnie. 'I mean. Zara*ji* has been in this industry for so many years, she has been around all through my teenage years. I remember going to the cinema to watch her movies, and I am only just starting out. I have such a long way to go before I get to her level.'

'Do you feel the pressure of being compared to your mother?'

'Not at all, I don't think anybody can ever be Laila Chopra. She's one of a kind.'

'How did you find working with Ajay after all these years, Laila*ji*?' asked one brazen journalist. They had all been told not to broach the subject. There was a moment of silence as the entire ballroom went silent.

'We are here this evening to raise money for a charity supporting street children. I find it rather upsetting that the focus is on something so banal,' said Laila politely but cuttingly. 'Still, I know there is speculation and what is there to say? Except there hasn't been an issue. I have been an admirer of Ajay's work for decades, so it has been a pleasure to work with him again.'

Ajay remained silent. That would be the news story tomorrow, he knew.

'Zara, ma'am, have you felt less threatened in London than you have in Mumbai of late?'

'I love Mumbai and it is my home, and I can't wait to go back. I think though that we needed this space, like a quarrelling couple. Time apart to realise how much we miss each other.' There was a quiver in her voice as she added, staring at the cameras trained at her, 'I have missed you, Mumbai. I hope you have missed me too.'

The audience applauded at this point, and Zara wiped a tear from under her eye, which felt real.

—

The bathroom was empty when the three women entered, apart from a female attendant.

Jackie looked around for the extras that were available in the bathrooms at the Mirage, and couldn't find them. The bathrooms there had practically every product you might find in a Chelsea housewife's boudoir, whereas here there was just soap, moisturiser, hand towels, and perfume.

'You know you've been spoilt when even the Dorchester fails to deliver,' she said. 'How will we ever go back to the grime of Mumbai?'

'I can't wait,' said Rani. 'I am a Maharashtrian and Mumbai is in my blood. I miss the dirt and dust and people. It feels so empty here in comparison.'

'I can't wait to see my children again,' said Sasha.

'I don't know how you bear it. Mine are all grown but I miss them, and my grandchildren especially.'

'Bobby is here with you,' said Sasha. 'That's good, right?'

'Yes,' Rani said hesitantly. 'I don't know what's going to happen next though. I feel so scared of the future.'

'Listen, doll, don't worry. We could all be dead by morning, so just enjoy every second. You look amazing tonight, and fuck that *lullah* head for not knowing your worth.'

Sasha started laughing at Jackie's outburst, using the Punjabi word for dick.

'I've had an idea,' Jackie said. 'Sasha, I'll direct your movie, maybe, if I can hire Rani as my assistant for the shoot.'

'I don't... what... why?' said Rani.

'Just think, two months in the Emirates. We can go shopping in Dubai, hang out in Abu Dhabi and enjoy the emerging eighth Emirate with the Walid clan.'

'That would be brilliant. In fact, I couldn't think of a better way for me to start my film as a producer than with you both on board.'

Jackie spat on her hand and offered it to Sasha to shake. Sasha looked horrified, so Jackie washed her saliva off and offered her hand again. Sasha shook it, and Rani added her own hand to the mix. The three of them left the bathroom hand in hand, determined to call the shots in their lives.

Chapter Twenty-Six

Dinner was a strange affair, as Jackie and Sasha were joined by their husbands, but Ajay sat at a different table.

The menu was staggering. For starters there were salmon kebabs, lamb kebabs, chicken tikka, potato pakoras, and four types of chaat. The mains consisted of lamb shank nihari, Mughlai chicken, nargisi kofte, hyderabadi biryani, paneer tikka, and the softest naans. In between they were served amuse-bouches and palate cleansers of sorbets, and dessert was ras malai with silver paper, with an incongruous chocolate cake for those that didn't want the traditional sweet.

Rani sat between Bobby and Raj, and Jackie decided to tease her husband with her false assumptions that something had been going on.

'Bobby looks amazing,' she blurted out to Raj, who looked annoyed. The Pol Roger was in her blood though, so she didn't care. 'He'd make a great toy boy, what do you say, Bobby? Fancy an older woman? He got his looks from you obviously, Rani. You must be so proud of him. Investment banker, own place in London, so well-mannered. He'll make a great catch for someone. Right, Raj?'

'You're so not funny,' he said in response, but he had a massive grin on his face.

'Isn't it amazing about the Ambassador?' Jackie said. 'She started off as a diplomat's wife, but she was so talented, the government gave her the top job. And her husband is so supportive, happy to accompany her on postings. I think the Indian man has finally come of age. Don't you think so, Imran?'

Imran looked sharply at her, fork full of biryani heading to his mouth. 'I think that's a very backward opinion of Indian men. We came of age a long time ago. We have been worshipping women for centuries. Our most famous monument, the Taj Mahal, is a testament to the love of a woman.'

'Try the chicken, Jackie, it's amazing,' Sasha said.

'God, I'm drunk,' said Jackie, squeezing Raj's hand.

'Aren't you always?' said Imran icily, then laughed.

'I love you,' Raj said jovially.

'I hope so,' Jackie said, thinking how in a year's time they would be parents. She just hoped Raj could lay to rest some of the demons in his head before then.

-

Zara, Minnie, Laila, Ajay, and Rocky were at a separate table with James Kapoor, who was clearly showing off to everyone in the room. James was richer than all of them, and with the Ambassador also at his side, he was definitely in peacock mode. Penny Kapoor was at the same table, fawning over the Ambassador, and loudly saying how she would be making a personal donation to the street kids' charity.

'*Personal* from the money my father gives her,' Rocky whispered to Zara. 'She's such a leech. Hasn't done a day's work in her life.'

'That's unfair, isn't she playing by the same rules you have been?' Zara said.

'He's my father.'

'He's her husband.'

'I didn't get a choice, she chose to be a kept woman.'

'We all have choices, Rocky. I can see one of your worst ones right across from me,' Zara said, pointedly staring at Minnie.

'Brutal,' he said.

'How is filming going?' James Kapoor asked very loudly. 'Is my son the next Ranbir or Aamir?'

Zara smiled graciously while Minnie snorted with laughter. Laila dug her nails into Minnie's bare thigh under the table.

'He's very talented, and I think will have a great future,' Laila said.

Penny had disdain on her face. 'When he starts doing movies his father isn't bankrolling, we will see.'

'That's rich, coming from a woman whose very existence is being bankrolled by the same man,' Rocky said snidely. His father shot him a thunderous look, and Rocky shut up.

'Madam Ambassador, tell me, how much are you hoping to raise tonight?' Penny said, totally ignoring Rocky and carrying on as though nothing awkward had just been said. Zara had to give it to her, she was a consummate networker. She felt tired suddenly, and it all felt surreal again. What was she doing, sitting with these people in one of the most famous hotels in the world? And the anxiety hit her again, and the apprehension.

Zara found herself struggling to breathe, the cloying heat and perfumes mingling with the food and wine, everything nauseating. It was the smell of money and power, and she needed to get away from it all.

Abruptly she got up and made her excuses, rushing from the ballroom.

–

Zara stood in the lobby, contemplating what to do. She had obligations to the event, but she wanted to leave, get away from everyone. She had the sensation she was being buried alive, and it was causing her to panic. What had she done? What had she done to Pari? What had the world done to Pari? She pulled her phone out of her purse, a drawstring pouch that had been created to match her outfit, to call for her car, when she was startled to see Raj.

'Zara, can we talk please?'

Zara followed him onto a vacant couch for guests. He looked around to make sure there was no one eavesdropping and kept checking throughout his conversation. His eyes were red as he spoke, and he let the tears fall on occasion.

'I need to talk to you about something. Something important. You've asked me many times why I took you for this movie. Well, the truth is I saw what was happening to you. The way everyone was out to get you, I thought doing this, shifting this movie to London would be a small way of me repaying the debt I owe you.'

Zara was confused. 'Raj, how can you say that? Your family gave me my big break. You have always advised me and supported me. You are a true friend, Raj, and I have so few of those.'

'Zara, please, stop, you are making me ashamed of myself.'

'Raj? I don't understand?'

Raj took a couple of deep breaths, wiping away his tears. His head was lowered now, and he spoke to her in soft tones.

'Zara, what happened to you… it was wrong.'

'It's ok. I think things are changing now, I think when we go back to Mumbai…'

'No I don't mean that. I mean back then. I mean when my father signed you. Zara… I was there.'

Zara didn't understand him, didn't want to understand him. What was he saying?

'The night my father… I was meant to be out at a party, but I felt ill, so came back early. When I came to the house, it was empty. Mum was away at her parents', the servants weren't around either. It was all so crazy silent. But there was a mess in the lounge. There were empty drinks bottles, cards, and mock casino tables. I saw cocaine lines. Dad had obviously had a party that night, and I was looking at the mess. I was thinking, *I need to clean all this up before Mum gets here*. You see, it wasn't the first time. I knew his assistant cleaned up after him usually and didn't let on to Mum. I always could tell, though. The servants would all be given the day off because the mistress of the house was away.'

Zara stared at his sunken head, and her heart was in her throat. She felt sick at what Raj was saying, and was trying to control her own breathing, trying to stay still, when she wanted to run before he said anything else.

'I went up to his room, Zara, to check on him. There was laughter coming from inside, and the lights were on. I opened the door, and... Zara, I saw what he did to you.'

Zara let out a choked sob.

'I watched as he assaulted you, in front of two of his friends. And I knew they had all used you. I stopped him, Zara, I shouted and screamed, but it was too late. I was too late.'

Raj was crying now, his voice broken. Zara stared at him, torn between sympathy, anger, hatred, and the need for revenge. She was ashamed of that night, of what had happened to her, but what could she do?

'I'm so, so sorry, Zara.'

'I get it now,' she said, through her own choked-up voice, 'why you were always so kind to me. You were trying to get rid of your own guilt.'

'I'm sorry...'

'Sorry? You think that will make it ok? Do you have any idea what I've been through, and what your father did to me? The worst thing is, I can't even remember.'

'He drugged you, that's why.'

Zara looked at the broken Raj in front of her. She felt sick again.

'Why didn't you tell me before? Why now?'

'I suffered after that, I want you to know. I can't have sex... every time I try I see his face... see yours, so out of it. The reason I married Jackie is because there, in New York, it was all ok, I was away from Mumbai, and reminders of my father and you... but then when we got back here, it happened again. And until I make this right, I won't ever be well.'

'How can anyone make this right, Raj?'

He looked at her, his eyes beseeching. 'You can. And I will help you to.'

Zara felt as though her heart was about to explode, and she ran out of the hotel and onto Park Lane. Someone grabbed her arm, and she was about to scream, when she saw it was Dan.

'Not here, there are press everywhere,' he said, and forced her limp body into a limousine that had just stopped near them. The door closed, and he got in beside her, as the car sped off into the London traffic.

-

Dan asked the driver to park up in a side street in Mayfair. It was a mean little back alley lined with trash cans.

'Charming location,' she said, her head still full of what Raj had told her.

'Sorry, I shouldn't have done that, maybe planned it differently. I was waiting for you with the driver, and when we saw you come out, we drove around.'

'That's ok,' she said. He looked good. She hated to admit it, but he did. She turned her face away before she fell into his eyes and started feeling things she didn't want to. She was a mess tonight. Raj's revelations had brought it all back to her, and she couldn't cope. 'What's wrong?' she said to Dan. Maybe he was going to apologise for using her. Thinking about that night, she felt the anger again. The same anger she had felt for Amol Dillon and all the other men that had used her. One of the men from that night must have filmed it, which was how VJ had the footage.

'Hopefully nothing is wrong. I wanted to tell you in person, though. I dealt with VJ.'

'What do you mean?' For a second Zara thought he had harmed him in some way. She felt glad, too. One of the men that had ruined her life had been dealt with at least.

'It doesn't matter. I just wanted you to know. You don't have to worry about him any more, or about the videos. They are gone, all deleted.'

'Are you sure?' She didn't even dare to believe it. Not on this night when her past had come back in such a dreadful way.

'Yes. And even if he hasn't deleted them, he won't risk leaking them. I made him aware of just how vulnerable he is.'

'Thank you, Dan,' she said weakly. It didn't seem like enough. But it was all she could manage right then.

'It's fine. I thought I should tell you. Anyway, Eamon will take you back to the hotel. I'm getting off here.'

'Dan... why did you do this?' she asked. 'After that night...'

'Let's not talk about it,' he said. 'I suppose that's the way your kind behave.'

'My kind? What do you mean?'

'I suppose you just used me for whatever reason. Maybe it gave you a kick to do so.'

'Dan, what do you mean? You're the one that used me. I heard you on the phone. To your mother-in-law. I'm guessing Amy is your wife, the one you said you loved more than anything?'

Dan looked confused, then started to laugh.

'Yes I was on the phone to my mother-in-law. Amy is not my wife, she is my daughter. Her mother and I divorced years ago when Amy was born.' He looked maudlin at the memory. 'Jean, my mother-in-law, looks after Amy when her mother and I can't. You see...' His eyes darkened. 'Amy is sick. Very sick. She has a rare form of cancer in her brain, and there is only one treatment available. It's a pioneering laser treatment in the US. But it's expensive. It's why I took on your security; it's why I work with the James Kapoors of this world. Their security is the most complicated, but they pay the best.'

Zara stared at him as he spoke, feeling foolish, but at the same time, her heart breaking. She hadn't even stopped to let him explain, just rushed out of his life without a backward glance, assuming he was like every other man out there. And here he was, the hard-working father, the most honest, true man she had met in years. A man whose daughter was dying, and who had to put up with the dramas of women like her to help his child.

Without thinking she pulled him close, and kissed him, needing him to make her feel ok.

'I'm sorry, Dan. I thought...'

'It's ok, I should have asked you,' he said, kissing her back.

'Can we start afresh tomorrow?' she said. 'I'd like to.'

'Isn't it complicated?'

'I've waited my whole life for you, Dan. I don't care how complicated it is.'

Dan watched Zara's limo pull away, alerting his team members that she was on her way, feeling emotions he hadn't left himself feel for a long time. They had agreed to meet the next day after filming, and talk through whether there was a possibility at all of starting anything. Dan was about to walk to Green Park station when he got a call from one of his contacts at the forensics lab he used.

'Deb, everything ok?'

'Sorry, I know it's late, but I thought I'd better do your stuff today before I forgot. So I processed the samples you gave me, and I got a match. The same DNA is on all of them.'

Dan had sent Zara's tampered make-up, the blood rose, and the cut rope from the falling chandelier to Deb to analyse. He had suspected there was something on the rope from the way it was cut, and hoped whoever did it hadn't used gloves. He was glad his intuition had paid off.

'Do you have a name?' he asked.

'Yes.'

When Deb told him, Dan thought at first it was a mistake, and then slowly realisation dawned on him. He hailed a cab and rushed to the Mirage after Zara.

Chapter Twenty-Seven

Zara was still a mess when she entered her hotel room. There was no security, they were still at the Dorchester, but she didn't care. It felt so unfair, her life caught between two states all the time. Just when she thought she was about to hit a port, another storm would drive her further away. She had Dan, finally a man she could love, who loved her. It should be the start of another future, a world where she was free of VJ and in Dan's arms. Only, Raj's revelations had rocked her. She thought his father had taken his price for her big break, and she had quietly held that poison inside her. Only the truth was so much worse. How could she face the day and love Dan completely, knowing what had happened to her? No, he was strong enough to handle this. She was sure of it.

She collapsed in the middle of the floor, clutching her phone to her stomach and wailing into the emptiness, then stopped abruptly and gasped when she saw a figure standing by the windows. He stepped forward, and she saw it was Kasim.

'You frightened me,' she said. 'What are you doing here?' Kasim was staring at her, a kitchen knife in his hand. 'Kasim? What's wrong? Is everything ok?'

Kasim stepped towards her, the knife pointed downwards and away from him. His eyes didn't seem to focus.

'Can I talk to you, ma'am, please,' he said.

'Yes, of course,' she said. He wasn't right, and she felt frightened of him, her mind thinking what she could do to get away. What was happening, why was he in this state? She clutched her phone tighter, tapping the screen discreetly. The emergency app button filled it, and she pressed on it. 'What's wrong?'

'You remember, ma'am, I told you about what happened to me?'

Zara nodded.

Kasim continued in the same monotone voice. 'And you said something similar had happened to you. Imagine, ma'am, if your abuser was here. What would you do to him? If you got the chance, for revenge, would you take it?'

Zara didn't reply. What did he mean? Had he lost his mind? Did he think she had done something to him? She hadn't even been a bitch to him like she could be to people. She had an affection for him which she always tried to convey and he seemed to feel the same. She was confused, and the knife was terrifying her. Was this it? Was this how her life would end? Murdered in a seven-star hotel in London, the rise and rise and then the dramatic fall of a star? She felt panic as Kasim came towards her.

'I've done something terrible, Zara ma'am, and I don't think I can come back from it. I think this is the only way to finish things.'

'Nothing is that bad,' she said, trying not to let the fear she was feeling show in her voice. She looked at how far the door was. If she wasn't wearing her ballgown and heels, she might have made a run for it. She wouldn't stand a chance, she had to talk him down.

'This really is. I have destroyed everything. I tried to get away from it, start again. This was my escape. But my past can never let me be free. And now it is all over.'

'What do you mean?'

'Do you remember what I told you? About my past? About why I came to this country for asylum?'

Zara tried to think, and then yes, she did remember. He said he had been abused by a gang of paedophiles who filmed it all and threatened to upload the videos if he said anything.

'Kasim, what happened to you was horrible. It was truly, truly awful. And the same thing happened to me, just tonight I know for sure the same thing happened to me. This is no way to end things though. You've made a fresh start. Look let's just walk away now, give me the knife and walk away. We can pretend this didn't happen. I swear I won't tell anyone. There is still a chance before you do something that you can't come back from. And we can both deal with this together. I promise, trust me.'

'You are not listening to me, ma'am. I am telling you this. I have already done something so bad I can't come back from it.'

'What did you do, Kasim?'

'Salman... it was me, ma'am. I am so sorry, so so sorry, that I did it in your room. I had no choice. I am so sorry. I killed him, ma'am. Now tell me, how can I escape that?'

Zara was still, unable to move. How could Kasim the mild-mannered, always polite young man have done that? Was that what he was about to do to her? Had he lost his mind?

'I don't understand,' she whispered. 'Why did you kill him?'

'It was him, ma'am. The gang in Pakistan. He was one of them. They were a group of powerful men, celebrities, spoilt sons of rich fathers. And Salman, he was one of them. Filming it. So many innocent Pakistani boys like me, being abused every day. And we are silent, because it would bring shame on our families if we said anything, it would destroy them. And so I ran away, I claimed asylum here, and I hoped I could move on. And then he came back into my life. And all the pain and hurt came with him, ma'am. And I wanted revenge so much, I wanted to hurt him for all the times he and his friends hurt me. Zara ma'am, I am sorry I involved you.'

'Kasim, you poor soul. I understand, I really do. But this isn't how to deal with it. Let's go to the police, we will explain, you were provoked. He deserved it. Please don't do anything stupid now that will ruin your chances.'

'What chance do I have, ma'am? I am on a refugee visa, if I commit a crime I will be sent back. I have done this. And I

326

will be sent back, and I don't want to. I can't bear to be used like that again. Please, ma'am. Help me.'

'I will, I promise,' Zara said, feeling a surge of hope. He wasn't going to kill her after all, he just wanted her help. 'What do you want me to do? Put the knife down and let's talk.'

'No,' he said sharply. 'I don't want to talk any more. I want you to use this knife, and take my life. I am too scared to. And suicide is a sin. Please. Take my life, and tell people, that I wasn't a bad man. I just needed to be free.'

Kasim walked towards her, knife outstretched in his hand, and was about to hand it to her, when the door to her room opened. Dan stormed in, but halted seeing the scene in front of him. He was in a rage, and Zara didn't understand why. Kasim panicked seeing him, and lunged for Zara, who tried to run, but her heels and dress tripped her over. She screamed as Kasim grabbed her and put the knife to her neck.

'Let her go,' said Dan. 'What are you doing?'

'Stay away, I need you to leave, now,' said Kasim testily.

'Please, Kasim, let me go,' Zara said. 'Dan won't tell anyone, we can sort this out. Please.'

Dan slowly edged towards them, pleading with Kasim to let her go. Kasim backed away slowly, but Zara was unmovable in her outfit.

'Dan, please, don't let him hurt me,' she said.

Dan ignored her, keeping his eyes in Kasim. He had made steps towards them and was within touching distance now.

'Kasim, I don't believe you want to do this. Please let her go and let's talk about this.'

'No, this is the only way,' said Kasim.

The next moments were a blur as Dan leapt forward, grabbing Kasim's knife hand. Zara's neck was scratched in the process, and she let out a scream, as Dan pushed her away, and toppled Kasim, forcing his hands behind his back. Kasim let out a cry, and began to weep, as Dan ordered Zara to call the police.

Zara was seated in the lounge, the police having taken Kasim away. She promised to get him the best lawyer she could before he went, but he looked so dejected, as though life had ended but he was still being forced to live it like a corpse. She was craving a hot chocolate, but thought it would remind her too much of Kasim if she had some just then.

Dan came to stand by her, and she smiled up at him, emotion clouding her vision.

'My hero,' she said. 'Thank you for rescuing me. Again.'

'I think I just made things worse from all accounts,' he said coldly. His whole body language was off, as though he was angry. She didn't understand it; he was so different to the man that had waved her off in Mayfair. 'I came as soon as you pressed the emergency app on your phone. But to be honest I was already on my way here. I needed to speak to you urgently.'

'About what?' she said.

'I had a friend of mine run some tests for me. Forensic tests, to check for DNA.'

'For what?' she said, confused. She didn't know what relevance this would have for her.

'I gave her the rose that was left in your room, and the rope from the mansion, the one that was cut that led to the chandelier falling on you, and the make-up you thought was tampered with. She called me tonight, had pulled a late shift for me. Do you want to know what the results were?'

Zara stared at him hard, listening and waiting. She dreaded what he would tell her now.

'The DNA on the rose belonged to one person only. The rope had many samples on it, but there was one match to that left on the rose, the same that matched the make-up. Do you know whose it was?' Zara shook her head. 'I gave my friend a test sample, to eliminate you from enquiries over the sample of the bloody flower. Only you, see, she matched your DNA to that which she found on the flower, the make-up and also the rope. Now I know you handled the flower and the make-up, but you didn't touch that rope. The segment I gave for testing was from where the person that cut it had held it. I suppose it slipped out of your grasp, and touched your skin. I'm guessing you were shrewd enough to wear gloves while you cut it, so it must have been a mistake. So you see, Zara, I know for a fact that it was you pulling these stunts. Trying to make me believe you were in danger. No wonder you didn't want the police involved, were happy to go along with the hotel. What I want to know is, did you use me so that I wouldn't figure out what was going on? Was I part of the act as well? Someone to see your reaction shots to the incidents?'

Zara couldn't take her eyes off him. Her heart was breaking inside, as this man, the only one she thought she might be able to love, was pulling away from her. And she had no one else to blame. He was right. Her hand had slipped as she cut the rope, her glove had ridden up and her palm had scraped against the rope. The evidence had painted the very image she could see in her head. She thought about denying it, about lying, but she knew that this was a time for truth. That she might be able to save this if she was honest with him.

'Dan...'

'Are you crazy? That falling chandelier could have killed you.'

'I knew when it would fall, I timed it. I saw online how long it would take with the weight and the cut to the rope. I would have moved out of the way. It's why I kept messing up the scene, trying to prolong filming time so I would be there when it fell.'

'Ingenious,' Dan said sarcastically. 'Why did you do it?'

'You don't understand. I was about to lose everything after the Jhansi movie. I thought my career was over, that I was poison for any filmmaker to take on. And then the bomb happened, and people began to forgive me and be sympathetic.

I thought, stupidly, that if things kept happening, and if they kept getting leaked online, the sympathy would grow. That people would come back, that I could save my career.'

'No matter who you lied to or hurt in the bargain?'

'Dan, please. I didn't mean for you to find out, I never wanted to hurt you.'

'I felt so sorry for you, I wanted to protect you. You played with my emotions so well.' His face was red with the anger he was feeling, his eyes gone from piercing to dark and full of rage.

'That wasn't part of it, I promise you. The way I felt about you, the way I feel about you... Dan, please, I love you. I know it. Please, don't let this get in the way, please give me a chance. I'm sorry, I wasn't thinking straight. I beg you, don't punish me for what I did. I need you.'

Dan looked at her hard, but there was no let-up in his dark mood.

'My daughter needs me,' he said. 'And I will not let someone like you anywhere near her. I never want to see you again, Zara Das. I hope to God you find some solace somewhere, and stop being so fucking messed up.'

'Dan, please...' she wailed, but he was gone. Zara sat alone in her seven-star hotel suite, with no one to wipe away the tears.

Epilogue: Bollywood

Zara stared into the camera, feeling nauseous, her heartbeat hammering in her head. Raj stood behind the camera, and nodded at her, smiling at her to encourage her. She had rehearsed the speech she was going to make already, but now, in front of the camera, it was becoming real. Finally Raj gave her a thumbs up to get her started, and she began. In painful words Zara recalled how she had run away to Mumbai to follow her dreams and make something of her life. Only to find that in Mumbai there were men waiting for girls like her. She recounted how she was forced into situations that no woman should find herself in, with men forcing themselves on her, having no one to turn to. That everyone in the entertainment world told her it was normal and was the only way she could make it. And then she looked at Raj, before she spoke about her break into movies. About how a producer had called her for a casting and had forced himself onto her. Not only that, he had drugged her and let his friends rape her too. She looked again at Raj, at the hardness in his face, and he nodded. And Zara named Amol Dillon as the producer who had done that to her.

'So it's time now, India. It's time we stopped this. I am here to raise my voice and say, I am Zara Das, and I have been the victim of sexual violence and abuse. And I am here to say, *enough*. It is time we protected our children, our sisters, our wives, our mothers. And to the men who think it is ok to use their power to carry out this abuse, I am telling you now that your time is up and that every sin that has been done over the years will be told and you will be shamed in public, because this guilt and shame is not mine, it is yours.'

She had tears running down her face when she was done, and she saw Raj wipe his own eyes.

'I'm sorry, Zee, I should have protected you,' he said.

'It's ok, Raj. Help me put away your father and the other men involved, that's how you can absolve yourself now.'

Raj nodded, as he packed up the digicam, and started to edit the footage on his laptop. They were seated in Zara's Bandra apartment, the windows open, the cool breeze flowing in.

'Jackie tells me Sasha has roped you into her movie?' he said.

'Yes. It's a dynamite script, and I thought it might do me good to get out of Mumbai again for a bit, when this all kicks off.'

'You will be the face of this, you know that, don't you? It's only going to get worse.'

'That's fine. I'd like to make a kick ass movie to silence the critics when it does. Show them that while I'm winning they are about to face their worst nightmare.'

'Yes, I hope so.'

'What about your father?' she asked him carefully.

'He deserves everything he is going to get. I know you're not the only one. I hope the others come out to support you.'

'I hope so too,' she said. In the back of her mind she hoped Dan would see the video, and maybe understand just what Zara had been through, and maybe find it in his heart to forgive her, at least. *Kismet India* was hitting the cinemas in a week, Raj having completed filming without incident in Mumbai. The advance booking had already shattered records, the buzz was so strong for the film. It was why she felt comfortable doing this now; the film was already a success, and she couldn't be accused of pulling a stunt.

'I couldn't have asked for all this publicity, or paid for it,' Raj said, as Shanti brought them tea. She seemed elated that Zara was back, and that VJ wasn't.

'It's quite something,' Zara said. The headlines had poured out over the past few months: Salman's death, and the faux outpouring of grief online by people feeling sad that such a hot man had died so young; the scandal of Rani and Ajay's divorce; his pairing with Laila, and even worse, someone had leaked the rumour that he was actually seeing Minnie, all coupled with stories of Zara's life being threatened on set were making more column inches and driving more social media traffic than any marketing campaign could. *Kismet India* was about to smash every box office record going, with everyone seeing it as evidence of just what a superstar Zara was, and what a comeback she had engineered.

When Raj had finished editing, he played the video back to her. Zara then uploaded it to her Twitter, YouTube, and Instagram accounts, with the hashtags *#MeToo* and *#TimesUp*.

–

Zara looked at her reflection in the mirror and saw in her eyes a new confidence. Shanti was positively beaming next to her as she helped her get ready. Zara had given herself the usual facial and then completed her make-up using Zara X. The brand had become an international sensation, and she had just signed major deals with Selfridges and Harrods. L'Oréal were also in a fight with Guerlain to buy her rights.

For this night Zara had painted her lips poppy red and her eyes violet and gold, to match her dress. She had never got to show off her saree properly before, so Laura Kim and Fernando Garcia had made her another one. The violet and gold Oscar de la Renta saree was like water under moonlight, the silk and gold threading merging beautifully. Anita Dongre had made her special shoes to match. Yes, Zara Das was back. And when she stepped out of her Mercedes at the premiere, it would be the return of the queen.

Shanti stood ready as ever to put her black *kajal* dot on Zara's cheek, to avoid the evil eye. Only this time she smiled broadly and stood aside. Instead, there was another woman standing ready to do that. Zara held back her tears as her aged mother reached out a bony arm and applied the *kajal*.

Her father had taken his anger to his funeral pyre, but after he was gone, Zara had reconciled with her mother. Finally, after a decade of heartache and pain, and after a lifetime where they had all lived with the ghost of Dev's disappearance, Zara had found her family again.

As Shanti and her mother both waved her off, Zara's only desire was to hurry back home, into the arms of these two women who loved her selflessly.

Zara checked her phone as her Mercedes hit the thronging Bandra traffic, her premiere at the same Juhu PVR theatre where her car had exploded. She said a prayer for her driver that had died that night, while exchanging banter with her new driver. She checked her phone, a message from Colette Dove. It was confirming that Dan's daughter Amy had successfully completed the cutting-edge treatment she needed in Los Angeles.

Zara had made an anonymous donation, which Colette had managed, with no link back to her. Dan probably suspected it was from James Kapoor, and that was how she wanted it. She didn't want to risk him not accepting it if he knew it was from her, and he was too proud to ask anybody else for it. But he couldn't be too proud to reject a gift, not if his daughter would benefit.

Zara put her head back, and closed her eyes, picturing Dan and Amy, hope in their lives again. She was desperate to speak to him, but knew that their fates just weren't aligned. And the one man she had truly loved could never be hers.

–

The flashes were brighter, the voices louder than ever, as Zara's Mercedes stopped at the red carpet. Tonight there was no warning in place, and Zara would do her usual long walk into the theatre. Her fans were there still, thronging the cinema entrance, desperate for pictures and autographs. Zara took her time with her fans, her way of thanking those who had stood by her. These were her Instagram warriors, the ones who hashtagged her haters into silence. And around the country the rest of her audience was back.

Zara stood in the midst of the lights and the adulation, and she felt at peace. It had been a hard road, but at that moment she could forget the pain and the loss, and be grateful for what she had.

–

Inside, the auditorium was full of Bollywood's biggest stars. Miss X was doing a Facebook live broadcast, rattling off a list of Bollywood's who's who.

'We made it, Zee.' Zara turned to see Imran in a tux, with Sasha on his arm. She was looking gorgeous in red and black opal.

'I didn't think I'd ever get to another premiere, let alone my own,' said Zara. 'Did Sasha give you the good news?'

'What news?' he said.

'I had lunch with Zara last week,' Sasha replied. 'Emel wants her to play the lead in the film I'm making, and I agree.'

'And who's the hero?'

'No, *jaan*, you don't understand. I'm re-writing the script. The role you would have done, had you not been such a misogynist, is now going to be a female. And Zara is playing it.'

'That's right,' said Zara. 'The only thing that works at the box office nowadays isn't sex and Imran Khan. The only thing that works at the box office is sex and Zara Das. When they come for the queen, she takes down the king.'

Raj and Jackie came to join them. Jackie still hadn't much taken to Zara, but she was at least saying hello to her, telling Sasha on the sly, 'Well I guess I should be nice to the woman who caused so much drama my husband's going to make a killing. Just what I need when I have a baby on the way.'

Raj looked tired and stressed, the only evidence of the real battles that he and Zara were fighting still. But tonight they were going to forget about that and celebrate life instead.

'Thank you, Raj,' Zara said. 'You took the risk of casting me, and look how you've been rewarded for not being a coward like the rest. They hate you now obviously, but that's not my problem.'

'Indeed, but what's all this nonsense about you not starring in my next movie?'

'Sorry, I got an offer from a better director,' she said.

'Are you trying to butter me up even before we start?' said Jackie. 'It won't work.'

Zara laughed, and Jackie cracked a smile at least. They were going to make a movie together, no matter what their personal relationship was.

'When do you fly out?' Raj asked.

'We have a few months yet,' said Zara.

'Well, I want it all done within nine months,' said Jackie.

'I'll make sure it happens,' said Sasha. 'After all, I am the producer.'

'Any sign of the others?' Imran asked, referring to the other cast members.

'Nope,' said Jackie. 'Ajay is in hiding, apparently a gay son and divorcing wife can still cause shame. Although no one cares apart from him. Rani and Laila have gone to some weird spa thing to bond. Or maybe Rani's gonna drown the bitch. Minnie is tied up doing something. Obviously she lost the belt she was planning on wearing tonight. And Rocky and James Kapoor are waiting for the London premiere next week. Apparently Prince William and Kate are going to be there.'

'Well, it's their loss,' said Sasha.

'Yes, it really is,' agreed Zara.

They all turned to take pictures, as the press clamoured for the money shot of the evening, with Zara in the centre of the group.

-

Later, Zara stood on her balcony, admiring her view: the dusk, the Arabian sea, the shadows of palm trees dancing in the distance, the scent of Mumbai. She was home, this was where she belonged and once again she was being called queen of all she surveyed. But that didn't matter anymore, she had finally released her demons, and waited for them to be unpicked and destroyed one by one. She had taken charge, and had done something meaningful for once. And for the first time, in a long time, she felt content.

Glossary

Agarbatti incense sticks

Bachao save me

Bas enough

Bhajia fried snack

Chaat savoury starter

Choli blouse

Chutiya fucker

Daal Lentils

Desi term used to describe something that originates from the Indian sub-continent

Desis people that originate from the Indian sub-continent

Dupatta shawl made from thin material that can be plain or heavily embroidered

Filmi dramatic like a movie star

Ghagra flowing ankle length skirt usually worn with a *choli*

Hijra transvestite/eunuch

Hoors beautiful females in heaven

Hyderabadi biryani Biryani style from Hyderabad

Jaan Means life, used as a term of endearment to a loved one, especially a romantic partner

Kajal black eyeliner

Kurta knee length loose shirt

Lengha Heavily embroidered flowing skirt usually worn by brides or at special occasions

Loris lullabies

Lullah penis

Mandap temporary erection under which Hindu wedding ceremonies are conducted

Mazel short for Mazeltov, Hebrew/Yiddish for congratulations/good fortune

Mithai sweetmeats

Mughlai chicken chicken made with cream and almonds

Nargisi kofte half cut boiled eggs covered in minced meat

Nikaah Muslim marriage ceremony

Pakoras fried snack

Paneer tikka cheese cubes with spices

Pheras circling the sacred fire in the Hindu marriage ceremony

Puja Hindu term for worship

Randi prostitute

Rangoli colourful patterns made from rice or flour to decorate

Ras malai dessert made from dumplings and cream

Roti chapatti

Samosas fried snack parcels containing meat or vegetables

Sati Savitri a loyal and devoted wife

Shalwar loose material pants

Shalwar kameez loose short and pants worn by men and women

Sherwanis tailored/embroidered jacket usually worn by grooms

A Letter From Alex

Thank you so much for reading *Bollywood Wives*. It's the first in a new series and I am really excited to finally share it with the world.

I really hope you enjoyed reading this novel, and it would mean the world to me if you would write a review if you do. Reviews and recommendations are so important for an author like me, and every single one is gratefully appreciated. I love reading, it's my passion, and I hope I can make other people escape into a different world the way I do when I read.

This novel has been an absolute dream come true for me. I always grew up watching Bollywood movies and reading glamorous bonkbuster saga novels from authors such as Jilly Cooper, Judith Krantz, Shirley Conran, Danielle Steel, Barbara Taylor Bradford and especially Jackie Collins. Growing up with very little, I think for me both the movies and the novels were just pure escapism from real life. From the time I was a teenager I wanted to write a novel that would combine both, but I didn't think I would ever get the chance to do that, and I never really had the guts to try. Keshini and Lindsey through Hera have given me the confidence to write this novel, and are also there to make sure that it is the best it can be. Writing *Bollywood Wives* still feels totally surreal, and I am so grateful that I have the opportunity to share it with you.

And yet I am very nervous at the same time as it's such a big change from anything I've written before. It's almost like starting again and I really hope I've done this idea justice, because it is so important to me.

While the novel is centred around fictional stars from Bollywood, it is at its core a story of four women and how they navigate the world they find themselves in. I hope I have managed to show characters that are flawed and real, but also done it in an exciting, entertaining and fun way.

I have had so much support since the publication of my first crime novel, especially from the blogging and writing community. You welcomed me in, no questions asked, and really cheered me on, and I have made some lifelong friendships from it. For an author like myself who is new, that support is crucial, without that backing and help there is no way I would even be writing today. So thank you, and I really hope I can receive the same love and backing for *Bollywood Wives* that you showed my earlier novels.

I would love to hear your feedback, I am active on Twitter, Instagram and Facebook, so please do get in touch. And thank you again for reading *Bollywood Wives* and your support, it's greatly appreciated.

Alex

Twitter: https://twitter.com/alexkhanauthor
Facebook: https://www.facebook.com/alexkhanauthorpage

Acknowledgements

Alison Bonomi – it was always so perfect and now it's more so. You are my official agent for this one, I am privileged and totally grateful for it.

Keshini Naidoo – thank you for taking my dream and making it a reality. You loved the idea when it was just a vague fantasy of mine, and encouraged me to write it and so nobody else could have published this.

Lindsey Mooney – you I owe the biggest thanks to, for taking the risk and loving this novel without even meeting me. That more than anything made me feel as though this was happening, that this idea was kickass.

Luigi Bonomi – for all your guidance and support, still being the best and for being in my corner.

Team LBA and Team Hera. You are all magnificent.

A A Dhand, Vaseem Khan, Imran Mahmood, Ayisha Malik (my hero) and Abir Mukherjee – funniest most supportive people I know, on hand 24/7 to talk writing, books, *ladoos*, Nutella, *bakwaas* and spoons. Especially spoons.

Victoria Goldman, Joy Kluver, Anita Majumdar, Mita Mistry, The Whole Kahani, Vanessa Fox O'Loughlin, Gayle Curtis, Emma Mitchell, Katherine Armstrong – you know why.

Marnie Riches, Vicky Newham, Sarah Shaffi, Liz Mistry, Nicola East and Jacky Collins – for the panels.

Angela Marsons and Lisa Hall – cover quote queens always. Steph Broadribb, Susi Holliday and Samantha King for the same.

Syed Waji ul Hassan Shah – thank you for all the hotel research and the photos.

To all the bloggers, reviewers and readers – because honestly without your support there is no way this book would even pass take off. I love you for all you do.

Tracy Fenton – the blogtour. Yes!!!

MKAZORHZZI.

God, my family and friends – my first aid kit.